HANDS AND STRAIGHT LINES

A NOVEL

CARLA BRADSHER-FREDRICK

TAILWINDS PRESS

Tailwinds Press
P.O. Box 2283, Radio City Station
New York, NY 10101-2283
www.tailwindspress.com

Published in the United States of America
ISBN: 979-8-9886903-4-4
1st ed. 2023

Hands
and
Straight Lines

To H.
for Happiness

1   HANDS AND STRAIGHT LINES

Childishly, as a child, I heard people say, "I couldn't draw a straight line if you paid me" and "I can't draw hands." I wanted to think that I drew better than other people drew; therefore, out of vanity, I decided to master hands and I decided to learn to draw a straight line without material aid. (I would say that I decided to learn to draw a straight line freehand, but drawing a straight line precluded freedom.) I loved drawing hands. I observed hands; I paid attention to them. Drawing hands' positions and hands' attitudes, drawing hands at rest and hands in action, drawing mere samplings of shapes that infinitely expressive hands might assume came naturally to me; I, or my hand, seemed naturally given to drawing hands. Conversely, straight lines tormented me. Drawing a streak that didn't curve, drawing a streak that didn't deviate with distance from its initial point, presented an inhuman challenge. And observing straight lines or, rather, observing things that looked like straight lines (tick marks rimming dials of combination locks, violin strings taut on violins, razor blades' edges) didn't teach me anything that I didn't already know about the unbending essence called a straight line. Straight lines did not reward observation. Taken singly, exclusive of their use in designs, they did not invite mental involvement; they remained, to me, shadeless and single in nature, uninteresting. But I learned. I learned to draw a semblance of a straight line by moving my hand and arm lever-like, mechanically. Stultifying practice brought me a vacuous skill. I learned to fear what I might do out of ambition.

Hands and straight lines engaged me. I applied myself consciously to those two subjects to such an extent that, although I dimly mistrusted dichotomies, I divided the world into "hands" and "straight lines." "Hands" and "straight lines" became huge, ill-defined, virtually limitless categories into which I divided much of my experience. "Hands" came to cover all shapes, forms, surfaces, textures, all physical entities that I found pleasing, graceful, interesting (usually because curvaceous, irregular, or variously hued). "Hands" stood for curves. Immaterially, "hands" served humaneness, however I construed that; "hands" aided; "hands" liberated; "hands" covered just about everything that I personally considered good. "Straight lines," the abstract opposites of "hands," covered qualities I disliked: flat surfaces; level surfaces; slick surfaces; surfaces possessing sharp, distinct, curveless edges; geometric shapes that lacked curves; hardness in texture; hardness in consistency. Immaterially, "straight lines" meant obstruction; inhibition; constraint; discipline imposed upon me by others; all forces that I judged hostile to my interests or to my inclinations; all uncongenial demands from having to have my hair cut to having to go to school; all hopes, interests, expectations that didn't coincide with my own. Inconsistently, however, I did not dislike or suffer from everything stored mentally under "straight lines." Some objects with "straight-line" characteristics also possessed the attractiveness of "hands," and many objects shared qualities from both camps.

2   RAZOR BLADES

At around four years old, I believed that all razor blades possessed one sharp edge. I remembered holding that belief because I tested it memorably. I found a double-edged razor blade on a washbasin where soap might sit in edgeless innocence. I picked up the blade and examined it carefully. Its edges looked sharp. They also looked identical, but I believed; I had faith; I believed that one edge would cut and that the other edge would not, and I wanted to know which edge harbored the invisible bluntness in which I believed. I studied the edges, blind to their sameness. I believed simply that sight could not show me where bluntness lay disguised in a shining bevel. I decided to test an edge at random. Confident I would choose the blunt edge, I blithely sliced the tip of my left index finger. Blood welled; pain surprised me; I screamed. My great-aunt Estelle treated my finger and comforted me.

Although I remembered that incident clearly, although I remembered both the belief and the curiosity behind it, I did not learn anything from it for years. No one enlightened me about razor blades. (I'd told no one that an actual idea lay behind the incident, no accident.) Curiosity *had* led me to cut myself, but my curiosity had had a refinement about it not caught by the blundering kind of curiosity attributed to me. At the time, not explaining what I thought about razor blades had seemed far, far easier than the all but impossible task of explaining myself. At the time, true to my ill-founded faith, I merely assumed that, by some inexplicable failure of good luck, I'd simply chosen to test the blade's sharp edge. I didn't think about razor blades for years. I didn't revisit my ideas about them until one day when, not at school due to some minor ailment and desiring company, I trailed into the dimly lit living room and saw my great-aunt Estelle seated in front of a window, fabric heaped in her lap, yellow light from a floor lamp shining into her sewing. The window looked large and gray, shining rectangular behind her. Yellowish light suffused hairs at her nape below her usual chignon, the suffusion brighter on the lamp-facing side of her neck than on the other. Light emphasized the curved areas of skin separated by indentations in her forehead. I crossed the room and sat beside her. Without having seemed to notice me, Estelle said, "How many times have I told you, if you're going to be out of bed, you should have something on those feet?" "Those feet" sounded loving and Estelle's lit corner of the dim room felt comforting. I put my feet up on the sofa and sat behind highly bent knees, watching Estelle pull gray thread from gray cloth. In twitching runs, thread backed out of stitches it had formed. When the retraction stopped at a knot, Estelle cut the thread using a single-edged razor blade. The cuts made soft, popping sounds. Estelle shifted the mass of soft-gray, woolen cloth heaped in her lap. A shiny, silver-gray ribbon moved with the fabric. Soothed by Estelle's calm activity, soothed by the sounding softness of gray, excluded rain, I began to watch what she did. By pulling out threads, Estelle detached one edge of the shiny ribbon from the unshining cloth. Detaching that edge, Estelle opened a fold in the cloth formerly sewn shut. The shiny, gray ribbon, detached from the cloth along one edge, remained attached to the cloth along its other edge. The ribbon remained attached to the very edge of the part of the cloth formerly folded up in a band against adjoining cloth. The razor blade, which Estelle took up and laid aside repeatedly, looked consonant with the ribbon, with the cloth, and with the opening fold. A bright, shiny, silvery metal strip, folded closed—crimped closed on the blade—covered one of the blade's long edges. The blade otherwise looked gray and flatly rectangular. It had a small, round hole like a pinprick centered in its broad side. Its cutting bevel gleamed, narrow and straight. The folded-over, bright, shiny, silvery, metal strip edging the blade looked proportionally similar to the ribbon edging the once-folded band of cloth that Estelle released. Estelle held the blade between her thumb and index finger; the bright fold roundly pressed the crease at her finger's top joint. The single-edged nature of the single-edged blade gradually dawned on me. I stared at it. I thought, startled as if by a remarkable discovery, "So that's what one of those things looks like," a truly single-edged razor blade. I remembered, then, my cutting error; I saw it as error only then. I remembered my blindness to evidence that had virtually stared me in the face. I remembered my optimistic incaution, my blithe determination to learn which edge of a double-edged razor blade possessed a mysterious, invisible bluntness. I remembered faith upon faith, my certainty that I would choose, by chance, "the" blunt edge to test against my finger. I realized that my attitudes and my beliefs had combined, in that instance, to create a situation in which I could not have avoided hurting myself. I wondered almost fearfully: how many more such traps might my mind devise?

3   FULLNESS, FLATNESS

My parents owned the house in which my brother and I grew up. Estelle lived with us. She had owned the house for most of her long life. To me, it remained Estelle's house entirely, hers completely in spirit. Built before the Civil War, it originally lacked kitchen and bathrooms. Half-hearted additions and a converted room upstairs replaced the original cook-shed and outhouses. In the cavernous, cold, slickly white-tiled, converted bathroom upstairs, faucet handles labeled "HOT" and "COLD" in thin, stiff, black, unbending letters made me think that, in the late twentieth century, I owed the convenience of running water to Estelle's predecessors, thin, stiff, unbending, black-wearing Christians, who, having done without the luxury of piped water, begrudged it to others and covered it with print. A rubber drain plug, employed or unemployed, either plugged or didn't plug the drain hole in the oval washbasin upstairs. A brightly scoured, silvery metal cross meant to exclude fallen objects barred the drain hole, the dark way down into inscrutable plumbing.

Inside Estelle's house, plucked flowers lay crushed in dictionaries; flowers lost their small fullness under the weight of words. Depicted flowers filled wallpaper dimly. A white damask table-cloth, Estelle's favorite among tablecloths, lay folded away or outspread. Spread flat on a table, the cloth disclosed its pattern, a supposed fullness of wide-open roses, roses depicted with cut stems, roses which tried to deny their flatness, roses designed to look active, joyously tumbling into someone's—very large, very flat—abundantly gathering lap. Flat surfaces seemed to consume fullness, flowers.

Behind the house, along one side of the backyard, between lilac bushes and a street, stood a high, solid, board fence. To my eyes, the fence looked exceedingly substantial given that neither the immediate street nor the surrounding town posed much of a threat. But there the fence stood, a phalanx of gray-blue-stained boards nailed up with nails (Jesus Christ), rectangular board beside rectangular board, rootless and hard beside the rooted, soft lilacs. Although surely harmed by the fence, which deprived the bushes of light on one side, the lilacs appeared oblivious to it. They grew high. They rose above the obstruction; they curved over it. Estelle tended them, but the plants looked self-sufficient. They looked as if they just lived, grew, produced flowers, lost flowers, lost leaves, and reproduced both obliviously, year after year. They appeared to flourish in thoughtless certainty, as if sure that they could have thrived as they did without human help.

I considered the fence and the bushes from within the yard many times. I drew the lilac bushes in flower and out of flower and starkly leafless. I painted, in wet, spreading watercolors, the flowers' opulent muzzles, the countless leaves. I would sit on the grassy ground, lost in flowers, in leaves, in ways sunlight cascaded over bushes or hung in air's nothingness. Sometimes I tried to paint, with emphasis, the physical contrast between the bushes' loose limbs and the fence's tight boards, the slanting leaves and heaped flowers seen against weathered planks. Often, my painted splinters resembled fur. I labored to sharpen them, to make them look splintery.

I committed flowers to flatness by depicting flowers on paper. But, in my sensual mind, painting denied flatness. Color grew its own fullness although paintings stayed flat. Painting liberated color; painting allowed paint to flower in its own right.

Factory-made sheets of watercolor paper looked sharply and strictly rectangular. (I sometimes softened papers' edges by tearing them gently.) I disliked most of the qualities displayed by watercolor paper. But however flat in general breadth, however white before paint overlaid whiteness, however straight-edged and sharp-cornered a factory-made sheet of paper appeared to the mere sense of sight, watercolor paper seemed to me *other* than endowed with its factual traits. To me, watercolor paper contained its own opposites. It seemed succulent, deep, spherical, and brilliantly colorful: rich and round as oranges, the full, living fruit.

I loved paper. Painting wetly with soft, lissome brushes drenched in watercolor hues gratified me greatly, gratified me as nothing else did, "as nothing else" because pleasure felt in painting derived uniquely from the materials used. Paper seemed, for all its diversity, one thing and constant, whereas brushes and pigments had a difficult inconstancy. Extremely unnatural, bleached, rolled, pressed, textured paper, paper made from killed trees, carried no negatives. White paper did not look deathly white. Paper, taking on paint and taking in paint, actively created its own effects.

4   PAINT SET

I used simple, childish paint sets until my tenth birthday. Simple paints gave me so much pleasure, I did not think beyond them. I did not know that art-supply stores existed. (That ignorance shocked me, in retrospect.) Estelle bought paint for me when and where she bought groceries. If I wanted more paint, I wrote "paint" on her shopping list. Estelle bought paint and lettuce, paint and milk, paint and oatmeal, and paint and carrots; paint joined staples as another staple. Estelle laid the new, little sticks of plastic boxes on the desk in my room where emptied paint boxes piled up like train wrecks. The sets varied. Some included more colors than did others, but none contained many. The most expansive sets might contain a brown, a black, and a white. Most contained, in square, in rectangular, in round, or in oval shapes, cakes of bright, simple exemplars of yellow, orange, red, violet, blue, and green. (Even in my ignorance, such sets seemed almost foolishly redundant. They contained both primary and secondary colors. Ignorant of the terms, I knew that one could make secondary colors by blending primaries.) Given those simple givens, I blended simple colors contentedly for years. Then came a revelation of sorts. I did not learn, then, that one could buy watercolors in tubes, hue by hue, or that paint of great richness came softly packaged. But I discover colors undreamt of in my simplicity.

My parents wished that I did not like drawing and painting as much as I did. In spite of that, they gave me the paper I craved, blocks of thick, expensive watercolor paper. (How I knew that such paper existed, I have no idea.) My parents gave me drawing materials despite their misgivings. They did not give me paint until my tenth birthday, when, out of character, they gave me a revelatory paint set, a huge, spreading paint set containing one hundred hues. Untouched, the hues looked small and sharply rectangular. They lay as rectangles, row upon row, brick beside brick, all inset in bright, slick, white-enameled tin. Tiny black letters labeled every hue. That set, that collection of samples of hues with beautiful names, opened up worlds of color to me. No red that I had ever met possessed the staining power and the depth of alizarin crimson. None of my heretofore concocted blues had what cerulean had; none of my yellows looked primrose, none of my greens viridian. New hues bloomed under my watery brushes, colors the like of which I'd never encountered in paint. I delight-edly learned differences between three different yellow-greens, leaf green, spring green, and vert Veronese. I spread midnight blue and Prussian blue beside each other, enraptured by dark distinctions. I learned the range from dark to light of every color in the box. And, far from sated with the plain glory of single hues, I blended the newfound subtleties with each other after my old wont. Given one hundred named hues, I discovered, I sensed, infinitude.

The hundred-slotted box that my parents gave me did not, like Pandora's casket, release plagues upon the world, but it did generate in me a swarm of interests and wishes; it brought discontentment. When the small, hard, and hard-to-dissolve samples of hues in the given box disappeared, I desired more of the same. I desired to learn about further unknowns. Frustrated by the hardness of the wondrous colors suddenly given, I desired something other, something better, some soft, cooperative form of paint. Suddenly awakened to the world's diversity, I discovered, and secretly bicycled to, art-supply stores. Gazing at the stocked shelves, I desired to use much that I saw. If seeing things that I wanted to own for my use had spurred me to earn the money with which to buy them, my parents might have congratulated themselves upon advancing my maturation by giving me a paint box. I did not think far, however, about earning money. My sole idea consisted of asking my parents to pay me for yard work that I already did. "We already pay you," my father reminded me. (Oh, yeah, I forgot. I supposedly earned an evaporative allowance.) I begged to take over my brother's work in the yard. Faced with my request for increased pay for increased work, my father told me, "You're too young to use a lawn mower." Thwarted in that one notion, I dropped the idea of earning. I developed a plain-spoken way of begging from my parents: "May I please have ten dollars for a tube of phthalo blue?" I generally received what I desired. Sometimes one or the other of my parents asked, "What happened to your allowance?" Gone, of course.

The hundred-hued set, the last of my childish paint sets, had several qualities not entirely childish. To my eyes, its size made it significant, no mere stick of a plaything, and color as a subject sprang from its complexity. Further, like the severe, antiquated faucet handles in the upstairs bathroom in Estelle's house, the set assumed that one could read. It seemed bent on teaching, at least, colors' names. And some of those names suggested history.

Among the yellow-greens in my gift set, I esteemed vert Veronese above the others. (Childishly, I accepted each of the set's hues as an immutable constant, as the absolute essence of a particular color. Awakening to the world's offerings in art-supply stores, I learned that hues with the same name could vary greatly.) To my devouring eyes, vert Veronese, wetly spread on white paper, looked like velvety moss suffused with sunlight. I understood "vert" from school, but "Veronese"? How did one even say it? My brother told me that much. I approached my mother for more information. She sat, reading. (She favored published letters and published diaries.) Verbally, I tugged at her sleeve. She did not look up. She said, "Hmm?" Zealously curious about my new word, I asked, "What's Veronese?" Mother told her riveting pages, "Not 'what,' 'who.'" "Who's Veronese?" I persisted. Mother replied, ever to print-bearing paper, "Was." Although accustomed to such withholding, to such pedantic chipping-away at ineptly phrased questions (an approach not unique to my mother but shared by all of my family members except Estelle), I felt a little exasperated. I asked, with unnatural exactitude and with natural exasperation, "Who *was* Veronese, please?" Then Mother looked at me. She said, "He was a Venetian painter. Sixteenth-century." "Why's that green named after him, vert Veronese?" I asked. Mother said, "I don't know, Edward. Maybe he invented it. He was a great colorist." She returned to her book. Colorist dismissed.

When fully opened, when spread open, flat, the hundred-hued paint set from my parents resembled two white-enameled trays hinged together on one side, long side to long side. The halves, otherwise rectangular, had rounded corners. Deep grooves in the lid's exterior appeared as slant-sided, round-topped ridges on the lid's interior. The snowy, low ridges with flat, slanting sides bounded flat areas lower than the ridges. The low fields had straight sides and rounded corners. In use, they contained separate pools of liquid paint or they baked brightly behind paint daubs not very liquid. After use, the lid's lining looked splotchy. The shapeless remains of used colors, of blended hues without names, covered it, while across the great divide, beyond the hinges uniting the two halves of the set, the named colors still lay, row after row, in rectangular shapes. However flooded or eroded, rectangles in rows persisted. Regimentation remained—despite the lavishness of my gathering brush.

5   REFLECTOR, BLUE BUTTERFLIES

As a child, in a botanical garden with my father, I saw trees with plaques nailed into them. (Perhaps small tacks grew in my mind to nails' wounding size. Nails, Jesus Christ.) The plaques gave trees' names in Latin and in English. The rectangular plaques curved to embrace tree trunks. Hard brass, they had bent. But although weathered to a pleasant, dead-leaf brown and fittingly curved, the plaques looked alien against bark, discordant with branches, with everything natural. But the trees thrived, to my mind, despite their labels.

In that park of applied names, my father and I came to a water-filled depression across the path we'd followed. Around the water, black earth glistened like a paste made of mirrors, and on the wonderful mud, little slices of sky blue, cerulean, lived; very small, sky-blue butterflies walked the earth; their unearthly wings, basking, spread thinly above it. I watched the butterflies, the sky blue, the earth black, the trim wings, and the sticky mud. My father and I walked on. In a dry part of the same path, in dust that I remembered as cinnamon-colored, I found a bicycle reflector: fire-orange, rectangular, silvery-backed, flat. I instantly licked it. It seemed to catch fire with the moisture. Within the burning, little rectangle, a fiendish network of tiny hexagons filled the two rectangular halves of the whole. When I tilted the strip, light glanced in its two halves alternately. Dad and I came to a newly-made, plank bridge over a shallow stream. My father crossed the bridge. I stopped in the middle of it. Because spittle had brightened the reflector rewardingly, I wanted to see what a whole stream might do to the thing. Holding up the reflector, I shouted to Dad, "I'm going to throw this in." "Go ahead," Dad replied. I knew that my father would not allow me to wade into the stream to retrieve the reflector if it landed on the visible streambed with its silvery side upward; I had one chance to see the fiery side under water. I looked at the stream. Thinking that the current might carry the reflector under the bridge and onward, away from me, I threw the reflector well upstream. I saw it flashing and tumbling along the streambed toward me. It slid and lodged, orange side upward, in an ideal spot for viewing, in sunlight, near the bridge. As I moved closer to it, light flashed in my eyes. "There's light coming out of it," I shouted. My explanatory father, in a benevolent mood that day, called patiently, "That's the reflection." I watched the reflector. Light stood above it, steady in the passing water. Ripples on the water's surface picked up fire-orange in brief, snaking strands. I thought that the yellowish light shining upward, above the reflector, looked like light admitted into a dark area by an open door. The reflected beam, as if from an opening, invited entry, and the bright bar, the reflector itself, suggested a fiery layer spread everywhere, just out of sight, under ordinary earth.

I remembered that sight when, shortly before I turned twenty-three, I saw a man who changed my life, a man who welcomed my ardency for him. When I first saw Lawrence, Professor Baussan, he lectured in a darkened classroom, a room traversed by beams of light from slide projectors. Lawrence became the love, the fiery lining, of my life.

6   BOOKSTORE, TRAIN

As a good, staunch atheist, my brother, Burke, offended our great-aunt, Estelle, largely because he argued with her. My father and I shared Burke's beliefs, but we didn't argue them. Although Burke disturbed Estelle through argument and, further, through an early love affair, she gave ammunition to the enemy in his case: she gave the proceeds from sold, family farms to her foster son, Burke's and my father, with the provision that he pay for Burke's and my education. Burke studied history. He'd studied history assiduously ever since I could remember. He would earn a PhD in history. He would get a job teaching history, an obtainment which, given the rarity of job openings and the intense competition for available positions, he called "miraculous."

In the early summer just after he'd turned twenty-four and shortly before he finished a master's degree, Burke began a two-month-long language course in Germany. He already read German well; he wanted to learn to speak it fluently. Just before he finished the course, in July, I, not quite nineteen, joined him in the small town on the Rhine where he'd lived for two months. We planned to travel circuitously and cheaply to Turkey. We could not have afforded to travel even as economically as we did without Estelle's liberal interpretation of "education."

Burke far exceeded me in studiousness. During that summer's language course, when not socially practicing spoken German, Burke read *Buddenbrooks*. He called the book "difficult," verbally and culturally hard to understand. He hadn't finished it by the time I joined him, and his much-bent paperback copy had broken through the spine into several pieces. Burke told me, as if confessing to some dire, besetting complication, that he "had to" replace his disintegrated copy with a whole one before we left Germany. "So," I asked, "what's the problem?" "No problem," Burke said, "except." Except that an ordered copy might not arrive before he left his current address. Except that the little town where he lived—plate-glass shop windows daily washed, impeccable gardens fronting houses so neat that dust edging bricks looked applied with an eyedropper—lacked a bookstore. Except that, to buy a new copy, he, or we, would have to take a train to the nearest city, Koblenz, half an hour away, where Burke knew several bookstores from previous visits. Burke didn't need much persuading. We went to Koblenz.

A train made for commuters, nearly vacant due to the time of day and the slow, summer season, swayed along the river and among wooded hills and hills bearing vineyards. In Koblenz, we walked around. We watched a broad stretch of water where two rivers combined. We listened to an organist play dark, towering music in a soaring church. The music lingered indistinctly in my mind until we entered a bookstore and a shop bell jingled. One burst of tinny sound shattered the Himalayas.

Burke preceded me into the store. I stopped just within it, stunned by the bell's sprightly jingle. Hanging from a springy perch on the door, the bell looked like a sleigh bell: a shiny, silvery, golf-ball-sized, hollow sphere pierced with slits. The slits looked straight in their cut nothingness amid the curved shell. Together the straight-looking slits through the material curvature formed an absence shaped like a cross with equally long branches. Each branch ended as if tipped with a circular absence, lollypop-like. Had the slits not ended, had they extended in their given directions upward, through, as if around, the silvery sphere, they would have met at its top; they would have quartered it. The bell, whose shimmering, light, trivial, bright, tinny sound displaced the vestiges of somber, dark, glorious organ music in my mind, served a purpose, of course. Even as I paused, absorbing the appearance of the bell and savoring what its sounds touched in me (fondness for the world's small flourishes), the bell served its purpose. A bell-alerted woman greeted Burke. Burke returned the greeting and produced a further string of clear words incomprehensible to me. In the benign temper that the bell's jingling had just released in me, I reminded myself to compliment Burke on sounding fluent. The woman spoke cordially. As she walked, her shoe heels knocked cleanly on the wooden floor; strewn cordiality seemed to gleam from the floor. I tore myself away from the sight of the bell and followed Burke and the woman up a few steps, out of the front room, into a further room, and then down more steps, into a very large room brightly lit. Double-sided, chest-high shelves full of books formed aisle after aisle the short way across the room; long aisles surrounded the cross-aisles; books filled the walls to reachable heights. Through the shining brightness (bright wooden shelves, bright wooden floor, books' brightly colored spines and covers dazzling me like static confetti), the woman led Burke to drab sameness: a line of books shelved against a wall, books all the same height and all bound in white. The woman waved gracefully before the graceless paperbacks; she departed; I looked at the books she'd introduced. Amid the general incomprehensibility of small, black words printed on the white spines (printed with the feet of the letters pointing toward the spines' right edges, a European convention conflicting with my American way of looking at books' spines sideways), I recognized a few authors' names (running upward along the spines, not downward). I barely had time to notice that alphabetical order applied neither among the authors' names, nor among the presumed titles, before Burke pulled *Buddenbrooks* out of the level-headed lineup. "How did you find that?" I asked. Burke said, "What do you mean, 'How did I find it?'" I said, "Without the alphabet." Burke said, "Oh. By number." Sure enough: tiny, black numbers in numerical order dotted the books' spines near the top. The numbers, from book to book, aligned perfectly with each other. The drear sight of the colorless books worked against the shop bell's gift of brief blitheness, and Burke's refusal to answer a simple question in a simple manner irked me somewhat, but I asked equanimously how Burke had known that particular book's number. Burke gestured. He said, "I looked it up before in one of those." Looking as directed, I saw a large, glossy, bright-yellow rectangle chained to the end of a bookshelf. Print covered it. The object consisted of several layers, apparently of cardboard, closed against each other accordion-wise. It hung, as if by one corner, from a very long, bright, shiny sphere-and-rod chain passed through aligned grommets. Other such rectangles, all densely print-covered, hung from other shelves: slices of fierce, piercing yellow, strident turquoise, raging pink. The colors glared transparently. They looked like highlighters' colors, like colors from pens used (ruinously) for marking over print in books. Dense print in columns showed through the colors. "What *are* those?" I asked. Burke said, "They're lists." The lists listed publishing companies' publications. They cross-listed publications by author, title, and number. Print camped on colors in orderly columns, victorious.

Burke purchased his chosen book. He and the cordial-sounding woman conversed again. He paid her with bills, paper rectangles. She thrust the book, the thick multiplicity of paginal rectangles, into a small paper sack. The sack threatened me distantly because it bore, as decoration, a print designed by a graphic designer, and I didn't want to have to work designing commercial prints. In interesting umber against a handsomely drab, decaying-leaf yellow, the print on the sack suggested two eyes seen head-on. The eyes looked rapt and wide. They did not quite look owl-like and they did not quite look human. Owlishly human or humanly owlish, the eyes appeared amid, as if seen through, an upright book created by light strokes, little feats of linear unevenness suggesting the edges of pages. Wide strokes gave the book shape wings. The whole design preached silently, "Read. Become winged, wise, or imaginatively transported." Three letters accompanied the image.

Because I asked, Burke told me: the letters abbreviated a publishing company's name.

Burke and I took a train back the way we'd come. Vacant, swaying, it resembled, to the point of identity, the train previously taken. Big, rotund seats upholstered in durable fuzz (cattail-flower brown) faced each other sociably on either side of an uncarpeted aisle (flat, dull, rosy dun). Paired seats faced paired seats; groups of paired, facing seats succeeded each other, back-to-back, down the length of the car, to either side of the aisle. Amid the tempting plurality of empty seats, Burke and I didn't actually have to sit near each other, but our tickets assigned us to seats—ridiculously side-by-side—and Burke wanted no conflict or explanatory interchange with a ticket inspector (should one appear, which one didn't). Respecting Burke's wishes, I sat near him, merely opposite one of our assigned seats, within the same group of mutually-facing seats to which our tickets assigned us. Burke sat facing forward, beside a closed window. I sat in advance of Burke, on the aisle, facing the rear of the train. Someone had left the window open above the pair of seats behind Burke. As the train moved, wind poured in, and a rosy-cocoa-brown curtain, which might have covered the open window had the train stood still, twisted, and filled, and flapped, and fell in a continuum of contortions which made the cloth appear tortured by an outside force or by the ascribed life of an inward force, by a desire to break away, to escape its nature as fabric, as a piece of anchored material, and become anchorless and edgeless, boundless and flowing like wind, which the actual drapery could only clumsily emulate. Wracked by what happened around it and seemingly afflicted by its inability to participate fully in what happened, the curtain flapped and floundered while, beside closed windows, orderly curtains merely hung, gathered away from the glass into flat, metal crooks. Below the crooks, the gathered curtains swayed continently. Sunlight slid, slipped, returned, turned with the train's turning, flowed golden-brown over dark-brown upholstery. On the vacant seat beside him, Burke's new copy of *Buddenbrooks* lay face down, its largely white back stitched across the foot with a line and a half of small, black, printed words. The book's back blazed and grayed as sunlight crossed it and left. Despite the abundance of fresh air, I felt sleepy. I kept jerking myself awake, out of picture-thoughts verging on dreams, the seats around us becoming sea lions piled on a dock, the golden sunlight a caged tiger pacing, followed by sticky, tasteless innocence: boxed "animal crackers" which I'd liked as a child not for their taste but for their container, a circus-car / train-car box with a stringy, woven handle. As I sat trying to stay awake, gazing at Burke's white copy of *Buddenbrooks*, the rectangular, white back cover brightening and fading above the cliff-like surface formed by the edges of its many, many pages, *Buddenbrooks* turned into a stupefying sponge of words existing simultaneously in print, printed words touching each other face to face, page upon page, word-touching words with a page's thickness between them and other word-touching words, sentence after sentence, sentence upon sentence, a dense, black, riddled sponge of printed words. To what extent could a read book exist with that simultaneity, whole in one's mind? Making a real effort to awaken, I said something aimless to Burke; he replied aimlessly. I looked around the train car. I saw things previously seen: the billowing curtain; the crooked curtains swaying from their waists down; the dark, cattail-brown seats golden-brown in moving patches; the blur of the ongoing world rushing past outside. But then I noticed a paper sack on the floor, the sack that had slipped off *Buddenbrooks*. Flat as new, the sack lay on the aisle nearby, open end toward me. Small, angular points like sawteeth edged the paper opening. The figure printed on the sack, the winged-book-bird-human figure, faced upward, upside down from my point of view. I considered getting up and retrieving the sack. I considered saving it from its fate as litter. I considered claiming it, keeping it, making it my own. I considered keeping it in token of my fondness for slight things and for the sake of the contrast it offered with

Burke's meaningful volume: serious book, insignificant paper; product of long, sustained, mental effort, brief gesture, drawing; thickness, solidity, words, thinness, emptiness, image. I thought about saving the sack, but I didn't move.

7   HAGIA SOPHIA, POSTCARDS

In Istanbul, Burke and I visited a vast, ancient building, a building so large and arched and high in its central vacancy that people, all tourists within it, proportionately resembled ants wandering the high, bony hollows of an empty tortoise shell. The vast shell held an enormous, empty room. Complicated spaces lurked beyond columns along the long sides of the room, but the room itself did not look complicated. Successive, very high curves cupped it, covered it with famously "floating" heights. A great dome over the center of the room began the floating. The dome appeared to float because it rose above a ring of forty small, straight-sided, round-topped windows; weightless light riddled masonry around the base of the dome. Below the ring of windows, four arches arranged in a square carried the crown-like ring of windows atop the upper-most curves of their huge, curved heights. Two of the arches rose from the main room's side walls; two of the arches spanned the width of the room. Flat walls with windows filled the side arches' high curves. From the other two arches, curved shapes spread to the ends of the room, shapes of tawny-looking, golden-mosaic-covered masonry, shapes each like one quarter of a hollow sphere seen from within. At either end of the room, beneath each of the bases of the quartered-sphere domes, further curved spaces and curved shapes gathered: three arch-topped spaces, recesses or rooms. Too large to see completely from one vantage point, the building seemed to float and to flow in a harmonious sequence of one, two, three: three arched spaces spread away, beneath two domes shaped like quarter spheres' linings, and one whole dome surmounted those two. A vast, gray, stone floor spread flat—as the tortoise shell's plastron. Entering that room, I felt more than pleased. I felt molded by curves and uplifted by heights. Responding to the high, floating air of the place, I exclaimed to Burke, "What makes this stand up? What supports all of this?" Sounding gratified himself, Burke replied, "Nobody knows." He said that engineers who'd studied the building couldn't agree on that point, that the building stood buried in buttressing invisible from within, that external additions, addition after addition, built up over centuries, shored up the weight of the "floating" heights. Burke made the outward building sound like a jumbled mess of architectural accretions. "But," Burke said, something planned from the beginning, something rationally innovative, worked at the building's core.

We stood under the main dome, gaping up at it. "What do you see?" Burke said. He did not really ask; he meant, "Think about the structure." I stared at the dome, at the ribs which rose to its crown from between the windows at its base. I stared at the four huge arches arranged in a square under it. I stared at the massive underpinnings of the four arches. I finally thought that the four arches beneath the dome's base dropped in their curves "like the legs of a table," if a table stood on arched legs. Thinking of an abstract table's flatness led me to see the feature that Burke urged me to find. Over the arches and below the dome's base, curved, transitional areas spread; shapes like bowed triangles, like triangles with arced edges, united the curves of the arches and the base of the dome. The triangles bent transitionally, eliminating corners; the round-based dome stood over a square. I, who imagined a world of difference between circles and squares, I, who felt the two all but incompatible, gasped simply, "Those triangles." Burke said "yes" as if congratulating me, "Yes, those triangles." Burke said that the building's architects invented that arrangement, "the first really good solution" to an ancient problem: how to put a curved dome over a building with straight sides.

Staring up at the dome, Burke and I admired the inventive engineering, the practical reasoning, embodied in stone above us. We atheistically admired the reasoned structure, while on the great, curved, transitional triangles below the dome, mosaics depicted angels. An angel filled each of the rational triangles with the mystical uplift of three pairs of wings.

So, Burke and I thought about and talked about something reasonable in an empty building, in a building which seemed extraordinarily empty because extraordinarily large, full of vast, cupped quantities of unobstructed air. But the building's very antiquity made it seem unreasonable to me. By the time that Burke and I came along, it had stood where it stood for nearly fifteen hundred years. One empire had given way to another empire around it; that empire had vanished, leaving the motionless building standing in a republic. With each political change, the building's name had changed, and the way in which the building served people had changed. Originally a Christian church—and the main church and showpiece of the Byzantine Empire—the Great Church, the Church of the Divine Wisdom, the Hagia Sophia, had become a mosque, Ayasofya Camii. By the time that Burke and I arrived, it had become a museum, an empty museum, the Museum of Ayasofya, displaying no collection, only itself, only its own enduring structure, marble and columns, and adherent mosaics.

In the church-mosque-museum, religion seemed absent. Christian figures glimmered in mosaic; Moslem trappings stood and hung in the cavernous hulk. But, to me, perhaps because the building offered nothing small, no object or accommodation of human scale, humans themselves seemed irrelevant to the place. (Perhaps that alone should have made it seem holy.) Burke paced around the Museum of Ayasofya, trying to find the human. He repeatedly referred to the finely-printed pages of the *Blue Guide* to Istanbul. Waving the book, with fingers holding a place among its pages, he said things like, "The iconostasis ran along here, I think." "Here, I think, people knelt to kiss the icons. There're supposed to be worn spots in the floor where they knelt. Do you see worn spots?" To that, I replied, "It all seems pretty worn." We found a bolt in a column where an icon had hung. We looked at leaves of marble spread over walls, leaves mirroring each other's veining, creating repetitive patterns. And so, having considered contiguous stone slabs and the weightiness of stone, and having considered the building's age in general, I felt struck, in contrast, by the postcard vendors' postcards that greeted us when we left the building and entered a grove of mobile trees, a group of men carrying racks on poles, racks packed with stacks of single postcards, racks from which conjoined post-cards, unfolded from packets, hung as long streamers, with creases between every card. I felt doomed to love small pictures and to spend my life making them, while Burke did not seem doomed, did not seem wedded to ephemera, to paper sacks on train floors, to things like postcards, and sparrows, and litter, to all the living people and moving traffic that surrounded that place, that palace of perma-nence, the temple of Burke's god, history, the Hagia Sophia.

8   LILACS

Just turned twenty-one, Burke sat reading a newspaper in Estelle's backyard. I'd spent that morning painting watercolors based on lilac bushes in flower. The day neared noon. My watercolor things lay in the long, deep, lank grass. I lay on a swing above the lovely litter. Two paintings on the top sheets of heavy, deep blocks of paper lay in the grass, lay as if thrown to the growing green. I'd worked on the one while the other dried. Burke had come out of the house earlier. Barefooted, carrying a newspaper, he'd stood above my painting clutter and lectured me about "mowing the lawn." According to him, I should have mown the sweet grass long before then, long, long before it obtained the reclining, lank depth which I sensuously admired. (I did cavil in the manner of my family. Burke said that I should "mow the lawn;" I replied, "You mean 'cut the grass.'" "Same difference," he said. I said, "It is not." I honestly wanted to spare the grass, grown to rare luxuriance, the lawn mower's noise and its whirling blade. If I had to speak about cutting it, I wanted no gentle generalizations, no "lawn" for the live, long leaves, the so-called blades, no "mow" for the act of cutting, severance.) Burke had settled himself in a vile lawn chair, one of four spread in an arc around the stupendous (yet hideous) sofa-like swing on which I lay. All the chairs looked like grapevines turned into metal, tortured into chair shapes, and then painted white. The chairs looked like rusting, white-painted lies about nature: they suggested that no matter how badly one tortured a grapevine to serve a human purpose, the vine would still obligingly bear fruit. Fake bunches of grapes, flattened into groups of low nodes, studded the chairs. In general, what with the white-painted, metal shapes of leaves, the twining fakery of stems, and the crushed, pendant bunches of little, white, pea-sized curvatures suggesting grapes, the chairs looked appallingly lacy. They also looked ancient. A table in the same style, which had stood, coffee-table-like, beside the sofa-like swing, I'd dragged away before painting. The swing on which I lay looked ancient and awful, but it did not match the chairs. It had a white-painted, rusting, metal frame with white-painted, rusting, metal springs at the ends. (The swing wintered in the garage. Summers, Burke and I hauled it out. When not in use, a tarpaulin covered it. The thing gleamed despite its antiquity.) Pale stuffing showed through a split in its bright-red, vinyl upholstery, the thing's sole injury, not counting rust. The yellowed stuffing resembled discolored apple.

I lay shirtless on the plump, stuffed, tacky, vinyl-upholstered, red swing. Having painted, I felt almost contented. I even felt almost sexually satisfied. My heart shoved the red vinyl slowly. Sweat, seeping, leaking, building up between me and the hot, soft, plastic upon which I lay, seemed meltingly mutual, as if produced by two bodies, as if shared by two bodies lying together, sexually spent. The surface sealed to me actually bore a cold pattern. Modulations in its red coloration, dim, feathery areas in the red, suggested ice cubes' edges and ice cubes' centers. Thus, the taut, plump, soft smoothness, which I felt and which I visualized behind closed eyelids, seemed uneven, crowded, packed with chunky, red ice.

I lay, eyes closed, absorbing sunlight. Cars passed in the one-way side street, beyond the fence-screening cliff of flowering, cresting lilacs. Infrequent cars slowed and paused at a stop sign which I, in my dark, umber mind behind orange eyelids, visualized as unfixed, its bright particulars—colors, angles, letters—swimming in space above a silver pole. Slowing cars gusted softly. Because I'd spent the morning painting, the gusts touched me as brushstrokes.

Into that peace, Burke's papery sounds intruded. He kept shaking his newspaper, bashing it, folding and refolding it. Sometimes he seemed to hit it, to give it impatient-sounding flicks with the backs of his fingers. I lay, peacefully trying to ignore his illusory abuse of paper. But anyone hitting paper, even paper with print on it, would annoy me. Finally, Burke's paper sounded smashed definitively. I heard him say something I didn't catch. I slowly opened my eyes to the light. I saw Burke, his bare feet reflecting green more subtly than his outstretched, pool-cue-supporting fingers braced on green ever reflected the green of his pool table. I saw his cream-colored jeans catch the light fully. Sunlight made the light-colored denim look hot as horseradish. Burke's shadow moved over his feet as he stood up. He stretched, as if punching the sky, while still holding a section of newspaper. He turned and tossed the closed and doubled-over paper toward me, twirling it a little as if dealing cards. The paper landed in the grass, near the emptied remains of my last, childish paint set. That morning, I'd used the lid's lining as a place to mix paint from tubes. Dried paint daubed the smooth, white-enameled tin. Burke's paper landed near the set's print-bearing side, the side full of aligned names. The printed names labeled long-since-emptied slots.

9   LILACS IN FRONT HALL

Almost ritually, every spring, as long as the flowering lasted, Estelle cut flowers from her lilac bushes. She arranged the softly conical flowers and the soft, severed lengths of the leafy limbs that bore them in a hard, slick, glass pitcher decoratively cut with sharp patterns. (Pinwheels of extreme acuity, two sixteen-pointed stars, covered the pitcher's sides, one to either side of the handle.) She placed the pitcher-and-flowers on a small, marble-topped table shaped like a half-moon which stood in her front hall, its straight side against a wallpapered wall. (The table seemed grave-like to me because Estelle consistently referred to the cut-glass pitcher brought to it as "Margaret's," "the one that used to be Margaret's," and Estelle regularly set flowers on the base of another piece of white stone, a somber, rectangular slab incised with two names, Margaret's and that of Estelle's brother, Everett.) Darkly wooden, uncarpeted stairs rose angularly above the cut, arranged lilacs. A tall clock ticked in a corner. A leaded fanlight like an overgrown web hung over the front door.

Estelle lavished care on her lilac bushes. She said that they "thanked" her "by flowering." She reaped the redolent thanks. Outside, the line of flowering bushes did not strike me as oppressive, heavy, or conventional. The flowery abundance looked almost joyous, as if the bushes celebrated something, throwing their flowers upward slowly into the air. Once Estelle herself seemed, briefly, to my imagining mind, part of the celebration.

That morning, I heard her cutting branches. I tried to avoid hearing the tool she used to cut through the green wood, the blades grunting closed, the shaken leaves rustling. (Estelle biblically called the tool, a V of long handles conjoined through short, snub, flat blades, a "pruning hook." I harshly called it "the loppers.") I lay chest down, shirtless, on a soft, hot, vinyl-covered swing, my lower legs awkwardly athwart an armrest. Burke sat nearby, sounding increasingly impatient with a newspaper, folding and refolding it noisily. He'd lectured me earlier about cutting the grass. The grass needed nothing, but he wanted it cut. Estelle wanted it cut. I heard Estelle's sounds of cutting. Eyes closed in warm sunlight, I began telling myself that I had to cut the grass, that I would cut the grass, that I would, I would, I had to, that afternoon. I opened my eyes. Burke stood up, stretched, tossed his paper aside. It landed near my paint set. Estelle came walking toward us, the sun so bright, it made her hair look white, whiter than I'd ever seen it looking. She carried a load of cut, flowering branches so long and deep that it hid her lower arms completely; it hid much of her upper arms, too, and more. As she walked, the flowers nodded, all heaped to one side. Grass blades squeaked as Estelle's polished shoes pulled through them. (The grass, squeaking, sounded like a wet mirror rubbed clean, but given my senses, the grass leaves whimpered. They seemed to cling to Estelle's shoes, to her moving feet, as if pleading for mercy, as if they knew to appeal to her against their impending execution by lawn mower.) Burke said, "I'm going in," but he walked toward Estelle, his bare feet silent in the grass as far as I could hear. Burke and Estelle spoke. I didn't pay attention to them until Burke said, "Here. Let me take those for you," and Estelle replied, "Thank you, darling. That'll save me a trip." Burke's words shocked me. I thought that he offered to carry the flowers, something that I—selfishly, self-indulgently—might have done. I wished otherwise. I prized assumptions about Burke. I only then realized that I prized a belief in deep differences between us. (I might carry flowers; Burke should not do so.) But, whatever I wished to believe, Estelle shifted the cuttings as if she would hand them to Burke. I soon saw my error. Burke took the loppers from her, from underneath the flowers. Burke's taking the loppers "saved" Estelle "a trip" to the garage.

That morning, I'd painted expansively. I'd painted, in bright, springing tinctures, evocations of flowers, leaves, bushes, sunlight spilling over leafy tiers. I'd painted, that morning, as if no fence existed, as if no fence existed beyond the bushy fountains, as if no knives existed under cut flowers.

10   FOB

Depicted in the wallpaper on Estelle's bedroom walls, bunches of roses with cut stems seemed to fly in diagonal lines across trellises like ladders set against Naples yellow. Red roses turned to dismal mauve bunched with roses once red; white roses turned to pallid green bunched with others once-snowy; roses in segregated diagonals followed each other over the trellises and over the yellow. The rose bunches seemed to fly because ribbons tied into big, cheeky bows bound the cut stems together and the bows' streamers of free ends seemed to beat the air like wings, energetically rippling, carrying the bunches. Three photographs and only three photographs hung on the walls. Two of them depicted separately Estelle's parents, Joel and Adelia Rawlinson. The other depicted Estelle's brother, Everett, as a bridegroom with his bride, a woman named Margaret Burke. Ovals surrounded the photographs; curved glass arched over them. Estelle's parents' photographs hung, paired by proximity, on the wall beyond the foot of Estelle's single bed. The wedding photograph hung above a satinwood chest-of-drawers, facing the bed broadside: a terrible arrangement. Margaret Burke had died giving birth to my father. Everett had died of a gastric ulcer soon afterward. Estelle had raised their child, my father, Carl. Thus marriage, trauma, death, short life, responsibility assumed for other people, duty, love, and sex, sex-as-leading-to-terrible-things, faced Estelle's single bed from across the room. The glass in the picture frames curved. The walls bulged with wombs filled with dead parents.

Ovals framed the photographs and ovals lay on the floor: Rugs made of dull, brown braids wound around oval centers. An oval posed as the back of a chair upholstered in needlepoint. Small, silver, oval picture frames stood on the ends of a satinwood dressing table. (My mother called the table a dressing table; she would. Estelle called the same table a vanity, recalling Ecclesiastes.) The vanity matched the tall chest-of-drawers below the wedding photograph and occupied the same wall. A large oval mirror loomed over the vanity. If one sat on the vanity's caned bench, as I once did, one could see Estelle's parents' photographs reflected in the vanity's mirror from across the room: parents over one's shoulders, my paternal great-grandparents twice made of light—by light reflected, breathing through the leavings of light as if down one's neck. Ovals clustered obsessively, stuffed into a chair, hung around photographs, spread in rugs' dull lumps. Estelle had variously acquired the ovals. She'd bought them, received them as gifts, or inherited them. I knew that much rationally, but irrationally I felt that some ovals drew other ovals to them. The powerful ovals, the oval-attractant ovals, lay in a box, in a drawer, inside the vanity. They consisted of four stones of four sizes linked through silver rims: four thin, translucent, blue-gray-violet stones flat and unpolished on one side, polished and slightly convex on the other. The sequence of four stones linked in order of size did not close bracelet-like upon itself. A small, jawed hook soldered to a short, plain chain adjoined the smallest stone. Estelle called the stones moonstones, erroneously. Together they formed a fob; she explained fobs to me. In the past of her parents, fobs decorated watch chains or clipped directly to pocket watches and dangled ornamentally from pockets. Fobs facilitated withdrawing pocket watches from pockets. Faintly splendid, modestly ostentatious, gray in its slithery glimmer, Estelle's fob looked as if it might have belonged to a Victorian lady. Perhaps for that reason, Estelle's fob offended its first owner, Estelle's father, Joel Rawlinson, who'd received it as a gift from colleagues when he'd retired from teaching in a rural school. Estelle, reminiscing while running the fob through her fingers, said many times that the gift-giving teachers should have known better Joel's simple taste. Joel Rawlinson had privately called the pendants "indecent." "Indecent": a condemnatory gout that sailed through three generations before it hit me, Ed, Joel's "indecent," gay great-grandson. Unlike me, Joel Rawlinson had had the decency not to explain himself, not to say, exactly, what he meant by "indecent." The fob, slick and glimmering, dripping in polished pendency from Joel's vest-wearing side, might have resembled viscera escaping when he did wear the thing as politeness required. Whatever reasons, whatever qualities caused Joel to deem the four stones "indecent," I added my own indecency plenteously to them.

I would stand or sit around and listen or not listen to Estelle talk about family, about religion, about religion and Rawlinsons, and Rawlinsons and religion until the two drear subjects seemed one and the same. I would stand sometimes with my back to Estelle-in-bed and surreptitiously untwist the curtains' ropes or dig into the curtain-ropes' tassels, searching for color, for the deep sheen of pomegranate-seed red beneath their faded gloss. Estelle talked and talked. She talked about Rawlinsons, Rawlinsons, Rawlinsons: Joel, Everett, Carl, Margaret, Adelia. Joel, Everett, and Carl predominated. Sometimes, glancing, I saw the stones, the supposititious moonstones, slip through Estelle's hands as she talked. And I, indecently, with my sex-saturated mind, thought often, as if I could not keep from thinking, "begat," "begat," "begat," "begat," one "begat" for each stone. I would see, in flashes, Joel, Everett, Carl, and my brother Burke, Joel, Everett, Carl, and Burke all actively begetting: hale, rigorous Joel pitching and heaving to an invisible wife, plying his moonstone-tipped penis to the glories of God; Everett beneath an invisible Margaret, moonstone delivered in a panting of lavender, romantic love; Carl bobbing in pragmatic haste, afraid that my invisible mother might change her mind about receiving his moonstone-tipped length unsheathed; Burke speaking, through his applied gem, love to an invisible woman who did not love him. Distended states ascribed to family members attached to Estelle's guiltless stones in my prurient head.

Estelle, talking, gesturing, nodding the fertile fob in my direction, repeatedly told me, "I mean for you to have this," or some such words. Estelle did not mean to sound threatening, and I did not mean to sound obstinate, but each time that Estelle referred obliquely to her death and expressed her intention to leave her talisman to me, I said something blunt and ungrateful, like "Give it to Burke," "Burke should have it," "It should go to Burke." Estelle sometimes gazed at me searchingly when I said, "Burke should have it," but she didn't ask me why I said what I said. I don't know why Estelle's chain, with its four obviously finite, gray-violet stones, suggested continuation, generational continuation, to me, but it did. The chain obviously ended. To my mind it ended with the largest stone of the four, the stone furthest from the chain-and-clip end, the glans-stone that I secretly called Burke's. Nonetheless, to my mind, the stones in finite sequence suggested sexual reproduction without known end, and I knew that I had no role and no desire for a role in that fundamental aspect of biological life. I also knew that Estelle meant what she said about giving me the fob. After many cryptic protests, I stopped resisting; I stopped referring to Burke when she brandished the fob.

I felt steeled to accept Estelle's gift in general. But I didn't expect her to give it to me when I came into her room to say goodbye to her, right before I left to begin work on a master of fine arts. Although elated about my prospects in general, I felt wretched when I approached Estelle to say goodbye. Entering her dismally, cheerfully wallpapered room, I felt crushed by a sense that I would not see her again. She sat in bed, hair in a braid, a book in her lap, pale eyes reading unaided. Seeing me, she laid the book aside. A crocheted bedspread, under which Estelle never slept, lay folded across the needlepoint chair. I sat on the bed, near Estelle's feet. Darting patchwork covered them, a quilt wild with contrasts, satin, corduroy, maroon, orange, turquoise, vividly patched; straight-edged, sharp-angled patches, triangles sharp as broken glass, stabbed every which way throughout the bending fabric. I sat. Estelle spoke of my MFA. "This is what you've always wanted." "I'm happy for you." "I'm sure you'll do well." "Take full advantage." Estelle repeated, "I'm happy for you, Edward." She seemed happier for me than I felt for myself. She said, "Promise me? Take care of yourself?" I froze utterly. I sat, eyes on the slicing patchwork. I heard what Estelle said, but I also heard an implication: "Take care of yourself. After I'm gone." I squeezed her covered feet. I wept with my face against them; Estelle made soothing sounds. I dived into hugging her wholly, feeling her living fragility, sensing her living—hair, scent, skin, warmth—a terrible complex that would soon disintegrate. I said gasping, "I'll miss you, I'll miss you." Estelle said gently, "I'm sure you will." She wiped my face with her fingers, said, "Take care of yourself. You hear me? This is exactly what I mean. You take things so hard. I worry about you." In a guilty rush, I tried to reassure her. I said that I would "take care of myself," that I would try "to keep things in perspective." Estelle said, as if properly satisfied by my worthless pledge to work against my temperament, "You can start by cheering up now." I sat up, sat averted and holding her hands. Eventually, Estelle said, "Will you do me a favor, now, Edward? No argument?" That I had ever argued with her seemed inconceivable. Moving her soft face, Estelle said, "Take that fob now, Edward. Bring it to me, please."

I had to stand up. I had to cross the room full of oppressive, obsessive ovals. I had to confront the dressing table and touch a drawer handle that Estelle had touched countless times. I had to pull out the drawer and see long, thin, narrow boxes like coffins stacked inside the drawer. As I stood looking down, Estelle prompted unnecessarily, as if she supposed that I hesitated because I didn't know which box to extract: "It says 'Hamilton' on it." The "Hamilton" casket lay uppermost: ivory-white plastic with the name "Hamilton" printed in small, blackened letters which looked as if etched into the plastic between molded scrolls at the lid's either end. I had to pick up the Hamilton box, Estelle's casket-in-miniature, Estelle's little body, just memories, which I, with my sex-saturated mind, felt unworthy to carry manually or mentally.

When I did manage to return across the oval rug, when I extended the Hamilton box to Estelle, petrous corpse in it and all, she waved it back to me, saying, "That's yours now. Keep it, Edward. Please." And I, tears seeping through my patched, leaky manliness, hugged Estelle, kissed her warm, yielding cheek and her barely present, presented lips, and even then I made demands upon her. I said that I would take the moonstones out of her (living) hands, "Not in a goddamned box." Estelle, her facial skin in thin, soft ridges all tending downward, smiled forgivingly. She said, "Don't swear, Edward. Promise me you won't swear." I promised. I extended the box to her. I had to see her eyes touch it, her hands receive it. I had to see her skin-veiled fingers turn back the box lid and lift, out of velvet clips, the small spine of family, the four so-called moonstones that all but had names.

11   TROPHY KNIVES

Estelle kept silverware in a silver chest. Lavender and pink fabric with a soft flannel-like nap lined the chest completely. The lavender seemed dark gray, violescent. A gray-violet ridge slotted to hold silverware crossed the pink-covered floor of the box. Transferred tarnish streaked the pink cloth and the weight of stacked spoons and forks that had lain upon it for decades (decayed, decayed, one might have thought) had dented the box floor, depressed the underlying padding. I supposed that Estelle valued her chest-stored silverware because, despite her religious abhorrence of pride as a sin (and the worst of sins, the opposite of humility), she took pride in the long-stretched genealogical web in her mind that connected every piece of silver in the box with someone whom she'd known (and who had died) or with people known to her only through reminiscences or through relics like letters and headstones and inscriptions on endpapers in her berg of a Bible. Estelle's silverware might remind her of her parents and of her brother, Everett, and of her pride in belonging to what she would call, unfortunately, "a good, Christian family." Her silverware might remind her of family members lost to death. It might remind her of a religious world lost to her with its proponents and lost, also, through my father's intellectual rebelliousness.

Estelle talked so much about which of her long-deceased relatives had acquired which clutches of silver and how and for what reason they'd acquired what they'd acquired that the utensils seemed transmogrified people, the bodies of people so long buried that, like coal to diamonds, they'd turned into silverware, small, silver bodies of compacted bones. The bodies seemed honorably buried, sealed away into an unworldly compartment, reverently laid to rest even when they lay stacked on top of each other. I didn't think of the knives, forks, spoons as people while eating with them, only when I saw them lying reposefully outstretched, arranged in kindred groups inside the silver chest (casket, crypt, barrow). Knives with pearl handles stood, handles uppermost, upright against the lid's lining when the lid stood raised. Seen against the upright lid, the knives looked fine and upstanding, vigilant and guard-like, above all the other pieces in the box—spoons and forks and serving pieces and oddments like hat pins and napkin rings and sets of children's silverware and sugar spoons with scoops like small scallop shells. Everything in the box except the bright fence of knives seemed subordinate to a ladle which lay, cloth-enfolded, along the front of the box, at the feet of many little families, stacked forks and spoons. The ladle loomed large in the box as Estelle loomed large to me.

My parents had bought the "coin-silver" ladle on their honeymoon in Mexico. Estelle had wrapped it in old cloth as if she meant to invest it, the base newcomer, with respectable age. One night, Burke untucked a corner of the ladle's shroud. He showed it to me. The corner lay on his palm. The cloth looked sallow. The crochet edging it looked limp, like white lilac flowers wilted. Little balls of thread edged the edging. Showing me the sallow cloth edged with heavy crochet, Burke said, "This is Victorian, very Victorian." I didn't know what he meant. I saw what Burke showed me, but I could not see what he saw. Trying to hide my ignorance from Burke, I didn't ask, "What's 'Victorian'?" I did not ask, with the unbelievable correctness drilled into me, "What does 'Victorian' mean?" I asked diffidently, indirectly, "What's 'Victorian' about it?" Burke replied. At first, he said unhelpfully, "Everything." But then, tucking the edged corner back under the ladle's cranium, making a dithering, pinched motion with his fingers in the air as if sifting it, he said, "Everything, then, had to express this," the sifting motion, "this fussy, prettified idea of refinement. Despite the viciousness of their society." Excited by the collision between "refinement" and "viciousness," I lost diffidence. I asked questions which Burke tried to answer at length until, patience exhausted, he said, "Don't they teach you this in school?" "No," I didn't say. No one taught as Burke taught.

Pink and lavender fabric in separate swaths lined Estelle's silver chest. Pink and lavender both lined the lid. If the lid stood raised, lavender lined the upper third of it; pink lined the rest, and pink fabric, without interruption, without break for the hinges, lined the back wall of the box, and covered its floor. Pink fabric bands, bands enough to hold fourteen knives by the blades with two bands for each blade, protruded lowly and flatly from the pink lining the lid. To put knives away, one slid the blades downward through the soft, pink loops. Knives occupied twelve of the fourteen sets of bands. Knives slipped down, between lid and loops. The loops offered no resistance to them, consisting, as the loops did, of given openings.

The knives stored inside Estelle's softly-lined chest, sometimes aligned against the upraised lid, looked extremely mild, extremely gentle, as knives went. The blades had round tips. The blades lacked effectively cutting edges. The blades bore decorative bevels on the edges not meant to cut. Ornate ferrules masked the mating between handles and blades. The knives' handles consisted of deep, rounded, curved pearl cut from the thick of pearl oysters' shells. The deep, naked nacre, the curved mother-of-pearl handles, looked subtly, discreetly iridescent in patches. Burke explained the iridescence. Given his information, I thought about the soft, deep handles and the hard, shallow blades. The handles seemed to analyze, to split, to divide, light to the iridescent end of something like understanding, while the hard, bright, brave blades, acting without hesitation, reflected light instantly. Each knife as a whole seemed very well balanced.

41

12   WIND CHIME

As a child I received a gift in passing from one of my parents'
friends. The gift, a wind chime made of glass pieces, strings, and
tin rings, delighted me. The clear, flat, glass pieces—squares and
rectangles—bore paint: daubs something like blue-petaled, yellow-
centered flowers, more like cats' inartistic footprints. Nine blue
strings came together at the top of the chime; the strings knotted
as one around a ring from which one could hang the chime. Held
horizontal by strings wrapped around them, two blue-painted,
circular, tin bands hung well below the topknot, one band smaller
than the other, the smaller band above the larger. From the
uppermost band, four long, flat, glass rectangles hung vertically.
From the lower and larger band, four flat, glass squares hung
tipped. Each square hung from one of its corners, with two of its
corners pointed sideways. One string, ending in a pendent square,
hung straight down from the topknot, through the center of the
system. Hanging from the larger of the two bands, the pendent
squares surrounded the pendent rectangles. The squares hanging
from the band could only just touch the rectangles. When the glass
pieces touched, they sounded marvelous, crystalline. That gift
offended my father. In the absence of the giver, he called it "no fit
gift for a boy." The chime's glassy ringing, which delighted me,
seemed effete to my father. He disliked my liking the thing and
its sounds: blue rings, glass pieces, effects produced in the air by
fragilities meeting.

13   RED KNIFE, CLAMS

My father gave me a knife for one of my birthdays. On principle, he gave me things that he deemed suitably boyish. Neither he nor I liked the knife, the appropriate accoutrement dutifully given. The knife possessed two bright blades; a levelheaded screwdriver with a nick near its base for stripping wire; a stubby, flatly curvaceous can opener; a deeply curvaceous corkscrew; a straight, pointed jabber with a hole through it like an eye in a substantial needle. When closed, the corkscrew lay along an outer side of the knife, as in a slot cut out for it in one of the knife's scarlet scales. The corkscrew's coils curved regularly over and over beside the flat, bright-red, plastic plating, which they exceeded in height. The knife crammed with flat things could not contain such emphatic curves. The side of the knife that didn't hold the surpassing corkscrew had the knife-making company's insignia printed on it. The slightly recessed insignia in silver paint consisted of a short-armed cross with all the arms the same length and a shield-like outline surrounding the cross. The cross appeared as if on a shield.

Neither Dad nor I liked the knife, but I thanked him for it politely. To me, the scales' blood-red hue looked so assertively bright that the blades seemed fitting extensions from it. To my father, the cross-within-a-shield seemed an emblem, not of protective faith, but of faith ready to war. The emblem offended my father intellectually; the scales' bright-red color repelled me emotionally. But I used the knife. I used the wire stripper to expose copper wire bundled inside rubber-coated snippets that men building new houses sometimes left at construction sites. I sharpened drawing pencils with the blades. (I had used a very old, hand-cranked pencil sharpener which gripped pencils between grooved cylinders and tore at them with the cylinders. Peeling seemed more torturous of pencils than did cutting with edges.) I used the knife's longest blade to kill clams for their shells.

To find clams, at summer camp, I broke rules. I repeatedly broke a rule against going anywhere into woods without a companion. I repeatedly broke a rule against going anywhere without telling an authority where one intended to go. And best, to my greatest delectation, repeatedly, year after year, and many times each summer, I broke a rule against swimming in lake water not approved for swimming: water which no guard watched, water free of floats and buoys, water free of lanes and lines, water in which no one raced or trained, water relieved of regulation, of discipline, and of competition. I broke those rules repeatedly and with unaccountable impunity. But I respected the rule against swimming in unapproved water enough to check for hazards before swimming freely. I hunted for clams by feeling for them with my feet in mud like superabundant finger paint.

I killed clams because I desired to own their shells, because I admired clamshells. I admired clamshells' peripheral curves and the curves of their inward and outward slopes. I admired how every shell half—purged of its maker—curved in many directions as a single form. I admired how the shell halves, which I had cut apart, fit together naturally, perfectly. I admired, above all, the colors lining the shells, colors like dawn light reflected on rippling water. The colors touched me in the quick of my mind, where my love for watercolor painting lived.

The knife that my father gave me did display curves, but, to me, it looked straight, as if absolutely curveless, beside a curved shell. Sometimes I paused before working the tip of a blade into a shell's hinge. I saw the knife in my right hand, the knife straight and bright, blood-red and chrome-bright, beside the shaggy, dripping darkness of a living clamshell.

At summer camp, I collected shells slowly. I stood the shell halves on end, paired as if still hinged together, along the edges of boards that reinforced the inner walls of camp cabins. That my fragile collections on precarious ledges survived year after year gratified me. No one smashed them; no one blundered into them; no hurled object hit them, remarkably. I felt that friendships and respect, more than mere chance, contributed to the survival of my collections.

14   THREE OF SWORDS

Over and over, growing up, Burke tossed me the comic sections out of his newspapers. I read the "funnies," I enjoyed them, and I studied them as drawings. But Burke's manner of tossing them toward me (or at me) irritated me. He probably tossed the comic sections aside, in my direction, without meaning anything by the tossing. But I felt that he acted lofty and dismissive. I felt that he acted contemptuous of comic strips and cartoons, that he tossed the color-bearing pages aside with an air of snobbish high-mindedness, as if telling me, by the tossing, that he had no time for such nonsense, no time for drawings, for trivial pictures. In revenge for this perceived slight to drawings, I sometimes called Burke "Val," the nickname of the comic-strip hero "Prince Valiant." Because Burke looked broad-shouldered and dark-haired and facially symmetrical, the ludicrous nickname stuck. Other people used it. Burke hated it.

Burke gave me a set of tarot cards which someone had given to him. "Maybe you'll like the pictures," he said. He disliked the cards. (He pointedly said so; I did not imagine his expressed dislike.) Burke disliked the irrationality of the tarot cards' intended use. But Burke's words, "Maybe you'll like the pictures," implied that I might find redeeming traits in the cards, whereas the figures on their fortune-telling sides couldn't possibly interest him.

I did like the cards. A person named David Palladini had drawn them at age eighteen, a fact which made me mildly jealous and emulous while it also sparked hope for my artistic future. The cards looked like Art Deco drawings: no human represented on them looked realistic, and flat patterns attended the stylized people. I wanted to think that drawings (and paintings and all other forms of visual art) did not mean anything beyond the registered immediacy of their formal qualities. A booklet that came with the tarot cards asserted a completely different principle. The booklet listed, in a few words, meanings for every card: one group of meanings for a card's image turned right-side-up and another group of meanings for the same image seen upside down. I resented the booklet, the little catalog of gists, for giving words primacy over silent drawings. But I looked at it. I looked at it so often and for so long in conjunction with the cards that I inadvertently learned which cloud of concepts applied to which view of which card. This inadvertently acquired knowledge of the cards' formally unjustified burdens served me well at summer camp, where I used the cards to tell fortunes, engagingly dire fortunes for fortunate people.

From a booklet, I learned meanings assigned to tarot cards. I also learned that I responded tellingly to the sight of certain cards. I could not see the card called the three of swords without feeling guilty about Estelle.

In the set of cards that Burke gave me, in the middle of the card called the three of swords, straight shapes representing swords transfixed a curved shape, a heart shape, left, right, and center. The dark-pink heart shape looked weirdly like and unlike a valentine heart. A firm, black outline defined it. Sword shapes interrupted the outline, but had the outline appeared in its entirety, its curves would have flowed together continuously, unlike the symmetrical curves of a valentine heart which terminate sharply, at abrupt junctions with each other. The tarot card's drawn heart also looked wider, more spacious horizontally, than did a valentine heart. Within the wide heart shape, within its evenly dark-pink area, a few sketchy, little black streaks, penned or penciled, suggested depth and texture, fullness and softness. The card's puffy-looking heart seemed to give softly, as if it sank around the swords, where they, as three unbending, firmly defined shapes made of straight lines, seemingly entered it. And where the drawn sword points appeared to exit the heart, near the heart's rounded tip, the heart's illusory softness appeared drawn along, as if it adhered to the transfixing blades. I could not see that card, that image, without thinking that Burke, my father, and I tortured Estelle. We grieved Estelle, in her heart of hearts, by our atheism.

15   AZTEC KNIFE

Adolescent, I stood in an immaculate museum in Mexico City, looking at a black, glass knife in a clear-glass museum case. Small, unobtrusive clips made of transparent plastic held the Aztec knife in position, not quite upright, against a pale, grayish panel within the case. In silhouette, seen broadside against the panel, the blade's shape resembled that of a magnolia leaf (minus the stem), a leaf also seen broadside. Its two edges curved symmetrically. From the end displayed as the lower end of the blade, the long, curving edges diverged gradually; they converged steeply near the upper end, where the blade looked widest. Both ends pointed. Someone had shaped the thing by chipping; light reflected variously from its surface when I moved my head. Print labeled the object "obsidian." "What's obsidian?" I'd asked Burke. He'd replied dramatically and directly, "It's glass made by a volcano when it melts silica." (Never mind, "What's silica?") Volcanoes and molten glass and an Aztec maker's living hands seemed worlds away from the quiet museum. The clear glass of the museum case, the neutral gray of the display panel, and the bits of unobtrusive plastic supporting the blade, all seemed to hold the shape carefully, carefully, in the very clean clutches of studious respect.

Burke had told me that Aztec priests, some with their teeth filed to points, their bodies painted black to symbolize War and Religion, their hair matted with human blood, cut open live human bellies and live human diaphragms, reached into live human chests, seized live human hearts, and tore live human hearts out, away from arteries. Burke said that priests raised the hearts to the deified Sun or crushed them as gifts against other gods' statues. When I, revolted, asked Burke why, why did they do that? Burke said that the Aztecs believed that they owed everything to their gods; that their gods had sacrificed themselves, many by giving their living hearts, when creating man and the world; that men consequently owed the gods an unpayable debt; that people should abase themselves before their gods; that people's spirits lived in their blood, in their hearts especially; that blood, hearts especially, represented the most precious offering that people could make to their gods; that spiritual energy given by people to gods by the gift of live, excised hearts fueled the universe, kept the Sun moving. When I, still revolted, asked, "Why did they think like that?" Burke shrugged. He replied, "We generally believe what we're told to believe."

Staring at the carefully preserved, carefully presented artifact, remembering Burke's talk of sacrificial slaughter, I almost feared the black blade. I wondered if it had served, in priestly hands, to cut open chests, to kill for live hearts.

16 CARDS WITH BURKE

Burke and I sometimes played the card game hearts, modified for two people. Burke, who coached me to excess, told me that when arranging cards in a hand of cards fanwise, I should arrange the cards by suits and the suits according to their hierarchical value in the card game bridge, with the most valuable spades on the far left, followed, from left to the right, by hearts, diamonds, and clubs. I usually did what Burke told me to do; I rarely had the nerve to disagree with Burke or to oppose Burke's suggestions. But, in that matter of cards, Burke surely erred. Surely one should not keep all those red cards together. Further, Burke erred in the mere sense of things. In rare and secret disobedience to Burke, when arranging a hand of cards fanwise, I separated hearts and spades. I kept the lobed emblem, love, away from the knife.

17   DROPS OF WAX, ESTELLE

One night, after an elaborate dinner which Estelle and her paid helper, Barbara, had prepared and arranged with all the icy, white trappings—china, cloth, candles—by which Estelle ritually recognized special occasions, my mother moved one of the two candelabra. The wicks of its three candles still smoldered; vapor roiled above the blackened wicks; liquid wax filled the small craters atop the candles. Without waiting for the wax to set, my mother lifted the holder; she tilted it slightly; I reached out, interfering. (My father later told me that he didn't like seeing me help clear the table. Anyone else might have helped without incurring his disapproval. But domestic helpfulness in me offended my father.) I reached out, meaning to right the candles. Molten wax splashed the back of my hand. The small drops clouded instantly. They had a fine, pointed whiteness. They hurt with a fine, pointed whiteness, like a kitten's teeth latched suddenly in play.

I liked the shapes that raindrops sometimes made, fallen on pavement, dashed against dusty grit by accident: spots like bottle caps deprived of a dimension, rounds with points around their perimeters. Such spots had impact—past—expressed in their shapes. They seemed more like exclamation marks than exclamation marks did. They conveyed actual shock, real transformation.

The night that wax caught my hand, I wished that I could have observed the small drops, the little, waxen, white drops with splashed points pointing, starting out from their edges. I wished that I'd had time to attend to their appearance and to appreciate the slight justice, the minor rightness, in the fact that the drops bit the hand that drew them, that had drawn other drops like them, rain dashed on pavement. I wished that I could have seen, but people rushed in upon my sight. My mother set down the candles. She grabbed my precious paw. She said, "Darling, I'm so sorry" at the same time that my father snapped, "Can't you be careful?" His "you" might have applied to both Mother and me, but then he said, "And you, Edward Rawlinson. What do you think you're doing? Hovering around. Always underfoot. Go to your room. I'll have a word with you later." I dreaded nothing so much as my father's "words." I pulled my hand away from Mother's. I ran out of the room.

Later that night, I came downstairs under the soft sound of rain. Dad had told me not to enter the dining room except for meals. Wilting in intended obedience to him, I stopped in the archway leading into the dining room. Beyond the table, on the far side of the room, stood Estelle. That night's tablecloth lay heaped in front of her. The cloth moved as Estelle, examining it for traces left from the meal, spread it flat against the table section by section. Around her left wrist she wore a pincushion on a clear, plastic band. Little gold-colored safety pins perched like insects on the wrist-worn cushion. Straight pins also studded the pad. Pinheads glistened like bubbles in soda water.

Estelle would wash the tablecloth by hand. She marked, in dry cloth, with gold-colored safety pins, the small, rare spots which she would address individually, with her scrubbing hands. She marked the small spots so that she might find them again, amid a sink full of the wet cloth's sopping, seemingly endless coils.

Golden pins with firm catches would hold fast to blemishes which Estelle would wash away. Straight pins, with their slippery straightness, might have slipped from the cloth. Straight pins would not have served her purpose. Golden pins would hold.

Sounding rain draped the house and made it seem limber, bending. Against the beat-less creak of rain, the hall clock ticked mechanically. In the center of the large, bared, glossy, almost-black table, light from an overhead fixture reflected. The reflection looked like a bushel-sized mass of thistledown flattened. Knives, used that night, lay on a sideboard behind Estelle. Silver and white on the almost-black sideboard, the six knives, grouped together, not touching each other, looked only slightly more substantial than did the thistledown glare. Examining the tablecloth, Estelle looked downward so steeply that I could see nicks made by hairpins in the foremost base of her chignon. I almost grieved for Estelle, for her firm sense of order trivially expressed. I did not grieve for her then, however, because I remembered that her principles transcended pettiness.

Finished pinning, Estelle gathered up the cloth. She stood upright, holding the cloth cradled in her arms and against her body. The cradled mass made her seem many things: vaguely bridal, vaguely pregnant, vaguely god-parental-at-a-baptismal-font, vaguely ready for death, posed and prepared on some stygian shore beside a black, burning lake, the dining-room table. Estelle cradled the tablecloth against her body, the colorless, rose-patterned cloth valuable to her for its descent from her parents, the thing patterned with flat images of cut roses, of abundant, tumbled roses, of roses pressed flat, pressed to near-extinction in the gleaming weave. Whatever anti-sensual principles religiously enforced, whatever unkindness against senses Estelle's tablecloth suggested, she spoke to me kindly, as usual. She said brightly, "Ah, Edward. There you are. I was wondering what had become of you. If you would like to help me, you could put those knives away." In Estelle's suggestion, I heard a moral thrust. She had preached mildness to me. She'd urged "forgive," "forget," "turn the other cheek." She'd tried to soothe away sharp emotions so softly, so often, with such gentle assiduity, with such persistently uninsistent tenderness, that when she said, "If you would like to help me, you could put those knives away," I heard her suggest that I might help her by forgetting (somehow, magically) every grievance, every resentment, every bladed bit of rage that I'd ever felt.

55

18 SOLDER

When days of rain and hours of ambitious drizzle almost guaranteed that no workmen would work on worksites, I bicycled out to find unfinished houses. Young enough—and timid enough—to feel agreeably frightened by my venturesomeness, I biked long distances and I trespassed, onto raw lots and into future houses. I saw soft wood with hard nails driven into it (nails, Jesus Christ). I saw brown water pooling in pits with cut, earthen walls. I gripped knurled reinforcing rods and smelled curing concrete, felt concrete warm in the grip of molding skids. I touched, smelled, and saw lumber, dead wood, killed trees, milled trees: two-by-fours standing in vacancy, making thin claims for walls. I looked at insulation, yellow wool, pink floss. I admired sheet metal's mingled flecks of grays. I learned that sheet metal reverberated readily, with the least touch released. I looked at broad sheets of paper-sandwiched chalk, at heaped plastic sheeting, rainwater cupped in its hollows, at bricks in strapped bales and at bricks tumbled loose. I saw black tar in tawny cardboard drums, the black like stubs of gigantic crayons paper-covered. I saw. tar-melting machines, tar-covered maws. I saw small, encrusted cement mixers and exhausted-looking tractors, the tractors' scoops lowered and slack on torn earth. I wandered into rooms-not-yet-rooms, rooms not-yet-private. Sometimes saws stood in rooms, saws with hook-rimmed discs for cutting, saws with an obviously dangerous, voracious, waiting quality. I picked up things and put things down.

I marveled and felt repelled. And, of course, I stole. I stole small scraps, scraps which I supposed no one would miss: metal slugs punched out of electrical housings; short, cut, dropped lengths of pipe; snippets of copper wiring, little bundles of copper wires covered in white, or red, or black rubber; piteous little wooden blocks with saw-torn small sides. I collected scraps. Manliness seemed to saturate them (and manliness reeked from everything encountered). I found small scraps attractive. But, among all the things that I saw or touched or smelled or heard, solder impressed me most vividly: silver-bright splashes on littered subflooring, splashes of once-liquid solder, silver-bright drops pointedly edged. Workmen, whom I avoided, I imagined as gods—and solder as the gods' lavish, loosed ejaculate.

19   JACKS

Christine played jacks on my parents' basement floor. She used twelve jacks. Each consisted of six extensions centrally conjoined. From the conjunction, four bars in the same plane formed a completely symmetrical cross. The small, cylindrical cross arms ended with balls. The balls, all the same size, looked large in comparison to the cylinders. (To me, the balls looked as if they sprouted from the ends of the bars.) From the conjunction and perpendicular to the budding bars, two cones extended from their bases to equal heights. In length, each knobbed branch exceeded each cone's height by some slight extent. The balls or spheres, of course, curved. They didn't point. The cones pointed. When tossed onto the floor and come to rest, each jack stood with two curves and one point touching the floor. If the cones formed an axis, each jack's axis tilted. Each jack tilted necessarily and stood in a manner determined by its structure.

While Christine played jacks, I lay sprawled on the floor, drawing with crayons. The floor looked even, level and smooth, but edges of its hard, dark-brown, square linoleum tiles projected minutely. When my drawing crayon crossed one of the minute projections, it left more wax on the paper than it otherwise did; extra wax showed as a dark spot in a passage, and dark spots, appearing near each other, added up to streaks as straight as the edges of the underlying tiles. Unless I moved the paper, which I peevishly and repeatedly did, straight streaks entered my drawing unbidden. I associated straight lines, even then, with discipline, and straight lines, coming into my drawing uninvited, suggested the presence and the operation of a force against which I could not contend. That day, I contended against an inhibition.

Christine's jacks attracted me. She shook them together in cupped hands; she tossed them onto the floor. They gleamed on the floor like a swarm of storybook stars, silver-bright on tiled darkness and three-dimensional. Christine, three and a half years older than I, sat cross-legged on the floor, her legs in red tights, her red-dressed feet shoeless, a gray-red-black plaid skirt flexibly spread—fanwise and bending—over her upper legs and behind her scarlet calves and feet. She played jacks using a golf ball. (Later she showed me, and I used, a true jack ball, a small, soft— spongy—sphere with a bright, slick, scarlet skin.) She bounced the golf ball on the floor; she picked up jacks quickly, between the bounces. The golf ball hacked at the floor and each bounce sounded: chop. (Chris later told me that she used a jack ball on wooden floors, a golf ball on surfaces harder than wood. Tame differentiation charmed me.) Watching Christine, I wanted to try to do what she did. And I felt shame that I felt interested in what my father would call a "girls' game." (My father had strong and well-rehearsed views about what boys should do and what girls should do and how the two should not do what the other group did. Jacks ranked rankly as a "girls' game.") Still, despite shame (what would *they* think?), I felt drawn to play jacks. I saw what Chris did, saw she made it look easy. She lofted the ball and caught up jacks; her jack-stuffed hand caught the ball before it struck the floor twice. She bounced the ball and picked up jacks singly, one per bounce. She strewed the twelve. She picked up the jacks by twos between bounces. Strewing and picking, strewing and picking, she picked up the jacks by twos and by threes and by fours and by all other numbers consecutively through twelve. She gathered leftovers from the counted groups in a single pass. The gathering and the catching happened quickly. If Chris moved a jack that she didn't catch up, she began plucking the jacks up singly again; she again progressed through the ever-increasingly challenging sequence. Sometimes Chris positioned her left hand wall-like on the floor and, instead of clutching the jacks caught up between bounces, she carried them across the hand wall and dropped them. Sometimes her left hand formed a cave, and she brushed the jacks into it. Sometimes she gathered jacks very rapidly and circled the falling ball with her jack-holding hand before catching it. My chance to join Chris came amid that maneuver when she struck the ball by mistake instead of catching it. The ball leapt down the room and rolled under a sofa. We both moved the sofa by one end; I retrieved the ball and returned it to Chris.

I must have mumbled. I must have spoken shamefacedly. But somehow I asked Chris if she would teach me her game. "It takes practice," she said. I did not tell her that I couldn't practice. I didn't own jacks, and, even if I had owned them, I didn't have the nerve to practice—behind Burke's and my father's backs. But, however abashed I acted, Chris acted friendly. She encouraged me in my bungling attempts. She seemed to like me. When our parents called us upstairs, I thanked Chris for the lesson, and I begged her, "Please," please, please, "don't tell anyone." Don't tell anyone that I tried to play jacks and liked it. Chris said, "I promise." As far as I ever knew, she kept her promise.

20 HAY

Friendly, Christine treated me as a friend. I bungled jacks; she encouraged me. The pattern begun with jacks continued for years. Christine remained the teacher, I the learner. Christine, whose parents could afford the sport, became an expert equestrian, a trainer and an exhibitor of hunters and jumpers. I abidingly feared horses. For four years, until shortly after my seventeenth birthday, Christine gave me access to the farm where she boarded horses. The farm went far beyond horses. It spread into cows and crops and into a near-wilderness of woods and ravines. I greatly enjoyed exploring it—far from the horsey precinct with its drills and demands. While at the farm, I tried to avoid horses and horse people, including Christine, although I felt grateful to her for farm-afforded pleasure. (On my first visit there, Christine released me to the place as if she owned it. She said something like, "Stay out of trouble. Don't get hurt. And I'll see you later." After my trips with her, as she put it, "out to the horses," had become routine, Chris complained, "You're like a dog. The car door opens, you're off. I don't see you for hours." Blissful hours wandering.) I felt grateful to Christine for that enjoyment. I should have felt more grateful to her than I did, considering, but I felt sufficiently grateful that when Christine specifically told me that she wanted to "show" me something or when she pointedly said that she wanted to teach me something, I cooperated. At her instigation and under her instruction, I learned how to groom a horse and how to drop clumps of hay into horses' mangers from wooden catwalks above two rows of stalls.

In a hayloft, Christine demonstrated how to open and how to take apart a bale of hay. A bale lay on broad boards at her booted feet. Piled bales in the loft formed walls and platforms like the ruins of buildings built by a people too peaceable to survive. The barn's far, opened end lit the loft duskily. A disused light bulb dangled from a rafter. The loft's strong floor ended abruptly, below a fence-like barrier. The barrier looked substantial, but not substantial enough. Too much thin air enveloped it. Christine would have my attention. She said, "Look. You take this." Her splotched arms moved in the dusky light.

Christine deplored what she called her "freckles." I did not admire Christine sensually, sexually, as Burke did. (Burke loved her for years. He virtually lived with her for several.) I did not admire Christine's skin as Burke did, as her unique integument, but even I felt that the words "freckles" and "freckled" disgraced it. I admired Christine's pigmentation in a painterly way. Accustomed to blending watercolors wetly on slick, white enamel, accustomed to seeing how paint behaved on such a surface, I felt that the skin of Christine's arms and of parts of her face bore an attractive resemblance to areas on which a thin, tinted liquid spread, spread and broke and contracted, not into beady dots, but into areas less large than those originally covered.

In the loft, over a hay bale, Christine said, "You take this." I did not want to look at the tool she held. She called it "an old pair of hoof clippers." I looked at her face which, in outer contour, seen head-on, widened smoothly upward, from a small chin to a wide forehead. To call her face "egg-shaped" would demean the effect. But some suggestion of an egg's shape hovered in my mind when I, sometimes, thought about drawing Chris's portrait full-face. Amid the clean rise of curvature from the chin upward to the composed closure of her forehead, a straight nose looked decidedly narrow. Chris's friendliness lived in her other features, in her edgy lips and her quick eyes, playfulness in the former, interest (generally) in the latter.

Chris said, "Look. You take this." I felt obliged to look at the lifted tool. Its head had jaws edged with edges like chisels'. Its shut mouth resembled the beveled edges of two chisels set edge to edge. Chris parted the chisels by parting two handles which joined, bolted, through the snub head. Chris hooked one chisel underneath one of two parallel wires which, embedded in the dead grass, bound the bale of hay. Christine pried up the wire with the chisel. She closed the tool on the wire, moving chisel to chisel. The wire parted, grunted. Chris said brightly, "You do the other one." Christine extended the hoof clippers to me. I hesitated before taking the object.

I disliked seeing Christine or anyone bridle a horse. I loathed seeing metal bits eased into horses' soft mouths. Once, when I'd turned away to avoid such seeing, Christine called me "impossible," "ridiculous." Christine said defiantly, of horses, "They're used to it." As if that justified bridling. Christine all but told me, "They're used to it. You'd better get used to it to. You can't go through life like that, turning away." Gentler than my father in speech and in method, Christine nonetheless seemed to share a project with him: to work me into some blunt, tough, practical sense about life.

I took the hoof clippers from Christine's milky, splotched hand. I cut a baling wire. Chris smiled mockingly, as if to say, "There, now. You see? That wasn't so hard." She pulled the severed wires off the bale. She bent them into a bundle. She dropped the bundle into an old oil drum kept in the loft for that purpose, to corral the potentially dangerous wires. She pulled the unbound bale apart. From the first, opening cleft, the bale separated strangely into segments somehow created in its packing, segments like large birds' nests pressed into square molds. Christine split the bale. She lifted one of the shedding sections and said, "You take this." I said, "Wait a second." From the compressed, silvery face of the unhappy grass, I detached a spray of dried vetch, once purple-flowering. I held the dead flower out to Christine, giving it to her. She laughed. She took the flower. She said, "That's what I like about you. You're so romantic." She spoke in mockery, but not quite mocking.

Baled hay disturbed me. To my mind, baled hay seemed grass, stuff of the natural category, hands. But baled hay also seemed grass cut and packed into unnatural shapes, grass packed into blocks with roughly straight sides, grass held in block form by straight lines, wires.

One might have thought that I would have appreciated Christine's lesson about distributing loosed hay, that I would have enjoyed freeing baled hay from constricting wires. I didn't. Perhaps hay seemed grass past saving (although saved, cut-and-dried), grass so past saving in any living sense that its brief liberation from binding wires—brief before its consumption—effected nothing: too little, too late.

21   HORSE FIGHTING LINE

Christine told me that horses usually learned certain lessons as foals. They learned ropes. They learned to remained tied by the head, not to break the ties that tied them, and they learned "to lead," by which Christine meant, they learned to follow the lead of a person walking beside them. Christine said that a foal, tied by the head to an object, might try its (small) strength against the things used to tie it, and, failing to break them, accept, thereafter, all bonds as unbreakable. (Horses, however dimly, made a false inference. Horses, fully grown, could readily snap halters and chains and straps and ropes.) Chris said, in effect, that horses usually didn't question lessons learned when young (when small and easily coerced, she did not say). Although I feared horses, I also admired them. I also pitied them for their biddability, for their disposition to obey. I pitied them for traits that I found in myself.

At the farm, with Chris, I saw, at a distance, a grown horse learning one of those lessons about ropes. The horse fought against a rope that would hold it tied. The horse did not wear an ordinary halter. It wore a sort of noose, a rope of bright-yellow nylon, one end of which encircled a tie rail (rife with a separate grief, dead trees, telephone poles, a horizontal beam beyond budging by horses). The rope's other end formed a halter. When the horse pulled back, straightening the bight between the beam-encircling coils and the halter, the loop around the muzzle tightened, forcing the nostrils closed. Nostrils forced shut, the horse couldn't breathe.

Nonetheless, it fought. It threw itself backwards, onto its hind-quarters. It scrambled and scrambled, trying to back up. It grew still while pulling, suffocating itself. It leaned sideways, as if it would lie down. It leaned. It swayed. And it jumped forward, loosening the nostril-depressing loop, breathing with honking sounds. Repeatedly, repeatedly, it threw itself backwards, scrambling, slipping. Repeatedly, it stilled. Repeatedly, it leaned. Repeatedly, it jumped forward. Sometimes it struck the tie rail. Repeatedly, the horse breathed, trumpeting.

I wanted to free the horse, but I lacked the nerve to do so. (Not my horse, not my place. Excuses, excuses.) I stood with Christine, who watched obedient horses and riders in an enclosure, circling. I asked Chris, "What's the matter with that horse?" as if I blamed the animal for its behavior. Chris looked at me. She said, "What horse?" I nodded; Chris glanced. She smiled. She said, in a smug, clubby tone which irritated me, "Oh, nothing. He's just young. And a Thoroughbred."

22   HORSESHOE NAILS

I learned, at the farm with Christine, that most horses calmly tolerated shoeing, that most horses would stand still while a man, skilled in the use of many tools, wrenched old shoes from their hooves; clipped and filed hooves; formed new horseshoes from given forms to fit individual hooves; affixed new horseshoes to hoofs using eight nails per shoe (nails, Jesus Christ). Horseshoe nails, flat and pointed, looked like very small swords with oblong heads instead of hilts. Shoeing, the farrier, facing the opposite direction from the horse and stooped over an upturned hoof held between his knees, set a nail to a hole in the shoe and hammered in the nail. The nail's point and much of its length emerged through the hoof's outer surface. Nail by nail, one nail at a time, one by one for eight nails per shoe, the farrier cut off most of the exposed length of each driven spike. He used several tools to flatten the stub against the hoof face. Finishing, he filed all the flattened stubs and did further filing. I watched, secretly daunted by the whole operation, secretly daunted by horses' tolerance.

While I watched, the farrier talked. I hadn't noticed until he showed me: each nail bent as he hammered it in. Each nail bore a stippled patch near its oblong head. The patch told the farrier by touch which way the nail would bend when he hammered it. The patch told the farrier which side of a flat-sided nail should face the hoof's rim, so that when the farrier hammered in the nail, its tip would turn outward and exit the hoof. The man explained that refinement. Having learned that horseshoe nails possessed, by design, a predictable pliancy made me respect them somewhat. Horseshoe nails seemed highly evolved, refined to their ancient purpose. They seemed less blindly straightforward than did most nails. But they still looked like tiny swords, flat and pointed, hopelessly vicious.

23 CRUCIFIX

My aversion to nails began in southern Mexico when, feverish, I followed Burke and a guide into a church. On low platforms, on the floor, candles flamed, dark-pink, pencil-sized candles spirally fluted. Around the platforms, around the flaming groves of overgrown birthday-cake candles, women sat ritually atop folded legs. Fabrics covered their legs completely. The fabrics looked powdery, pale, washed-out, exhausted. A woman sprinkled petals over the flames; another, pine needles. The guide told Burke something about "Indians" using the building, in the absence of Catholics, in non-Catholic ways. Wax ran down candles and pooled at candles' feet. The guide genuflected, which caused me to look from the altar-platforms on the floor to the high altar, and to the wall above the high altar where hung a huge, crude painting of the crucified Christ. The painting conveyed a tortured man and nails used tortuously. From the painted rendition of pierced hands, from the painted gash among painted ribs, from the painted depiction of transfixed, overlapped feet, painted blood flowed copiously. Painted gouts dripped from the hands; painted cords ran down the body; painted blood, cumulatively abundant, pooling and thick, crawled from the feet. The painted blood moved. The painting lived. I fainted.

24   ROBERT'S DRAWINGS

Robert, a friend of mine in high school (and well before high school), drew hard, blackly-lined, line drawings: thronged battle scenes full of swords. Robert specialized in drawing battles bristling with medieval weaponry—lances and maces and, especially, swords. Robert called the swords "long swords." I loved Robert in a timid way, in a way which did not involve touching (though not for lack of desire on my part), and I appreciated Robert's zeal for drawing, a rare quality, but I did not like Robert's drawings. His black lines, his thronged clashes, his seemingly bloodthirsty enthusiasm for murderous, medieval, hand-to-hand fighting, made me uneasy. I thought that Robert could have a bright future designing armor for movies. He could probably turn his skill to lucrative use. I envisioned no such prospects for myself. My drawings looked nebulous, uncommunicative, willfully obscure. They consisted of shades added to shades and of shades erased. They formed shapes vaguely. They shaped forms of such hazy hesitancy that they seemed to beg people *not* to look at them. I drew murk, not honest subjects as Robert did with his sprawling, cinematographic, medieval hack-fests. My drawings looked soft. Robert's active, anecdotal storyboards looked, at least to my eyes, unambiguously hard. Ironically, Robert drew exclusively with the softest of all common pencils, a yielding B3. I used many hard Hs (and Bs for darkness as well). Robert erased smudges from his finished drawings; I smudged and erased as a way of drawing. But, valuing Robert's friendship, I forgave him his subjects; I forgave him his style. I tried to ignore his principle drawing method.

Robert drew many parts of his drawings, his numerous "long swords" included, using a ruler, anathema to me. He used a flexible, thin, transparent ruler. (No ruler, no matter how limber, seemed flexible to me.) Robert drew with both hands. His left hand managed the ruler, swinging it, stopping it, frequently pivoting it against the tip of a pencil held in his right hand. In one motion, as soon as the ruler stopped, his right hand drew a streak along the guiding edge. The ruler slid over paper like a planchette on a ouija board; a pencil tip whipped; a line drawing built quickly under the blade. Inevitably I saw Robert's hands work in rapid concert, although I tried not to watch. I tried not to see fingertips posed in their press against hands' enemy.

Watching a farrier shoe a horse, I saw a small, square, yellow cardboard box among the farrier's tools in the back of his truck. I lifted the box. It felt heavy for its size. I asked the farrier if I might open it. He smiled. The sides of the box lid completely covered the sides of the underlying box, for strength, I supposed, given the box's heaviness. I removed the lid. The box contained horseshoe nails, many, jumbled. I recognized the nails as nails, but I saw them as swords collected from the slain in one of Robert's fields.

25 TARGET

Burke shot arrows into a paper target, bright red arrows with pointed tips. The circular target—concentric bands and circular heart—occupied a large paper square spread against baled hay arranged as a wall. The smooth, new, undisrupted target glared. Burke hit the bull's-eye with every arrow. I walked to the target, through the radiating harshness of its coloration. I removed the arrows, outstanding sticks. I looked at the holes in the target, round holes with torn edges bent—forced inward—into the hay. I fingered the torn openings. Burke shouted, "Just bring them back." He supposed me a retriever. I'd approached the target, I'd rid it of arrows, not as Burke supposed, to help him, but for paper's relief.

26 APPLE

Burke loved Christine. For her first two years in college and his last two at the same school (the small, local college where Burke's and my father taught), Burke and Christine virtually lived together, the closest they came to the marriage that Burke desired. Burke had plans for himself: graduate school, eking out a living as a history teacher if, as he put it, "by some miracle," he could find a job. Burke's plans, Burke's desire to live an academic life much like our father's, conflicted diametrically with his loving Chris. When Burke begged Chris to consider marriage with him (long forestalled), she answered scornfully, "What would we do for money?" Christine had to have money because, by her lights, she had to have horses, and she "couldn't imagine" affording horses—her kind of horses—on a teacher's salary. Burke left for graduate school mortified. "Money" and "horses" covered nothing. Christine did not love him.

My first year and Christine's last year in high school coincided. When at school in the same building as Chris, I sometimes saw her at a distance, between classes, while she moved along as if on a tide of friends, greeting people left and right. Across the trudging concourse, Chris discreetly called to me or waved or, less than discreetly, kissed her fingertips and waggled the kissed fingers at me. She called familiarities like "I missed you yesterday" or "See you later." She seemed to like everybody. She seemed beyond the mean distinctions of social cliques. Nonetheless, I, shy freshman, felt fearfully distinguished, splashed publicly with the wide-flung signs of her liking. And her behavior worried me for at least two reasons. First, because inconsistent; Christine seemed more affectionate toward me in that publicly brief, casually passing way than she did when she drove me—just the two of us—out to the farm; second, because her gesture, her fluttering kissed fingers at me, however playful, however frivolous, would have pained Burke, had he witnessed it; he felt that insecure in her affection.

I rarely saw Christine in the school's clamorous cafeteria. (It seemed all clashing, hard, flat surfaces graced only by the curved corners and the arched rims of the plastic trays frequently clapped against tables.) I rarely saw Christine there, but once, in November, among the cold grays of plastic tables, plastic trays, and overcast windows, while I sat facing Robert and eating a sack lunch, someone came up behind me and squeezed my shoulders. Christine said, "Don't be surprised. It's just me." ("Don't' be surprised" sounded like "Don't be ridiculous," which sounded like Chris.) Turning, I saw Christine's lively features, her joking air, her earlobes dotted with tiny, agate spheres, the feathery, wispy, gray-green knit of her sweater foil to the darkly red-brown curtain of her thick, lengthy hair. Jokingly, Chris said, "I bought you something." She pulled an apple out of a dangling backpack, a large, dark, purplish-red Delicious apple ("named for what it is not," my family would scoff). I said ungratefully, "Did you buy that here?" Chris said lightly, "Just now." I held out my hand and said thank you. Christine put away the apple, saying, "Well. Actually. It's not for you. It's for you to give to Eustace later." An absurd dread flooded me. Of all Chris's horses, I feared Eustace the most. Christine laughed. She grasped my shoulder goodbye and, leaving, said, "I'm warning you."

That afternoon, Christine, wearing black leather gloves lined with gray rabbit fur (cut shorter than rabbits ever bore it in nature), withheld the dark Delicious apple from the nuzzling muzzle and the nipping lips of a fabulous-looking horse named Dancing Pearl (called Eustace, for Useless, although a mare). Chris gently fended off the horse's head with one hand, while in the other she held the apple in an attitude which clearly indicated that I should take it from her. "Keep your hand flat when you give it to her," Chris instructed. "So she won't catch your fingers." I looked at the apple in Christine's dressed fingers. Smooth, glossy, dark-red, the apple bore reflected light on a telling curve as its upright shape, tapering downward to the small, rounded prominences of its flower end, occupied Chris's gloved fingers. Chris's fingers looked loosely wrinkled, black, and only subtly lustrous, holding the taut-skinned, smooth, upright, shiny, and single apple. Chris turned her head expressly with the beginning of a reproach or of an admonishment, which I did not want to hear. I took the apple. I let it lie on my flattened (or backward-bent) bare palm while the dappled animal bore down with blunt teeth, tore the apple, and consumed it in two bites separated by chewing. "That's a dollar a bite," I commented. "So?" Christine asked. "So. Nothing. Only," I said. "Only what?" Christine asked. "Nothing," I repeated, thinking of Burke. Burke grieved in the present over his future inability to afford expensive horses.

27 TROPHIES

At thirteen, I did not consciously assess anyone's temperament, but I registered differences between people, and I recognized that Christine, whom I viewed as calm, confident, strong-willed, and sociable, did not resemble me in that she possessed those qualities. She adapted quickly to unforeseen events; she faced surprising developments with poise; she displayed deliberate decisiveness. As far as I could tell, she rarely doubted the sufficiency—or even the excellence—of her abilities in any field, athletic, social, academic, whatever. Most remarkably to me, Christine actually liked—she positively welcomed—challenges. While she did not make insistent or willful demands upon other people, firmness in having her way showed in her conduct with horses. (When she rode, her objectives became the horse's objectives even when the horse initially displayed a mind of its own.) And, outgoing without pushiness or boisterousness, Christine's interest in other people made her generally well-liked. At the farm, she helped the owner and principal trainer teach riding. She encouraged his numerous students by words—encouragement, tips—and by her example. If Christine ever felt fear, if the heights of jumps confronting her (and a horse) ever gave her shrinking pause, she didn't show it. She took obvious pleasure in a dangerous sport, and she communicated pleasure as something that anyone could share. All as a group, Christine and other devotees from the farm took horses to horse shows where everyone from the farm supported everyone else from the farm in every event in which any of them participated. I exaggerate, but not by much. The group amounted to a loud, rousing club, Christine its president—elected perpetually by acclamation. Christine took a considerate interest in everyone in the group, the numerous girls and the few boys. She comforted; she encouraged. She even encouraged people against whom she earnestly competed. And she usually treated me with the same kindness despite my standoffishness, despite my reservations about her sport, and despite my decided distaste for training, discipline, and competition. As I said, Christine liked challenges.

Christine enjoyed and enjoyed. She enjoyed horse shows. She enjoyed the efforts they entailed in preparation and in performance. She enjoyed the camaraderie and the competition. She enjoyed testing her training and that of three of her horses, two hunters (judged on the smoothness with which they moved through a course of jumps) and one jumper (judged on cleanness in jumping, speed sometimes a factor). Christine enjoyed and enjoyed. She frequently won competitions; she enjoyed winning. The few times that I glimpsed her bedroom in her parents' house, I saw no further than a line of trophies and ribbons arranged on a shelf high up, near the ceiling. There Christine's most prized prizes stood and hung—silvery (silver-plated, she told me) plates, bowls, and trays, each with a multicolored ribbon clipped to it or near it. (Multicolored ribbons meant more than a single win.) Each ribbon consisted of a large, ruffled rosette from which long streamers hung, each streamer a strong, bright exemplar of white or of a primary color: yellows of daffodils turned to satin; blues like night air glowing at dawn; reds of high, shining scarlet (forgiven for inevitable bloodiness; I frequently forgave reds); whites each by each all seeming different varieties of immaculate snow. Letters and shapes in simulated gold drenched the ribbons with sheen upon sheen. The colors spilled and hung pointed; each streamer ended sharply angled. Despite that jaggedness and despite the singleness and separateness of every hue in the cascade, I admired it. The ribbons looked, if anything, louder and bolder than did the trophies themselves, trays jittery with ornament, smooth replicas of Revere bowls, platters like full moons. Christine's trophies looked grand, but by my standards, they looked overly bright. Chris's trophies, right for their purpose, right as objects won in competition with other people, right as objects won under the sun, in a public way, had none of the inwardness of my violet clamshells aligned on camp-cabin walls. And beyond alignment and silvery brightness, the true trophies in Christine's room had little in common with Estelle's trophies, with Estelle's familial silver, with pearl-handled knives stored away, entombed.

28   RED SILVER

Age seventeen, I saw a man who aroused me greatly. In bodily form and in clothing, he impressed me so greatly that the other people, gathered together in the marble-clad foyer during a concert interval, lost all distinction and became mere obstructions to my sight of him. The man's body sloped, from top down and from knee-height upward, toward an outstanding center. Over that form, from throat to groin and all down his arms, the man wore bright-red velvet, and over the red a Navajo belt made of thick, silver plates, each lobed as if it had sprouted ovals, each slightly convex, each studded in its center with a chunk of turquoise. Plant-like starts of small silver—small, leafy silver pieces—intervened between the plates; leather united the plates and the pieces; one plate hooked buckle-like into the leather; three plates hung below the closure, hung in magnificent excess from magnificent excess, hung in prodigious sway, down from the man's left side.

Having seen that man, that body, that boldness of clothing at a classical concert, feeling helplessly aroused—engorged as if in emulation of the red-dressed man overall—I forgot about music just heard and about music anticipated. Needing privacy for relief, I virtually ran to the car I'd driven, fumbled with keys ceremoniously bestowed upon me for the evening by my father, and drove home through the campus of the college where Dad taught and at which Christine lazily pursued her junior year absent Burke (gone for further degrees). I drove home and rushed through the house, past my unobservant mother—"How was it, dear?"—past my observant father—"You're home early"—and up the stairs, into a lockable room, where I hastily stripped and lay down to the first of many encounters with a figment whom I named, beginning then, Red Silver. Despite my seeming fixation upon the real man's clothing, I imagined Red Silver as naked, as a mass of receptive bulges happily heaped either before or under me. My excitement thrived on imagined male curves; in fantasy I climbed, hiking, into those curves.

Red Silver, the figment countless times conjured, seemed many things: feast to my famine; ease to my constraint; a dream of bigness on the part of my penis; a Bacchus born of appetites often suppressed. But besides appearing to my fantasizing mind as an affable—and oddly mature—mass of bodily compensations personified, the red-dressed man whom I'd seen also impressed me in a social sense. I saw the actual person as socially brave, as unafraid of what others might think of his form, of his taste; as unafraid of unconformity; as inclined to celebrate his corpulence, to advertise it. I admired the man both for that inclination and for that bearing. In my conceptions, the two of us differed greatly. I craved invisibility; I dressed in faint blues, denim and broadcloth. I feared other peoples' judgments upon me in general, which reflection led me to recognize the red-dressed man's essential appeal: warranted or not, I saw him as gay, as openly gay and proud of himself.

At age twenty-two (almost twenty-three), I met Lawrence Blay Baussan. Until I met Lawrence, I had no sexual experience with anyone but myself. I fantasized often. I feared many things in fearing shared sex. I feared untempered lust, the plain expression of bodily need. I feared casualness and carelessness and betrayal in caring. I feared ridicule and illness and emotional devastation (knowing myself readily devastated). I feared many things in fearing shared sex. And beyond fearing the normal risks that one would run with a partner, I also feared shocking Estelle with what she would see as my willful embrace of sinful aberrance. I feared losing Estelle's love by shocking her. I feared causing her grief. And, further, I even feared offending nonexistent people: the paper shades of my grandfathers, the photographs displayed under glass on Estelle's bedroom walls, Joel and Everett Rawlinson. Their narrow miens and lean frames sat in judgment upon me, somewhere in the inconsistent and diverse court of my conscience. When Estelle gave me Joel Rawlinson's watch fob (or chain of putative moonstones), she gave me a pretty, little reminder of my shackles, constraints.

I saw the red-dressed, silver-spangled man, Red Silver's progenitor, as a liberated figure. The whole of his stupendous belt, especially the dangling plates, suggested a broken chain. I responded to the sight of the man as if I believed that he'd stepped straight out of a logically ludicrous, but heroic, myth; as if I believed that he, once chained by the waist—in an impossible prison appointed with treasure—had broken away and made good his escape; as if I believed that the man wore the chain—the remains of the chain—as a personal trophy, as an array of silver plates affirming liberation.

29 BATHROOM

An unusually hot day during the summer before I turned eighteen, I lay in bed. The house, Estelle's house, Estelle's three-dimensional model of order and décor long, long, long out of date, Estelle's house technically owned by my parents, who unbelievably altered nothing, not one room's wallpaper, the house sounded empty and open, as if every window in it—all filled with black screens—gaped to admit the slightest breeze. Cicadas sounded. I wore a thin, off-white bathrobe which Estelle had kindly made for me without considering that I might have appreciated color. Feeling sticky, pulsing, greasy, alive, free from nausea, I lay listening to cicadas, golden scrolls scratched on the black screens. I felt almost well. Feeling that well felt like adventure. I heard Estelle climb the stairs. I heard her courteous knock on the wide-open door. From the doorway, Estelle said something about "picking up a few groceries." She asked if she might bring me anything. I heard her leave, steps on stairs, car sounds, cicadas' hot maracas, burning fronds. I felt rich in privacy, a luxury so great that I didn't know what to do with it. I got out of bed. Barefooted over floorboards, I walked into the upstairs bathroom, a graceless room which seemed to hate bodies. Square, white tiles the size of large (four-part, four-square) soda crackers covered the walls unremittingly in milky slickness. (Two windows interrupted the tiled grid with other grids, panes.) Beyond a tiled passage, the room opened up, yawning in gauntness the size of a racquetball court. Down the left-hand wall as one entered, toilet, basin, and bathtub stood plunked down, one, two, three, one after the other, colorless. The bathtub stood on scaly feet; rust tinged their cracked paint; the sphere-clutching talons resembled chickens' feet. Two thin, dim-chrome legs supported the basin's front. Against the wall to the right, around a right-angled corner where the passage met the main room, a washing machine and a clothes dryer carried on smoothness and whiteness from the tiles. Towels and towel-like mats didn't relieve the room's pallor.

I stood before the washbasin, looking down into it, avoiding the round-cornered, mirror-covered door of the medicine cabinet above the basin. Feeling slightly nauseous, I gripped the basin's rim. I stood, eyes closed against reflections, against the sight of the white tiles, against the sight of the basin. I tried not to feel self-piteous, holding the thick, curved basin rim, missing, missing, missing what? Red Silver's live prototype, the real, glimpsed man whose scarlet-and-silver-dressed torso curved to the fore like the hard, smooth, white, hollow, lifeless basin's opposite.

The full man whom I'd seen had worn a blue-eyed belt over scarlet fuzz. The basin in front of me dangled a chain made of dull, little spheres the size of peppercorns, dull, little, gray spheres connected by minute rods. The chain connected a rubber drain plug to a chrome boss on the flat, vertical back of the otherwise ovoid basin. Estelle had evidently used the basin last. Only she bothered to set the drain plug up, just so, on a level area beside a faucet handle, when she removed it from the drain. Because of her placement of the plug, the bead-and-rod chain draped the level porcelain and hung in a curve from the level area's edge to the anchoring boss inside the basin. The chain hung inside the basin in a deep, sidelong curve. The curve resembled the curve of a watch chain in one of Estelle's photographs of Joel, my paternal great-grandfather.

30 AFGHAN

In her so-called free time, in her scant hours of leisure, Estelle read. When she didn't read, she crocheted, or she knitted. Although she spent little time doing it, Estelle crocheted many things: slippers; covers for cheap, heatproof discs used (when crochet-covered) as trivets; shawls; caps; mittens; afghans. Most of the things she made went, through her church, to charities. Out of string and "free time," before my lifetime began, Estelle crocheted a star-patterned bedspread in which the stars consisted of diamond shapes, the diamond shapes of triangular shapes, and every star shared a diamond with six other stars. The spread looked evenly repetitive and obsessively abstract. I ruefully considered it one of Estelle's two masterpieces, one of Estelle's two limited masterpieces. The other masterwork, an afghan, usually lay folded in half over the back of a sofa in a room called "Burke's study." (The room bore that name not because Burke studied there—he didn't—but because the room contained books and a desk, and it adjoined Burke's bedroom through one of its three doors.) The afghan in Burke's study consisted of bright violet shapes combined with bright green shapes. The violet shapes, crocheted discs and parts of discs, coarsely—painfully—imitated grape clusters. The green shapes tried to suggest grape leaves' silhouettes. Little ligatures of glaring green connected the grape shapes and the leaf shapes closely. The abstract bedspread in Estelle's bedroom displayed no color stronger than that of rolled oats. The figurative afghan displayed color, but color in such garish hues and in such disharmony that I almost wished it colorless. Estelle's masterpiece-afghan, Estelle's web of woolly grapes, hung over the sofa in such a way that its travesties of grape clusters appeared as if they hung downward, as actual grapes might hang in an actual arbor. The afghan, which I grudgingly liked despite my dislikes, bothered me because I liked it. Estelle had invented its design. I sometimes wondered—without a word, without a praiseful question to her—why Estelle had made it, the sole exception (as far as I knew) to her usual, uninventive, conventional webs. What had possessed her? A sense of biblical vineyards? A hint of paradise? What had she imagined that led to fibrous grapes? What vision beyond the reach of yarn? A spidery ruin of lushness, an ugly form of something beautiful, a sad attempt to net fullness embraced me, to my humiliation, every time I lay down on the sofa and pulled the afghan down and around myself.

31 BASKETBALL

Sometimes I lay on the sofa in Burke's study because I felt sick. (The sofa surpassed my bed in softness.) Sometimes I felt lustful. Sometimes I felt disgusted with my drawings or with my paintings; the afghan's travesties reminded me of my own travesties, flowering purple lilacs ineptly painted. Sometimes I lay in the study, punishing myself, in morose retreat, staring at the moral baggage on the walls, trunk after trunk of it: my grandparents' books full of sunless sermons. Sometimes I lay there in pain. I managed to break my right arm, my vital, drawing right arm, twice—not once, but twice—during high school.

I broke my arm playing basketball in gym class. I broke it by extending it—stupidly—toward the on-rushing floor. Both times, I felt shame. The first time, having fallen, having gotten to my feet, I stood hunched over, hoping that the pain would just go away. The second time, I knew what had happened the moment it happened. I felt a rage almost equal to the pain; I felt both painfully hurt and furious with myself. (And, despairingly I thought, "Not again, not again.") I felt some wordless, searing equivalent of "How could you be so stupid as to do the same stupid thing twice?" That second time, I saw a black stripe on the golden-wooden floor close to my face. I saw the basketball net, the pale, diamond-shaped meshes drastically foreshortened, tapering down, below blissful orange distantly circular. The person called

Coach barged, bellowed, demanded, "What happened?" Coach yelled at me to get up. I got up. Coach stared at me saucer-eyed as if he hated my guts. I felt hauled off the court, hauled into court, publicly and suddenly convicted, proven guilty of—heinous crime—structural fragility, unmanly weakness.

After the second break, I brooded. I lay, cast on arm, sullenly wrapped in the violet-and-green afghan in Burke's study. (I did not impinge upon Burke; he lived elsewhere by then.) I felt feverish and achy and furious with myself. I considered the cliché, to give one's right arm for something. My right arm felt taken; I would never have given it for basketball. I resented my bones for breaking. I resented failure in my frame, failures plural, failures which seemed to confirm a humiliating judgment, "fragility," a real slap in the face—in my so-called pretty face. I humiliated myself willfully and intentionally by thinking things like, "If I'd stuck to playing jacks with Christine, none of this ever would have happened." I recalled twelve-year-old Christine's jack balls, little, spongy, red, rubber jack balls. Little red jack balls, lodged in my brain, stung my conscience. I wanted to get my hands on a basketball. I wanted to feel the ringing, pulsing, big curve, the brown-orange burr, the seam-like dents. I missed basketball; I missed drawing; and I blamed myself—up and down—for not having gotten my priorities straight: drawing, painting incomparably more important to me than basketball. I felt told undeniably that I couldn't have it both ways, that I couldn't practice both art and sport. I sulked; I ached; I considered my vanity.

I'd liked to think that I played basketball well because I sank threes reliably given a chance. I'd felt proud of my height, proud of my reach, proud of my quickness. Pridefully, I'd ignored my liabilities: flimsiness, skinniness; lack of interest in teamwork; a tendency to become confused under pressure. I knew that I'd had something to prove, of course. I might paint flowers in watercolors; I might suffer from indecision, mull, moil; I might back down from arguments; I might comply with other peoples' wishes quickly; I might even look like some sickly El Greco brought to life, but I did not want every macho jock in the universe—or even one of those few in my school—thinking that he could push me around. I would sometimes stand up for myself. My righteous pride, blended with a generous dose of delusional vanity, had had consequences in basketball which I, in and of myself, viewed melodramatically as disastrous. I'd felt compelled to "prove," to demonstrate convincingly to myself at least, that I possessed "manly" qualities: durability, assertiveness, toughness, ability to hold off opponents. Of course, I proved the opposite.

Lying in Burke's study, lying on a sofa as if helpless, lying down wrapped in Estelle's masterpiece-afghan as if in a mantle (over my clothes), I felt as if I'd capitulated to every effeminate strain in my taste, in my ways, in my mind, in my temperament. I felt given over to the binding ties of an old woman's love.

32 BURKE'S STUDY, EFFERVESCENCE

In the room called Burke's study, a faded leather sofa stood along one of the book-lined walls, a narrow table beside it. A mouse-gray carpet looked more beaten into the floor than laid upon it. A wide, plain desk barricaded the only window, a narrow aperture at the far end of the room (as seen from the entrance to the room, in the area around the stairs). Maroon curtains smothered the window. (I might have called them wine-red. My father liked to quote a wine critic who criticized another wine critic's taste, "Red wine should not look black." The black-red curtains suited the room, the walls packed with my grandparents' preachy books. The curtains, of course, had nothing to do with grandparental aversion to wine not churchified.) To reach the curtains, to perform the obviously discouraged act of opening them, one had either to reach across the desk or to maneuver around it, neither option convenient. (The window, through screen mesh and sash panes, let one see across a side street, into a neighbor's maples. The window's lower sash stuck; one had to work to raise it.) Despite the room's narrowness, a dictionary managed to fit, wedged-in yet outspread, on a stand near the desk. One of the room's doors led, through a wall of drear books, into Burke's bedroom. The main door offered a way to or from the stairs. A third door, immediately perpendicular to the stair door, gave access to an afterthought, a small, tacked-on closet. The end of the sofa that I habitually viewed as the foot abutted the closet's doorless side. On that wall hung a plain, round-faced clock. Black dots arced fixedly between its hour numerals.

When I lay on the sofa feeling sick, when Estelle supposed that I might "try to eat something," she invariably brought me a soda cracker and soda water. She set them on the table beside the sofa. Invariably the water, bursting with activity, filled a cylindrical, plain, clear glass. Invariably the cracker lay rigidly across a small, round, white plate. The plate, any one of its tribe, looked as if it might have done hard time in a diner. The cracker bore a cross in pin pricks; minute pits in straight lines crossed it symmetrically. To my mind, the pits said: Break here; divide this whole into quarters, neatly mind you; break on the dotted lines. The pits, like plans, prescribed action. Of course, I disliked them. And, of course, the cracker didn't bend. It didn't slump; it didn't lie comfortably within the plate, nestled against its contours. It stretched a brittle roof from rim to rim, over the small plate's mild concavity. From the sofa, I repeatedly watched soda water go flat. Countless teeming bubbles diminished in number; bubbles, thinned from profusion, moved in small streams. The fleet, gleaming streams reminded me pleasantly of key chains consisting of minute, bright spheres connected by minute rods. From points of origin on the inside of the glass, bubbles sped to the surface. When the water moved—because I moved the glass—the bubble streams bent and changed. They clearly flowed. Thus, apparently freely mobile, the bubbles did something, in my mind, to offset the starch cracker's rigidity.

33 HAT

I once covered my face with the veil of one of Estelle's hats. Alone
in the house, I went into her closet, took a hatbox from a shelf,
set the hatbox on Estelle's crochet-covered bed, and opened the
box. My conscience certainly told me to stop right there. I'd
invaded Estelle's privacy already, first, by entering her room and
second, by entering her closet; opening one of her boxes represented at least a third degree of invasion. Tissue paper in the
opened hat box stayed me—momentarily. Tissue paper hid the
hat from immediate view. I parted the paper and lifted the hat, a
short, columnar stack of black-velvet folds. One end of the hat
bore a veil, a short piece of black net which Estelle called an eye
veil. I carried the hat to the vanity-dressing table and sat down. (A
cane lattice filled a gap in the vanity's bench. Straw-golden cane
matched the sunny satinwood. The lattice's interweave teemed
with eight-pointed stars. Each starry portion of the weave enclosed
a small, octagonal gap.) Crocheted pieces made by Estelle lay,
custom-shaped to their locations, on the side heights of the vanity
and on its central level. A hand mirror lay, glass side downward,
on the central net. A matching hairbrush lay near it. Pale bristles
pointed upward, high antithesis to the hidden glass. Below the
vanity's comb of tall, oval mirror stood a small, clear-glass box in
which Estelle kept hairpins. The four glass legs of the box looked
bowed, as if they bent beneath the weight of the hairpins, bent
wires shaped like Vs but curved at the convergence and rippled

evenly along the divergent lengths. The hairpins combined curves and straightness. An indirect interplay between curves and straightness had confronted me the moment I'd entered the room: over the window at the far end of the room, gauze hung in long, quiet, almost tubular folds, a glowing screen against sunlight. Weighty drapes flanked the glowing sheers. The sill's shadow, cast from beyond the gauze onto the tubular folds, curved in deep, complementary curves, curves which, despite countless disparities, reminded me of the high and deep, curved teeth edging a giant clam shell. The straight sill's shadow didn't look straight.

I sat, hat in hands, hands in lap, facing Estelle's vanity. Cicadas sounded more distantly than they had sounded in rooms open through screens to the air. I closed my eyes and brought my head to the verge of entering the hat. Satin cool to my forehead, I wondered wordlessly and without savagery a version of my father's favored and stinging question: What did I mean to accomplish? Did I intend to humiliate myself? To see myself dressed in part as a woman, which I benightedly would find humiliating? Did I mock? Did I acknowledge? Did I acknowledge Estelle's power over me? Estelle's influence? Did I even begin to try to think about Estelle? Did I crudely use a physical prop, one of her churchgoing hats, as an aid to a sense of her spiritual life? No physical thing or act could illuminate that. Pushed to find a conclusion by sight, failing to fumble my way to one through my mind's blind alleys, I sat up straight. I pulled the hat onto my head, as far as its smallness allowed. I pulled down the eye veil and held it. The real challenge emerged: I had to open my eyes. I had to look up. I had to confront my face in the glass.

34 CROCHET, BRAIDING

Burke directly opposed Estelle's crochet. Estelle crocheted edging. She sewed crocheted edging to the edges of the open ends of pillowslips. Burke asked her to spare him her edging. He asked Estelle not to trim pillowslips for his use. Estelle obliged him. I sensed that she perceived his request as a snub. (If love went into crochet, did Burke reject love? He argued with Estelle. An air of antagonism prevailed between them.) When Estelle put away laundry, she stacked things like sheets neatly in a cabinet; she put freshly laundered things on the bottoms of piles of kindred things. She maintained a pile of untrimmed pillowslips for Burke. The distinction must have irked her. She thumped his pile roughly. A forbidding distance of an extra inch surrounded it.

Estelle edged pillowslips with crochet called tatting: strings of tiny, conjoined circles along a crocheted footing. A tiny offshoot of a few knots or loops sprouted between each circle, and each circle sprouted a minute, knotted beard. Estelle called tatting "nothing fancy." Burke brought historical understanding to edging on a cloth wrapped around a ladle, but he found plain—white or off-white—tatting too fancy to tolerate or to use.

I remembered Burke's resistance to Estelle's edging when Christine asked me to learn to braid horses' manes. Christine braided horses' manes for horse shows; she said that she "could use some help." In grateful obedience to Chris, I learned to braid manes. I disliked the activity; I disliked the appearance of braided manes. To my mind, which admired as if starved for what it admired, which admired hungrily almost any instance of ease, of laxity, of freedom, or of general largess, Chris's horses' manes looked mutilated even when loose, without braids. Excepting the silvery cascade that draped the neck of the "useless" horse, Eustace, Chris kept her horses' manes about four inches long. She used scissors and thinning shears (a weird tool like scissors with one blade a comb). Chris wanted a thinned, trimmed mane further reduced—for show—to a row of braided nodules evenly spaced. Teaching me to braid a mane, she demonstrated. Starting behind a horse's ears, she braided evenly spaced sections of mane into sticks; she tied off the sticks with rubber bands. She then folded sticks, hiding the elastics, and sewed the little, braided bundles shut. Sewing, she used yarn something of the color of the mane. A black mane's bundles resembled blackberries—without berries' appeal.

Braided manes grieved me in the same way that the sight of grass as hay—in wire-bound bales—grieved me. Constraint lay in man-made compression; constriction lay in interlacement. I disliked braided manes, and that I braided them worried me. I remembered Burke's objection to tatting on pillowslips used on his bed. Burke, the paradigm of manliness to me (whatever "manliness" might mean), avoided trim, and there, I *made* trim; I made something like tatting, along horses' necks.

Teaching me to braid manes, Chris actually touched my reluctant hands. She actually moved them for me into braiding motions, into passing one bit of horsehair over another. "Like this," she said. I learned to braid quickly, and I braided quickly. Chris said, "You have smart hands—for a boy." She had no idea.

In each three-stranded braid, strand covered strand. Braids, when finished (as sticks), looked as if each consisted of two strands, not three. A braid's bulges appeared as if paired in regular sequence. But every strand hid part of another strand. No one strand stayed hidden. Strands wove in and out of sight. Yet braiding with three strands, making the three appear two, ever losing sight of a third strand, reminded me that I should remember Burke when working with Chris, that I should remember Burke when spending time with her. Burke loomed in my mind—unduly—when Christine, teaching braiding, touched my hands. Burke loomed in my mind when Chris, as if playing with me, or truly playing, threatened me with her friendliness.

35 CROWS

For something like two and a half years, before I could drive legally, Christine drove the two of us "out to the horses," by which she meant, to the farm. When I could drive legally, she turned the driving—of her car—over to me. She said that she didn't care for driving (an odd inconsistency, considering how avidly she, as a rider, drove horses). I drove with pleasure. One could get to the farm by two routes, neither more expeditious than the other. Something other than scenery—overhead trees, river glimpses—attracted me to the route I favored: people less well-trained than I, less timid, less tractable, less fundamentally law-abiding than I, abused cars for the fun of it on the River Road, laying down rubber in gripping, whipping, black turns, as if drawing with cars. (I wouldn't have known, even in the abstract, how to make such marks, if I hadn't asked Burke, who told me. "Don't even think about it," he said. But he also told me: Step on the gas and the brakes simultaneously. "Brake torqueing," he called it.) The black swerves on the River Road thrilled me as marks. And they suggested nocturnal wildness beyond my ken. I said something admiring about the tire marks—and their presumed makers—once to Chris. She dismissed the marks, or my admiration of them, with a bored-sounding sigh, saying in effect, "How tiresome," and she condemned the drivers who drew with cars by saying, "I think it's crazy, that they do that." I didn't agree, but I didn't argue.

My favored route to the farm turned from paved road to gravel.

The gravel road ran for several miles beside fields. Wire fences in deep grass—in deep, free grass—bounded the fields. The bodies of dead, shot crows blackened one of the fences for something like twenty stinking yards. The bodies, hung by the feet, ranged through every stage of decomposition, from clawed shreds and feathered tatters to glossy, black wholes freshly killed. Seeing the black, knotted mane of carrion, Chris complained once, "I don't know why you come this way." I said, "Neither do I." Another time Chris honestly wondered. She wondered why the unknown shooter of crows displayed the bodies. "Why do you think he does that?" she asked. I said, "I don't know. Maybe they're trophies, like yours." Christine dismissed the cockeyed comparison, "Hardly."

36   CHRISTINE'S HAIR

Most people said that Christine had red hair. "Red" registered with me as the color of blood, as a primary color. By that literal standard, of course, Christine did not have red hair. Her hair looked richly, darkly reddish-brown, not quite as dark as raw liver, but unusually dark for red hair. She usually wore it in a single plait down her back around horses. She wore it unbraided at school. For horse shows, when Christine usually wore a large number for identification on her black-coated back, she kept her hair off her back (number clearly visible) by coiling the usual braid, pinning the coiled lump through with pins, and covering the pinned-through coil with a hairnet all but invisible against the severely compressed mass. The netted lump rode, lodged low on her nape, below the hard rim of her hunt cap, a black-velvet-covered helmet with a short visor, a velvet button atop its crown, and a small, black, grosgrain-ribbon bow sewn flatly to its rear. Although accustomed to seeing Estelle's long, pale, gray hair coiled and pinned through and worn high on the back of the head, Christine's similar treatment of her own hair impressed me adversely as excessive, as grievously excessive in its degree of control.

37   SAM, DANCING PEARL

One day, at the farm, Christine told me, "Wait here." I waited, feeling dread, in a wide, earthen-floored hall between rows of stalls. Christine led a saddled and bridled horse out of one of the stalls. She led the horse to me as if she would introduce us. Chris said, "It's about time you learned to sit on a horse." I wanted to say, oh, no. No, no, no. But obligation to Christine—for the farm's pleasures—stopped me. Recognizing the horse with Christine, I knew that she had borrowed and prepared—bridled and saddled in advance—the least threatening, the least excitable, the most stolid and placid, animal readily available, a horse called Sam, whom the farm's owner had bought to carry very small children in their first riding lessons. The farm's owner had bought Sam at a price determined by the animal's weight. If unpurchased, Sam would have died in a slaughterhouse. Sam sinned in men's eyes not by age or unsoundness, but by shape, by the unlovely combination of short neck, long head, low-slung belly, short legs, and big hooves. A slightly pendent lower lip made Sam look dully sorrowful. When I'd first seen Sam (before Christine presented him), I'd thrilled with a single, naïve question. Enraptured, I'd asked, "What color *is* he?" I'd asked that question as if, contrary to my principles, I wanted an intellectual label to clarify the naturally unclear. In Sam's suffused coat, hairs of a nameless yellow like yellow ocher blended plenteously with black; shoals of not-quite-ocher lit the darkness like sparks. When I'd asked about

Sam's color, Chris had glanced at him. She'd frowned. She'd said dismissively, "I don't know. Some sort of roan. A black roan, maybe." "A black roan, maybe," I'd marveled. When Christine introduced Sam to me—with the proposal that I sit on his back—I remembered Sam's apparent patience and apparent gentleness. I'd seen Sam carry very small children. I'd seen small heels pummel his sides. I'd seen Sam, battered into a shambling trot, soon subside into a shambling walk. Something like pity moved me to think that if ever I might like any horse, I might eventually like Sam. I told Chris, "All right. I'll sit on him." Chris looped the reins up, over Sam's head; I stayed her. I began unsaddling Sam. Chris asked, "*What* are you doing?" I said that I would sit on Sam, not on a saddle. Chris sighed. I unbridled Sam. Chris said, "You *can't* ride him like that." Typical of my pedantic family, I said something like, "I said I would sit on him, not ride him." Chris laughed. She said, "I guess that's a start."

I learned to sit on Sam. I learned to keep my balance on saddle-less Sam while he stood still, while he walked, while he reluctantly trotted, and while he rarely cantered. I learned to guide Sam, using a rope attached to a halter around his head (no bit in his mouth). I thought that I literally learned to sit on a particular horse. I associated riding with a higher degree of direction than that which I imparted to Sam.

Christine owned four horses, three "good" ones plus Eustace. She called Eustace "worthless"—and Worthless and Useless. The "good" horses jumped well, the hunters smoothly, the jumper high; Worthless did not jump at all. And Christine loved Worthless. She hung on the animal's neck and purred "worthless" to her: "You're utterly worthless. You know that? Worthless." Worthless, monetarily worth plenty, leaned into Chris's rubbing her behind the ears. Chris sang Worthless's demerits as she would sing other horses' praises: "She overflexes like crazy." "She doesn't track straight." "She couldn't jump a straw, not to save her life." Worthless (or Useless or Eustace) actually had another name,

Dancing Pearl. That name suited the mare, a dapple-gray Anglo-Arabian, half Thoroughbred, half Arabian, "the worst halves of both," Chris lovingly said. When ridden, Dancing Pearl appeared, to my eyes, to live in such foment, in such restless motion—fidgeting and sidling at the very least—that she seemed to generate the beauteous foam of her own coat, churning the bubble-like dapples up into her chest, neck, sides, and hindquarters, out of her jet-black legs, through their ceaseless action. Many of the pale, round spots in the horse's coat looked rounded: so subtly shaded at their edges that they appeared globular (yet not in conflict with, but conforming to, the animal's contours). And the round dapples themselves looked energetic, as if they actively emerged, as if they broke through and displaced a preexisting layer of pure black hair. On those parts of the horse's body where no pale rounds appeared, black hairs and white hairs mingled, and the mingled mist, too, suggested energy, as if it seethed with potential bubbles, or as if it derived from previous bubbles' sudden extinction. Dancing Pearl's coat possessed a fascinating, dynamic beauty to my eyes. And even though I feared horses too much to want to learn much about them, even though I feared Dancing Pearl in particular, even though Chris's talk of equine conformation slid through my mind without sticking, even I could see that Dancing Pearl possessed a beauty of form independent of her boiling, roiling, fabulous coat. What Sam lacked in length of neck and leg, Dancing Pearl had in spades. Where Sam looked sleepily long-suffering, Dancing Pearl looked high and bright and wild. Sam slumped and shambled. Dancing Pearl arched through the neck and through the tail, and usually moved as if she could not move enough.

I supposed that Christine enjoyed riding Dancing Pearl because, as mentioned, Christine liked challenges. The horse capered sideway; Chris laughed, "She's a handful." The horse plunged over nothing; Christine laughed, "Oh, come on, now, mare." I supposed that Christine enjoyed riding Dancing Pearl as a break from training. Chris didn't try to accomplish anything with Dancing Pearl. Chris didn't attempt to correct, in Dancing

Pearl, any of the faults of carriage and of conduct which she, Christine, lovingly enumerated ("She doesn't track straight," et cetera). Chris acted more permissive with Dancing Pearl than I ever saw Christine act with any other horse. I supposed that riding Dancing Pearl amounted to pure riding for Chris, to riding with no end in mind. If she entertained a purpose while riding Dancing Pearl, perhaps Chris intended to benefit the horse, to give it the pleasure of exercise (however constrained).

While I didn't exactly ride with Christine, I frequently sat on plodding Sam while Chris rode the "handful," Dancing Pearl. Given the mismatch between Sam's favored slow pace and Dancing Pearl's abundant energy, Chris often let the mare gallop in far-reaching circuits around Sam-and-me. When Chris brought Dancing Pearl back around to us from such a run, the mare usually looked more excited than ever, taking three steps to Sam's one, staring wide-eyed, the mane-draped neck bent in such a curve that the whole horse appeared to attempt to get ahead of itself—to flow on forward, over and above the short, taut leashes of the so-called laced reins. Held to a barely-contained approximation of Sam's unambitious pace, Dancing Pearl worked the bit in her mouth, a bit with a flexible joint mid-mouth and large, flat, metal rings beside the mouth—rings hard in shape, although round, in contrast to dapples. When Christine and Dancing Pearl left Sam and me behind, Sam would continue to walk calmly forward in whatever direction he'd previously headed. Sam acted mindlessly certain about where to walk, about how to proceed, for example, through a pathless field of high grass not yet cut for hay. Sam merely walked straight ahead until he realized that I neither guided him nor impelled him in one direction or another. Eventually, he would notice his relative liberty. He would drop his head and graze peaceably until Chris and Dancing Pearl returned (like a whirlwind on four legs).

Christine usually acted sensibly (if one could call the fundamentals of her sport sensible). Christine usually didn't "ask," as she put it, Chris usually didn't direct, impel, or command a horse to perform any feat beyond its ability to perform. However, one November afternoon, Christine did not act sensibly. She rode Dancing Pearl directly toward a gully full of brushwood. Any one of Christine's "good" horses would have passed over the gap without blinking, without breaking stride. Not Dancing Pearl. From Sam's back, I watched Christine canter off through high grass. Chris's hair, in a single, long braid, made late-afternoon light a localized sunset. The braid lay still along the center of her inclined back as if no motion enveloped it. Dancing Pearl's bicolored tail—black above silver—bobbed with the roll of her spotted haunches. Chris rode toward bare oak trees. I simply watched. I noticed the November scent, dead leaves, the chill, the light's angle. Sam picked up his four feet in pairs and set them down simply. All seemed well, until I remembered the ravine in the grove. Then I feared sharply. And what I feared happened, even as the fear formed: Dancing Pearl skidded into rearing, stood high in the air, and fell, sliding sideways into the brush-filled gap. Chris seemed to stand on her left foot momentarily—as her left foot met the ground. But she didn't stand; she fell, sprawled. And she, too, slid into the chasm. A terrible snapping of dry wood filled the air. I jumped off of Sam and ran toward the ravine. Dancing Pearl floundered up the far bank, vacant saddle perched on her incongruously, like a shining piece of shelving fungus. Christine followed almost immediately. I felt faint with relief.

I ran around the gully. Some thirty yards from Chris, I had to stop running. Chris, squatting on spur-less heels, one arm through the horse's downed reins, clutched a high part of Dancing Pearl's left foreleg with both hands. Chris's helmeted head inclined toward her hands, as if she would rest her forehead on them. The horse, looking all wide-eyed—plum-eyed—stared at me. It would have bolted—gripped foreleg notwithstanding—had I not stopped. My first fear had shifted, but I still feared. I feared. Yet I saw. I noticed mere patterns. (Buckled together as a loop, the broad reins, down from around Dancing Pearl's neck, contained small straps worked through the main straps. The small straps formed patterns along the main straps: a sequence of little Vs, one after another, all pointing, acutely angled, the same direction. Christine's long braid, hanging down, near the reins, also looked like a series of Vs. The lustrous strands forming the braid cut off views of each other at acute angles. The visible parts of the braid's strands—plump, curved shapes like garlic cloves in shape only—all pointed downward and inward, pair by pair, along the braided sequence. The cable of hanging braid crossed the reins' curve.) I approached; Chris turned a set face toward me. Amid the fixity, which suggested grimness, freckles—irregular stretches of pigmentation—looked blotchy-dark against unusual pallor. I gasped, "You okay?" Chris said, "Yeah. But she has a puncture." "A puncture?" I felt sick, even then, asking. And for no good reason that I could think of later—unless for reason of ease, preferring simple demonstration to difficult explanation—Christine released Dancing Pearl's leg. Out of the part of the horse called its forearm, out of a large black-white-suffused bulge of muscle, a bright red jet curved into the air. The scarlet jet curved so far outward from the leg that no red showed around the jet's origin. Blood arced; scarlet curved; blood splattered dead leaves. I gagged and reeled. And yet, I saw: Christine looked disgusted with me. She turned back to the horse. She returned her hands responsibly to the leg that she'd irresponsibly injured, to the leg to which she'd caused harm through her foolishness, through her recklessness, through her daredevil spirit (usually expressed more judiciously than she had done that day). Chris obviously felt shaken by her fall and irked by my squeamishness. Perhaps easing nervous tension, Christine shouted at me. She said something like, "You chicken shit wimp pansy puking little faggot you goddamn queer." She later apologized. I said it didn't matter.

38 BLOOD ON THE LEAVES

A year after Dancing Pearl's puncture, in the autumn just after I'd turned sixteen, Burke, then a senior in college, called me up at home. (I answered the only phone in the house, an old, old, archaic, low, black, toad-like phone crouched squatly on the marble-topped table below the front stairs: a phone forever in the center of things, where anyone might overhear whatever anyone on the phone said.) Burke said peremptorily that he had to "talk with" me "face to face." Feeling dread, I stood speechless, a perforated black lump—one end of the receiver—near my mouth. Burke asked crossly, "You there?" He told me to meet him at a certain coffee shop. When I met him, he said, "Let's go for a walk." I'd seen too many gangster movies to welcome that suggestion, generally a prelude to execution.

I feared that Christine had somehow upset Burke. That I had ever had anything to do with her became an unfathomable enormity around the sliver of a conviction that I had done nothing wrong with regard to her (apart from exploit her as a free pass to the farm). I viewed Burke and Christine as adults, as glamorous, sexually active adults, as autonomous and responsible adults light-years removed from my dependency and confinement, light-years removed from my grubbing sphere of masturbatory visions. Burke and I had little to do with each other. But Chris could have provoked him into remembering my existence.

Burke said, "Let's go for a walk." We walked and walked, Burke striding along, hands jammed in pockets, I virtually trotting to keep up with him. He looked unshaven, unkempt, unrested, waxen-pale, ill and harried. Even so, he looked powerful and orderly by virtue of his bones. Leaves poured over the ground; wind battered; the left side of Burke's head flared with a shifting cowlick. We followed an asphalt bike path; the black sometimes gleamed with gritty silver. Poplar leaves scraped the asphalt, ticking, skittering, profuse as cornflakes. Two boys passed us on bicycles. Burke finally stopped. I said, "I'm freezing." Burke inhaled; his aster eyes watered. He said, "I'm sorry, Ed. You must be wondering—why I dragged you out here, like this." I shivered some mute, dread-filled equivalent of "no kidding." Burke said deliberately, as if temperately, "I'm going to ask you something that I know I shouldn't ask you." Burke's tone did nothing to alleviate my dread. "Ask," I said. Burke seemed to grasp after a thought as if gasping for air. He said, "Edward. I know you and Chris are friends. But. I guess. Uh. What I want to ask you. What I want to know is. You wouldn't sleep with her, would you?" I'd pitied Burke—briefly—for his obvious distress; I'd felt worried sympathy. But that question irritated me. I disliked Burke's questioning me on my principles while Christine, Christine herself, must have caused his worry. I should have answered Burke calmly. I should have said, in Burke's protracted manner, "Of course not. How could you think such a thing?" (Clearly, he knew little about me.) Instead of answering Burke calmly, I said unkindly, "You mean, if she asked me to?"

For that impertinence, Burke hit me in the mouth. I saw his facial expression: hard, staring. I saw how he moved, how he turned toward me. I even saw Burke's fist closing in, his fist-bearing arm greatly foreshortened along its length. My teeth felt incandescent in the ringing taste of blood. I must have fallen. I stayed rolled up, near the ground, kneeling, typically wallowing in pain. Burke, some alien giant outside my blindness, pawed at my back. He said things like "Jesus, Jesus" (and he a good atheist). "Jesus, I'm sorry." "Jesus, I didn't mean." And sorry, sorry, sorry.

Burke tried to get me to face him. When I could see, when I unclenched from my doubled-up, kneeling knot, when I unclenched just enough to see—through a watery slit—I saw Burke's right hand, the knuckles kind as concrete, gripping my left hand's wrist through its sleeves. Burke gripped the wrist of the hand clapped to my bleeding mouth. I waved him off. He stepped back; I eased my eyes open. Leaves in immediate view, below my face, lay motionless. Perhaps my body shielded them from the wind. Blood trickled down leaves. Spots of blood lay, and more came: round and bright red, on bright yellow leaves.

39   LEAVES SWEEPING

I tried to draw softly things like tar mends in streets, tar poured in rubbery flood into miniature canyons; bare tree limbs' shadows across tarred cracks; elm leaves rotting under shallow water; maple leaves' shadows on columns at night, shadows which changed as cars' headlights passed. I could draw leaves; I could draw leaves' shadows; I thought vainly that I could draw color in black and white. But I could not draw the shock that I felt when leaves shrieked across Christine's umbrella. Walking with her, I stopped. Leaves lay flat underfoot, silver-red maple leaves flat on wet grit. The sound struck my conscience: I should not see Chris; for Burke's sake, I should end our acquaintance—right then. Chris, who'd stopped when I did, began some question. I hastily said that I'd forgotten something. I could not explain; I could not say that I could not explain. I took off running. Over my shoulder, I shouted, "Sorry."

40   MARKS, MOON

One November night, more than a year after Burke hit me and mere weeks after the conviction that I should not see Christine had prompted me to run away from her, she invited me to supper at a restaurant. I accepted the invitation. I felt so guilty about seeing Chris—with Burke newly away at graduate school—that I lied to my parents about where I meant to go and with whom. I told them that Robert and I would spend time at his place (Robert, still the only other person in the universe of high school who took drawing seriously). That night, having supper with Chris at a Lebanese restaurant full of college students, I felt glum, evasive, vague, indecisive, and irritated with myself. I didn't know why I'd agreed to see Chris. I resembled a foal taught "to lead," taught to follow; Chris pulled; I followed, resistant yet obedient. No sooner had we ordered than Christine said, "You've been avoiding me. Why?" I shed enough vagueness to say of my seeing her, "I don't think Burke would like it." Christine's attempts to talk me out of that perception bored and annoyed me. Chris seemed flippant about Burke. I couldn't bring myself to argue his case, to say stupid, blatant things like, "Doesn't it mean anything to you that he loves you?" when it evidently didn't. I should have asked Chris why she wanted to see me, but I didn't want to hear any more stupidity, any statements like "I like you" and "What's wrong with that?" I simply did not want to talk. I imagined Burke's grief-to-come over losing Christine completely.

After the uncomfortable meal, I compounded my initial mistake of seeing Chris by helping her on with her coat, a costly load of fur-lined suede softly cocoa-colored. The coat had bothered me throughout the meal. Chris had dumped it over a chair, and there it had stayed, as if staring at me, its soft surface appealing to my eyes in the way that deep drawing chalk heavily expended on paper appealed to my drawing senses. At the same time, the suede's nature as animal skin repulsed me. After the meal, I helped Chris on with that coat, a ridiculously improbable courtesy for a seventeen-year-old to enact, but, absent-minded or letting my mind drift permissively and luxuriantly into chalky worlds of drawing, I must have copied my father's routine coat-holding for my mother. My fingers left shadows in the suede, areas where they'd overturned its minute pile. The finger-induced streaks looked literally shadowed, darker than their unreversed surroundings, as if something about the suede's raised texture actually cast shadows, and thus made the streaks appear dark. I, not thinking, ran my hands over the streaks; I smoothed them back into conformity with the rest of the deathly field. And Christine possibly thought that I caressed her. She glanced around, smiled brilliantly.

We left the restaurant. We'd walked to it separately. I thanked Chris again for the meal (for which she'd paid) and said goodbye. Chris said, "What's the hurry? Would it kill you to walk with me a little?" Of course, it wouldn't kill me. Chris took my arm. Again, with no more sense than a foal, I followed her lead. Chris suggested going to her apartment, having a glass of wine. I disliked the suggestion, and I disliked feeling childish—extremely young—sheltered, naïve. I'd never drunk wine except in occasional sips in my parents' presence. Christine said, "Don't worry. I'm not trying to seduce you." "Or," she added lightly, "Is that what you think?" I thought that I had avoided thinking precisely that. Before I could figure out a reply, Chris said something flippant and presumptuous about "respecting" my "gayness," and she told me again not to worry. I disliked appearing worried. We walked through the campus. A flagpole in the distance sounded coldly hollow, wind-blown rope pulleys clinking against it. Wind blew snow from a tree branch through the lit area around a streetlamp. Seeing that dim passage, I stopped. Chris said, "Come on. Why are you stopping? It's freezing." I said, "No. For Burke's sake, I really don't want to see you again." Chris looked surprised, disbelieving. She said, "You're kidding." I said, "No. I'm not kidding. Goodbye, Chris." I walked away from her. I felt rude and cruel and stupidly inept. I knew that I would have to learn how to treat people decently, not mutely, not bluntly. And I grieved for Burke. Although the night felt very cold, unfrozen water lay cupped, pooled in steps that led up a hillside. As I climbed the steps, a full moon's reflection appeared, disk after disk, near my trudging feet.

41 SNOWBALLS

In high school, I incurred an unusual punishment. I'd heard of the punishment; I'd supposed it legendary, unreal, never exacted from a student with rights. While I knew that my school had a rule against throwing snowballs, I never supposed that anyone in authority, any teacher or administrator, catching a student throwing snowballs, could ask—or require—that student to pack snowballs, in stated number, with his or her bare hands. I broke the rule against throwing snowballs, and I ran into an anachronism, the school's one Latin teacher, a Mr. Altquist, possibly a man of antiquated persuasions, possibly a man of sadistic inclination, possibly a man all too glad to inflict corporeal punishment (of an indirect sort) upon a suitable subject. Then again, possibly, Mr. Altquist felt persecuted by students. Perhaps he wished to assert himself. Whatever the case, no school policy could have sanctioned Mr. Altquist's request, but I didn't think to accuse him of abuse. We meshed, he and I. He gave a faintly cruel order; I weakly obeyed.

Running into that punishment, I felt wonderful. Winter had finally lifted; the air felt warm—above freezing—for the first time in months. Snow in front of the school building blazed—a deep, gashed white in noon brightness, melting. Robert and I had run and chased and scrubbed each other with snow. My hands hurt from cold gladly. I stood still, catching my breath, looking up at the school's cliff of windows. Dark-green blinds showed through the glass. Snowmelt fell from limestone trim amid bricks rich as scabs. Water riddled the drifts between denuded bushes, below the windows. Bright-colored clothing glowed in the light. Robert's sky-blue ski jacket glowed, unzipped, open. He moved, circling, watching to see if I would chase him again. I watched him as he blindly walked sideways. Of course, the world seemed to revolve around us. Behind Robert passed a bicycle rack, all large, silver-painted rings which, although showing only partially above snow, wholly suggested a spiral notebook's wire binding. The high and dry sidewalk leading into the school appeared and disappeared behind Robert as he moved sideways. I began packing a snowball; Robert motioned, "Don't"; I threw the snowball aimlessly aside. It broke on the sidewalk. I felt joyous. I felt only incidentally glad that I hadn't hit a passing person. The dark streak of a person stopped at the shattered snowball, stopped comically, I thought at first, as if a giant feather blocked his way.

I didn't resolve the streak into a specific person, the Latin teacher, Mr. Altquist, until he shouted at me, "You there. Come here." I walked over torn snow. Cold rose to notice. (I wore no coat, no jacket, but a loose, loosely-knitted, drab-green sweater—Estelle's handiwork—and a dirty-beige muffler with long fringe at either end. Cold fingered through the loose knit.) Mr. Altquist looked professionally intimidating. He wore an overcoat like blackboards, only slightly more pliant. He'd furled his dark trousers' tops into ferocious galoshes, galoshes closed with latch after emphatic latch, latches like bitterness given many mouths. He wore a wedge-shaped hat or cap of crinkly black wool; the fleece of dead sheep—of dead, black sheep at that—gleamed in the sun. The cap remarkably suited his angular face. His cheekbones tapered steeply to a chin with a deep indentation; the sides of his cap tapered shortly upwards to an indented crown. Because his face so suited his hat (or vice versa), and because I had stringiness in common with my muffler, I imagined the two of us, briefly, as a cartoon. I labeled the cartoon in my mind, "Militant Wedge meets Penitent String allergic to scissors."

Mr. Altquist barked inquiry. He asked my name. He asked if I knew the rule against throwing snowballs. I began rapid apologies (all too joyously). The man said, "Very well," as if bored, and I thought, okay, over and done with, easy enough, end of the matter. Wrong. I stopped apologizing. Words seemed to freeze in my throat. Mr. Altquist smiled; teeth filled his leanness. He said, "So, you didn't mean to hit me with it." I said, "No, sir," contritely. "No, sir. I didn't. I wasn't thinking." He said, "Well, you should learn to think next time." A self-pitying sense of injustice pricked me. My throat hurt. Mr. Altquist said, "Get busy." He told me to pack six snowballs and to do so quickly because he didn't have all day.

I obeyed. I bent my spineless back; I packed the snowballs. Scraping miserably at the snow, which I had previously grasped with pleasure, I saw my eyelids flash orange against the sight of my hands. I saw the snow-matted fringe of the fore end of my muffler double up against the snow. It had caught the snow previously; I hadn't noticed until then. I threw the fore end of the muffler over my shoulder. I felt miserable, in part because I obeyed and in part because experience with my father had taught me the crushing lesson that, at least in the short term, obedience cost less than did resistance (however justified). My submissiveness grieved me. I packed the snowballs. I set them, one by one, in a line on the snow. Finished, I stood straight. I didn't look at Mr. Altquist. I heard him say, "All right, now. Step on them." An unheard-of detail and a crowning pain. I stepped with my hiking-booted right foot. I crushed each snowball, one at a time.

42 EDWARD'S SITUATION

My father, who'd effectively planned his own life, had plans for me. He planned for me to go to college. He planned for me to learn enough in college that he might consider me, in his words, "well rounded in the basics." And he planned for me to go to graduate school, learn a skill, and earn a degree that would attest to that skill, and thus make it, my unspecified skill, marketable. Thus, prepared by training and education to lead a good, sound, middle-class life, I should live that life properly, according to Dad's lights.

My first conflict with my father over his plans for me concerned college. I wanted to go to art school. My father said no, absolutely not; he wouldn't countenance such an idea. He said that he would allow "no son" of his "to specialize at the undergraduate level." (His phrase "no son" amused me. Saying "no son" of his, my father sounded hounded by countless sons.) When I pleaded my native narrowness, when I told my father, exaggerating only slightly, that I had no talent for and no interest in anything besides art, Dad countered with galling, adult logic: so much more the need for me, Edward, to "broaden" my "horizons." (For horizons, I liked the edges of sheets of watercolor paper.) My father insisted: no art school. But he treated with me, out of love, I supposed. He said that if I did his bidding in college and studied hard and took *no art classes*, then, if I could get myself accepted into a master's program in fine arts (despite my lack of preparation), he would pay for me to "study art" in such a program for four semesters.

Dad couldn't have afforded to make that offer if Estelle hadn't given him money earmarked for Burke's and my education.

I bowed to my father's strong will and great generosity. I went to college; I studied diligently, as Dad wished. Well before I graduated, I applied to MFA programs. I'd done enough work on my own, without taking art classes, that I could submit the required portfolios. I wrote admittance essays about my desire to learn printmaking as a desire to draw more out of drawing than I'd previously drawn. The school that I most desired to attend accepted me. My father, true to his word and good beyond it, agreed to finance me as promised. He also gave me a car, an old, black Mitsubishi. I affectionately named the car Bit-n-Pieces, it seemed so pieced together, so compact of other cars. Estelle gave me her moonstones and, saddened but selfishly joyous (intoxicated by a newly-acquired illusion of independence), I drove away to my chosen school. Arrived and enrolled, I worked zealously at that school, grappling greedily with new tools and with new materials. I worked zealously until just before the end of the first semester, when Estelle died. I then flew home, witnessed the alienating, religious spectacle of her funeral, and grieved sorely in private, stiffly otherwise. I returned to school in January, made good the projects left unfinished in December. I worked, submerged in lithography, through the second of the four semesters promised. Over the summer following that semester, my father resumed needling me with his plans.

For a while, following Estelle's death, I did not feel like resisting people. I did not feel like contending with or against anyone or anything. Near the end of the second semester of my work toward an MFA, a friend, Mike, readily convinced me that he needed a car over the summer far more than I did. I signed over half of Bits-n-Pieces to him with the understanding that, come September, Mike would return full ownership to me. (However much people tired me in my mournful state, the impersonal bureaucracies involved in altering the car's title, registration, and insurance didn't. Indifference served as patience.) I noticed, with rational annoyance, that I actually—abjectly—welcomed the prospect of living at home over the summer without a car, without means of easy escape from my parents, without means of easy escape from that old trough of shadows, Estelle's house. I wanted to live in Estelle's house, swaddled in loss, without moving.

That summer, my father's concerns about me transcended irritation about Bits-n-Pieces. Dad seemed to have forgotten that he'd promised me four semesters in which to work to my heart's content (and to earn a master of fine arts in the process). Over that summer, Dad repeatedly told me to think—and to think "hard"— about applying to graduate schools for *the fall after next*. He verbally granted me the further semesters promised, but he skipped over them in his admonitions. That projected good, an earned MFA, meant little or nothing to my father. He considered the degree worthless as a qualification for paying work, and he stormed at me with sibilant vehemence about his intention that I earn, in the future, "at least some semblance of a decent income." I listened in my unresisting mood. I realized that I would have to resist my father as I had never before resisted.

Dad talked and talked—with belated, pathetic desperation— about my supposed need to choose a career and to pursue it through schooling. I thought mournfully about the menial jobs that artists often did to support themselves. I thought about those jobs—waiter, house painter—while Dad's word "career," in Dad's urgent voice, disturbed the air. I heard the word "career" pronounced so frequently that I eventually learned the sense of it in Dad's accents: Dad's word "career" exceeded the word "care" by two repetitive letters. Dad might have stormed, not "career," but "I care, I care, I care, I care." How could I contend against his loving care?

Lying around Estelle's house, I felt that I had neither a leg to stand on nor a penny to my name. But I did, suddenly, have pennies. Estelle had willed her remaining funds to Burke and to me. Burke shockingly called the gift "a pittance, not a legacy." As to the leg to stand on, although spineless in slumped posture before my father while he browbeat me at a pathetically late date about the fiction called "my," Edward's, "career," I knew that I had a grain of talent and a vein of grit to go with it. I just felt temporarily incapable of action. I couldn't even bring myself to offer reassurance, to say to my overly anxious father, "Don't worry, Dad. Don't worry about me so much. I'll be fine." I did not seem at all fine to him.

When I failed to tell my father anything about plans for or preferences about a career for myself—mention of my indefensible art enflamed Dad's contempt—he began flogging his own preference (or pathetically vain hope) for me. He began urging me to study architecture. I told my father that "pre-architecture," like "pre-med," existed, and that people began "studying architecture" as undergraduates. Dad ignored those facts. He knew that I had no special interest in buildings; he knew that I disliked working on projects with other people (as an architect would have to do). Dad knew all that, but he had faith in me, inconveniently. Discounting all drafting technology, he believed that I could "at least" paint pictures of buildings—pictures of unbuilt buildings—to promote investment. Dad tried to qualify the word "architecture" to me, but he persistently used it. I heard the word "architecture" pronounced sharply so many times that, whatever the merits of the field, whatever the powers of the "built environment," whatever the culturally telling expressiveness of buildings, the word "architecture" became "Architecture" to me: a threat, which Dad leveled, the great A like an arrowhead aimed at my chest.

43 FLOOR, PAPER, CRAYONS, TRASH

My father urged me to think "hard" about my future. I understood that I should think seriously about earning a living. I understood that I should not just lie around, that I should not lie on my back on the bed in my old room in Estelle's house, watching cigarettes undo themselves, watching burning cigarettes do nothing—because they could do nothing—to contend against the fire that writhed through their fibers and turned the fibers to ash. I should not see cigarettes' lengths of drooping ash in the light of a spring day out-of-doors, when Estelle, having finished cutting flowering lilac branches from bushes behind the house, stood in sunshine facing me, holding a heap of cut lilacs, the drooping, mildly purple—sun-blanched violet—flowers of which did not look like cigarette ash.

I understood that I should not lie around, idly considering words like "hard" and "soft." I should not dwell on memories of bright-red arrows, arrows which Burke, as a child, shot into archery targets. I should not remember Robert zealously drawing marks using a transparent ruler, marks which suggested swords in thronged—clanging, hacking—depictions of battles. I should not shrink from bright red or from sharp lines as "hard."

I knew that I should not lie around thinking about tarot cards, about Burke's backhanded gift to me of tarot cards which someone had given to him, cards which he passed on to me, saying contemptuously, "Maybe you'll like the pictures." I should not remember having learned the cards' gists and "telling fortunes" at summer camp using the cards. I remembered "telling fortunes," but in my old room in Estelle's house, I avoided thinking about hopes, fears, and expectations, collectively called "the future."

My father urged me to think "hard"; he urged me to think seriously; he urged me to think constructively. He urged me to develop plans—plans, plans—plans for the year after the next and for years following. Lying on the bed in my old room in Estelle's house, burning cigarettes solely for the sight of will-less smoke, I thought about how, as a child, lying sprawled on a floor with paper and crayons, I'd burrowed my way into a world of making so gratifying to me that I wanted to stay there for the rest of my life. How had I arrived at the age of twenty-two (almost twenty-three) still wrapped up in paper?

I tried to think "hard" while watching soft smoke. I tried to think as my father wished me to think—seriously—about "a career." I tried to think as my father wished me to think about earning an income, about earning "a decent income," through the use of a skill, a "marketable skill," which I had yet to identify and yet to learn. I thought about the skills which I already possessed. They earned nothing; they cost to use. I thought about how I craved their use and augmentation as a way of life. My father passed ringing judgment upon me. Dad said that I'd "lived a pretty rarified existence up to this point." His tone plainly implied, "This has got to stop." I had to end the indulgence, the rarefaction, he'd sponsored.

That summer, that mournful summer after Estelle died, I recognized that I would have to get a job. True to the skills, to the temperament, and to the wayward, subterranean, impractical ambition that I, in fact, possessed, I could not let my father direct the rest of my life. But what could I do? I could possibly work as a dishwasher, busboy, waiter. I could possibly clean houses. More in line with my skills and with my gift for triviality, I could possibly work for a decorator, converting solid walls, for example, into Italianate, cracked ones. Having several jobs at once, I could possibly afford an apartment shared with other people. Thus employed and thus splitting expenses, I could possibly afford life, but not my true work.

I did not think "hard" well. Watching smoke furl and bend, watching smoke marble the air (the soft air, marble-less), I did not think "hard"; I indulged in soft reveries. I developed an extended fantasy about what I "should" do morally to atone for my "rarefied existence," to atone for my deepest sin, love of inhuman paper: I should get a job as part of a crew picking up trash beside highways. I should collect trash by stabbing, by using a litter harpoon against sacred paper. Thus, I should work to conquer my aversion to pointed sticks—arrows, pool cues—by using one against paper. I should work against my love of solitude by working with other people, people who, although armed with pikes, might refrain from using the supposed tools to murder me for gayness (however contained, another offense). Like them, I would wear a required uniform of sorts, bright orange additions to ordinary clothes, orange warnings to motorists. (In my favored clothes, all gray-blue, I avoided attracting sight like the fog.) I imagined myself wearing bright orange patches. I imagined myself wearing my native vague blue and uncongenial additions, strident orange, wearing orange and blue and standing amid tall, blanched, exhaust-blasted grass beside a highway, looking down, standing immobilized over some dull, filthy, sodden clot of once-white, weak paper, unable to do my prescribed job (jab) because even that paper, as paper, trailed glorious strands from my former life.

I imagined picking up, piercing, pricking up, trash as penance. More than I enjoyed imagining that work, I enjoyed imagining presenting that labor to my father as my chosen "career," mocking his concept of "career," of course. I enjoyed imagining standing in front of my father, he behind a forbidding desk, I upright, on the exhausted carpet of his study, looking downward deferentially but staunchly telling him that I'd "finally decided what I should do with my life"; telling Dad that I'd decided to spear trash for a living (fantasy within fantasy); acting staunch as Saint Francis in the face of paternal outrage; speaking serenely to the grayed remains of carpet underfoot; speaking as if nothing could dissuade me from "this course of action," a phrase of Dad's own. (He would stare at me, hearing me use the phrase, hearing me misuse the phrase by applying it to an activity that he would deem unworthy of the expression.) I enjoyed imagining Dad trying to joke with me initially, then sliding, sliding into declining to "dignify this ridiculous notion"; Dad finally cracking, Dad spitting tacks, saying, "I didn't pay for your education in order to have you throw it away like this." Of course, he didn't (I wouldn't smile). I most enjoyed imagining the most far-fetched part of the scenario: Dad driven to distraction, saying, "Edward, Edward. Forgive me. I pushed you too hard"; Dad begging me, begging me, not to turn beggar ("trash-picker," "trash-picker-upper, Dad"); my father's final pleas, "Listen to me, Edward. Please. Please. Will you? For once in your life? Be reasonable?" None of that happened; none of it would happen, of course. I didn't bait my father, but I enjoyed imagining.

44 CHECK

The summer after Estelle died came to an end. I felt as if I'd spent it entirely listening to my father's words, Architecture, career, decide, apply soon, listening to his invocations of my need to plan, listening to talk of my need to determine what I would "do next." My father's desperate talk ignored the immediate prospect of the coming year. I'd spent hours listening and listening and impotently disapproving of my deep, eager willingness to exploit my father. (I knew what I should do to avoid exploiting him: I should not return to art school; I should forfeit the remaining semesters promised; I should start supporting myself—all sound judgments, all vacuous, all lifeless.) In that spring of motivations called my heart of hearts, I wanted those remaining semesters; I wanted the excitement, the discovery, the thrill of making they promised.

So, I made plans—to return to art school. Listening, listening, I'd occasionally assured my father that I'd heard what he'd said. (He asked me if I had point blank more than once.) I'd said, "Okay, okay. I'll think about it." He'd replied, "Edward, you have got to do much more than think." I'd murmured, yes, sir, archaically; that smoothed his Jovian feathers. I made plans to return to art school; my last night at home for that summer came. My mother had an amateur-theatrical rehearsal that night. Without her, Dad and I would have dinner out; he would drive me to the airport. I would return to school.

When seeing me off to school as he had done, semester after

semester, for five years before that night, my father had personally given me a personal check for what he called my "personal expenses." Handing me a previously written check, he'd said things like, "Take care of this," "Make this last," "Put this to good use," and I'd thanked him concertedly. But the night at the end of the summer after Estelle died, just before leaving the house to see me off, Dad did not give me a check prepared in advance; he wrote out a check in front of me. He acted as if he'd forgotten to write it beforehand. I wondered. Did he think that writing the check in front of me might stir me to refuse it? Did he mean to augment my sense of indebtedness? Did he wish to remind me from whom, from whose literal hand, "my" funds derived? Did he dramatize the handout?

Preparatory to writing the check, Dad unclipped a pen from his suited depths. He laid the pen's cap aside. He opened a leather-housed checkbook. With his left hand, he held the small folder flat against the dining-room table. With his right hand, he wrote on a check the date, numbers, numbers' names in script, and my name formally. He included my middle initial, A for Arthur. The A jabbed: Architecture remembered. I felt guilty, watching the clean, golden nib of Dad's pen form crossed strokes like Xs, which stood for zeros, watching the nib fling out words for numbers and words, my name, the emergent turns, lengths, and bends of trained ink briefly shining bright black and quickly drying dull on the pale-blue-hatched surface of the check made of burnished paper. Soft, pervious, unburnished paper, like the paper of a paper napkin, would have drawn the ink far away, into itself; its fibers, claiming ink, absorbing ink as if drinking it, would have turned the nib's narrow tracks into spreading clouds. Such paper would have subverted the nib's intentions; meaningless clouds would have followed the pen. The hard check, right for its purpose, did not let ink get carried away. I felt guilty, watching wet ink stay put, watching wet ink dry quickly. I felt guilty of frivolity, of thinking of what paper and ink *did not* do together while my father wrote. I felt guilty of exploiting my father and guilty of sticking to my childish passion—making clouds on paper, essentially—while my father deeply desired me to become responsible in his eyes, adult. I felt guilty, guilty, seeing my name written out in script on hard paper, above a long, thin, black, printed shape called a straight line, a line labeled "pay to the order of," a very thin strip of unwavering blackness.

Dad wrote out the check. He ripped it out of the checkbook. He extended it toward me. I saw, in the still-open checkbook, the binding ridge from which he'd torn the check, a strip rough with the edges of checks previously torn. Vanished checks had all torn away from the binding in a regular manner. Each check had left a small blur or burr of torn-paper raggedness, like a sedimentary layer in the low cliff of leavings which rose above the newly uppermost check, the blank check newly disclosed by the check extended. Past checks and the check then offered had all torn away from the binding, not through aligned perforations consisting of true, gaping holes, but through subtle weak spots like pinpricks which pierced without removing paper. I wondered guiltily, seeing the signs of past checks and the deck of checks remaining in the checkbook: How much paper like that had gone for other paper? How many checks had I spent on watercolor paper?

I knew that I should stop taking Dad's money then and there. But I didn't do so. I stretched out my docile paw; I took the check offered. I thanked my father. In a ritual which had not become routine, I acknowledged his generosity and I promised conscientious use of the money. But what I considered the good use of money—spending it on rolls of deep paper, on watercolor fields, for instance—my father would have considered waste (and worse, the purchases illicit). That night, at the end of the summer after Estelle died, I thanked my father more earnestly than ever for the check guiltily received. But by mistake, through nervous distraction perhaps, I actually treated the check negligently. (And contrary to my usual treatment of paper, a substance I hated to see folded, I also treated the check cruelly.) I folded the check sharply in half, short end to short end; I slipped it into my shirt pocket. An inconsiderate thing to do. No way to treat a man's money. Show some respect. Dad didn't reprimand me. In a lenient mood that evening, he corrected me gently, as if he spoke to a child (perhaps he did speak to a one). He said, "You won't lose that, now, will you?" I instantly transferred the check to my wallet, another rectangle folded in half, but a rectangle crushed by use into compound curves.

45 RESTAURANT

After I'd housed my father's check respectfully (deep in the craw of my exhausted wallet), we went to a restaurant for supper. Dad then drove me to an airport so that I, as planned, as arranged, as funded by him, might fly back to school, to the life I coveted, life in a graphics studio, life among good instructors and high stacks of paper, ever-renewed stacks of paper, paper that posed as free for the taking. My father seemed unusually relaxed and expansive that night. Perhaps he felt glad to see the last of me for a while, after months shot through with "Architecture," months pierced by his talks about "my," Edward's, "future" and about "my," Edward's, "plans." Besides acting relaxed and expansive that night, my father also seemed subtly, lovingly apologetic to me, possibly because his beloved Margaret, my mother, had expressed no interest in seeing me off ("Well, goodbye then, you two. Enjoy yourselves"). She had a rehearsal dependent upon her presence that night. She had good reason for abbreviating the leave-taking, which my father protracted, but she'd sounded flippant.

Although Dad kindly pressed me—"Where would you like to go?"—I felt beneath speaking of restaurants that night. I expressed indifference while trying not to sound ungrateful. My father chose a place and I followed him into his choice, a lugubrious Italian restaurant which contained, to my mind, far too much red in its décor. A dark-haired woman led us to a table. (Her long, gathered hair stirred against her back as she walked, live darkness against almost equally dark fabric.) Throughout the restaurant, mitigated in force by low lighting, scarlet miters—folded napkins—projected from white tablecloths. Someone had placed the white tablecloths diagonally over red tablecloths; the tables showed red, as if they had red, triangular corners. Dad and I sat down at such a table, within a lugubrious booth consisting of high-backed, dark, rubbery seats. At the closed end of the booth, the seats and the table abutted an incongruous brick wall. Low light shone over the table out of a hole in the wall, out of a niche deep in brick, a low-down niche very close to the table. We received into our hands, from the woman who'd led us, huge, padded books, thick pages printed with listings, descriptions of food. "Hungry?" Dad asked. I said, "No, unfortunately." Dad glanced humorously and fully at me. He said briskly and again, as to a child, "I doubt that they give you much to eat on that plane." I said quietly, "I'm sure they don't." We ordered food and drinks, I didn't notice from whom. I felt too full of the sense that I might have to work as a waiter to notice the waiter until he returned with the drinks. I then watched a tanned, shapely right hand deposit a white paper square on the white tablecloth to my father's right, in the fullest light on the otherwise dimly pale, white-draped / red-draped table. The right hand then placed a rock glass, a stocky cylinder full of ice and golden liquid, upon the appealing if folded scrap of soft, soft, soft, white, absorbent paper. Light passed through the drink; yellowish light fissured with an intensely crumpled-looking sheen from the ice appeared where a shadow might have appeared, at the base of the glass. Marvel enough, but more marvels followed: with a flowing gesture, the man working as waiter laid white paper on the cloth to my right and lowered a tall, stemmed glass of pinkish wine to the paper. He lowered the wine with his left hand, and his left hand didn't leave. Its lingering surprised me. And I noticed: the man wore an ID bracelet, a long, slightly arched, rectangular, silver plaque on a broad-linked, flat-linked, heavy silver chain. The plaque bore the name "MILO" in stiff, upright capital letters, machine-engraved. The manacle lingered. The man labeled Milo

seemed to linger and to linger left-handedly. He seemed intentionally slow to release the glass, as if he meant for me to see, to read,
to register, his name. The man's perhaps-imagined behavior
thrilled me. I felt too shocked, too thrilled by what I perhaps
imagined, to look from Milo's hand to his face. Had I looked up,
I might have seen Milo simply looking elsewhere, distracted in
mid-task by some claim on his attention unrelated to me. Or I
might have seen confirmation, in the form of a smile, for example,
of what I clearly, embarrassingly desired: that the whole man
beyond the hand take a sexual interest in me, and that he, due to
the circumstances of his employment, had only limited means to
suggest that interest. Perhaps, those possibilities aside, had I looked
up I might have seen in the man's face an ordinary expression, one
that I could not have milked for meaning. Whatever Milo meant
or did not mean by his lingering, I felt a full charge of lust, and I
embarrassed myself both by my sexual starvation and by my
inconsistency: I'd gleaned slenderness in Milo from his hand; I
usually lusted for corpulent giants.

Milo brought the dishes we'd ordered. As he right-handedly
lowered an oval platter before my father, Milo said, "The plate is
very hot, sir," but nothing protected Milo's fingers from the heat.
As he began to serve me in the same bare-handed manner, I said,
"Don't you burn your fingers?" before he could speak his routine
warning about the heat of the plates. I could not tell if our minds
met as our eyes did, but as he set down my radiant plate, Milo
leaned down close to my ear and said, as if whispering without
actually whispering, but as if imparting a secret, "I'm used to it,"
and he smiled as he withdrew, and my shocked timidity warred
with other thrills, and I almost expected my father to ask, "Do you
know this fellow?" I imagined gladly answering that question, "No,
Dad, not yet."

My father and I ate. Doing so, I curbed my expressivity with
regard to Milo, who came and went. I lacked confidence, ease, and
experience in flirting. If I *had* actually, already flirted with Milo
the least little bit, I'd gotten away with it (before my father), and

I didn't dare more. I didn't want to discover that I'd misinterpreted Milo. I didn't want to antagonize my father, with whom I'd never discussed my gayness, and who, while not oblivious to it, brushed it off with evasive comments. I wanted to imagine Milo as living a good, strong, full gay life above boards, not in the shadows of a gloomy restaurant: he should have much better things to do than to flirt with me, however much I enjoyed perhaps-imagining that. Thus, wanting to think better of Milo than to think what I thought—that he flirted with me—and wanting to spare my father the discomfort of seeing my gayness in action, however constrained, however little the action; wanting to spare myself feeling ridiculous, mistaken in Milo, and convicted of my mother's sin, physical vanity (imagining myself so compellingly attractive that a beautiful man working as waiter couldn't help but flirt covertly with me); desiring, in effect, not to deepen my distraction, I conversed intently with Dad, ignoring Milo while Milo brought plates and took away plates and refilled water glasses that did not need refilling. When the meal finally ended, my father said to Milo, "You could bring us the check, please." Again, I regretted the check in my pocket.

Milo, coming and going, brought the bill for the meal in a thick, padded, dark vinyl folder. The folder resembled an elongated wallet. Milo left. Dad opened the folder, read through the tally printed on paper, paper which, like his paper check, did not attract my sympathy as such. Dad extracted his billfold, extracted a credit card from it, and laid the small, flat, gray plastic rectangle with rounded corners on the open folder. Dad closed the folder; Milo arrived, bore it away, returned with it, and with a yellowish-white, plastic ballpoint pen. Dad, armed with a golden-tipped pen near his heart, used the plastic pen to write digits—as on his check for me—digits meaning money. This time he wrote on a small, white, rectangular piece of paper much longer than wide. He added a tip to the printed tally and signed his name to the straight-edged paper. I didn't bother to watch how the pen's (stiff) ink behaved.

46 PLANE

After supper, Dad drove me to an airport. I sat as if dumped in the seat beside him, watching highway signs that seemed to sweep over us. The green signs bore pale-grit letters and glowed in light from lamps projecting from their bases. The signs had sharp—right-angled—corners. Each sign also bore a border in the same pale grit that formed the letters. The borders had rounded, hence mild-seeming, corners. The round-cornered borders caught the light clearly; the signs' true edges and true corners didn't; thus, sharpness—sharp corners—seemed to lurk in darkness; the round, gleaming, mild-seeming corners suggested my naïveté. The signs began reading "Airport," "Airport," "Airport." The As touched "Architecture," "Architecture," my father's plans for "my" future. I supposed that "the future" lived as people's thoughts and emotions, in their hopes and expectations, and that decisions and actions in the inescapable present had effects in the present-to-come, whenever that present came about. The present, from my point of view that evening, seemed more than usually fraught with projected future. Intermixed with airports and airlines and schedules and motion, the present, my present then, seemed to exist only to fulfill the intentions that directed it, as if people and machines worked only with purposes, impelled (directly or indirectly) only by aims, the actual present counting for nothing. Presuming upon the future, I would board a plane. A plane would take me to another state (geographically, socially, and probably mentally as well). The friend to whom I'd more than loaned my car would meet me. We would talk, drink, see other people. The next day, some far-distant tomorrow, I would move into an already-assigned dormitory room, part of a set of two rooms shared with someone whom I already knew and liked. Life, such as I'd known it during the most gratifying parts of the previous year, seemed prepared to resume because presently arranged. I had good prospects, pleasing prospects, agreeable prospects, but. Dad's plans for "my" future oppressed me. And my dishonesty with Dad concerning those plans oppressed me. I felt that I should not board the plane that I intended to board. I felt that I should not return to school. I felt that I should begin working somehow, that I should somehow begin, right then, to support myself. (I might "act" renunciatory in fantasy, as in my fantasy about telling my father that I would collect trash for a living, but when it came to giving up something I really wanted, like art school, I could not make the sacrifice.)

Despite my preoccupations, Dad and I spoke during the drive. We said goodbyes at length. Once he echoed Estelle: "Take care of yourself." He also said, "Let us hear from you." He meant write letters; I loathed telephones. Highway signs read "Exit," "Exit," "Exit." "Exit," without a curved letter, began to apply to "Airport." Dad turned the car; we turned, leaving one gem-flood, entering another: headlights, taillights, red-white light streams. We turned several times. Blue highway signs replaced green. Pale-grit letters on blue began reading "Terminal," "Terminal," "Terminal A," "Terminal B." "Exit" and "Terminal" seemed deathly. A large building with a long curb beside it emerged, orange-lit with glowing haze. Cars made for the curb; cars drew away from it; Dad expressed irritation, "What does this idiot think he's doing?" Dad didn't mean me. We stopped at the curb. Dad cut the engine, opened the trunk remotely; we both got out. I hauled my bags out of the trunk and sent them on the pavement. Dad and I hugged and thumped each other goodbye. I resisted referring to Mother. (Give her my regards. Regards? For shame.) Stronger than spite,

I felt a conscientious need to warn my father about my resistance to his plans, as if I had not already demonstrated, if not overtly spoken, my opposition. When Dad and I embraced, I said faintly, yet to his ear, exactly where he should hear me most clearly, "What if I don't—do what you want me to—next year?" Dad dismissed that, or seemed to dismiss it, jocularly. He said, "That'll keep. You'd better get going now."

I got going. I waved goodbye to Dad, a shade in a moving car. I towed my bags into the building; "Architecture" reeked from the rafters, from the handsome, steelwork roof. I had made a reservation months previously for a round trip, then half expended, for which Dad had paid. I had made a reservation months before, long before the capital letter A had begun to sting, "Architecture." Having found the correct counter for my chosen airline, I regretted my choice. The airline's logo consisted of two flat-topped— lopped, defanged—capital As, one blue, one red, and an eagle shape, the wings raised to form a V over the valley between the two letters. A form of that logo dominated the wall behind the long counter staffed by airline employees. Everywhere, people worked. I would have to work soon. I stood in line among burdened people, between webbed, dark blue, nylon straps on shiny, chrome-bright stanchions into which the straps could retract. I stood in line until no one stood in front of me. With a clear view of the high and deeply, regularly notched counter, I saw, among the many working people behind the counter, the one who called, "Next in line." I moved forward, put my bags (towing handles thrust back into them) onto the scale flooring the notch in the counter nearest that person. I handed my driver's license, and the bent-but-not-creased paper recording my reservation, over the counter to a woman who looked at the license photograph, at me, and again at the license, a slick, flat, plastic card with round corners. The woman's fingernails looked clipped to the card. She placed it flat on the counter, brushed it toward me an inch. She asked questions; I answered, observing her air of fatigue, the steepness between her cheekbones and chin, the lustrous darkness half-covering her ears, ears pinned through with small, bright ornaments. The woman took my reservation paper down, onto an area like a desk behind the counter / barricade. She typed, nails ticking. I couldn't see the type as it appeared on the averted screen, although I leaned forward slightly, trying to see it without moving much. (Computer terminals near the line in which I'd stood—and which still snaked, its population shifting between the straps-and-the-stanchions—offered a means around using another person to register one's presence, to state one's business with the airline. One had, then, a choice between using a computer directly and using one indirectly, through another person. I chose the archaic route.) The woman typed; long, strap-like baggage tags emerged from a slot just below the desk, well above the scale. The quick-fingered, diligent, efficient, employed woman, inadvertently setting an example to me through working, expertly grasped the long tags one at a time; looped each large-letter-marked, bar-coded, strap-like tag through a bag's small, not-extensible handle; ripped paper off the tags, exposing adhesive areas; peeled from each long strip a small strip bearing adhesive; stuck the small strips to the immediate desk edge; bundled away into waste the other paper removed; aligned the looped, long tags' free ends and lengths; ran fingers quickly along the strips, from the far ends up, almost to the handles that the tags then surrounded in a single layer beyond the long, double-layered, stuck-together portions. Other paper emerged from another slot. The woman grabbed it; stuck the little strips from the desk edge onto it; passed the slip to me; spoke numbers; directed me to "my" "gate"; called out, "Next in line, please!" I murmured, "Thank you," hauled my bags off the scale, and towed them to a conveyer belt, which bore them away into an X-ray machine, an ominous-looking large box into which they disappeared.

I moved on; waited in another line; removed shoes, jacket; placed shoes, jacket in a round-cornered, gray-plastic tub; placed the tub on a conveyer belt, which bore it into another X-ray machine as into the tunnel of an amusement-park ride. I put my pocket change into a small tub different enough from the first tub to seem a different species. On signal, I walked toward someone through a metal-detecting frame. I regained change, shoes, jacket; restored them to my person appropriately; proceeded. Everywhere people worked. I would have to work soon. I began thinking that I would have to get a job soon, in order to soothe my conscience about letting Dad support me while I intended to oppose him over his plans for me. I would have to get a job soon, soon, soon, not in nine months, when, presuming upon the future, I would have finished earning an MFA, not in nine months, but almost immediately; I would have to "do something, something." My mind rattled grievously. I would have to do something immediately—almost immediately—to prepare myself for work beyond art, work which I dreaded. I would have to look into finding such work *the very next day*. I could not let my guilty, vague, conscience-appeasing semblance of a resolution to find work (slight work at first, symbolic work at first) grow stale, evaporate, desert me, fade, become buried, lost, among other and much more welcome challenges, distractions, projects. Thinking vaguely yet grimly that I would have to work, that I would have to find some sort of not-very-time-consuming, little, symbolic job very soon, the next day if possible, I strode along corridors, ignoring people, windows, reflections, distant lights, nearby lights outside; ignoring shops, food-stops; not quite ignoring people, struck by the sight of a man cleaning small spots off the largely clean floor. (Someone, at a less populous time of night, must have driven a floor polisher, working; the huge floors gleamed.) I walked rapidly along corridors, following overhead signs which directed people to gates: long, thin, horizontally rectangular signs, slick overhead signs with right-angled corners, without textural differences—reflective grit—between backgrounds and numbers, backgrounds and letters. I stood impatiently on and walked impatiently on-along-with several long, depressed, flattened-out escalators set into the floors. Having reached the waiting area for the flight I intended to take (but which I shouldn't take), I dumped myself into one of the many empty wide seats arranged in fixed rows over a napless gray carpet. I sat, eyes closed, until boarding began and I had to stand up; wait in line; hand over a white, sharp-cornered, paper scrap to a woman who fed it quickly to a slot in a box which chopped through the scrap, executing the paper. I had to receive the stump, the stub, the paper scrap's tag end; it bore links to my luggage. I had to hear a woman say "Have a safe trip" repeatedly, before me, beside me, and after me. I had to say "Thank you," compelled to empty politeness. I had to walk down a gray, not-entirely-steady chute to a plane's door, a large, bowed, round-cornered chunk of the fuselage standing against the fuselage and beside the opening into the plane. The door's shape gave me pause; I stopped; I stepped out of the way.

The door's shape, perhaps in conjunction with the staid gray of the plane's exterior, reminded me of the credit card that Dad had just used to pay for our meal. The enormous credit-card door caused me to feel the enormity of both my debt to my father and of my self-serving behavior, my willful use of my father's money. I felt deeply indebted, and I felt as if I betrayed my father. The door said: Last chance to turn back. I heard that stern message in my brain, but the graphics studio (far away) beckoned. The studio represented a whole and hopelessly desirable way of life to me, a life of learning through working without practical concerns. I entered the plane, found my seat, and sat down.

I sat in my assigned, cramped space, eyes closed. I'd shut my eyes almost immediately upon sitting down because, directly in front of me, all too closely in front of me, another credit card loomed: a gray, plastic tray-on-hinges folded up and away into the back of the seat in front of me. The tray, showing its underside, looked credit-card-like: gray, round-cornered, rectangular, plastic. Plastic inlaid within a matching gray, plastic frame, the tray repeated the door's message forcefully and at short range. I shut my eyes and my mind against the strident object.

I sat beside a small window, eyes concertedly closed. If the deep, small window's shape looked too mildly oval to join the door and the tray in shouting "credit card," "indebtedness," "indebtedness of the sort you cannot repay," the window, essentially a sealed perforation, nudged me gently with its cornerless form, a shape verging upon oval, oval, oval; I missed Estelle. I did not think about how Estelle might have counseled me about my various conflicts; I simply missed her. And, tired of my self-involved emotions, I tried turning my attention, through listening, to the outside world. That didn't work.

I heard trite music; I heard people engaged in settling into the plane: a child crying amid hushing murmurs, a plaintive recommendation in a woman's voice, "Why don't you put it here?" Under and around human sounds, the plane shook as, I supposed, unseen people, beyond the immediate unseen people, loaded luggage into it. The impact of heavy objects, objects landing as if someone had thrown them, shook the plane subtly. And, although the shaking thumps and the vibrations caused by shifting objects came from below the area in which I sat, I remembered blows from above shaking a different structure.

I remembered hiding, age thirteen, in a small, run-down barn on the farm where Chris kept horses. I hid when a truck with two men in it drove up. One of them climbed a board ladder to the hayloft and opened the hay doors. The other man, standing in the back of the battered pickup, threw four hay bales, one at a time, up into the loft. The bales landed heavily; the barn shook subtly. The man in the loft dragged each bale aside as soon as it landed. Bits of hay sifted down, across my view of sunlight framed by the dark barn. In the sunlight, the shirtless man in the back of the truck dazzled me. My mind would later—much later—tell me that the man in the truck looked like a collection of erotic clichés: stubble of stiff, blond hair; sweat glistening through the crewcut and upon chest and abdomen; bits of hay sticking to the glistening torso; waist disappearing lithely into washed-out blue jeans; large-buckled cowboy belt rimming the denim where the waist disappeared. Later, those details suggested clichés, but at the time, hiding in the barn, I did not see clichés. I saw an actual man working and an actual body that aroused me—unbearably. The man from the hayloft climbed down the ladder; the half-naked prodigy in blue jeans swung himself down, over the side of the truck. As he turned, I glimpsed parts of letters on a patch sewn to the jeans, under his belt. Recognizable by their parts, the large letter parts spelled the brand name "Lee." The men left. And I, closing my eyes to the barn-gloom, confused the touch of my fingers with the bright sight of "Lee."

As the plane shuddered, struck in its interior by objects arriving one after another, I felt slightly, bleakly, bearably, contemptuously—not contemptibly—lustful, considering men amid work: unseen men loading luggage (men, I assumed, although women might have worked, too); the man labeled "Milo"; the bale-throwing "Lee." I felt contemptuous of my faint, faint, echoing lust because it assailed me as a distraction when I had other concerns. (I would rather think about men working than think about work itself. Easy to think of sleek "Milo" naked.) I did not rank sex among my immediate problems. But my fear of sex (with another person), along with my fear of work (beyond paper), suggested a general immaturity, some general fear of the rest of the world. (Conquer one, conquer all? I would have to find, to try to find, some kind of work the next day.) Sitting on the plane, I told myself: I should also try, try to meet someone, to overcome my extreme sexual diffidence. (I feared what I called "intimacy," bodily "intimacy," more than I feared work.) I sat in the plane, eyes closed, trying not to think about men, trying to think about fear. What did I fear? What did I fear? What did I fear, really?

I heard recorded announcements, talk about seatbelts, safety. (If "cabin pressure" dropped, oxygen masks would also fall, umbilical cords, placental sacks dangling. Under some black circumstances left to imagination, lights along the aisle floor would illuminate. I'd already noticed the nearest exit: "Exit" in red light shining through plastic pierced with the letters' shapes, "Exit" in red illumination, without a curved letter.) The plane talked to itself; it moved backwards, turned, lumbered. The plane lumbered and lumbered. I glanced out a window, out the cornerless, partially straight-sided, deeply double-paned shape immediately beside me. Small blue lights pricked the darkness. I shut my eyes again. (Why should blue lights take on sensual loneliness, shine like beaded saliva on a detached hair?) The plane rolled, seemingly for miles, as if it meant to take a land route to its destination. But then it stopped. It sat as if gathering itself, raced, took off; vibrations lessened. I kept my eyes willfully shut against the underlying city's vaunting splendor, the city turned into lights. I did not feel up to seeing shining magnificence full of economic meaning. I did not wish to see height, distance, and light falsify the world by making it—a great, man-made part of it—stunningly beautiful. I did not want to see "little" chemical plants and refineries, their lit, clustered towers looking beautifully intricate, like flutes' and oboes' keys and rods, fit to serve music, not the processes that the towers actually served. I did not wish to see Earth turned to utter blackness, mere background like velvet, to man-made gems. I did not wish to see lights, like stationary fireworks, praising corporate capitalistic spread, lights proclaiming fabulous wealth, the gemmed tips of a developed country's infrastructure. But I did look out the window when the worst of the glory had passed. I saw highways like smoldering leis, orange-marigold-gamboge-colored light shining in lei-like lengths, darkness deep black amid the burning flowers. (Dad, I thought, drove on such a highway, Dad with his thoughts, his preoccupations, a particle in the fiery orange.) I saw, I didn't know what: light in mysterious patterns, like some god's dropped horseshoes. The plane flew and flew. Lights began looking distantly tentative. Towns, clustered lights, began drifting by, stunningly dynamic, clearly alive: small, luminous bodies, beads and soft, yawning clouds, lights like angora, lights like gases. Roads spread from the light-bodies: hair-fine tendrils, glowing, pale. Towns looked beautiful beyond human nature. Towns became silvery spots like lichens, like flat, little patches of much-wrinkled tinfoil. As one of the distantly dime-like patches seemed to approach, I raised my right hand. Its reflection, ghostly, appeared on the window. The dime-patch appeared as if it moved into my hand's reflection. It crawled along, as if within, one of my outstretched, reflected fingers. (What did I expect to feel? Ladybug feet?) When the small light reached my palm's reflection, I closed my hand; the reflection closed around the starry spot. The small, small body of light, caught in an impalpable illusion, didn't notice my grasp. It kept on moving of course, moving evenly, obliviously, utterly undeterred. The spot moved into my reflected wrist. It then suddenly disappeared. I felt vaguely hurt. To allay that vague, irrational hurt, I reasoned. The plane's wing behind me had simply cut off my view.

Returning to school, at the end of the summer after Estelle died, I decided to find "some kind of work." I would have to find true—demanding, time-consuming—work soon enough, in two semesters. But, in the meantime, I merely had to "do something." I had to express my determination to oppose my father's plans. I had to act upon that determination. I had to keep that determination alive in my mind. The day after a plane's door stayed me with its resemblance to a credit card, I set off—in my car, Bits-n-Pieces—to the Student Employment Office. I would go there, I told myself. I would go there. And I did go there, eventually, after the wayward side of my brain created two long delays.

On the way to the Student Employment Office (known from a glass door seen in passing, a glass door labeled blackly, plain as day), I stopped at a traffic signal. Looking away from the light (waywardly), I noticed a laundromat, a small building among other small buildings with which it shared a parking lot: much fresh-looking asphalt barred with sunflower-yellow stripes. Coal and gamboge glistened appealingly. The laundry looked transparently trusting. Its front wall consisted of very large windows atop a few courses of brick, a civil conjunction. (The bricks looked too tame to rebel, to arise rebelliously against the glass.) The building had no central door. Two glass doors, one at either end of the building, interrupted the huge, frontal windows (and the well-behaved bricks). A "Help Wanted" sign showed through the glass beside each door. The signs scared me. Their white-bordered, red letters glared. Black rectangles, also white-bordered, surrounded the red-and-white print. The black added gravity to the letters' message. The signs made me think: What would "help" do in a laundromat? Repair machines? Mop floors? Assist customers? How? I felt told, by the signs, "Help Wanted," "Earnest Help Needed," "Not you, Ed. Not you, with your precious, little notions about 'symbolic work.'" The traffic signal in front of me turned green (green, ever-springing, hope). I might have escaped the reproachful signs. Instead, I pulled into the parking lot. I parked immediately facing the glass-fronted laundry. I sat, looking—as one could look—directly into the place.

Within the building, clearly visible through my scrupulously clean windshield and through the trusting, big windows, washing machines stood side-by-side in double rows perpendicular to the glass. Smoothly cream-colored, the machines looked almost cubical. (Coin receivers and control panels projected from their lidded tops. The machines' heights exceeded their widths. Their planar sides and tops merged, with mild curves, into each other; the machines lacked sharp edges. Yet they looked cubical.) Back-to-back, in double rows, the machines must have shared plumbing, or, at least, all of the requisite pipes and drains must have run through the same area, behind the machines. But one saw none of that, none of the connections, none of the plumbing. Someone had masked the gaps between the back-to-back machines with simulated window boxes full of artificial flowers.

Seeing the artificial flowers, I began to feel nauseous. I could not blame feeling sick on drinking the previous night. I hadn't drunk much. I couldn't blame the misery on apprehension about applying for the job advertised by "Help Wanted." I had no intention of applying. I dreaded the Student Employment Office—as if the office itself threatened me. But I did not really fear work; or I thought that I didn't. I knew the disgusting truth: I felt sick because, even at the remove of two layers of glass, the sight of artificial flowers disagreed with me. And the travesties in the laundromat looked particularly awful.

I sat in Bits-n-Pieces, trying to take comfort in its dust, in its familiarity. I reminded myself that the last time that I'd seen Estelle alive, I'd told her that I would try, try "to keep things in perspective." Keeping "things in perspective" meant much the same to me, then, as "Don't overreact." Breathing through my gaping mouth while it sweated saliva, I told myself that whoever had bought and arranged and positioned the boxed imitations meant well. The false flowers truly had color. They added color to a room packed with beige machines. And the plastic flowers far from fresh—daffodils-not-daffodils, ersatz hydrangeas—might recall, to some people pleasantly, the real things, the subtle, delicate things behind and beyond the betrayals.

Trying to think of other people didn't quell nausea. Neither did criticisms such as: You don't know anything about hardship; you need to learn; you need a good, stiff lesson in unloveliness. I bounded out of the car and vomited into a gutter. Much heaving delivered me of a few bitter strands.

I sat inside Bits-n-Pieces, gazing into the laundry. Something about the washing machines inside the building appealed to me. Something about their smooth, boxy shapes, something about their lidded tops especially, wooed me with increasing strength as I felt increasingly well, increasingly recovered. The lids fit smoothly into the machines' smooth tops. The lids had straight sides and rounded corners. The lids largely filled the washers' tops. Some numen of childish happiness lived, in my mind, beneath an enameled lid, inside an enameled-metal box. The pleasure resided, in my mind, inside an object merely *like* a washing machine, in an object that merely resembled a washing machine in a few particulars: in a smoothness of cubical, enameled metal, in a box with a lid set into the top. Wasting time luxuriously, delaying confrontation with the Student Employment Office, delaying making my embarrassing request there for almost no work, I sat inside Bits-n-Pieces, relaxed, eyes closed, in search of a remembered—something. What?

I remembered. I remembered a baby-blue cube, a jack-in-the-box. I'd absurdly loved the abrupt, bobbing Jack, the footless clown, the puff of nothing—the comically-hatted, spherical head, the extended arms, the bodiless fresh white smock—attached to the box. The remembered pleasure gave pleasure again, and yet I felt tired of my childishness; I felt impatient with myself. I'd done lots of laundry using dormitory washers. I knew the difference between a washing machine and a jack-in-the-box. Washing machines worked; jack-in-the-boxes didn't. Washing machines served a purpose, Jacks none at all—beyond amusement, beyond the contradictory absurdity of an expected surprise. When washing machines finished washing, when they'd gone through their cycles, their lids unlatched automatically, and they did nothing more. One had to open a washing machine's lid oneself. One had to see ordinary things, heavy, wet, twisted fabrics plastered thickly against the machine's interior. One had to extract the wet coils oneself, hand over fist, in matted hanks. And the clothes hauled from a washer would fit a mortal, human body. They bore no resemblance to a bodiless little hanky-of-a-smock.

Sitting in my car, I thought, "Grow up, Ed." Did I resist growing up, taking on "adult responsibilities," things like laundry and countless other tasks? Did I resist much dull work out of an overly-developed love of pointlessness? Love of art could seem pointless, could resemble a fondness for antic toys. I told myself that I would go to the Student Employment Office. I would go there; I would go there. But first I wanted to see the interior of the laundromat—without intervening glass. I entered the hive, pointlessly, without laundry.

The place smelled good, looked active, and sounded loud. Machines gushed and churned; machines gurgled. Everywhere, people worked, tending laundry, tending children, tending both at once. Children ran, shrieked; clothes dryers pinged. Dryers plated the room's end walls, and, visible through the dryers' huge, beautifully circular, transparent doors, cloth in abundance, cloth in diverse pieces, cloth in colorful confusion, rose and fell, borne aloft and dropped by the dryers' revolving drums. I knew from dorm experience that if one spread wide the door to such a dryer, the door's full opening stopped the machine. I watched as a woman opened a dryer door partially, not wide enough to stop the whirl within. (Although stuff didn't jump out of a washing machine, as out of a jack-in-the-box, cloth did try to come flying, light and dry, out of a dryer.)

Within the room, people worked. People worked without disturbing each other, without obstructing each other. They moved loosely, separate from each other, yet close together. A loose, light activity, like that of the clothes dryers' contents, pervaded the room, as if people rose and fell through it while merely doing laundry. People moved wet cloth to the dryers in rattling carts: shiny, white-metal baskets—chrome grids—on long, wheeled legs. The long legs meant a short reach between washing machine and cart and between cart and dryer. People carted dried cloth to long, smooth, pale, aquamarine, plastic tables. The tables had rims around three sides, like street curbs. The curbs controlled the piled laundry, keep piled things from intermingling freely with nearby, neighboring piles; the tables touched, side-by-side and back-to-back. Each table had legs like Estelle's hairpins overgrown: thin, steel, rod-like legs. Each leg-rod curved, bent smoothly in half, where it met the floor. Each leg section, above the curve, angled gently away from the other. On their inconspicuous, thin-if-double legs, the tables appeared to float, arranged as if moored together in groups. A wide, aisle-like space ran centrally through the room, lengthwise, between the banks of beige washers and the blue tables' marina. Along the main aisle stood many large, dark, boxy objects: change-making machines; vending machines; sinks set in cabinets. The room's handsome, chip-dotted, terrazzo floor (which "Help Wanted" might mop) spread everywhere. At the room's long, back wall, the terrazzo floor stopped at a ledge some eighteen inches high made of undisguised concrete. Stainless-steel washing machines with round, frontal doors stood side-by-side along the ledge. A few chairs—orange-plastic scoops in fixed groups of four—faced the round-fronted washers. I crossed the room and sat down in an orange scoop, facing the round-fronted washers.

Inside the washing machine across from me, someone's washing, awash, rubbed against the porthole-door like a bad dream about drowning. Each of the machines on the ledge had a large, flat, brown-painted, cut-out plywood panel fitted around its barrel-like body. One could see through chinks between the panels; the machines backed into a further room or passage. Yet a wall rose directly above the panels, a wall made of plastic boards designed to resemble rough, gray, weathered planks. Arrayed against the false planks, large, shiny, black plastic letters, and numbers which matched the letters, all in three-dimensional, frontally bloated, flat-backed pieces of Courier type, read in three lines: "Texas Machines / Average Load / 14 to 16 sheets." The words and the numbers puzzled me. ("Texas" might mean "big." But "sheets"? Bedsheets came in many sizes. And could one wash things other than sheets in the "Texas Machines"? And why not say "15 sheets," averaging fourteen and sixteen? Did "sheet" represent a unit of measurement which measured only evenly, so that, in "sheet" language, one could not say "fifteen"? Spans of even numbers might represent odd averages.) The letters and the numbers on the partition-wall confused me, and they threatened to keep on confusing me, until I noticed—and *how* could I have missed it in the first place?—a terrific decoration above the letters: a huge, fake, fake, fake, giant leaping sailfish. The fish shape seemed to leap over the lettering as if it had leapt from the sea. It leapt over the machines, over the little, stainless-steel bins of pent surf. The fish shape seemed to hang in an arc, like a rainbow, blessing the room full of work. Someone had zealously painted the object. Someone had painted it fantastically, with an airbrush, chartreuse and turquoise and cadmium yellow, with an abandon beyond all natural colors. Wondrous splattering covered the suffused bands. I liked the false fish. (I obviously didn't care about falsity in fish the way I cared about falsity in flowers. I obviously didn't care much about falsity in printed letters or in weathered planks, either. And I obviously didn't care about incongruity among the three.) The wall in front of me, above the pilloried—panel-collared—"Texas Machines," ridiculously parodied, if not a great divide in my life, then, at least, my conflict with my family. Mute form and problematic print did not contend on the wall. They simply hung there, ridiculous, balanced.

I sat, eyes closed, amid amniotic gurglings. I sat, listening to the room, hearing dryers ping, hearing hard objects hitting and scraping dryers' interiors, hearing change-making machines thump and rain change in jingling cascades, through metal chutes. (Change-making machines gave the impression that, if you hit a dollar bill hard enough, it would break into pieces.) I sat blindly, eyes closed, hearing carts clash, children laugh, children scream. A little girl sat next to me for a while; I glanced. She played a video game. Her small, whorled thumb kneaded a button on a box. The game kept producing short tunes like runs of bubbles—going up? going up?—under surging sounds, water. I paid attention when a guy my age dropped two large, tightly-packed, shiny-black garbage bags not quite opposite me. The guy—face feline, cheeks creating the feline effect—dug in one of his blue jeans' pockets, extracted change, examined it, walked away. The very large, very shiny, black, black, black plastic trash bags stood on the terrazzo, claiming a machine to my left. (Among the countless stony flecks which filled the smooth, concrete floor with neutral tones, black chips contrasted strongly with pale bits of faint gray and pale bits of brown-almost-white. When the shiny, black trash bags landed on the chip-filled concrete, the black chips near the bags looked sharp with new prominence.) Guy returned. Working expeditiously—setting an example to me by working—he dragged one of the sacks away. The floor snapped with shattered blackness as the unified blackness slid over it, hissing. The remaining bag sat on the terrazzo. It shared an intense, black-plastic, glossy convexity with the Courier lettering on the wall above. It outdid the lettering vastly in convexity. Guy returned. He swooped down, grabbed the remaining sack by the bottom and raised it. The black disgorged red, nothing but dark-red scraps. Abundant as fallen leaves, dark-red scraps heaped the floor: hundreds and hundreds of restaurant napkins. Guy leaned over the napkins. Swinging his arms, not watching where he put the napkins, he thrust them by handfuls into a nearby machine. Although he worked quickly, he shook each bunch of napkins hard before throwing it—thrusting it, shoving it—into the washer's body. A French fry flew from one shaken handful, from another, a small, white paper napkin. The white disappeared into the shifting red pile. It reappeared when Guy, having packed and closed the washer, kicked the remaining scraps along the floor toward a vacant machine. The napkin flitted out of sight, under a nearby chair. I stood up abruptly. I left the laundry. I'd frivolously spared paper in my fantasy about spearing trash for a living.

48   FAST FOOD RESTAURANT

I parked a few blocks from the Student Employment Office. Approaching the dreaded office, I walked along a side street. Large, red-brick buildings darkened the street. Along one side of the street ahead, a few small buildings, beyond the large ones, ended the darkness. Red brick gave way to dingy-yellow brick. Yellow brick housed a post office. Over the sidewalk, outside the post office, an American flag hung twisted upon itself on its horizontal pole. Only the blue and starry union hung straight downward, decorously. Red-and-white stripes in funnel-like shapes hung, clustered, from the pole's fore end. One of the flag's (properly lower) corners, caught over the flagpole, overlapped the union from above. The overlapping triangle appeared diagonally striped. Had I felt more exuberant than I felt then, I would have jumped up, as in basketball; I would have tapped the flag to undo its bad drape. Instead, I walked on; I passed beneath it. Just beyond the yellow brick, rosy-sandy-pale brick housed a fast-food restaurant. Historical preservationists, clinging to straws, meaning to spare the small buildings at the far end of the street, had allowed the construction of the fast-food restaurant. As a sop to preservationists, the building had an unusual design for a fast-food restaurant. It stood in a scant courtyard formed by token walls. A few relic elms—scrappy elms—grew in the courtyard. A circular, stained-glass window, bastardized by containing a stained-glass form of the fast-food restaurant's corporate logo, occupied a high, peaked gable in the building's second story. (Not every high, peaked angle should remind me of "A," the acute initial of "Architecture." Not every hint of architectural planning should do likewise.) I stopped. I gazed at the circular glass in the gable. I thought about clothes dryers' windows in the laundromat. I thought about practical purposes served by the circular windows in dryers' circular doors. Looking at the fast-food restaurant, I reluctantly saw—faint— decorative value in the false rose window (and in the gable, and in the softly-mottled, rosy brick). I saw the logo-filled glass as practical only in that, to anyone familiar with the logo, it identified the building as a restaurant of a particular kind. A sign in one of the restaurant's windows nagged, "Now Hiring." I did not intend to apply for work in the fast-food restaurant. But the sign, harping on a theme, entailing an involved suggestion, invited me to delay, to forestall, to put off facing, once again, whatever the Student Employment Office might or might not offer.

I entered the restaurant through a roomy airlock. The airlock gave access to restrooms. The airlock's floor of large, brick-red, red-clay tiles (credited with earthen authenticity despite my prejudices) continued in the restaurant's main room. The main room stank of fry-grease, but the place looked inviting: airy and open, with big-windowed walls. Everything looked bright and shiny and (while stinking) clean. The building's second floor consisted of connected balconies—seating areas—reached by a central staircase. The staircase slanted, escalator-like, through the middle of the room. Chalk-white walls, not banisters, bounded the staircase. Above the projecting rim of balconies, a ceiling of highly varnished, golden-oaken boards athwart highly varnished, golden-oaken beams repeated the angles of the street-facing gable. The long, oblong beams, in shape and in color, suggested French fries. Only a few people sat eating. Only a few people stood in line to order. Only one person took orders. I debated. (I did not eat meat. I did not want to give the restaurant's corporation—or the owner of that franchise—so much as the price of a cup of coffee. But I wanted to delay. Indulgently, I delayed.) I ordered coffee from a woman who could have used help despite the low volume of business (midmorning). Her eyebrows looked as if a high wind blew them backwards, along her head's curves; her whole face appeared shaped by the same—pleasantly—distorting force; her face advanced, streaming. She wore a nametag and a uniform. Hand-written letters in broad, black print on the little, round-cornered, white-plastic rectangular nametag read "Lisa." The letters, written in marking pen, looked as if they'd rushed onto the slick, little floor of the nametag and all but fallen over backwards. Setting an example to me by working, Lisa brought coffee in a large, white, polystyrene cup. She placed the cup—with hurried fingers, with fingers possibly hurt by the coffee's heat—on a bright-orange, round-cornered plastic tray lined with advertisement-splashed paper. She looked at me fully, her irises dark in their whites as the coffee in the white silo. Looking down, she fitted a white, perforated, elaborately molded plastic lid to the cup. Her eyes bounced up; she said brightly, "That it?" I said, "That's it." Opening my wallet to pay for the coffee, I saw my father's check. (He might have questioned, demanding, "What do you think you are doing?" I knew what I did: I delayed.) As Lisa released change into my hand along with a paper receipt, I asked, "Is there a smoking section?" She said brightly, "Upstairs." I thanked her and carried the coffee on the paper-lined, bright-orange tray up the white-wall-bordered staircase. As I climbed, the stained-glass window, in the gable beyond the staircase, came into view. It appeared to rise as I mounted the steps. It rose like a glowing, bright-orange sun.

Trash cabinets flanked the stairhead. I looked at one of them. It had a closed, hinged door. Immediately above the hinged door, a flap, part of the cabinet, read "Thank You" in letters cut through plastic veneer into an underlying layer (something like sawdust powerfully compressed). The dark letters curved in depth, as if carved with a curved chisel. The ends of each letter curved, semicircular. The letters also curved where their parts converged (the T's right angles non-existent, implicit). Why on earth that curved style? If the letters' curves would not catch dirt, as corners might; if the letters curved to facilitate washing, why make them in depth at all? (One could wash a flat surface faster and more effectively than one could wash a flat surface elaborate with alphabetic indentations.) Did letters' depth serve permanence, as gravestones' letters did? Deep letters might not soon wash away. But the cabinet's cheap construction belied such concern. Did the letters' depth merely make them look emphatic? Eye-catching, as they had caught mine? The sides of both cabinets flanking the stairhead extended above the cabinets' tops on three sides. The cabinets did not, otherwise, resemble the laundromat's blue tables. Orange plastic trays lay neatly stacked in the incomplete corrals atop both cabinets. I set the tray I carried on the nearest stack. I removed the lid from the coffee and the paper liner from the tray. I thrust lid and paper through the flap marked "Thank You," making both instantly, wastefully trash.

I carried the coffee silo—too hot to hold comfortably—to a table beside a window on the side of the restaurant that faced the post office. I sat down. I stood up again immediately, found an ashtray, and sat down again—stricken by the ashtray, a tinny little buttercup-of-a-thing made of virtually disposable, gold-colored foil. The little dish had a circular bottom and a low, crimped rim. The dish resembled the stained-glass window in circular shape and in bearing, within its circular bottom, the restaurant chain's logo. Around the logo-embossed disk of the bottom, the low rim wavered regularly with an endlessly circular series of softly-meeting, softly-bent-into-the-tin triangular shapes with apexes pointing alternately into and away from the little tin pan. No true triangles possessed such softness. But triangles bent into the tin, curvaceous through bending, surrounded the bottom of the dish as if they trimmed it with a ruffle. I remembered Estelle's way of shaping the rims of pie crusts before baking. She formed an upstanding rim of soft dough and then bent the rim at even intervals by twisting it, over and over, between her thumb and the midst of her index finger. She called the bent pattern "rickrack." I could not put the little dish to foul use; I could not dump ash into it.

I remembered sitting with Burke in a room in Istanbul. The room contained many small tables made of boards nailed together. Slick fabric covered them. I'd thought that I might light a cigarette. A man, serving as waiter—but not, then, setting an example to me by working—set a tin can beside my elbow: a shallow tin can, outwardly bright as chrome, inwardly golden, gold-tinted. The can had a golden, concentrically rippled bottom. I looked from the can to Burke. He said gently, "Ashtray." He sounded tired, tired of explaining the world to me.

I sat. I touched the coffee to move it. I pressed my palm to the warm spot in the table left by the coffee. I bathed my fingers in light reflected by the ashtray. A boy and a woman came up the stairs. The boy bounded around the woman. She carried a tray concertedly level. She must have asked the boy, "Where would you like to sit?" The boy shouted excitedly, "Over there." The woman steered the tray, herself, and the boy to seats facing mine at a distance. The boy bounded into the low booth. He stood on the seat. He pressed his hands to the immediate window. He shouted, "You can't see nothing here. Just the United States flag, a tree, a store, a skyscraper." The woman, skin dark under eyes, hair pale with age, looked straight at me. She said apologetically, "We don't come here very often." I said, "Me neither." The boy turned from the window. He shouted to me, "What's your name?" I said, "Ed." The woman all but bowed to me apologetically. She diverted the boy's attention to food. He picked up chunks of it with his hands. I looked out the window, looking at what the boy had seen: "tree," a ragged elm; "store," a dry cleaner's; "skyscraper," an apartment building twelve stories high. (I counted the window tiers.) The "United States flag" looked awful, all red-and-white seen from that side, the red-and-white contorted. I sat, drinking coffee. A loud sound—from downstairs—startled me. The crack changed to clatter; sounds sounded of many pieces, but of nothing broken. The clatter sounded plastic, like many hard, plastic things slipping and sliding, striking each other. Over the slithering clatter, a woman yelled, "Bruce, you shithead." A man responded unintelligibly. Plastic sounded, clapping, slithering, plastic on plastic, as if scraped up. I imagined that people raked plastic trays, not autumn leaves, into a heap and stacked them. I glanced at the stairhead. Atop the trash cabinets, plastic trays sat silently, stacked, behaving themselves. Frivolity threatened. (I remembered a witless, childish prank, no fun for the person who hadn't heard of it, a card game proposed, "fifty-two pickup"; drop fifty-two playing cards; say, "Now, pick them up." If I had to work as a waiter, I would learn that one must not drop trays.) The tray-scraping, tray-clapping subsided. I sat. I began thinking about the Student Employment Office. I told myself silently, "Get moving." I replied to myself, silently, "All right, all right. Just a minute. Just another minute."

While I sat, bothered by my orders, "Get moving," and by my suppliant, plaintive begging yet to delay, I realized that something outside my head also bothered me: threshing, papery sounds. Paper sounded crushed, not far away. Paper sounded stirred—as if misused, as if badly hurt. Polystyrene foam, breaking, cracking, shrieked. I looked at the stairhead. One of the trash cabinets stood open. Its hinged door spread beyond a shiny, black trash sack sitting on the floor. A flushed, tense—angry-looking—man, who had "Bruce" written all over him as well as on his nametag, held the mouth of the sack forcefully shut with one hand while, with his other hand, he rammed a chrome-bright rod down, into the sack, through his sack-holding hand. He pulled the rod up, through his fist, and plunged it down again. He plunged and lifted repeatedly, jabbing, stabbing, stirring. I wanted to stop the atrocity, but no atrocity occurred. Neither bag nor—compressed— trash suffered. Yet Bruce seemed to murder the sack by raping it with an object. Bruce finally withdrew the implement completely. It emerged, long and smooth: a long, shiny cylinder ending in outspread extensions, like a five-footed cane, only worse. Having compressed the trash, Bruce strangled the bag. He tied its neck in a knot—as if to make absolutely certain that he had killed it.

Leaving the murder / rape weapon behind—and the trash-cabinet door standing open—he dragged the corpse down the stairs. The sack hissed as it descended, scraping a wall.

I sat, unduly shaken, tired of my idleness, tired of imagination. I also felt guilty because I'd feared Bruce. Desiring to stop the trash compaction, desiring to stop it simply because it looked awful, I'd considered approaching the dewy, flushed, curly-haired Bruce and saying something innocuous, like, "One of those days?" I hadn't dared to do so. I'd feared that the man labeled "Bruce" would take one look at me and say something mildly brutal, like "Fuck off, Nancy." I also felt guilty because that summer, at home, I'd fantasized about telling my father that I would pick up trash as a "career," while there, in the fast-food restaurant, someone actually handled trash. And Bruce actually wore orange. He had no choice in the matter. His obligatory uniform included a dark-brown tunic with bright orange sides, pants similarly striped, and an orange baseball hat. In fantasy, I'd martyred myself, in part by wearing an orange safety vest. I'd frivolously fantasized about doing things that other people actually, honestly did. I stood up to leave, to face Employment. I took the polystyrene cup with me, not for the sake of the remaining coffee, but because I didn't want the cup bundled away, into landfill.

49　HIRING

I tore up the polystyrene cup and pocketed the scraps. Thus, feeling even more inefficacious than usual—for trying to save the world from polystyrene one cup at a time—I entered the Student Employment Office, a gray-carpeted, L-shaped room housing computers on tables and notebooks on shelves. A counter faced the entrance. A woman behind the counter said, "May I help you?" Whatever I'd dreaded (taking a numbered slip, waiting, waiting in a packed room, trying to find my way to some negligible job through a computer) fell away before her stare. I said that I "hoped to find a job" for "something like three hours a week." "Three hours?" the woman asked. (I'd feared out-of-hand dismissal. I'd feared reproof for wasting a serious person's time. I'd feared sarcasm and condescension. I'd even feared expressions of plain incredulity, all as imagined responses to my request for work for "three hours a week.") To my relief, the woman behind the counter sounded matter-of-fact. She sounded non-judgmental. She even seemed—amazingly—interested in my request. I instantly liked her—out of relief, out of gratitude for that relief. (I'd almost instantly liked the gray room—out of relief upon seeing only a few people in it.) The woman (myopic eyes, false eyelashes) said, "Three hours? Seems I heard something like that just now." (I later learned that she'd received a telephone call.) She searched a desk. Leaning over the counter, I watched her touch recumbent papers and pluck paper slips out of a vertical rack. She touched with long,

long, tong-like false fingernails, all dark red except for the squared tips, which bore small, diagonally slanted areas of pattern. A pale-yellow memo stopped the search. The woman looked up. Heaviness beyond my ken seemed to live in her irises. Again I felt shameful, even ridiculous, in my quest. But the woman, looking again at the memo, said in a neutral tone, "H. A. need a slide operator. Urgent." I learned that "slide operators" operated slide projectors, and that "H. A.," without joking (ha!), stood for "History of Art." I knew, from brief experience, that slides, as light projected through transparent photographs onto screens, some-times illustrated teachers' lectures. I'd taken one out of two history of art courses required for an MFA. I'd seen slides-as-light used in a classroom; I'd noticed the projectionist. Projecting slides seemed easy work. I asked how to apply for the job. The woman wrote a note on archaic paper. The small scrap looked cut savagely, cut at odd angles with a paper cutter. The note summarized spoken instructions: I should go to a room called the "Slide Room" on the "1st floor" of a building called "Seekford Hall." I should see "Mrs. Callender." I thanked the woman and escaped the Office. I felt—exuberantly, foolishly—that I'd already accomplished something. I had not gotten a job, but I no longer dreaded the prospect.

I found Seekford Hall, a small, purplish-brick Victorian building, crouched behind a museum. The little building's doleful appearance should have daunted me. Half-basement windows in wells looked up imploringly out of the ground. A flight of steps lolled tongue-like out of a deep, dark porch-mouth. Anti-pigeon defenses—clustered spikes—crowned the building with thorns. I stood on the sidewalk in front of the building, looking up at it. In the back of the building's throat, on a window above the door, severely dignified golden letters with black edges formed words in two lines, "Seekford Hall" and "History of Art." Those words gave me pause. The words "Seekford Hall" told me that I'd found the building that I needed to find and that I would have to proceed into the building if I really intended to embrace employment (however slight, then, however much a mere whiff of a foretaste of work to come). Doubts on that point alone might have stayed me, but the black-and-gold words "History of Art" really engaged me (in further delay). I'd never felt impressed, until that moment, by the little word "of" between "History" and "Art." As I stood on the sidewalk outside Seekford Hall (delaying), the "of" in "History of Art" suddenly impressed me as the keystone in an arch, uniting opposing concepts. If I had ever thought about "history" and about "art" in the abstract, I had not considered them together or as anything like equals. Despite Burke, I had not viewed "history" as an academic discipline involving interpretation. I'd considered "history"—dimly—a collective term for everything known to have happened anywhere. I considered "history," in general, an unremitting ordeal of human suffering. I thought of "art," in general, as any manipulation of materials undertaken out of interest in form or with expressive intent. I thought of "art" as humanity's gift to the world, as something that came into existence *despite* "history," as something benign in contrast to the overpowering malignity of "history." Stopped in the September sunlight, standing on a busy sidewalk with people passing around me, standing there, seeing the words "History of Art" spelled out in black-and-gold letters, I suddenly thought of "history" as a positive force, as a creation of minds similar to the creations of artists' hands. Nonetheless, seeing the black-and-gold lettering, I thought, as if my dim view of "history" still held, "Black for history, gold for art."

Burke had earned a PhD in history. He'd gotten his "dream job," teaching history, the previous year. Dad approved of Burke's work; Dad disapproved of mine. No wondered I considered "art" embattled. Seeing the lettering on Seekford Hall, I longed to see worded intelligence turned to the service of art. I longed to see my family's distain replaced by informed and inquiring admiration.

While I stood on a busy sidewalk, wistfully considering powers implied by words, the door below the black-and-gold lettering opened. Three women, as a group, passed through the doorway.

One of them hit every nerve in my mind where Christine lived. Forgetting "history," forgetting "art," I stared at her, unintentionally, rudely. The woman, descending the steps, did not really look like Christine, not really. She did not have Christine's frame or facial turning. But her hair recalled Christine's rich, rare dark red. She carried several books, using both arms to carry; her shoulders stooped. Her nose looked painlessly broken—and more beautiful, to my eyes, than any perfectly straight, undeviating fragility of a nose could have looked. I stared at the woman so impoliticly, so impolitely, so openly, and for so long, that she (and I, only then) noticed my gaze. She looked at me directly, quizzically, as if she would ask, in Chris's arch manner, "Are you lost? Do you need directions? Isn't there something you should be doing?" With eyes the green of Chris' eyes, the woman seemed to ask, "Are you lost? Don't you have," et cetera, so directly that I actually shook my head no. Her presence lingered behind her, upon the vacant steps.

I wanted to meet the Not-Christine for Burke's sake. I suddenly wanted to attach myself to Seekford Hall in order to meet her. (Had her pile of books suggested that she studied there?) I had just learned that the Not-Christine existed, but already I wondered, how could she and Burke meet? Could I bring about their meeting? I, who had not even met her myself. I cursed the presumptuous, the busy-body, the match-making part of my brain even as I encouraged its impulse to scheme. I also felt dismayed by my instantaneous identification of the red-haired woman as Burke's type, as if he might utterly claim her, as if she did not exist in her own right. I regretted that, in ignorance of real traits, I'd leapt presumptuously to type. I knew nothing about the woman on the steps beyond her appearance (whatever beyond appearance an appearance might suggest). I regretted my response, yet it persisted as a sense, as a sudden, instantaneous, irrevocable recognition. Wishing to put my wrong-headedness behind me (believing, perhaps wrongly, that I could not correct it), I rushed up the steps and into Seekford Hall.

Having plunged into the building, I discovered that I hadn't really entered it. I stood in a bleak, little airlock. A makeshift wall containing another door faced me immediately. Stairs dropped blankly down, to my left. A paint-caked radiator—cream-colored—stood to my right. I went through the second door, into a large, square room with one door in each of its four walls. Across from the entrance, a wall like the inner wall of the airlock, a wall made of crudely framed glass atop an opaque foundation some three feet high, contained in its center a solid oaken door. Visible above and beyond the oaken door-amid-glass, an oaken staircase, clearly original to the building, led to a landing half a story above the room in which I stood. The staircase divided at the landing; separate staircases, of which I could see the banisters and the ceiling-like undersides, slanted upwards and toward me from either end of the landing. All along the landing and tall above it, an uninterrupted line of windows with many small panes imposed the panes' smallness on a deep, rich view of thriving chestnuts. Seekford Hall seemed a series of airlocks: the true airlock behind me, the room in which I stood, and the glassed-in space around the stairs.

To my right, black stenciled letters broken with gaps labeled a windowless door in a stale wall "Library." To my left, letters in the same style labeled another door in another stale wall "Slide Room." I had no reason not to proceed to the Slide Room. (I blamed the note I carried for directing me to the "1st floor" of Seekford Hall; Seekford Hall, with its half-basement, had no true first floor.) Glancing around (for distraction), I regretted seeing a soft, soft, soft cork bulletin board near the library door. Someone had used far too many tacks on—in—the bulletin board. Someone had affixed far too many rectangular, print-bearing pieces of paper to the bulletin board in even rows; a tack pierced every corner of every piece of paper. The tacks gleamed as nothing should gleam in the fluorescence: shiny, chrome-like, white-metal thumbtacks with slightly convex, circular heads, tacks driven in needless numbers through every page's every corner, into soft cork. My head began to ache. I felt as if struck—hard—by the Not-Christine and then punched by tacks. I remembered the anti-pigeon defenses. I went to the windowless door marked "Slide Room." The door asserted immobility without doing anything; it looked locked. Should I knock or try the knob? I tried the knob. It turned.

The door disclosed a dense arrangement of low filing cabinets, all gun-metal gray, all blocky, all containing very shallow drawers (full of slides, I later supposed). The cabinets stood side-by-side in banks, like washing machines in the laundromat. Aisles between the banks of low cabinets suggested streets through a small city. When I entered, a woman bounced up. (From beyond cabinets, she popped up like a jack-in-the box.) She looked very young and very wide, braless in a dark-green T-shirt. Wedges of thick, brunette hair stood out, as if they rested on her shoulders. Her complexion looked stunningly, perfectly bread-and-jam, with planar cheeks pale and rosy. In a tone that suggested that I'd intruded, the woman demanded, "May I help you?" I said, "Mrs. Callender. Is she—" (uh, here? Uh, in?). The woman waved negligently toward what seemed like the first open door I'd seen in weeks, a door propped open with a brick to which someone had, as if lovingly, glued much bright-green felt. The bearer of green darker than the doorstop's said, "Go on in. She's in there."

The next room looked murky. The far wall, opposite the door, glowed faintly, barely visible beyond hulking lines of tall file cabinets piled with unhoused papers in unaligned stacks. The file cabinets' deep drawers suggested much—more—ancient and undisturbed, decaying paper. The room smelled strongly of papyrine death. I liked the odor. I liked the whole shambling, moldering, outmoded archive. To my left, an aisle led past the ends of cabinets to an unobstructed window beside which a woman sat at a desk, writing intently in the shadow of her hand. (Had she turned on the available desk lamp, or had she sat with the window to her left, instead of to her right, the shadow would have fallen away from the area in which she wrote. I wanted to tell the woman, who brought out a certain soft confidence in me, "If you turned the desk around, you might see better." I kept my suggestion to myself.) I approached the poorly-oriented desk; I stood facing the woman. Without looking up, she said, "Yes?" I said something about having come about the "slide-operating job." The woman looked up as if awakened. Her eyes looked almost dog-like, almost all brown, with little white showing around the irises. Her eyelids, peaked at their centers, slanted downward from the centered peaks. She wore her hair in a—roughly overgrown—hairstyle like a helmet. With lips bearing traces of lipstick, she said incredulously, "You have?" Her tone dismayed me a little. If it didn't actually carry a note of the skeptical ridicule that I'd previously dreaded, it reminded me of my previous dread. But, as Mrs. Callender spoke on, as she told me that "a regular" had "backed out" on her "at the last minute" and that she hadn't expected "a replacement" to appear "out of the blue," my favorable impression grew. I began to appreciate her lack of demanding vanity. (The undyed hair, which some might have thought needed cutting, and the lack of makeup beyond vestiges of lipstick, suggested a pleasing ease with her natural appearance. Mrs. Callender's appearance suggested grooming standards far less exacting than my rampantly vain mother's.) Surprised that I'd surprised Mrs. Callender by appearing "out of the blue," I asked, "Didn't the Student Employment Office call?" (The Office woman had said she would call.) "No. No, they didn't," Mrs. Callender replied. She spoke warmly, likeably, rapidly. She spoke as if, call or no call, she didn't care. She seemed eager to hire me. She asked if I'd ever shown slides before. I said no. She said, "It doesn't matter." If I hadn't undergone "training" by that department, I would still have to do so. "Training" consisted of "one session." Mrs. Callender pushed back a sleeve, glanced at a minuscule watch. She said, "And that's today. One o'clock. Room two-oh-three. Upstairs. Can you make it, by any chance?" I said yes. "Good," Mrs. Callender replied, "assuming that you do that." Her dog-like eyes met mine. I nodded vaguely, wondering silently what "training" involved and what I'd gotten myself into. The small job that I hadn't wanted, but which I had sought, had gotten me—with extreme rapidity—more than I had gotten it. "Have a seat," Mrs. Callender said (as if light with sudden, kind interest). "We might as well start the paperwork." (She would say "paperwork." "Paperwork" would end in pixels. A new computer sat on her battered desk.) Mrs. Callender nodded briskly toward a folding chair stacked with papers. I set the papers on the floor, sat. Mrs. Callender extended a clipboard to me. "If you would just fill this out," she said. "Mark in when you have classes." As the clipboard's clamp end tilted toward me, a ballpoint pen, tied to the clamp by a string and (until then) loosely lodged behind the vicious clamp, slid from behind the clamp, dropped and swung. The pen hanged itself in front of me. I caught its body out of the air, slackening the string. Mrs. Callender's dog-like eyes seemed to absorb me. I took the clipboard, released paper from the clamp, filled out a scheduling grid. Having printed my name and other information, I returned the sheet (loose on the vicious clipboard) to Mrs. Callender, who appeared surprised by the lengthy marks I'd made across rectangles representing hours in days. I explained, "MFA," "studio art," "long studios." "Ah," said Mrs. Callender. Again, she seemed to assess me. I looked down after confronting her odd and oddly observing eyes. I scrutinized the various blues in my blue jeans' knees. "So, you're a graduate student," Mrs. Callender said thoughtfully. I said, "Yes," and, "Can you still hire me?" Mrs. Callender continued to look at me. I thought that she looked at me more carefully than she had previously looked. Finally, she said, "Yes. Yes. But. Do you really think you have time for this?" "Barely," I said. Mrs. Callender looked at the scheduling grid I'd filled out. She turned to the computer. She typed. She regarded the screen. She regarded me. Finally she said, in a tone both cautious and reverential, "Professor Baussan is teaching four-ninety-five this semester. Monday, Wednesday, Friday, eleven to twelve. That fits your schedule." I said that "that" sounded "fine." I filled out more forms. Mrs. Callender typed. She asked questions, typed. She told me to return after "training" that afternoon, and that she would then "transmit" my approved application. Mrs. Callender asked if I had any questions. I did have questions, but I didn't ask them. I wanted to know why Mrs. Callender had intoned the name "Professor Baussan" as if telling me, by intonation, that I should feel honored to show slides for that person. Perhaps she thought that I should have heard of the person. Should I have? I wanted to know what went through Mrs. Callender's head when she registered my status as a graduate student. Why all the ponderous, assessing staring? Instead of asking my real questions, I asked, "What's four-ninety-five?" Mrs. Callender looked—almost grandly—satisfied. She sat back in her chair. She said simply, "Just a minute. Let me give you the title." She shifted papers. (Her fingernails looked neat, pleasingly and simply neat enough and natural.) She found a shallowly buried list. She said, "Let me see. Four-ninety-five. History of Medieval European Architecture." "Architecture," I said. "Architecture" hurt, as Dad's word. But "medieval" sounded past, full of stonework, enduring.

50 TRAINING

I attended the short "training" course required of "slide operators."
The training left me feeling untrained. It introduced me to
complications that I hadn't known existed. (In that respect, it
mirrored, in miniature, the general effect of my entire education.)
In "training," I learned that the Department of the History of Art
used two types of slides: large glass ones and small plastic ones. I
learned that the two types of slides required two types of projectors.
I learned that, although teachers in the Department of the History
of Art had agreed to avoid requesting the simultaneous projection
of more than two slides at a time, teachers might—and very often
did—request the simultaneous projection of two slides *in any
combination of the two slide types*. (Simultaneous projection of two
large glass slides required two projectors for glass slides; the same
went for small slides and their projectors. Thus, I would have to
learn to use, not one, not two, but four slide projectors. And I
would have to learn to feed slides into the correct projectors for
their types rapidly.) Naïveté, combined with forgetfulness of the
one art history class that I had taken (in a modern building, not
Seekford Hall) had led me to expect simplicity: one slide projector,
one task at a time. I learned that I would have to do something
four times more complicated than anticipated in my simplicity.

Other basics covered in "training" lacked complication. I (and
some ten others) learned that, at the beginning of each class period,
at the beginning of each lecture, the teacher would hand the

projectionist a slide box: a wooden, lidless box containing slides, each slide tucked neatly into a thick, cardboard holder (which held a delicate slide by its inured edges only). I learned how to remove slides from holders; how to hold slides, in my fingers, by the edges only; how to tell the front of a slide from the back; how to turn each slide (upside down and backward) when placing it into a slide projector's "carriage," a rack that would carry each slide individually into the machine's inner light (and thus cause light, a projected slide, to appear on the screen). I learned how to adjust a projected slide's focus and how to change the light bulb inside a projector (of either type) should its bulb fail. I learned what a lecturer's directions, "right" and "left," meant, as in "Next slide, please, on the right." (The directions did not mean to the left or to the right of the person speaking. They meant right and left from the point of view of a person facing the screen.) In "training," I practiced— briefly—handling slides and projecting them. I emerged "trained," ill-prepared. Despite my confessed incompetence, Mrs. Callender hired me. She told me that I would work in Room 203. "Oh," I said, further daunted. (Room 203, where "training" took place, looked blind—with blinded windows. Behind a very large screen lurked a built-in chalkboard.) I thanked Mrs. Callender for having hired me. I felt that she watched me curiously as I left her musty archive of an office.

51   ROOM 203

Room 203 looked unremittingly dismal. Its battered antiquity disturbed me. A segmented chalkboard plated the room's front wall: panels of dull, ashen black standing together as one, panel-by-panel. A huge, white, rectangular screen hung in front of the chalkboard. The screen did not cover the chalkboard completely. Ends of the black, segmented chalkboard showed, framed by everlasting woodwork, beyond both sides of the screen. (After "training," as people left the room, I surreptitiously peeked behind the screen. What had I hoped to see? Some break in the chalkboard? Some intervention of innocent wall? No pallor divided the solid shadow.) From the back wall of Room 203, a low, square platform extended. A painted table with unusually long legs stood on the platform. Visible brackets and screws held the table in place. Four slide projectors sat in an immobile row on the immobile table. Screws anchored the projectors. I understood the rationale behind the screws and the brackets: screws kept slide projectors from moving, kept the lenses in slide projectors parallel to the screen. Without that parallel alignment, an image projected onto the screen would appear distorted, the greater the angle out of parallel, the greater the distortion. I understood that much. I also understood that someone had determined where—exactly where—the projectors should sit, so that simultaneously projected patches of light on the screen might sit at seemly distances from each other—and not overlap. If the table moved, it would undo that planning. Hence the screws, hence the brackets. But only cheapness and expeditiousness might excuse their ugliness. (Naïveté struck again: in a classroom in which people academically studied art, I apparently expected something other, something better, something more subtly sensitive to aesthetic matters, than a brutal crudeness of screws and brackets.) Around the platform bearing the slide projectors, chairs with spatulate arms for notebooks covered the floor in wavering rows. I should have appreciated the lack of fixity among the chairs, the randomness that had crept in among chairs aligned to face the screen. The heavy, old, battered, light-colored wooden chairs looked likeable enough. Each chair's single broad arm (made of stout, varnished plywood curvaceously shaped almost like a palette) bore chiseled, written-in, or otherwise incised marks: interesting graffiti. And the screen-facing rows of nicked chairs wavered; here and there a chair sat, turned at an angle suggesting that the last person to leave it had only just managed to stagger away. Across the front of the room, below the screen and the largely but not entirely screen-covered chalkboard, a narrow stage provided a walkway for lecturers, an elevated path to pace before glowing pictures (projected). Hard, plastic tile— linoleum tile—plated the long, low—foot-high—stage. The same material plated the projectors' platform. The dark, chocolate-brown linoleum tile clashed with the virtuous wood of the original floor—long, narrow boards, boards which I forgave for their parallels, for their close linearity reminiscent of "narrow-ruled" lined notebook paper. On the low, plated stage, to the left of the screen (as one faced it), a boxy lectern stood, a small, dull-brazen, cylindrical lamp clamped to the edge at the height of the lectern's slanted top. Wing bolts—incongruously shaped like maples' paired seeds—secured the lamp, which crouched close to the lectern's slanted surface made to hold notes. To the left of the lectern, a free-standing chalkboard, framed and on legs ending in long feet on wheels, stood on the floor. Clamped-on lamps all but dangled over it. Its slaty surface had a fresher complexion—some fineness of light shag or slight roughness about it—than did the built-in chalkboard, and, although black, the free-standing chalkboard looked lighter than did the ancient stretch of (worn-smooth?) gloomy, built-in board. The row of straggling chairs closest to the door off a hallway, the row of chairs closest to the only door in the room that I saw used, and the mobile chalkboard, together framed a narrow way—the only obvious route—from the door to the stage and the lectern. But in a far, deep corner of the room, almost obscured by the chalkboard-on-wheels, another door darkened the drably-pale wall at the front of the room. Across the room from the door on the hallway, across the choppy wrack of all-but-drifting, nicked chairs, another door hid in white paint, dull among windows that did not admit light. Something opaque masked every pane in each window, and over the door surrounded by grids-once-windows, an unillumined, rectangular, maroon-and-white sign read "Exit" (without a curved letter, the letters maroon). I only slowly deduced that, given the windows, and hence an exterior wall, the door labeled "Exit" must lead to a fire escape. My mind thrust a black, metal raft made of flat bars and a black, folding ladder into thin air, beyond the "Exit" door. Six lamps hung from the ceiling in two lines of three parallel to the screen or in three lines of two above the chair rows. In shape, each pendent lamp—of dusty-dull, rosy glass—resembled a turnip with a flattened root tip. Metal sheaths covered the screen-facing halves of the three lamps closest to the screen. The sheaths closely followed the lamps' napiform shapes.

Room 203 looked gloomy. (Even its name, said with a certain intonation, "two-oh-three," could sound sadly, wistfully indecisive.) Room 203 got under my skin. It reproached me for my own—person-excluding, light-excluding—devotion to paper, to the making of drawings and prints and paintings on paper. Every feature of the room appeared devoted to the screen, to the large, white, blank thing that resembled paper, frost-covered, frozen paper. Everything in the room, in an inanimate way, attended to the screen. People had arranged everything in the room to provide optimal viewing of projected lights on the screen. Masked windows excluded daylight. Sheaths banked the light from the old, old, old pinkish-glass lamps hanging overhead. (New light in old bottles, I'd seen. A rheostat allowed one to dim or to brighten the overhead lamps gradually.) Subsidiary lamps drooped over the lectern, the mobile chalkboard, and a visible portion of the built-in chalkboard behind and to the right of the lectern (as one saw it, facing the screen). All the lamps bowed, as if differentially, to the enormous screen. (They would cast their light downward, not into the screen.) In typical overreaction, I felt that even the likable chairs worshiped the screen: their spatulate, single arms for notebooks tilted upward slightly, away from their backs, tilted as if hailing the screen, the vast, brooding specter of rectangular paper. So Room 203 disturbed me. I took it personally. (Of course, I would.) Room 203 struck me as both an unflattering reflection of me and my reclusive monomania and as a dark judgment upon me. The gloom of Room 203 and its desuetude condemned my bright wish, my central ambition: to spend my life making works on paper, works analogous to slides-as-light projected onto the screen.

52   PAPER NAPKIN DISPENSER

Newly hired and poorly trained—or, rather, fearfully inexperienced—as a projectionist of still pictures, I left Mrs. Callender's office in mid-afternoon. I felt ravenous. I hadn't eaten since the previous day. Ordinarily, I would have bought groceries for lunch, but, that day, I indulged myself by going to a vegetarian restaurant, a minuscule place with two tables and a counter. I ordered pita bread, hummus, and olives. While I sat, eating ravenously, something began to bother me; something cut through the bliss of delectable food. A paper napkin dispenser sat on the counter, almost in front of me: a black, boxy thing with two open sides stuffed with folded paper. I stopped eating. I stared at the dispenser. I picked it up. It weighed like a little refrigerator (if refrigerators came in that size). It had two solid sides, one solid top, and one solid bottom with four small feet. Overturned, the box sexlessly displayed its feet: little, round, black nubs like prolegs or outgrowths from its flat, black base. They looked tender, absurd, helpless, innocent. The little feet tapered roundly in the way that pendent raindrops taper, clinging to the underside of anything flat. (Drops shaped by surface tension taper to their round ends without developing points.) The blunt, round nubs budding from the dispenser's underside struck me as absolutely the only thing to like about the black, incomplete box, the hellish bed, the cruel rack for paper-not-made-for-respect. I set the dispenser upright again where I'd found it. Its little feet somehow offset the bulletin-board thumbtacks seen in Seekford Hall. I shoved the dispenser aside, but I couldn't take my eyes off it. Of course, I empathized with paper, the bearing flesh of my art. And there, weak paper stood trapped, under black rims, under marginal frames bent from the box's two solid sides. The rims framing the rectangular display of proffered paper lacked corners; they didn't meet to surround the paper completely. In the corner gaps, where the narrow black metal strips framing the inserted paper did not meet perfectly, I saw the corners of many stacked paper napkins, fold upon fold: many corners made of paper many plies deep.

Having just gotten myself hired and nominally trained as a "slide operator," I wondered: What had I really done? What obligations had I incurred, if any, beyond those already known to me? I felt trapped. I realized that I did not feel trapped because I had just suddenly accepted a trifling, "symbolic" job. I felt trapped because I feared offending my father. Dad's personal check for my "personal expenses" stirred like a wild thing inside my wallet. Dad's check, which I had absent-mindedly folded in half in front of him, Dad's check, once folded in half, occupied my folded wallet, while paper napkins, folded in several ways—folded in half across and lengthwise upon themselves—paper napkins, bent double and sideways, would stare at me because I stared at them: docile, pliant, white paper napkins.

Eyes on trapped paper, I considered what Dad called "my," Edward's, "future." If I did what I usually did and obeyed him, if I went to graduate school (beyond the MFA) as he desired, if I studied something to Dad's liking, "something practical this time," something like Architecture, I might well end up trapped in a job I disliked. I would have sold my little wisp of papery spirit to my father's good sense. If, on the other hand, I did not do what I usually did, if I did something uncharacteristic and defied my father, if I did not bend to his wishes, I would soon lack money. I would soon have to scramble to support myself. I might well end up trapped in a job I disliked. Paper in the dispenser looked trapped, coming and going. Paper in the dispenser looked trapped, facing two ways.

53   BAR GAME, FLYING PAPER

The night before the day on which I went to work for the first time as a slide operator, I stayed up late, playing a demented game learned in a bar. The game, more a brooding pursuit than a game to me, consisted of torturing paper. To play, or to engage in this activity, one spread a ply of a paper napkin over the rim of an empty glass. (One moistened the rim to hold the paper.) On the paper tympanum, one placed a coin. One then touched the tip of a burning cigarette, turn by turn, touch by touch, to the paper spanning the glass. One tried to keep the coin from falling as one burned away its support. Touch by touch, paper went up in smoke. Paper smoldered; holes in it multiplied. (Cigarette paper burned without seeming tortured.) The paper over the glass, the paper supporting the coin over a void, changed from an intact, white round into a blackened, browned network of slender, slender unburnt bridges. The coin, of course, didn't change in weight, but it appeared to weigh more and more heavily upon the paper, as the paper, giving way, vanishing, turning into a burnt-out, blackened, increasingly fragile lattice, lost strength as support. Eventually, one had to burn something essential, some last, sustaining thread. The coin might slip; it might hang, balanced slantwise, supported by next to nothing. But then, with another touch or two, the coin would fall. Whoever made the coin fall lost the so-called game; anyone else engaged in the game won by default. If one engaged in this activity alone, one inevitably lost.

The night before I went to work for the first time as a slide operator, I stayed up late in a dormitory room, burning paper, leaning to the wretched arena—a covered glass—in the light of a lamp, while my roommate, in a separate but connected room, slept audibly. I pitied the paper I tortured. I saw it as tortured for the sake of money, as tortured not by fire but by the weight of money.

I "played" that demented game morosely and late. And I felt punished the next morning for having done so. Early morning, before waking, I had a dream. I dreamed that paper meant to kill me. I dreamed that I'd engendered hatred in the generic substance, paper, by my treatment of it, by having tortured one defenseless paper napkin saved from a dispenser for a fate far worse than its intended use. I dreamed that paper, ruthlessly enraged, desired revenge. I thought other things, too, about that dream, but, as a visual dream, there seemed nothing to it: I dreamed that I saw, far away on a barren horizon, a large, white mass like whirling fan blades. I knew that the mass, unlike fan blades, contained many straight edges. The mass, the enraged spirit of paper, flew whirling toward me. It meant to kill me, to fly through my neck. I couldn't move. Just before the paper reached me, it shrank to the size of a diamond-shaped paper kite; it hovered. Seeing the hovering paper, I registered *its* animus; I felt its hatred; I knew its intent. I bounded awake. I felt told by paper that paper hated me, that paper hated me murderously. I felt shaken, desolate, bereft, and scared.

54 PAPER COLUMN

Having dreamed of a white, whirling, indistinct thing which I interpreted as representing paper; having felt, in a dream, a terrifying sense of the extreme ill will—the hatred, the malevolence, the deadly intent—borne against me by the flying, whirling, white spirit of paper, I sprang awake, terrified. Terror subsided. A sense of abject disarray replaced it. I felt both betrayed by paper and convinced that I'd sinned against it, an inanimate substance (become animate with animus, the dream's whirling white). My whole life seemed wrong in some ineffable way beyond the usual points on which I felt guilty. Paper had meant to kill me. I needed to beg for forgiveness. I needed to appeal to the chastising god, to swear, with humility born of grief, that I had never, in all my born days, intended to offend it, paper, the very entity that I most desired to serve (as if paper had goals of its own and might pursue them through me). (Did paper view me—with good reason—as a mass murderer? I had laid waste to countless paper sheets. Had my long history of spoiling paper finally caught up with me? Had I, by my latest burning of a defenseless paper napkin, simply gone too far, committed one crime too many, added a last straw to the sum of my misdeeds? Or had that last act, my latest sin against paper, exceeded the gravity of my previous sins?) I needed to address paper by gesture, by a gesture silently saying: Whatever your justified wrath, please, please, pardon me, forgive me, give me—sinner, yes, but your servant—a second chance, any chance to regain your good graces. The exact nature of my offence eluded me, but I repented, if one can repent in ignorance. Rationally, I noticed a pattern in my dream and in my responses: Edward subject to a god-like force much like his father exaggerated, Edward suing for return to loving equilibrium with the offended party by showing grudgeless, pure, unresisting willingness to take blame for the other's irate condition. But I had mixed feelings. (Paper betrayed me; betrayal hurt; I resented betrayal.)

A vague but rational sense of my psyche's understructure didn't dispel my emotions. I sat in bed, first awakened, gasping as if I'd struggled up, out of water, into an alien state and place. I then began to recognize "my" dormitory room. (A lamp in the quadrangle outside illuminated it dimly.) I stopped feeling terror, but dreadful, repentant aftereffects persisted. I got out of bed, put on a bathrobe, opened the door to my room, entered my roommate's room, saw Gerald asleep, his sheet-draped body spewing breath loudly. He lay with his mouth darkly open, his throat exposed—as if to the whirling white that my mind retained. Seeing Gerald sleep unguardedly, I felt more sinful than ever: I felt as if I had endangered Gerald and untold others by offending paper. I felt as if the straight-edged fan blades of which I'd dreamed really existed and that they might kill other people because of me. I entered the bathroom (situated between two sets of connecting rooms), turned on a light, urinated, showered, shaved carefully. (My razor seemed capable of taking murderous inspiration from the paper of which I'd dreamed.) I returned to my room, dressed, packed breakfast (apples, bread). I left my room. I left Gerald's room by the door to the corridor. (Three doors opened into or from Gerald's room. In some voluble life that seemed long-past that morning, I had called the dormitory a "door-matory" and the door-lined corridor, which I then entered, a "cori-door.") From the blue-gray-carpeted hallway, a steel door, dull cobalt blue in electric light, led into a stairwell. A further door, black amid glass, led into the out-of-doors.

Beyond the doors, I walked downhill, past a pond where I

sometimes dropped (pleasurably-crushed) crackers (bought with soup) onto the water for carp. I walked past the Music School building, across convergent streets to the Art and Architecture building. Brass letters labeled the building with a person's name and with the words "Art and Architecture" near the double front doors. I'd walked past the brazen name and the brazen words many times, sometimes ignoring them, sometimes blind to them. That morning, I stopped. The separate, polished, brass letters, including capitals, looked softened by the dawning light and by the air's dampness. "Architecture," sharp with its high A, contained the word "art" within its first six letters. But the three letters "chi" seemed to bite through the "art," and I felt excluded from the circle of unity suggested by the "and" between "Art," unbitten, unbiting, and fanged "Architecture." I reached up and wiped the humid film from the capital A of the whole word "Art." Inside the building, the air stank of carrion: oil paint, turpentine, artistic ambition. I walked along a hall (lined with short, bright-red lockers) and up a staircase. On the ground floor, below the staircase and visible from above through its airy structure, three huge, rough-plaster copies of statues by Phidias lay. The vague so-called copies lay warehoused in full view under the minimal staircase. They reminded me of Gerald asleep and seemed deathly in general. I entered the Graphics Studio, the first person to do so that day. I did not turn on the lights. I approached paper. Partitions formed a room within the room; the partitioned space lacked doors; the incompletely enclosed space housed equipment. Near one of the partition-room's open ends stood the communal paper supply. People took paper from the stack whenever they needed it for their work. The stack stood with three sides exposed, within easy reach. From day to day and during each day, the pile's height varied. People removed paper from it in great quantities. Teachers brought packaged paper from a locked storeroom and restored the stack's height. Although I had seen the replenishing, I felt that the paper stack replenished itself. It lived, like a sacred tree, growing and dwindling, beside a doorway without a door.

I might have supposed that the paper stack, the white stump, the white trunk made of killed trees, possessed a benevolent nature, that it existed for the general benefit of art. It supported all students' efforts, all stages of nascent, artistic prints. I might have considered the paper pile in the Graphics Studio generous, giving of itself unstintingly, asking nothing in return. But all paper cut, and even that paper stack, or rather one of its previous versions, spit strictures: Don't touch. I'd cut my hand on some previous pile in that location by tapping projecting sheets, intending to realign projecting sheets with the majority. Paper edges cut, for the wrong touch, for a meddling touch, multiply.

The morning of my dream about whirling paper, I went to the paper pile as to a temple. I knelt in the obscurity, beside the altar.

55 LECTURE

The first day that I worked as a slide operator did not begin well. I dreamed that paper meant to kill me, and I actually tried to tell a stack of paper that I, a mass murderer of paper sheets, meant no offense to it, but rather the opposite. (The unresponsive dimness, the paper stack, seemed unforgiving. It seemed to know that I had no intention of mending my murderous ways.) The morning proceeded. I spilled ink, thick tusche. I wrenched my previously broken right arm moving a lithographic stone, which I almost let fall; unwonted pain from my past shot through my arm. Someone offended me. Further, I felt frustrated. A morning class in the Graphics Studio presented a technique new to me; I had to delay using the technique—trying it for the first time—because I "had to go to work." (An inner refrain mocked, "Showing slides? 'Slide operator?' You call that 'work?'") I took a bus. I walked to Seekford Hall. I trudged up the stairs in the building's third airlock. Dreading work ("You call that 'work?'"), I looked at the stair steps as I surmounted them. Pinkish rubber covered the steps. The rubber had texture molded into it, a level field of shapes above a lower background. The flat, round-cornered shapes wedged together without angularity reminded me pleasantly of pads on cats' feet. Sure-footed cats seemed invoked by pads intended to improve human footing. The rubber, which completely covered the steps, seemed promising, considerate, effective, and generous. I remembered bleak, exiguous and ineffectual—soon bald—

narrow, gritty, black adhesive strips applied to steps in my high school building. I'd broken my arm in high school, not on steps, but on a basketball court. My arm hurt. Pads underfoot said: "Relax. You'll survive simple 'work.'" I waited outside Room 203 in a large, central, foyer-like room. A chairless, cheerless refectory table stood in the middle of the room. (What immaterial feast did the bleak table serve?) I sat on a bench. Classes continued audibly in nearby classrooms. Through an opened door's doorway and across a narrow hall to my right, I could see the entrance door to Room 203. (The door would block the hallway if not opened completely, if not moved all the way to the wall that it had closed when shut. I judged the potentially hall-blocking door hazardous. If opened suddenly, it might hit someone in the hall. In case of fire, it might impede evacuation.) I sat waiting, trying to calm myself by reviewing the little I'd learned in "training" about glass slides and plastic slides, about how to turn slides when setting them into carriages, about which type of projector to use for which type of slide. The process of turning slides upside down and backwards when feeding them into projectors actually seemed familiar. (Drawings reversed when turned into prints.) Nothing seemed particularly threatening or difficult about projecting slides. But whatever calmness I'd attained, whatever benefit I'd done myself by trying to think about a dreaded task rationally, vanished when the treacherous door to Room 203 opened (slowly and fully, evidently pushed by someone aware of the risk the door posed to passing people). People emerged from Room 203. I stood up.

Among the emergent people merging with others emerging from other rooms, I did not notice the slide operator, but I did see slides ride by, carried in a lidless, slotless, wooden box proportioned something like a boxcar. The sight of slides made me feel dreadfully unprepared for work ("You call that 'work?'"). When people ceased exiting Room 203, I entered it. I glanced at the screen, almost afraid of it because of that morning's dream. I sat down, in the last chair in the row of chairs closest to the door. I should have sat behind the slide projectors, but dread and timidity stayed me from climbing up one step, into that place of relative prominence, before I had to do so. I sat, looking at marks on the chair arm in front of me. The chair's right and only arm spread into a broad, round-cornered, likeably palette-like area intended to support a notebook. Archaic pencil marks scarred the golden, oaken uppermost layer of the strong plywood arm. Blue and black penned marks also scarred it. Things happened. Things kept happening as if inexorably, one after another. People entered the room, sat, and sat talking. The room filled. The great screen played dead, played innocuous, played innocent, played meaning-less in blankness, played incapable of dispatching dreams. I sat, avoiding the screen, looking at marks on the chair arm in front of me, until a tall, broad—corpulent—fair man entered. Then I saw him. He seemed to move inside my chest, as if every turn he made in motion and every turn in his physical shape grazed me or displaced something in me sensitive to touch. I did not precisely feel lustful watching him, but whatever great want beyond lust had ever wracked me during lust thickened as if in my throat at the sight of the man: Professor Baussan, identifiable as the teacher because he carried a slide box terribly full of something like forty slides. He also carried a manila folder from which dull-yellow, lined paper splashy with list-like handwriting protruded; the raggedly-torn ends of the yellow pages showed unkempt beyond the trim, slick, otherwise continent folder. Professor Baussan also carried, draped over one arm (dressed in its part of a ridiculous, golden-brown corduroy suit), a deep pile of white, print-bearing paper. The pile, the many, many white, rectangular paper sheets, lay bent in a relaxed curve over his forearm. The carried stack showed where staples—vile, insistent staples, staples insisting upon separation as much as upon unification—divided the draped whole into many, many subgroups of equal thickness. In a beautifully resonant yet soft, deep voice, Professor Baussan greeted as "Susan" the person seated nearest the door. Susan rose from her seat. She lifted the staple-bitten paper from Professor Baussan's forearm. Distractions assailed me. I felt that I could not see, merely see, enough of Professor Baussan. I felt that I could not endure the details about Professor Baussan that bit into me while normal things happened, while Susan distributed the white-paper stack's subdivisions, or page groups, using an oppressively familiar method: she walked across the front of the classroom, before all the chair rows, pausing at each, counting the people seated in each row, counting meticulously off the stack a corresponding number of page groups, leaving the counted-off page groups with whoever sat in the foremost chair in each row; each foremost person then took a page group and passed the remaining groups backward. White paper in waves passed over the room.

Susan began the oppressive distribution. Professor Baussan gazed (with golden-brown eyes) calmly at the unmanned slide projectors where I should have sat. He tucked his overflowing folder under his left arm. With his right hand, he raised the slide box as if showing it off modestly. He said, with such confidence in his booming, calm, carrying voice that the question did not seem to question, but to state an assumption, "Somebody's here to take care of these?" I had to stand up. I stood up. I even tossed back my hair and squared my shoulders, vanity, vanity, that Professor Baussan, a tall man, might witness my height. I should have gone to meet Professor Baussan; I should have taken the slide box from him; I should not have made him approach me, but, having lifted my chin to the height of my vanity, I could not take a step. Professor Baussan, however, came toward me. He seemed natural, even avid, about it. He held the slide box extended, as if he would shake hands with me through it. I heard words he voiced: "You?" "Okay." "Good." I grasped the slide box; Professor Baussan released it; I didn't drop it. Professor Baussan said, touching me with his vocal depths again (and with the spread of his girth and the wealth of his neck), "Now, you're, uh, what did they tell me your name was? Edward, uh?" "Ed Rawlinson," I supplied, as if speaking my own name made me cold or cost me something. Professor Baussan said, "Pleasure," and, "You're new at this, I understand." I assented without looking him in the face. Professor

Baussan said, "Well, this is a lot for a first day. But it's pretty straightforward. I'll let you know when to change them. Oh, uh. But. Here." He began explaining complications. Stiff, white, lineless index cards with bold, black numbers written on them stood up among the all-too-numerous slides. Professor Baussan touched the slide in front of the first card. I should have paid attention to what he said, but instead I noticed his fingers: thick, softly tapered, shallowly wrinkled over the knuckles. Fair hair on their backs spun with bodily implications. Professor Baussan said, "After you've used this one," touched slide, "you move it here," in front of another numbered card. "Here to here" and "here to here, uh, you see." I didn't, but I didn't speak. Perhaps I glanced at Professor Baussan; perhaps I glanced at his face with something like amorous panic. Professor Baussan said, "You'll get the hang of it, don't worry." "Don't worry," he repeated. He seemed to clench me with his eyelids avuncularly. He went to the lectern, I, to the slide projectors. I saw Professor Baussan labor to step up one step onto the stage. I wished that he'd gripped me, that he'd let me assist him.

I sat behind the slide projectors, looking blindly downward into the slide box. I sat registering my reactions. Professor Baussan's painful-looking effort to step up one step onto the foot-high stage wracked me. I desired to assist Professor Baussan intimately, physically, to help him live with his body. In that desire, I felt utterly hopeless. But I also felt, looking down into the slide box, that if I could not help him intimately, personally, I could at least "help" him then and there by doing my job properly. Feeling strangely changed—changed and charged—I no longer felt dread. I felt hopelessly motivated, desperately purposeful, determined to show slides correctly despite their daunting number and those extra, unforeseen cards. What the lineless, stiff, white, rectangular index cards meant that I should do, in exceptional instances with particular slides, became clear. While I crouched studiously over the slide box, Professor Baussan called roll. I noticed peripherally: Professor Baussan opened his folder against the lectern's tilted face. He lifted a single sheet of paper from it. He read the roll from the paper, but he seemed not to read. He nodded to acquaintances; he looked attentively at each name's owner. No name made him falter. Asian names, Spanish names, names of no origin known to me followed each other mellifluously. I envied all the names' owners. They, the names' owners, had legitimate claims on Professor Baussan's attention; I didn't. The sonorous roll call, the deliberate, attentive noticing, ceased. Professor Baussan lifted out of his folder a page group like those previously distributed. He left the lectern; he stood, broad in his unbuttoned jacket, soft in his ridiculous, wide-wale corduroy suit, stage front and center. Professor Baussan lifted his page group. He said, once again with such confidence that his question did not sound like a question: "Everyone's got one of these?" Papers rustled responsively. Professor Baussan talked about the page group's contents—"course outline," "required reading," "recommended reading," "course requirements." He requested that, if students would take notes, they take them in writing, without recording or typing. People groaned. He said "I know" as if mocking his own requirement. Some whispers, some shuffling ensued. Professor Baussan continued to speak. He talked about the "vastness" of the "subject matter" that the course, History of Medieval European Architecture, encompassed and about how he'd decided "to organize the course" around "sixteen major monuments," "all important examples of religious architecture." "Today," he announced. At that word, work really threatened. I looked up. Professor Baussan motioned to Susan who, having resumed her seat nearest the door, stood up again. She closed the door and dimmed the overhead lights by turning a wheel near the door. Professor Baussan, again behind the lectern, switched on the lectern's lamp. Amid the room's new obscurity, light from the lectern's lamp suggested candlelight. My mother favored candlelight because she thought it flattering. The lectern's lamplight did not flatter Professor Baussan. His wide, square chin, catching the light first and holding most of the light that his face caught, looked bloated and belligerent. His small lips appeared sourly jammed upward, his lower lip undercut by shadow. His beautiful, intelligent, quick light-brown eyes became fiendish-looking glints in dark sockets under eyebrows shaggy as ripe heads of wheat. His full head of smooth, orbicular, dense and very fair hair lost its solar radiance and became moon-like, silvery. Lit from below, Professor Baussan looked, I imagined, like some bloated, gorged potentate from deepest hell: decidedly unsuited to begin talking about churches. Touched anew, touched newly by the obviously unfair, fleshy ugliness that light gave him, I turned on two slide projectors. I set the first two slides into the carriages that would pass them into the projectors' internal light. (Slides entering projectors would displace "dark screens," devices which, until displaced, prevented projection. No naked light would ever glare on the screen.) Professor Baussan's eye-glints turned toward me. He nodded. He said, "First slide, please." I moved a carriage-rack; a slide as light opened on the screen. The light depicted a black-and-white drawing, a floor plan magnified, shining in immaterial whiteness. I checked the projected slide's focus. I thought that I might—just—survive work, that supposedly simple job.

Professor Baussan presented what he called an "overview" of the course. He introduced "sixteen major monuments." "Lectures," he said, "in the coming months" would "touch upon related structures." The sixteen selected exemplars flew past, summarized in importance. Professor Baussan directed me, saying, "Next slide, please," "Next," "Next," "Next pair." I took slides out of holders, replaced slides in holders, set slides correctly (upside down and backwards) into carriages, shoved carriages carrying slides over into machines. I checked the projected light's focus repeatedly. I felt sternly excited, working, attuned to the lecture and thrilling to what I heard. Professor Baussan spoke. Sometimes he stood behind the lectern, speaking, not reading. Sometimes he stood near the lectern, near students, as near as the stage allowed, looking over the class. Despite work, I heard pens, note-taking on paper. Buildings, slides as light, spilled through the air, spread as shafts across the room, and illumined the screen. Buildings flashed, pictured. Buildings appeared resurrected, represented by drawings, or as ruins, or as wholes. "Old Saint Peter's," Rome. "San Vitale," Ravenna. "The Hagia Sophia, Church of the Divine Wisdom, in what is now Istanbul." The Byzantine paradigm passed and other lights followed: "the Palatine Chapel," Aachen; "Saint Sernin," Toulouse; "Abbey Three," Cluny; "Durham" and "Speyer" cathedrals; "the first completely Gothic structure," "the choir of Saint-Denis," Paris. I set up slides down the line, listening, drinking in light: "Chartres," "Salisbury" cathedrals. Amid Salisbury, a student asked, "What do you mean, 'clerestory windows?'" Professor Baussan answered. He entered the light of a slide. He stood in the projected image, designating windows. Unreal church tinted him. Colored light ripped on his ridiculous corduroy. His shadow cut sharply into the light. His shadow touched me. It reminded me of something that I couldn't remember, something lust-inducing. Without attending to the quest, I began trying to remember where I had seen such shadow, a vertical shadow near an attractive man. Professor Baussan left the light. He told students that they should "familiarize" themselves with "these terms," the names of parts of churches. "You're going to be hearing a lot about them in the coming months," terms "clearly presented" in such-and-such a book. Resuming his lecture, Professor Baussan swept through "Fontenay Abbey," "Freiburg" and "Pisa" and "Florence" cathedrals. Then "King's College Chapel," Cambridge, sprang. He called it "old-fashioned" in its Gothic style, "built in the Renaissance," and the "overview" ended. A second introduction immediately began. Professor Baussan discussed the need to see buildings "firsthand," to walk through them, "to get a feel for them." He talked about "our unhappy reliance" upon "photography," about cameras' limitations. He discussed architecture in general. And he began teaching the course in earnest, I thought, by saying, thrillingly to me, "Early medieval architecture was Roman architecture." He talked about Greek and Roman architecture in opposition to each other, calling Greek temples "aloof," on "high plinths," and Roman temples "more approachable" than Greek ones, with "portals," doorways "at street level," "reaching out," not on "high plinths." Slides, flying through my hands, leapfrogging from note to note, showed Roman "porches," "precursors" to "Gothic portals." Professor Baussan roundly talked about the round Pantheon in Rome. He called glowing Greek buildings' forms, in contrast, "generally rectilinear." Then he paused. He said deeply, in his stirring voice, "Wednesday," and "We'll take up from this point." Class ended. I felt many things, including relief.

Moved by Professor Baussan and by his subject (as conveyed by him, his mind, his voice); struck by stony power and beauty; feeling transported by worded knowledge; feeling hopeless / helpless, admiring / adoring, I deadened the slide projectors. I remained seated behind them, watching processes reverse: Susan, turning the rheostat wheel, brightened the overhead lighting. She opened the (criminally, inwardly painted) door carefully, slowly, fully. Students closed notebooks, stowed objects, rose, talked, milled, left the room. Professor Baussan turned off the lectern's lamp. He stepped down, off the stage, without hesitation. People clustered around the golden teacher. Through the crowd, Susan passed the remaining page groups to Professor Baussan who, receiving them, acknowledged Susan by dropping his head sideways and half-closing his eyes. Kindness, smiling, seemed to overpower his eyelids. I watched him talk, nod, incline his head affably. I watched him turn his attentive, light-brown eyes as if fondly upon people whom he held in his gaze, people who would question him, an "approachable" man, ahistorically "Roman," I supposed, in contrast to me, ahistorically "Greek" on a "high plinth," the slide projectors' platform. When only two questioners remained—one asked, could Professor Baussan "recommend a good introduction to Piero della Francesca," a request without bearing upon the lecture just heard—I took the slide box in hand and waited near the door. The last questioners left. Professor Baussan came toward me, shaking his head, muttering, "First day of class and already worrying about the final. I don't schedule these things. We'll work something out." (The last student to speak with him had had a "schedule conflict"; two university-scheduled exams coincided.) I extended the slide box to Professor Baussan. He arranged the things he carried and took the slide box from me. He said, "Thank you. Excellent job. Nothing to worry about, you see. There won't be nearly as many next time. Ten or twelve, maybe. Going down?" He gestured with his overflowing folder through the open door, a gaping rectangle, a straight-sided absence beside his full form. Professor Baussan motioned across the corridor as if the stairs began there, which they distantly didn't. However much I wanted to walk with him, or at least in the direction indicated, I shivered negatively, no, not "going down" yet. (Why did I do that?) Professor Baussan looked at me as if deciding something. Finally, he said, "Uh. Well. Then. When you do decide to leave. If you would, please. Cut the lights. And lock the door. Just pull it to. All right?" (No classes met between twelve and one o'clock.) I agreed worshipfully, without saying anything. Professor Baussan said, "See you Wednesday, then, Edward." He turned left into the corridor. Floorboards beneath him sounded taxed. I reached into the hallway and closed the treacherous door quickly. I stood, leaning against it, face to the deep, angled recess where door and jamb met.

56 JANITOR

Professor Baussan, standing, moving, talking about "clerestory windows" amid light that suggested a cathedral's high nave, Professor Baussan and his shadow amid the projected light, reminded me of something that I couldn't place, until it came to me. One late afternoon during my senior year in high school, I'd returned to the school building. I'd just had the cast removed from my arm (broken in gym-class basketball). That afternoon, before I'd had the cast removed, I'd decided defiantly that I would not do homework that night. I'd wanted to celebrate the return of my right arm by drawing. (I'd longed to draw for weeks; weeks had turned into months.) But then, typically, indecisively, after the cast had gone, I'd changed my mind. I'd felt discouraged by the sight of my arm. I'd decided penitentially that I *would* do homework that night, that I would, in fact, embrace my worst subject, chemistry. I'd returned to school late to retrieve the necessary book. I then changed my mind again. I saw the thick chemistry book lying on my locker's shelf. I lost dispatch. I lost resolve to study, not because the book reminded me of its difficult subject, but because the hardback book's stubbed corners touched something in me. The book's corners looked soft. The book's broken corners spread, showing the hard binding's cardboard as an inner softness. The sight of that softness released by corners made me feel generous, or not generous exactly, but as if freed from immediate limitations. Perhaps the nearing end of my high-school years occurred to me. Perhaps enlargement of my future promised. I decided that I *would* draw—and not do homework—that night.

Closing my locker door, I noticed something well-known about it: like all of the other locker doors, like all of the tall, narrow, gray-glazed, metal doors, which plated the sides of the hallway then devoid of people, the locker door required force to close. One could not simply, slowly, quietly shut the door. One had to slam it a little to get it to lock. Pressing the thing gently didn't engage the lock. I stood, looking at the door, looking down at the vents nearest its top: four parallel inclines, four gray, metal slats fixed in one position, unadjustable. I touched the locker's handle, a long, sleekly molded piece of chrome-shiny metal, which one could raise, or slide upward, when unlocking the door. The handle did not project far. It had no sharpness about it, which made it safe, I supposed, unlikely to wound anyone run, or shoved, or punched, or otherwise impelled against the door. The same sparing lowness showed in the combination lock, a low, black, bluntly truncated cone flecked with white dashes, slight indentations, line segments, which divided the dial evenly. I looked at one of the lockers next to mine. Lined paper projected downward through one of the locker's lower vents, several overlapped sheets with blank, rounded corners. A punched hole, round near a rounded corner, showed vaguely, its openness blocked by an underlying sheet. A few pale blue, parallel lines printed on the paper showed.

I slammed my locker closed as quietly as possible. I turned around and leaned back on my arms, my newly freed arm happily naked in its sleeve. I stood looking up at the lighting fixtures high overhead: trays of fluorescent tubes shielded by slats. The hallway seemed smooth, quiet, absent people. Amid the vacated planes of the physical school and with eyes closed against the known-more-than-seen pale blue lines of the fluorescent tubes and against the pale blue lines on lined paper, I felt suspended in an institutional mold. I saw in my mind the long, wide hallway plated up to a certain height along its sides with tall gray locker doors, doors,

doors, doors shut, slammed, locked fast, closed in deceptive uniformity, concealing the lockers' diverse contents. I saw in my mind what I had just seen without registering: the broad, smooth, high hallway along which, at lengthy intervals, classroom doors, taller than the locker doors, stood open, open, opened, fanned at random angles into the hall. The classroom doors to the west admitted afternoon sunlight. Where the late sunlight, reaching deep into the building from the far out-of-doors, touched the floor, the floor looked scratched like soft, milk chocolate; elsewhere it looked smoothly, darkly umber. Sunlight slanted edgeless in the imprisoned air. I wanted to draw. Slave to realism, I wanted to draw what I'd just seen: wide open, opened classroom doors, narrow, shut, locked locker doors covering the walls between the light-admitting openings—liberating light in the binding tightness. I clenched my right hand's fingers. Then a booming sound startled me. From the sight in my mind, I looked down the hall. Amid all the flatness, all the straightness, all the rectilinear subdivisions in the plated walls and in the tiled floor, beyond all that hard, strict, straight flatness, I saw the likely source of the booming sound: a newly-arrived, large matte clay-red canister strapped to a dolly. The trash canister glowed in the light admitted by an opened door. Far away, it resembled a nub of sanguine chalk. A strip of its interior looked warm, brightly-lit, ocher. As I, surprised, admired the distant canister, the round peg set down in a large square hole, a man joined it. A broad, thick-bodied man dressed in one-piece gray moved in the doorway light. His shadow raced up the canister. He stood briefly beside it, emptying a gray, metal, fluted wastepaper basket into the canister. The man stood in wide, full—abdominous—profile to me, his shadow patching the canister before him. Late afternoon light covered his back. He looked full beyond flatness. He looked variously curved beside the cylinder.

57 CLASSROOM DOOR

Leaning as if dropped face first into the small corner formed by the door and the jamb of the one frequently-used door in Room 203, I felt desirous and unrequited and wracked with the crime of my sudden admiring: "falling in love" with a teacher. I agonized: How could you, Edward? You of all people? "Fall in love" with a teacher? Having known my father, a teacher, all my life, I should have known better. I should have acquired at least some immunity to the reeling, responsive idealization I felt. In some ineffable way, Professor Baussan seemed married and happily married and sexually prolific. He seemed old enough to have children at least as old as I, and he seemed like the loving type who would have loved to have many. Did I seek a "warm" father to replace my "cold" one? (I would not call my father "cold," but he ran hot and cold, and he would qualify, by most measures, as a "strict disciplinarian." What other kind existed? How could you, Edward?) *I* did not gush "love." *I* did not become rapturous over lectures. *I* did not conflate lecturers with their lectures. So how could I, how could I develop a "crush" instantly? "Crush," shameful word, fit for teenage girls. I had my pride and my naïveté hurt it.

As I leaned into the crease formed by the door and the jamb, I suffered admiring / desiring. I suffered such conviction of the hopelessness of all of my wishes that the mere existence of wishes seemed nothing but proof of the logically impervious nature of hope. I condemned myself for not condemning myself on moral grounds, but rather on the petty grounds of injured pride that I, I of all people, committed cliché upon cliché, "falling in love" with a teacher and tumbling so at once, at first sight. I leaned into the door wracked every which way; self-consciousness mauled me. But I also reached outward: I listened after Professor Baussan as he walked down the hallway beyond the door. I heard him walk away and turn left. I heard him because the building's old, decrepit floorboards squeaked. Something covered the boards in the hall. Nonetheless, they squeaked. And their faint, squeaking, creaking noises wracked me: Professor Baussan bent boards with his tread. He treaded down straight lines. Every miserable, pinched constraint, every drear, restrictive inhibition conditioned into me and created by my temperament, by my indulged timidity, seemed exercised, flexed, with the sounding boards. I'd built myself into a box. That box became Room 203. And I craved liberation. I needed someone to help me out of my crate, out of my closet, out of my prison of rules.

Professor Baussan did not seem that person. Professor Baussan did not seem someone who could help me. He did not seem gay. And even if he had seemed gay, I would have believed him married in fact or married virtually, endowed with a loving partner, happy in a long-established partnership.

Leaning into the door of Room 203, I heard floorboards. I heard a remote door sound; whether closed by His hand or not, I couldn't tell. I listened hard for anything that might relate to Professor Baussan. Tired of unrewarding stillness, I turned around. I leaned back against the door and stood looking up at the ceiling, at the six pendent lamps.

58   OFFICE DOOR

Room 203 looked so bleak, so dull, so dead, so unenlivened after
the light had passed out of it, after the light of the mind of
Professor Baussan, that I felt almost as if his lecture hadn't really
taken place, as if his lecture should have affected the very room.
How could Room 203 remain as battered and plain as before he'd
spoken? Newly stricken with Professor Baussan, I tore myself away
from the door. I walked up and down among the chairs, dragging
my fingertips along their single arms. Whatever plain lust the man
working as janitor in my high school had evoked in me—and he'd
evoked plenty; I'd fantasized about him repeatedly—a deeper and
a graver desire followed Professor Baussan. I told myself that I
would not, would not fantasize about the golden teacher. I would
not savor thoughts of his form in solitude. I would not think about
his brown eyes; I would not imagine them soft with affection or
lidded in a daze of sexual pleasure. I would not, I would not. Amid
thinking about how I would *not* think about Professor Baussan,
amid thinking about how I would not use thoughts of his body to
serve my own low, choking, solitary ends, I suddenly felt stung,
surprised, scared, tingling with shock: the hallway creaked. It
creaked exactly as it had creaked under Professor Baussan's tread.
I feared discovery. Having forgotten that the door to Room 203
locked automatically when closed, I feared that Professor Baussan,
passing in the hallway, would notice light under the door, that he
would open the door, and that he would stick his fair head in, see

me, and ask something like, "Everything all right in here?" I listened, tingling, pulsing, feeling fearfully guilty of staying in the room, which I should have left as instructed. The creaking continued; it didn't stop; it didn't pause at the door. I felt relieved and I felt warned: I should leave the room. I should leave it as Professor Baussan had told me to leave it. I decided to leave.

Walking among the chairs, I'd lashed myself with prohibitions. I'd bound myself to respect Professor Baussan's image; I would not base fantasies upon his fair form. Among other proscriptions: I would not pry, by any means, into his private life. I would not follow him, ever, without his knowledge. I would not seek electronically-provided information about him. And I would not even seek to glean anything of his mind by reading anything that he'd written. I would not do much. But I would do one slinky, little thing: when I left Room 203, I would follow the hallway, going and coming. I would follow the hallway as, I believed, Professor Baussan had just followed it.

I turned out the lights. I shut the door behind me. Its lock clunked. (Burke's slowly rolling pool balls, dropped into pockets, recurred.) Down the hall to my left, at the turning where the hall turned to lie behind Room 203 instead of beside it, a dark door faced me. The door bore a white rectangle centered on its upper panel. I walked to the door where the hallway turned. The floor's underpinnings creaked. They made as much noise for me as they had made music below Professor Baussan. A narrow, brass frame (seldom or never polished) surrounded a white rectangular card on the door. The card bore a person's name in clear print. Below the name, separated from it by blankness, abbreviations and numbers, in three lines, summarized when and where three classes met. Below the little sticks of information and separated from them by blankness, print on the white rectangle read, "OFFICE HOURS: TTh 3:30-5." The solitary white card with its impeccable print looked more firmly, more rigidly, more grimly imprisoned than paper napkins had looked, clamped as a mattress together, in a black dispenser. Another door ended the hallway behind Room 203. Two doors in the side wall perpendicular to the hall-ending door intervened, recessed in deep frames. All the doors bore white labels. Why had I deliberately entered that narrowness? I walked toward the far door. The doors to my right flashed their cards, "OFFICE HOURS," names, letters-and-numbers in printed sticks. The hallway looked very narrow, dark, lit solely by electric light: dim bulbs in pimply, clear-glass fixtures overhead. No light entered from the out-of-doors. No full-bodied male stood in slanted light beside a trash canister. The hallway looked hopeless. I reached the last door. I read the card on it. Flawless print, print which gave no hint of human hands, read, "LAWRENCE BLAY BAUSSAN." The belted "Bs" bulged erotically. Letters, numbers in two left-aligned sticks referred to two classes. The stick of information that applied to the class for which I'd just—and as if weeks previously—shown slides read, "HA 495 MWF 11 SH 203." The card on Professor Baussan's door concluded exclusively: "OFFICE HOURS: BY APPOINT-MENT ONLY." None of the other cards said that; the others gave office hours. That "ONLY" seemed the last word in bleakness. I stood, looking at print on trapped paper, looking at print on a white framed card, in a narrow place lit solely by electricity. I felt as if my high school's locker-lined corridor had suddenly, utterly closed down, closed in upon me. No opened doors showed. Doors looked dark, windowless, not very numerous. No sunlight entered the hallway. And the golden man, shaped like a man working as janitor, might as well have never walked along the dreary passage.

59   INVITATION

I thought that I'd come to a dead end among doors, that I could not get to know Professor Baussan, not as I longed to know him. A closed door, a hopeless situation, stared me in the face. Seeing the white card on Professor Baussan's office door, I told myself, "Be reasonable," don't encourage this mania; discourage it. I gave myself much good advice over the following days to little effect. Desire, admiring, a tormented adoring of and for Professor Baussan persisted in me despite efforts to understand myself and efforts to "listen to reason." I considered reasons—psychological, moral, social—why I might feel as I did and reasons why I should *not* feel as I did: obsessed with a teacher and that teacher possessing Professor Baussan's traits. I felt attracted to Professor Baussan as if by gravity. I wondered, while trying not to think about him, why, even if I saw him not just as a person, but also as some sort of figure—teacher figure, father figure, authority figure, figure figure—even so, why then, in all those extra-personal capacities, why did Professor Baussan attract me? Why did I bend inwardly, aching in sympathy, when he seemed pained in a knee? Why did Professor Baussan's occasional, wearied look of age make me feel—uselessly, tenderly—protective of him, desirous to spend my life to his good? I even tried, by writing down words, to grasp what factors might contribute to my attraction to Professor Baussan, an attraction which, by many lights, would seem at best inappropriate. Efforts to dispel that attraction by thinking about it failed. I could not, or at least, I did not manage to, conquer my adoration. I lived to see Professor Baussan, to show slides for him. And I did show slides. I received slide boxes from his hands. I returned slide boxes to him after class after class after class, after six lectures total. But although I felt sensually greedy when near him and intellectually rapacious while hearing him lecture, I behaved myself discreetly, I thought; I spoke with him once only and that once briefly. He asked me, after class, if I'd "declared a major yet." He seemed to think me at most a junior or something like twenty years old. I'd actually reached the—shocking-to-me—age of—almost, minus days—twenty-three. I supposed that Professor Baussan asked after my major out of generous, general, generic curiosity. When he asked after my major, I briefly explained my work toward a master's. He seemed surprised and approving, but then, gesturing toward the slide projectors in Room 203, he commented with a touch of asperity, "I'm surprised you think you have time for this." He valued time, I remembered: "OFFICE HOURS: BY APPOINTMENT ONLY." I behaved with Professor Baussan in what I considered a respectful, considerate, distant manner. I answered minimally when he spoke to me. I didn't stare—or gaze—at him. I returned slide boxes to him promptly after class without waiting for the room to clear. I considered all of that dampened, discreet, downcast, self-denying behavior all well and good, decent of me, sparing of him. I also felt such strain, maintaining that bearing, that I feared that I could not keep up the act for long.

My resolve to spare Professor Baussan knowledge of my— surely errant—attraction to him and my desire to spare myself a confessional ordeal, which would both humiliate me and mean that I would have to resign as "slide operator" and thus forfeit all future opportunities to see, to hear Professor Baussan, my resolve on those counts began to weaken under strain like a faulty dam. Ten whole days and two partial days after I'd first heard him lecture, after the sixth lecture that I'd heard him give (a lecture on the Hagia Sophia, and on light and mystery and Neoplatonism, as well as on pendentives, a lecture thrilling to me beyond the thrilling norm), Professor Baussan stopped me after class. (He wore a dark blue blazer that day. He looked especially well-groomed—fair, burnished, radiant.) I'd returned the slide box to him and moved to leave the room. He raised his broad chin. He pointed to me with it—without pointing—as if calling on someone in class. He said to me, in his genial, rich, deep, carrying voice, through the crowd leaving Room 203, "Edward, would you wait a moment, please." I felt certain that I'd done something wrong. Knowing my thronged wrongs, I would suppose that. I thought that perhaps I'd made a mistake showing slides. Had I projected one backwards? I thought that Professor Baussan intended to mention my mistake tactfully in private, after class. I thought that he might leave me with words like, "All right. You understand now. Don't let it happen again." The possibility that I had committed some slight misdeed and that I might receive some slight reprimand seemed disproportionately awful. I waited beside the door; people exited. When all of the students—all of the enviable, legitimate recipients of Professor Baussan's professional attention—had left the room, Professor Baussan shifted the slide box. He shifted his folder (still overflowing with raggedly torn, yellow lined legal paper). He fished, with his freed right hand, in his jacket's heart pocket. He extracted white paper, a sheet folded first in half, then again in thirds. With a broad, groomed-looking thumbnail uppermost on the folded white, he extended the paper to me. He said, "You may have seen this posted downstairs, but I doubt it." "What is it?" I breathed. Professor Baussan said, "Well, uh. I guess you could call it an invitation." I opened the paper (ever grieved over creases in paper), read: "Seekford Association / Potluck Supper." While I read the flyer, which invited all "students and faculty" in Professor Baussan's department to a "potluck supper" at a location indicated on a likeably sketchy map, Professor Baussan said, "This is something we do every year." He said something about "get-together," "meet the new students," "chance to catch up after the summer." I said—gauchely, naively, with

gratitude gushing, running, forming unconsidered questions—
"You're inviting me? Why?" Professor Baussan looked slightly
discomfited. Flesh around his eyes moved. He said deliberately,
"You're in studio art. We don't meet many artists." I started some
soft, surprised protest against his giving me "too much credit."
Professor Baussan moved his free hand as if he would pat back
speech needlessly filling the air. He said something further about
valuing whatever contact he could contrive between people
involved in "making art" and people who studied art already made.
I gushed, I exclaimed, "Thank you." Professor Baussan smiled.
His eyes narrowed genially. He said, "So. You'll join us?" I gushed
yes, sure, thank you, thank you. Still smiling, Professor Baussan
reached over and tapped the sketchy map and said, as if confiden-
tially, "That's my house. North off Shelby, like it says. I'll see you
tomorrow then." The flyer gave a date and said "Saturday." I
distractedly had to translate "Saturday" and the date into meaning
"tomorrow."

60   MEETING

I believed that I often deluded myself, that I leapt to conclusions. I'd deemed Professor Baussan warm, accessible, open; then I'd seen his office door, the cold, white card with print on it reading, "OFFICE HOURS: BY APPOINTMENT ONLY." I'd concluded then that I'd erred in my first impression of him, and I'd thought that, in general, I judged people on a basis of unreliable impressions, through a wishful haze, by the lights of my blind, self-serving desires. Handed white, folded paper, a virtual invitation, I tried to guard myself against deluding myself once again. I did not want to let myself think what I wanted to think: that Professor Baussan liked me despite my standoffish manners, that Professor Baussan took some sort of interest in me.

The next day, the day of the potluck, I had a headache. I hadn't slept. I drove at an appropriate time to Professor Baussan's house. It stood high above the street and well back from it, among woods brutally hacked away to accommodate it. On its street-facing side, the house had, instead of lawn, ground-covering ivy; railroad ties enforcing terraces; boulders; strategic plantings; natural trees left from the killing / clearing. A driveway skirted the yard to the right (as one faced the house). Cars lined the street below the house, but I, in reckless despair, drove up the driveway. It widened into a parking area behind an outsized garage. Four cars parked there left space for mine. Parked, sitting in my car, I observed the house. It looked large, expensive, shaggy, golden, wooden. No paint, no plane tamed the raging wood. The big, rough planks constituting the house stood side by side in their might, vertically aligned, stained golden with creosote (I later learned). The planks created an L-shaped structure. A smooth door—windowless, varnished, oaken—stood in the crux of the L, above a low, concrete stoop. A path, bounded by railroad ties, led from terrace to terrace, from the street to the door. Another path led from the parking area to the door. Behind the immoderate garage and beside the parking, firewood lay stacked in a black, metal rack: more arboreal destruction than I cared to contemplate. Professor Baussan's big, rough house, clearly out of line with what I knew well about teachers' salaries, Professor Baussan's house, snagging golden, autumnal sunlight among tangled trees, seemed to confirm what I'd suspected since Day One: that Professor Baussan had money beyond a teacher's salary and, probably, that he also had numerous children, now grown. Why else would he ever have needed such a house? I turned off my car's engine. My head hurt. I rested it against the steering wheel. (Given how I felt about Professor Baussan's house—wasteful of planetary resources—I shouldn't have driven a car. I should have walked or bicycled.) I sat with my head against the steering wheel until I feared looking peculiar; people approached. Women carrying dishes walked up the driveway. They walked behind my car and past the garage. They disappeared behind it. Because they acted as if they knew where to go, where to take their dishes, I decided to follow, not them, but their example. I took my potluck contribution, a red-net sack of tangerines, left my car unlocked (as a matter of principle), and walked downhill, beyond the garage, along a path bounded by two courses of railroad ties. (I did not like railroad ties. Trees died to form ties. Besides, Burke had once—grinning, friendly, pushing, playing—shoved me off of a railroad track's rail. I'd felt rebuked, then, for the game I'd played, until he shoved me: balletic balancing. Burke had run off, planting his feet, in great leaps, between railroad ties.)

The path defined by railroad ties led gently downhill, under oaks and pines, through peacefully dark-green ivy; an abundance of ivy shoots curved lightly, as a layer, over the older leaves. Low, little, durable-looking lamps, unillumined, burgeoned at intervals—every ten feet or so—from the dead-wooden ties. Translucent pebbles littered the path. The house loomed to my left. The garage jutted. A long, splintery, golden, rawly wooden section of house intervened, recessed, between the garage jut and another jut. Both juts contained doors; the doors faced each other distantly. More juts followed those with doors. A second story grew under the ground floor where the house overshot the hill. Where the second story and the whole house appeared to end along that side, juts seemed to accumulate in one painful corner. A wooden balcony with solid, horizontally planked walls surrounded a huge chimney pile made of natural stone. Wooden steps with gaps instead of risers slanted between the balcony and the ground. The balcony jutted; the chimney jutted in the balcony's grip; both together jutted off the last, big jut, some interior room. The path led to lawn, a level clearing at the end of the house. The brutally-hacked-into woods rose as a dusky wall beyond the clearing. In the wretchedly beautiful, still, golden early-autumnal air, people in the clearing stood and moved, laughing and speaking: many people, like pieces of a living, convivial wind chime meeting. Red-and-white plastic tablecloths covered two tables (painfully) above the glowing-green grass. I tried not to see the red-white, pattern-filled checks checkering the plastic with countless corners. Wine bottles, smoothly tapered, probed the golden light like gleaming shoots. (Wine bottles grew as a grove produced by one table. Dishes covered another table.) The circulating people ate, drank, talked. I tried to ignore crimes: white paper plates. The hopelessly perfect weather, the wretchedly lovely amber sunlight failed, lacked, wanted all, because it did not contain *him*. Failing to find Professor Baussan, missing Professor Baussan without overlooking anyone, I wandered around. (I laid my tangerines on a table, found a knife, slit the palindromic tender red net containing them.) I looked at the house again. Facing it, gazing up at it from the lawn, I felt prepared to forgive even it its sins, its wooden expense, its rugged splendor, because unlike the air around me, it probably did surround Professor Baussan.

The house looked best seen from the rear, its southern side, above the clearing. Banded with balcony where it had two stories, catching the light in its splintery pelt, the house did look handsome (despite its vanity, despite its implications, family, et cetera). Two smooth, glossy, oaken doors with windows in them gleamed with glass amid much glass. Shining glass afflicted me. But the house looked brave, as if it feared no storm, no molestation. It looked barbaric, aggressive, and proud. The house seemed to proclaim— to announce proudly of itself—that it had killed many trees or that people had killed many trees for it, trees that had turned into it. The craggy chimney, holding two flues, with turrets to keep rainwater out of the flues (not bag houses to scrub smoke), seemed to express an intrinsic appetite for wood, as if one would have to keep feeding the house trees as one would have to keep feeding a captive lion meat. While I stood looking up at the house, one of the two glassy doors—the one at ground level—opened abruptly. A woman carrying a heavy-looking dish in two padded hands emerged. However she'd opened the door, she tried to close it with an elbow. I almost ran up to her. I hastily asked, "May I take that for you?" The woman looked conspicuously not like a student. She looked puffy in face and hair and motherly several times over and I suffered to realize that I, jumping to conclusions once again, had instantly tagged her, because of her age probably, and because of her familiar manner with the house (her elbowing the door), as Professor Baussan's wife: someone capable of making me die of repining envy of her. I offered to take the dish from the supposed Mrs. Baussan. She, her round blue eyes cushioned on crescent-shaped pouches, her short, pale hair distended in many loose yet crescent-shaped locks, held the dish firmly with pads scorched and fraying where scorched. She looked at me seemingly with slight consternation, as she felt tired of encountering, every time she turned around, thoughtless, youthful energy misapplied. She said, in a tone which suggested that I should have figured it out myself, "No. Thank you. I've got this. But you could get the door." I said, "Oh, yeah, sure." And I importuned her further. While she stood, holding an obviously heavy object, I asked, "Do you have any idea. Where I could find. Professor Baussan?" The woman again, I thought, acted wifely. She looked wry at the academic title, I thought, and she again acted, I thought, as if she owned the house. She motioned with her chin, somewhat in Professor Baussan's manner. She said, "Straight on in there, upstairs. In the kitchen." I said thanks. The woman, her loose dress blue-gray like her eyes, moved toward the tables. I felt desperate. My head ached. I desired to see Professor Baussan. And someone had just—seemed to give me permission to enter the house. I agonized as usual. (Should I, should I not, enter? I should not, but I did.)

I rushed into the house. I rushed, as if to escape my conscience. I rushed across a large single room, which I scrupulously ignored. I plunged up a staircase (slick, bare, golden, oaken stairs with smooth round-lipped steps). At the top of the stairs, I stopped. Directly before me, a door, which would open into the small, square landing on which I stood, showed green, out-of-doors, through its window. My conscience told me that I should leave the house then and there, that I shouldn't have entered it at all uninvited. I should not have entered the house on the dubious strength of apparent permission. But, strong in hopeless desire, I did not leave. While I stood looking out through the window in the door (which faced a similar, distant door in a jutting part of the garage), I heard music, classical, discontinuous, piano music, played by someone somewhere in the house. The music ceased and resumed. It seemed to coexist with fond, demonstrative talk about it in a man's voice, not Professor Baussan's. I heard a woman's voice, too. The voices and the music reminded me of other worlds, of other people's lives, activities, interests. Feeling slightly calmed, grazed by audible traces of what seemed a graceful world, a world of people conversant with music, I looked down. I turned to my right and took one step up, the only step offered, out of the small landing. When I looked up, I felt mildly surprised. I'd expected to see a kitchen ("Straight on in there," "in the kitchen"). Instead, I saw a dining room: a large, teak table and eight teak chairs. (The wood-eating house evidently took its time digesting tropical hardwood.) The seemingly misplaced kitchen showed to my left, separated from the dining room by the combination of an overhead cabinet (glass-fronted, full of glassware) and stone-topped, solid cabinets below the overhead one. In the kitchen, partially visible, stood Professor Baussan, his broad back toward me. I had never seen him without a jacket. Gray pinstripes in the loose, white shirt he wore (above staid, loose gray trousers) looked widely spaced. Nonsensically, I felt that the music then coming from another room had modified the pinstripes, that it had magically made them few and faint and graciously spaced, drawn in their vertical flow to its own intervals. Professor Baussan, in his full, loose, barely barred shirt, stood facing a sink. I could not see as high as his shoulders, but his attitude suggested that he stood gazing calmly outward, through a window above the sink, while slowly moving something held in his hands. I feared approaching him. I felt desperate and intemperate, and my head hurt. I felt as if I'd intruded upon a calm, adult, orderly world, a world of amicable ease, sociability, and easy talent. (The intermittent music suggested talent.) I felt as if I'd intruded upon the very world that I hopelessly longed to share with Professor Baussan. Telling myself to (just) get it over with (just say hello), I went to the kitchen doorway, a wide, doorless gap. I knocked on a countertop. Professor Baussan turned toward me. He beamed. He looked as radiant as he usually looked. He laid aside a glass and a napless towel. Doing so, he said genially and as if surprised, "Ah, Edward. So. You made it." I entered the kitchen and extended my hand. Professor Baussan grasped it. He squeezed it between both of his and he didn't release it. He looked at me warmly and he said warmly—because, I thought, he did everything warmly—"Good to see you. Good to see you. I was beginning to think you'd changed your mind." My sanity wilted at his hands' soft embrace.

I felt given a touch, a taste, of what I could not, bodily or otherwise, ever know of him. Made desolate (more than ever) by that touch, that taste, that paradisiacal hint; given his hands' soft pressure, I said desperately, "You sound as if you cared about me—what I did—whether I showed up or not. But you. Can't possibly care about me. The way I care about you." Professor Baussan's eyes opened wide. He looked horrified, but he did not release my hand. I said, to eyes that I thought I would never see again, "You must have had. Your share of. Hysterical students. With." I floundered under his roundly brown-eyed gaze. I floundered on. I said, "With students who say. They're 'in love' with you. God, what a phrase. But I. Really am. I guess you'll have to. Find someone else to show slides. I can't do it anymore. I can't stand seeing you." Professor Baussan gazed at me. He looked wide-eyed, as if stunned. He showed set teeth for a moment, staring. I tried to pull my hand out of his grasp, but he held tighter than I pulled. He even pulled me slightly toward himself, as if he would tow me under his jaw to say—down, into my face, severely—"Let's get one thing straight." Instead, he said, "Edward. Good-looking boy like you. You wouldn't tease an old queer?"

61   DANA

As dizziness caused by motion doesn't end when the motion ends, so my desperation didn't ease immediately with Professor Baussan's message. His question, couched in clichés, told me plainly through the clichés, "I'm gay," "I find you attractive," and "I hope you mean what you've just said." I drank in the sight of Professor Baussan's eyes.

I had not hoped. I had not known what I would do when I entered the kitchen. I hadn't even hoped enough to hope for emotional relief through cathartic confession. Professor Baussan's unanticipated response to my unanticipated behavior seemed too gratifying to accord with reality. I barely dared to believe that I'd heard what I'd heard. Having misjudged Professor Baussan, having judged him off-limits to me, surely not gay, from Day One until then, my judgment had disserved me; perhaps it *could not* serve me well. I knew that I often deluded myself.

Professor Baussan's face relaxed; stern effects slid from it; he released my hand. He said, "You seem surprised." I said, "'Surprised' doesn't begin to cover it." Stretching his mobile face plaintively, raising his head-of-wheat eyebrows, grazing the ceiling with a glance, Professor Baussan said, "If I even looked at you wrong, you could sue me; I could lose my job." I desired to reassure him. I felt a powerful need to prove myself stable and sensible, patient and prudent. My recent behavior displayed none of those qualities; my recent behavior suggested their opposites. And I did not trust words to reassure him. (Words might sound of hollow protest. Words might sound slick—with an untrustworthy quickness to make promises.) Not trusting words, I looked downward contritely. I stepped backwards, away from Professor Baussan. Just then, someone entered the dining room (not from the stairs). High-heeled footsteps sounded: sounded, stopped, and sounded as if they would leave as quickly as they'd approached. Professor Baussan called genially, "Ah, Dana. Please. Don't go running off. Let me introduce you." The high-heeled footsteps, sounding, neared. I steeled myself to act sensible. I steeled myself to behave calmly. So steeled, I looked up. I received another shock. I saw the Not-Christine at close range. I nodded to her. Professor Baussan, who knew little more about me than my name, said formally, "Dana Ferris, let me introduce Edward Rawlinson." Dana told me, in a light tone of voice, "I think I've seen you somewhere before." (Christine might have said, "Haven't I seen you somewhere or other?") Without looking at the Not-Christine, I recited, "Front steps, Seekford Hall, September sixth, just after twelve-thirty." Professor Baussan laughed, the first time I'd heard him laugh—or chuckle. He produced a wonderful series of sounds, sounds like rocked water sloshing, soon growing still. "Unforgettable as ever," he told Dana. I glanced at her. I could not take back the awkward compliment that Professor Baussan had paid her, but I knew, guiltily (as if guilty of deception by letting the compliment pass), that I remembered the time of day, the date, and the place because I'd mentally scrutinized, in retrospect, every step of that day, the day that had led to my meeting—to my seeing for the first time—Professor Baussan. The steps down which Dana had stepped had led to my meeting him. Professor Baussan spoke on. He told me something about his "supervising" Dana's "dissertation research," and something about how she'd spent the summer in an archive named (in Italian?), studying a manuscript also named (possibly in Latin), and something about how he expected to see a "rough draft" of her dissertation "soon." And Dana (who did not look like Christine, but whom I could not see in her own right through the haze of Christine, through a crosscurrent of comparisons which told me, in detail, exactly how Dana did not look like Christine) banteringly answered Professor Baussan's reference to seeing the "rough draft" of her dissertation "soon." She suggested that he might see it by Christmas. She sounded lightly defiant. She said, "That should be soon enough. Honestly." Dana's Christine-green eyes moved evasively, as if she desired to change the subject. She announced, "Anyway." She asked Professor Baussan if he had tin foil. She wanted to save a portion of her potluck contribution for someone not present, someone to whom she'd promised "a piece." Professor Baussan said, "Of course." From a drawer, he extracted a long, small-around, pink-blue-silver box. He handed the box baton-like to Dana. I recalled his hands—with their fair crisping of hair—gripping slide boxes. I wondered fearfully, joyously: Could I really *hope, hope, hope, hope* to get to know him? Dana held the long box in one hand. With the other, she gripped the serrated edge of the foil coiled within the box and pulled out a large sheet of stuff like very flimsy, very dim mirror. Tiny, bright-metal triangles closely edging a box rim cut through the foil, not all at once, but in a running cut as Dana tightened uncut foil against the cutting teeth in a crosswise motion, maintaining pressure on the uncut foil as the cut crossed the sheet. The cutting sounded rending, and the sheet shook, resonant with sounds suggestive of visual shimmering. (My head hurt.) Dana passed the box back to Professor Baussan who, giving me a view, once again, of his large, loose, white-and-finely-gray-striped shirt's back, returned the box to the drawer from which he'd taken it. Dana folded the cut foil into quarters, said "Thanks" lightly to Professor Baussan. To me, she waved with the folded silver and said jokingly, "See you around." She left the way she'd come, along the length of the dining room, not by the stairs. Professor Baussan and I looked at each other.

62 PARTY

Professor Baussan told me that I looked pale. He asked if I felt "all right." He sounded just tender enough to suggest, to my wild, uncouth, greedily seizing brain, further—and voluptuous—tenderness. His forehead flexed with a minute tightening between his eyebrows. His eyelids lifted as part of the same tightening, revealing more of his pupils than they'd previously revealed. His jaw relaxed; his lips all but parted. Relaxation in his lower face, combined with tightening and heightening across his eyes, produced such an expression of concern that I unthinkingly, instantly told Professor Baussan the truth. I said that I had a headache, "a really murderous, splitting one." I regretted my words as soon as spoken. Professor Baussan became solicitous of me. He offered aspirin. Sunk in errors, I accepted. I regretted "troubling" him, but said, yes, that aspirin "might help." Professor Baussan lifted his right hand as if telling me to stay put, to wait a minute. He left the kitchen. He quickly returned, carrying a beautifully translucent, green-plastic bottle of aspirin topped with a white-plastic, ribbed cap. He, himself, gripped the bottle with his left hand and pressed his right palm down broadly, hard, on the cap. His lightly haired fingers held the cap as he turned it while pressing. (How could *his* hands do such ordinary things?) The "child-proof" cap resisted his first attempt to remove it from the bottle. "Adult-proof's more like it," he muttered. (Oh, the extraordinary ordinary.) With hurried, swinging motions of his body, he righted the glass that he'd laid aside when I'd entered the kitchen. He opened a refrigerator and took from it a tall, straight-sided, clear-glass pitcher of water. He, himself, poured clarity from clarity into clarity. (He filled the glass set on a tawny, stone counter.) From the opened aspirin bottle, he spilled many more than two aspirin into his palm. He shuffled the excess back into the bottle. And I, desiring to prove myself quiet, reliable, domesticable, tractable—not a disruptive force, not a mess or a mass of perpetual crises—said, "Thank you." I picked the two powdery white lenticular tablets off of Professor Baussan's very palm—as if doing nothing at all out of the ordinary. I took the aspirin with the water; Professor Baussan watched, soft-jawed, his fine, inquiring eyes opened observantly wide. And so I, I, who desired to serve Professor Baussan; who desired to aid him, to take on chores and errands, to do for him whatever petty, practical things he did not want to do himself; I, who desired to make his life as easy as possible in practical terms (and as gratifying as possible in all respects); I, who desired to leave Professor Baussan's time and mind free to pursue his scholarly work, spared small obligations and nagging annoyances, I, I, I let him bring me aspirin; I let him pour water; I let him offer me tablets. I let him wait on me.

Professor Baussan and I talked. He said, "I gather you found the place okay." I nodded and said, "It's quite a house." He talked about the house. He said that he'd lived in it "a long time," "longer than I care to think." I began something dismissive like, "It can't have been that long," but stopped short, seeing Professor Baussan's eyes; their sobriety stayed me. He said, "Excuse my bluntness, Edward. But. May I ask? How old are you?" Fearing his response, I said, "Twenty-three. Almost." I would turn twenty-three in a few days. Professor Baussan intoned, as if the thought plagued him, "I'm twenty years older than you are, Edward. Twenty years." I said, "I don't care. It doesn't matter. What does age matter? It doesn't." Professor Baussan touched my arm (saying "Enough"?). Half to himself, he muttered, "It could be worse. You look younger." Whatever he meant by "it," I thrilled unutterably.

Professor Baussan soon asked if I "felt up" to meeting someone. I asked, cringing at the prospect, "Not another student?" Professor Baussan said, "No, no, no." He said, "Herman's an old friend." By "old friend," I understood lover or past lover. I felt that Professor Baussan, like the god Krishna, could multiply himself among countless lovers and leave all of them feeling singularly requited. We left the kitchen. Walking through the dining room, Professor Baussan said, "I should warn you. Herman's a bit of a joker." I barely noticed the dining room. I barely noticed the entry beyond the dining room. I barely noticed the living room beyond the entry. I did notice a gaping, black fireplace set in craggy stonework in the living room's far wall. I did notice a grand piano, hard, prominent, and reflective in its shiny black (as opposed to the softly black, sooty, recessed, and not reflective fireplace). I did notice a chess set on a table, the small spires erect in unbroken ranks on a brown-and-blond-wooden board. (The black chess pieces had the same neatness, the same clarity of form—each on its small, square, wooden floor on the board—as did the piano, its black feet in transparent casters on the light-colored, highly polished oak.) I did notice the man seated at the piano. His face reminded me pleasantly of William Blake's drawing, *The Ghost of a Flea*. A unifying curvature carried his features; none projected far; what hair he had lay close to his head and far back on his scalp. We entered. The man whirled himself around on the tufted black bench-like seat at the piano, sprang to his feet, and exclaimed, "Now I can see what kept you so long." Professor Baussan glanced at me as if he would say, "I warned you." Herman Kuprin, introduced as teaching "piano" at the Music School, took my extended hand and made absurdly much of it, saying, as if imploring some cruel power above, "Why, oh, why was I not blessed with fingers like these? My life would have been so much easier." Professor Baussan replied placidly, "You do perfectly well with the ones you've got." When Mr. Kuprin finally released my hand (as if parting with his dearest possession), he told me "to remember" him if I ever considered "changing careers." An undertone of sexual invitation shocked me. But my father's word, "career," coming from the sly twist of Mr. Kuprin's almost lipless mouth, didn't sting; it flattered me with an unjustified assumption.

Before I'd entered the kitchen that evening, before I'd desperately thrown myself at Professor Baussan, I'd heard music and voices. I'd benefited from imagining, on the basis of a few hints, people living lives in accordance with their gifts. A sense of a calm, bourgeois solidity born of balance between work and domestic life had wafted into my mind as if carried by the chilled, air-conditioned air, as if reflected from the flooring's hardwood. I might have set foot in the house, but I didn't conceive of joining the life that I imagined—in the most spaciously vacant of outlines—as animating it. In retrospect, I suppose that I longed selfishly for people older than I to come along and help me out of my problems. I longed for the benefits of other people's attainments. But although I would doubt myself—down to the ground—on those points, although I would doubt myself as conniving and parasitical, as meanly manipulative (behind my own back), I also tasted a saving and a contradictory honesty: I did not doubt that I loved, with all the irrational force of love, my unknown savior, Professor Baussan. Whatever the lowness of my ulterior motives, a selfless ultimate drove me. Then too, of course, I jumped to conclusions. When Professor Baussan introduced me to Mr. Kuprin, I felt introduced to the world sensed at the top of the stairs. I felt that I had gained, in extraordinarily short order, not one friend, but two. I felt extraordinarily welcomed, extraordinarily accepted—on the basis of nothing—into two men's lives.

An extraordinary plural bathed me. *We* went out, onto the balcony. Professor Baussan stopped almost opposite the door. He set his forearms against the balcony's upper edge. His hands dangled, almost within one another. "Good turnout," he said, observing the party below. "Last year, almost no one brought food. We had to order pizza." Mr. Kuprin, standing, not leaning, to Professor Baussan's left, groaned. Professor Baussan turned his head to look at Mr. Kuprin. I felt as if I dreamed, seizing the soft emergence of Professor Baussan's lost profile.

I later wondered if the double dose of strong aspirin had actually drugged me, if it had actually interfered with my perceptions. I felt blinded to all beyond Professor Baussan's presence, and yet I saw and talked and functioned—as if part of the (apparently) normal. Professor Baussan joked about not needing but wanting "a bite to eat." We walked along the balcony, toward the steps. Mr. Kuprin followed Professor Baussan and me. Remembering the ease and the pleasure with which Professor Baussan had talked about his house while in the kitchen, I asked of the balcony, "This is cantilevered?" The moving—living, breathing—marvel beside me replied, "It is indeed." We walked into the very corner of all corners, into the furthest jut that the house threw from itself. Pointing to the neat, straight sequence of angles formed by the meeting ends of floorboards where the balcony turned with the corner of the house, Professor Baussan said, "There's an I-beam right under here. It runs back, into that," the massive chimney. Despite the gaps between the floorboards, we did not walk on air. We stood on solids. We talked about solids. Yet something dazzling—in the moment and in prospect— made me oblivious to solidity.

We went down the balcony steps and into the yard. Professor Baussan introduced me to more people than I could remember. In the dusk and in the darkness lit by starry lamps, Professor Baussan looked silvery, as in the low, occluded lights of Room 203. He acted as if intrigued and as if pleased by everything in existence. He laughed softly, often. I felt astonished that Professor Baussan said ordinary things to me like, "If you would go help Herman, over there, I'll find us some chairs." "Over there" meant at the serving table, but I did not understand what Professor Baussan meant by "help Herman." Smiling as if some joke awaited me, Professor Baussan said, "Oh, just answer his questions. He'll have questions, Herman will." Mr. Kuprin did. An expression of charming befuddlement suffused his features as I approached. Gesturing over the table, over candles in netted globes, wrecked casseroles, and deranged salads, he said, "I'm at a loss here. What would you recommend?" I said, "I really can't say." Mr. Kuprin looked as if he could lap up modesty for lunch. He said, "Ah, well. Perhaps you could tell me. Does *that* have a name?" He nodded toward a taco salad as if trying to keep the salad from noticing his nod. Someone, I thought, had expended considerable effort on the once-layered dish. Delved helpings had mixed and spread and obscured its layers. Mr. Kuprin had acutely chosen to question me about the very worst-looking mixture among the many on offer. I said, "Uh. That's. Taco salad." "What would you venture to say is in it?" he inquired. He looked up with a truly impish smile. (How did a lack of seriousness enter into pinched eyelids?) Mr. Kuprin didn't care about what went into taco salad. I soberly named every visible ingredient. Guacamole raised eyebrows. In response to questions, I blundered through disclaimers; I did not know anything about "Tex-Mex" food. "Texas. Texas," Mr. Kuprin intoned, as if trying to recall having heard of the place. Finally leaving the poor wreck of sour cream and shredded lettuce behind, Mr. Kuprin inquired into the "national origins" of several other dishes. He pointed toward a bowl of weeping cottage cheese containing chopped, black olives. He said, "This dotted mélange, now. Where would you say it is from?" I cracked. I laughed. I said, "Hell, I think." Mr. Kuprin lifted his chin and smiled as if finally satisfied: It takes you a while, but you catch on. Eventually, mincingly, he put food onto a plate.

We rejoined Professor Baussan, who sat as if lying in—as if poured into—a deep, black, canvas sling chair. (I later learned that he owned the chair, that its supporting framework folded, and that Professor Baussan usually stored the chair in a closet.) Seeing Mr. Kuprin and me, Professor Baussan bayed, "Am I glad to see you. I can't get out of this thing." He looked so stunningly beautiful, pooled in and overflowing from the curved thing of curves—from the chair's deep concavity, which rose in four parabolas around his body as if flowering—that I stared transfixed, holding the sight, one of life's small miracles momentarily manifest. When I recalled with incredulous joy that I might actually get to know Professor Baussan, I virtually swooped into kneeling beside him. I asked quietly if I might bring him "a plate," "that 'bite to eat' you wanted." Professor Baussan looked at me (as if more than contented). He said, "Thank you. That would be great."

I felt consumed with a mission: doing Professor Baussan a service for the first time outside of a classroom. While I put together a plate of samplings, Dana came up to me. In one hand she held a short clear-plastic cup dark with wine. She held it at an uneven angle. She looked down. The foremost strands of the long hair framing her inclined, shadowy face looked threaded with fire, reflected candlelight. I said hello. Dana looked up and tossed her head. (Competitive Christine, who unjustifiably considered herself plain, would have hated Dana on sight for Dana's even, soft-looking, unfreckled complexion; for the curvatures of Dana's cheekbones; for the flow of Dana's profile; for the very length of Dana's nose with its lilt of painless break; for the amplitude of Dana's eyes edged in extended, low S-bends laden with lashes naturally darker and longer than Christine's; for the unspeakable harmony between the rimming curves of Dana's eyelids and Dana's lips' outer edges; for the seeming repetition of those curves in undulant order, over and over, throughout Dana's long, dark, thick, luxuriant hair; for Dana's height and figure.) Dana said, without greeting, "You're the reason he's so happy tonight." I froze, rabbit-like. Dana patted my plate-bearing arm with the hand not holding the wine cup. I said nothing while she told me that she'd known "Lawrence," Professor Baussan, "a long time." She said that she wanted me to know something. I feared some awful revelation. But Dana just patted my arm again and said confidingly, "You're just his type. Type of his type. You should know that." I wanted to run away. I did not want to stay to hear how many "types" of Professor Baussan's "type" Dana had seen come and go. Unwisely, defensively, I replied, "You're my brother's type. I wish you could meet him. Forget that I said that." I virtually ran away, carrying Professor Baussan's plate. In taking his servings, I'd tried to spare nothing—except a look of ridiculous excess.

I brought Professor Baussan and Mr. Kuprin wine in short clear-plastic glasses. Mr. Kuprin raised his glass. He tried to find light against which to view its contents. Professor Baussan, eating, sitting up as much as the hammock-chair allowed, told him companionably, "Don't worry, old chum. You won't like it one bit." We talked and ate. What disturbance Dana had caused me subsided. Calm in bliss, but with headache recurring, I began to think about the conclusion of the party. (Where did the numerous folding chairs belong? They looked rented. Would someone sort the trash, glass from plastic, for recycling? Assuming that the potluck dishes left with their makers, would someone clean the plastic tablecloths? And what about the tables?) I asked Professor Baussan about the cleanup. He gestured generously, said, "You'd be surprised how quickly it goes." Like everything. Professor Baussan said something equanimous about letting "them," the lingering Seekford Association members, "take care of it." He sounded indolent, contented, content to sit and to talk. We talked. I finally asked him when I might see him again. He looked around as if startled. He said, "You're not leaving, now?" I said, "Yes." And I daringly asked him, "May I see you tomorrow?" Gazing at his face barely visible in the darkness, I told Professor Baussan that I'd seen a chess set in his living room and that, if he liked, we could "get to know each other better" "that way" (with a chessboard between us, I didn't quite say). He looked surprised and not entirely pleased. But, with a familiar gesture, he motioned to me to help him out of his chair. I helped. I felt his weight: thrillingly bodily.

63   CHESS AS BARRICADE

I suggested playing chess to Professor Baussan for many reasons; reasons ramified in my mind like a rational tree. Although I loved Professor Baussan, I needed to become acquainted with him before we touched bodily, as I assumed we would do. I supposed that he had many reasons to proceed cautiously with me. (I had, after all, burst into his kitchen, raving, "I love you," "I love you," like a crazy person. I needed to prove myself sane and trustworthy in his eyes. I needed to assure Professor Baussan, by my behavior, that we might touch, that we might proceed to touch each other's bodies, without my flying off the handle, without my wildly accusing him of sexual misconduct.) Professor Baussan and I had hastily expressed a lively interest in each other. I supposed that he might take alarm at the hastiness that we had already exhibited. I thought that he might repent in my absence, after I left the potluck party, of having acted so fool-heartedly as to encourage me to the extent that he had done. He had given me an inch, a very warm inch, admittedly; he'd given me an inch of encouragement, and I had run with it for miles—to life-altering assumptions: I would love him forever; I would serve his every whim with ardor; I would satisfy him as none of his previous partners had ever satisfied him; we would live together in sexual bliss and domestic felicity for decades; I would outlive him. Perhaps he had good reason to doubt my sanity. I rushed to glue myself to his ample side.

Professor Baussan, of course, did not know, on the night of the potluck party, the scope of my desire. He had had, by then, only a very small taste of my raving wisdom, of my driven love, of my ambition to enter his life (for his own good, of course, before my evident own). Professor Baussan might well think me reckless, impetuous, passionate, and misguided, as likely to come to grief, to wreck through frustration upon his staid routines. (Of course, Professor Baussan impressed me favorably as a rock, as a potential anchor, as a source of much-needed stability and support. I felt ashamed of the self-seekingness obvious in my desires. But self-seekingness aside.) What better way to prove myself a quiet, reliable, considerate, reasonably intelligent person than to sit in contemplation of chess pieces, patently exhibiting forethought and cognizance of possible consequences, for hours? What better way to spend time together without relying upon words to introduce us to each other?

I suggested to Professor Baussan that we play chess for reasonable reasons. But beneath my reasons, at the root of my reasonable tree, lay something that might seem neurotic and unreasonable. I feared sex. I even feared sex with Professor Baussan, whom I rushed to love, Professor Baussan whom I desirously viewed as a stupendous partner. My skittishness about shared sex derived, in part, I thought, from Estelle's influence upon me. I jokingly told Professor Baussan later, during one of our many talks following chess, that I had grown up "under a nineteenth-century stone," like a grub afraid of contemporary light. Estelle had raised me, and Estelle had never married; Estelle had surely never had a lover, and probably had never deliberately thrilled herself sexually. Burke had called Estelle unkindly, behind her back, "the absolute virgin." While I had stood quietly by like a little white sheep, Burke had, black-ram-like, battled Estelle. He'd tried, by words, by sustained argument, to savage her religion for its repressive rules, and he'd scandalized Estelle morally by, in Estelle's prim word, "consorting" with Christine. That stiff, that condemnatory opinion, that Burke and Chris "consorted," had grown in Estelle's mind, as far as I knew, from one instance, from Estelle's once having seen Burke and Christine kiss in public. Estelle actually said sharply to me, "I don't want you turning out like your brother." She judged Burke as having "turned out" badly when he hadn't "turned out" at all, before he'd finished college. And, to my knowledge, only Estelle condemned him. She condemned his very intelligence, "too smart for his own good." I had enough sense not to respect that opinion.

Estelle stood alone as the only Christian in my family, as the only puritan with any trace of a relationship to the capital P, Puritan. But even Burke and my father, good atheists both and self-proclaimed political liberals, even they impressed me as rigid and unforgiving puritans when it came to gay sex. So why didn't I feel guilty living among them, sitting there mum as a shut oyster around my big, fabulously valuable, pearl-like secret (probably no secret at all)? I knew that I had lusted for men ever since I lusted. I would lie in the book-lined room called Burke's study, under the narrow room's walls packed with published sermons, under walls packed with books that had belonged to my grandfather's grand-father; I would lie there in the valley of the shadow of bookcases and masturbate luxuriantly to imaginings of men ever receptive to me while the books frowned down with their faded spines, while a 1950s edition of the *Encyclopædia Britannica* gleamed with little thistle-like designs impressed in false gold upon and along its numerous black spines. I shuddered wonderfully, thinking, "Someday," "Someday." Someday the chesterfield sofa under me, the soft, soft, soft barge of buttoned-down bloats, would become an ample, masculine lover. I did not solely dream of full-bodied men, but full-bodied men predominated, in my mind, as desired figures. I dreamed and I dreamed. I dreamed, masturbating, of spacious figures in a narrow room, of massive, soft figures, all sensual liberation.

Did I behave as I did because I feared having shared sex? Did I fear having shared sex because I behaved as I did? I did not believe, as Estelle did believe, in the inherent sinfulness of people. I disliked the whole notion of the division of people into one thing called a body and another thing called a soul. I believed no aspect or element of any creature immortal. I did not think that knowing that one faced sure obliteration dimmed any of the wonder of all natural existence. But despite those far departures from Estelle's beliefs, others of hers stuck. I felt ruled by the conservative conviction that love and sex went together, that if one had sex with a partner, one should absolutely love that partner. I internalized an idea of desire as lust transformed through its infusion with emotion; great caring for another person changed rude lust into lucent desire. I suspected that libidinous energy generated some forms of love, but the puritan in me balked at giving flesh and blood that exalting credit.

Growing up, I did not want to lose Estelle's love. I did not want to offend her or to grieve her. I did not want her sorrowing for my so-called soul the way that she sorrowed for the same posited particles of Burke and my father. But I shared, I worshipfully drank in Burke's patiently explained and simply phrased postulates, high among which ranked: Don't complicate matters. Don't think that all things happen for a reason known only to a directive divinity; don't pile cause upon cause needlessly, in offense to reason. Estelle had just as much cause to despair of me for intellectual reasons as she did to despair of my other two mentors. But in my case, strangely, Estelle ignored their reign over my impressionable mind. Nonetheless, I feared that she would condemn, and that she would not forgive, me if I so much as declared myself gay. I did not condemn myself for what I embraced as my inherent nature, but I deeply feared condemnation by Estelle. If a mere statement would at least grieve if not completely alienate her, how much more would knowledge of an active, gay life—with an actual partner or partners, as opposed to imagined ones—grieve and offend? That she need not know what I did in the world beyond the preachy confines of Burke's study didn't embolden me to leave that book-lined den.

My grandmotherly but virginal great-aunt-of-a-mother thus formed, as a weight on my conscience, the "nineteenth-century stone" of which I complained to Professor Baussan in one of our many talks after chess. Professor Baussan kindly tried to avoid embarrassing me, yet he clearly enjoyed asking questions, probing my inhibitions, contemplating that entrancing—not-to-him-repelling—inexperience of shared sex which he couldn't restrain himself from labeling—as if a prize, not a pain—my virginity. He asked therapeutic questions, and so I spoke about Estelle and about my father, an on-again, off-again disciplinarian who cared more for the surface calm of family life than he did for honesty. I had feared grieving Estelle; I had feared merely irritating my father, a moody person capable of snapping at anyone (Estelle excepted) for minuscule disruptions such as dropping a fork, a man prompt with sharp, brusque, pointed little demands: Sit up straight; don't mumble; tuck in your shirt. My father merely tyrannized me in his exacting moods. He wanted no form of "trouble," and I imagined an active sex life for myself as fraught with potential trouble. I didn't want to take risks; I didn't want to court danger; I didn't have the courage to attempt to have a relationship as long as I felt the heavy hand of paternal rule. And, justifiably or not, I sensed that parental oversight while in college. I felt pathetically committed, if not addicted, to solitary sex until after Estelle died, and until I realized that I had to cease obeying my father as a child might obey.

I also told Professor Baussan about a whole different ballgame, my central ballgame, or rather I spoke about the high wall around my garden, art. I told Professor Baussan (without uttering the qualification, "until I met him") that I felt that I lived most vividly when actually alone or when my mind shut out surrounding people, when I concentrated upon the productions of my hands given materials like pencils and brushes, etching needles and engraving burins. I lived best alone, in the sight of my making, without knowing that *I* made, while following, or allowing, the making of "works on paper." In that blissful solitude, lacking consciousness of self, I experienced relaxation and gratification, the benefit of which could carry over into life among people. But because I disliked distractions (and became distracted easily) and because I felt irked unreasonably by interruptions, ungenerous with my time, and hostile to most external demands, I usually tried to keep people at a distance. Meeting Professor Baussan utterly confused—with new bliss— that self-centered compass.

Until I met Professor Baussan, I had feared giving up time to another. I had feared giving up some peace of mind, peace like uninhabited space, to the consideration of someone other than myself. Those fears vanished in my newfound desire. But learning that Professor Baussan and I might well meet as lovers forced me to confront another fear, bodily fear, not the fear of offending, not the fear of alienating love, not the fear of barked reprimands from an inconsistent disciplinarian, but fear of the deep degree of touch entailed in sex. (Ashamed of the euphemism, I called sex "intimacy.") I rarely touched even dressed people; I rarely felt them touch me. I felt deeply unprepared for the fearfully strange: contact with a naked person, bare genitalia involved. I swam laps for exercise; I felt at ease wearing little in public, yet I felt very shy of full disclosure even to the kind eyes and mind of Professor Baussan. I feared openness, opening; I feared sharing my body.

64   FIRST CHESS

In Mexico, the summer before I turned thirteen, I endured a bad fever. During it, my life became my body's life, suffering; I felt terribly plagued by my terrible body. Then one day I awoke, my body's hold broken. I could see, beyond fever dreams and hallucinations, the stark, solid hotel room that I shared with Burke. The immobility of furniture seemed wonderful; the freedom of things from suffering seemed wonderful; I saw without having to endure the seeing. And there, across the room, on a very even-looking, perfectly well-made bed, on a bed tautly wrapped in a drab blanket and barred with a white band of turned-back sheet at one end, my brother sat cross-legged, facing me but looking downward, into an assemblage of objects: a flat board supporting small knobs separable from the board. He held a parted book in his left hand. He looked from the book to the board-and-bobs in front of him. With his right hand, he moved one of the knobs on the board. He studied the result. He looked alive with bright thought, as if free of body.

Following my recovery, my parents, Estelle, Burke, and I moved from hotel rooms in a city to a pension in a small town. I loved—I greatly enjoyed—the place. Our rooms opened onto flower-lined courtyards: bougainvillea in magenta banks against turquoise walls and walls powerfully orange with flowering trumpet vine. A tiled fountain with ceramic frogs around its rim occupied one courtyard, a mosaic-lined swimming pool another.

I loved the colors—colors upon colors—the like of which I'd never seen before, or never seen before in such profusion. I loved—I greatly enjoyed—touching and seeing the chocolate-smooth, tiled floors. I enjoyed swimming underwater, eyes open, close to the pool's fantastic mosaics. I enjoyed seeing and feeding the frog-rimmed fountain's fan-tailed goldfish. (They smacked at bread-sticks, which I held in the fountain water for their crowding mouths to devour.) I loved the place—and even its proprietary people, who impressed me as extremely kind. But despite living for two weeks in an inexpensive garden of earthly delights, I spent much time ignoring it. I began learning to play chess from a ready teacher, Burke, who otherwise, as far as I could tell, spent most of his time reading. The sight of Burke studying a chessboard, when I'd awakened free of fever, had inspired me with an unrealistic, untenable idea: by playing a cogitative game, one could escape one's body. Seeing Burke reading might have suggested the same, but chess, as an unknown quantity, attracted me then as anti-corporeal.

Burke began teaching me chess. He called it "stylized warfare." He said that aside from the kings and queens, the pieces represented "the four wings" of ancient Indian armies. Bishops represented "war elephants," the pawns, "foot soldiers;" queens originated as "viziers," ministers of state. I learned that much reluctantly. I wanted to think of chess games not as wars or as battles, but as cities consisting of sheer planes of thought—immaterial, but much like the wind chime I'd once received as a gift, all glassy panes suspended tier upon tier. I disdained Burke's historical informa-tion. Gross, human failures—war, slaughter—and the base, conniving cunning of trying to gain advantage over an opponent had nothing to do with the games of my dreams. Despite Burke's talk of "stylized warfare," actual games of chess, as I learned to play them (after a fashion), actually satisfied my desire to exercise reason, to practice reasoning. I embraced reason: small defense against enormous life.

During my fever I had seen, or I'd thought that I'd seen, a vast pregnant woman washing the floor near my bed on her hands and knees. As in the cliché, she labored barefoot. Abundant fabric, skirt and blouse, covered her body, fabric printed with red-green hibiscus and fabric printed with blue-yellow parrots. She moved a galvanized-tin bucket of water beside her as she moved. Its handle rattled; its base scraped the floor. Sometimes she reared, like a walking house fly, up from her crawl, above knees planted and spread wide on a drab folded towel. She rinsed a cloth in the bucket-held water. She waved the wet cloth spread between her two hands. She slapped the spread cloth against the red-clay-tiled floor. The cloth circled, in circling folds, around her circling hand. Flesh on her working arm circulated; her fecund breasts swayed. Her body filled me with repulsion for bodily processes. Blaring hibiscus and screaming parrots covered the body of bodily Earth.

65 BURKE'S CHESS SET

Burke taught me the little I knew about chess. He showed me moves and taught me rules. He taught me to see the chess pieces as possessing powers invested in them by rules. He made chess-boards come alive with forces. He tried to teach me to see implications of implications of implications of moves. And ever welcoming Burke's company, ever welcoming Burke's attention, I desired to learn to play well enough to interest him. For my first lessons, in Mexico, we used a chess set which Burke disliked. He'd bought it indiscriminately in a little shop. "It was the only one they had," he growled. He hadn't looked further. The pieces, all knobs and points of lathe-turned wood, looked elaborate in shape and elaborate in decoration. Someone had decorated each piece—unremittingly—with knife nicks and incised bands, cutting through black paint to pale wood and through transparent varnish to the same. The black pieces looked lacy with flowery sprays, flecks, and rings. The same patterns on the pale pieces looked much less conspicuous. A bit of plastic, imitating ivory, topped every piece. "This is *not* what a chess set should look like," Burke announced. Thus, from the beginning of my experience of chess, an idea hovered over the material pieces: my idea of Burke's idea of what a chess set "should look like."

That chess set, which Burke disliked for its cheap plastic fake-ivory tips, teeth, and crowns, for its flowery, hand-gouged ornateness, and for its lathe-turned, individually-made, whimsical shapes, possessed a real flaw: incompleteness. It lacked a light-colored pawn. That fault appealed to me as an unworldly absence. The lack of a pawn bothered Burke. He substituted a fifty-centavo coin for the pawn-beyond-all-pawns. Teaching me, Burke would point to the coin and say, "That's a pawn, remember." I remembered. The coin-pawn came back to haunt me. The summer that Burke and I traveled together to Turkey, he produced a portable chess set. He unfolded it before me. I saw nothing but disks: little checker-like plastic pieces. The disks covered magnets by which they stuck to the board. The disks bore emblems of chess pieces, little plastic appliqués barely thicker than emblems in printed diagrams. Red disks bore white emblems; white disks bore black. Seeing the board and the emblems with their disks for the first time, I felt dismay. I felt uneasy. I felt pushed toward abstraction against my will. Burke saw my dismay. He said sweetly, coercively, "Don't worry. You'll get used to it. You'll see." I felt like reminding Burke of his old snobbery, of his old prejudice, about what a chess set "should look like."

Traveling, Burke and I played with that set for hours (for weeks, for months). I missed towers; I missed sculptures; I missed the third dimension all but squeezed out of Burke's extremely flat set. I wondered if I would ever become accustomed to the thing. The set possessed an intrinsic element that I strongly disliked. I disliked the little red disks abidingly. I wanted to think of chess as a reasonable game. And there the red disks lay—magnetically stuck to the board—clustered below my inclined face. The red disks reminded me, and the red disks reminded me. They reminded me unreasonably. They reminded me of unreason. They reminded me of drops of my blood seen—on bright yellow leaves—after Burke hit me out of grief over Chris.

66 TOMATO, MELON

Traveling with Burke in Turkey, I admired the produce in produce shops. I especially admired the banked displays outside the shops: produce used to advertise itself through beauty, bounty, freshness, and color. The displays usually looked unarranged, and even obvious arrangements looked natural. A cut melon might sit on a ledge in the open air, the removed wedge horizontal to the vertical wound in the whole fruit. Tomatoes might alternate with cucumbers, red-green, red-green, side by side, long-short, long-short. Seeing one such arrangement, I stopped Burke, who would have walked past it: an evenly dark-green watermelon the size and shape of a bowling ball sat with a golf-ball-sized tomato balanced on top of it. The arrangement looked ridiculous, as if the melon possessed some sort of dignity violated by wearing a topknot. Dignity and the lack of dignity in melons struck me as funny, but I told Burke seriously, "Those are very well balanced." "How do you mean?" he grumbled. I said, "That much green to that much red, that much cool, that much warm." Burke frowned as he usually frowned when something that I said didn't make sense to him. Talk of "warm" and "cool" colors made sense. But, fearing that Burke would dismiss my actual response to the tomato-and-melon combination, I did not tell him that, in the coloristic "balance" that I did discuss, I saw a metaphor for mental balance. Seeing the tomato-watermelon combination, I thought: the green fund of sweet reason, represented by the watermelon, needed its great size, vis-à-vis the tomato, to offset unreason.

67   TILES

Traveling, Burke and I got caught in rain in Istanbul. Running, we entered a small, empty restaurant, its emptiness very unusual. Burke sat down; I fell into a chair, badly winded, soaking wet. Touched by the table in front of me, a small, roughly-made table with turquoise-painted legs, I began laughing. Greasy-feeling, extremely slick, filmy material covered the table. The stuff had Delft tiles printed on it. Delft-tile-like patterns covered a table in Istanbul, a juxtaposition hilarious only if you'd just seen mosque after mosque, huge beautiful Ottoman mosques all lined with tiles: flat, floral stylizations many of them, patterns which didn't stop, completed within each tile, but which spread from tile to tile, each tile repeating the pattern of contiguous tiles, tiles meeting edge to edge and meeting with their matching patterns to form overall patterns, patterns which seemed to go on forever, glorious in abstract beauty, covering walls gloriously to the glory of God. The tile-like prints in front of me looked intensely domestic. They didn't aspire to glorify anybody's All-Mighty. Each picture in each tile print (some sticking to my wet arm with their oily surface) looked complete in and of itself; each looked separate from the others, as if framed by its depicted edges. I felt that the little pictures covering the tabletop breathed love of pictures, breathed love of painting. I felt that the prints reflected a tradition embracing Rembrandt and Vermeer. (Surely I imagined some of that, seeing in one tile imitation a flock of Vs, meaning birds, against curves, meaning clouds.) Seeing the tile prints, I felt welcomed by representation, welcomed by fullness, welcomed by illusions of three dimensions. I had felt oppressed; I had felt afflicted; I had felt as if personally stifled by a Moslem prohibition that forbade the depiction of any living thing, flowers alone excepted. (As I understood it, Ottoman custom permitted the depiction of flowers provided that one did not depict them naturalistically. Rendered abstractly, on tiles, flowers became flat, curvaceous, beauteous essences based on a few petals' shapes.)

So I sprawled, laughing, feeling relief from flatness despite Delft tiles' flatness and that—flatness—present in their imitations. Sensing Burke's discomfiture—more disapproval than worry induced by my behavior—I sat up. Tapping one of the prints, I told Burke, "These tiles. Are being. Disloyal." I stopped laughing, not because Burke facially ordered me to do so, but because I saw flypaper near the window facing the street, beyond Burke: a long, pendent, horn-yellow rectangle blackened with flies. The room revolved. I heard Burke say, "You okay?" I replied, eyes closed, "I will be—in a moment." The slow tumble ceased. I opened my eyes, saw earnest Burke looking dangerously comic: soaking wet, soaking serious. Burke's hair gathered into dripping points across his forehead; his white shirt stuck to his skin transparently in patches. Burke said, "Okay now?" I nodded. Burke lectured. He said, "It might help if you would eat something." I asked to see "our" shared backpack, a small, peacock-blue, nylon backpack with black straps and black zippers. Water-beaded, it hung off the back of Burke's chair like a raincoat for a ham just then removed. Burke, ever guardian and sternly supervisory, said, "What do you want out of it." He didn't ask. I said, "Aspirin. I have a headache." I did. Burke unhitched the dripping pack and handed it around the table to me. I dug cigarettes and matches out of it. Burke said, "I thought you said you had a headache." I said, "And so I do," in a tone that said, "Shut up, Burke."

We sat. We sat in the unusually empty one-room restaurant. I did not touch the cigarettes. I thought better of doing what I usually did with cigarettes, watch the smoke, given Burke's mood. A man who served as waiter appeared, dressed as a butcher, with gory apron frontally tied, strings barely long enough to reach around his corpulent middle. Burke looked agreeably at the man's face, pronounced a Turkish greeting agreeably, and said something brief in German while gesturing self-deprecatingly toward the out-of-doors. The man spoke a greeting and more in German. He seemed affable and ill, sick with some chronic ailment that affected his voice and his breathing. The man swung to my right, returned, set a tin can near my elbow, a goldenly-lined, low tin can, label-less, odorless; the can suggested packed tuna fish. The can had a golden, concentrically rippled, circular bottom. After more chat in German incomprehensible to me, Burke ordered two of something. The man withdrew. I studied the tin can. I looked from the can to Burke. I asked him silently, "What is this for?" And Burke told me gently, with a spoken word, and as if burdened with the never-ending task of explaining the world to me, "Ashtray."

We sat. Rain slated past the window beyond Burke; heavy rain dashed a narrow street. I did not light a cigarette. The flypaper hung, treacherous paper, fatal paper, paper thick with black death. The walls looked dimly glossy, turquoise-painted to shoulder height, cream-colored above that, with the turquoise painted onto the cream, the turquoise uneven due to the wall's texture where it ceased against cream. Evening seeped into the room. I asked Burke, "What did you order?" Burke replied seriously, potentially hilariously, "Water." "All this rain, and you order water?" I asked incredulously, verging on laughing again. Burke frowned; he didn't reply. I heard ringing sounds, glassy, not crystalline notes. I turned to see their source: the man who served as waiter approached. He carried clear-glass bottles, one in each hand's stocky grip. Inverted drinking glasses hung over the bottles' long necks, and the glasses swung without force, striking the bottles; dull music chimed to a swaying tread. Breathing with shallow breaths, rasping, the man set bottle and glass before Burke; Burke righted the glass. The man set bottle and glass before me, removed the hanging glass, and set the glass upright. I saw a wide, swollen-looking, blunt-looking hand, a thick golden ring on a finger that bulged around the barked gold unhealthfully. The man's breath rasped several breaths. I didn't look at him. The man stood beside me, breathing with portentous effort, bodily right beside me, and I acted as if I couldn't move a hair or a muscle. I acted that way because I found that man attractive, and I felt petrified before Burke, and afraid of myself. The man left us. The things he'd brought stood on the table, water bottles, glasses: tall, scratched clear-glass bottles, water in bottles under plain, dull, silvery thick-foil caps. The caps' edges rounded smoothly over the bottles' lipped rims. The bottles—heavily scratched, dulled by scratches everywhere, roughly recycled, standing among, not centered upon, the blue-and-white fake-Delft tiles on the table's square top—began to oppress me with thoughts of chess. I looked beyond Burke, out the window. Rain slanted. The air seemed scratched with flying scratches.

Had anyone told me then what my future held; had anyone told me truly then, when I sat with Burke, with an empty glass and an empty tin can, that in four years, three months, and some days, someone would change my life, that a beloved person would welcome me into his life, and that we would live together happily with no end in sight, with no term defined by that prediction; had anyone told me these things, I would have felt rapturous; I would have felt glad relief. I would have counted the time to come, the time to come before that meeting, as nothing. Four years, three months, and some days would have seemed nothing—given such a promise.

68　HOUSE DOOR

The day after the revelation of Professor Baussan's gayness, the day after I'd unwittingly solicited that declaration by my own declaration—by my raving "I love you," "I love you" in Professor Baussan's kitchen—I returned to his house. We'd agreed to play chess. My timidity about sex made me cling to the idea that we would simply play chess. (I'd confessed to Professor Baussan, "I need time—to learn to breathe in your presence." And he, with much at stake professionally, had reason upon reason to proceed cautiously. Professor Baussan had frowned at my first mention of chess. But he'd quickly come around to smiling, to agreeing that, yes, playing chess might, quietly and rightly, further our acquaintance.) The night of that agreement, after I'd left the party, incredulous joy had kept me awake. I'd tossed and turned joyously, incredulously, doubting the reality of what had occurred: Had Professor Baussan, the golden, the open, the Sun-like teacher, actually shown the liking for me that I thought that he'd shown? Sleeplessly, joyously—and shot through with joyously hollow doubts—I'd reviewed my memories of the previous evening, of Professor Baussan's turns and words and facial expressions. (Oh, the lowering of his eyelids when he spoke to me. Oh, the pricked attentiveness of his lifted eyebrows.) More soberly, I'd reviewed the circumstances that had brought about our meeting. I'd sleeplessly suspected, in joyous retrospect, that Mrs. Callender, who'd assigned me to show slides for Professor Baussan, and who, judging by her friendliness at the party, knew Professor Baussan well, had assigned me to show slides for him deliberately. (Did I have Professor Baussan's type written all over me?) I'd suspected, joyously, that Mrs. Callender had deliberately exposed me to Professor Baussan's view. "Thank you, Mrs. Callender," I'd mentally tolled. I'd tugged at the roots of my decision to find a job, and I'd touched upon the stunning coincidence, that I'd thrown myself at Professor Baussan just when I'd decided to assert my independence from my father. Had I rushed to attach myself to a provident man? "For shame, Edward," I'd happily condemned.

The desired day came. It rained; it turned sunny. I drove to Professor Baussan's house, parked, and set foot on his nubbly driveway. I smelled wet woods—damp earth, dripping trees— amid blazing sunlight. Thin shadows hugged the driveway's embedded lumps. A path bounded by railroad ties led, amid pines and much ivy, to the front door and stoop. Sand lined the path. Pine needles lay, matted in curved, linear drifts, on the sand. The path, strewn with the beauteous debris of insignificant and vanished torrents, widened gradually—with a subtlety that I wouldn't have expected from railroad ties—as it approached the stoop: one wide, concrete step and a wide, concrete platform. The platform and the step did their angled best to flow, like rapids, down into the path. Their low height contributed to the illusion of flow, but an eave's shadow lay across them, and the shadow's edge switched jaggedly, from perfectly vertical against poured-concrete verticals to sharply angled across hard horizontals. Where sunlit, the concrete glistened as if laced with mica. It also contained black grains, like the remains of a bonfire ground into wet sand. A coir doormat lay next to the door, the fibrous shag crushed, down-trodden, hard-used (past crying out against the exploitation and the poverty of people who made coir doormats). I rubbed my feet on it. A sizeable, unused clay flowerpot sat in an unused clay saucer on a back corner of the stoop. Forsythia bushes grew against the house. Water drops, falling from someplace, from somewhere beyond my interest, smacked as if they hit gravel. The drops smacked at peaceful intervals. Listening to the sounds with my eyes closed, I saw in mental darkness imagined flowers, small, bright-yellow, forsythia flowers: star-like bursts, yellow joy. Open-eyed, I absorbed the appearance of the front door's wooden grain. Although I had lamented the deaths of trees, the high number of trees killed, turned into the lumber used to build Professor Baussan's house, and although I had lamented, only the previous day, trees turned into lumber and trees felled on that lot to accommodate Professor Baussan's proud, high, mighty ark of a house, then, on the very brink of meeting him to play chess, I did not lament; I admired. I admired the oaken slab of the windowless door. Under transparent varnish, the grain of the door's constituent planks looked watery, as if the trees-become-planks had, while living, mapped rivers, currents, shorelines, and sandbars, curve within curve, in their very substance. Looking at the natural moiré, at the wood grain in front of me, with its concentric ripples surrounding islets, I wanted to think that trees knew something mystical, something nonsensically mystical, like where all rivers went, and that trees naturally recorded their knowledge in cellulose. I did not have religion. I did not believe in ultimate tendencies, in Providential plans. I did not believe that things happened because divinely ordained. Facing Professor Baussan's front door, I felt that no purpose, but rather that everything within me—plus a generous addition of chance, sheer luck—had led me to that door and moment, to the brink of meeting Professor Baussan alone for the first time, momentously. I remembered his bleak-looking, locked-looking, dark office door, the door with a curt card on it reading, "BY APPOINTMENT ONLY." I remembered the despondency I'd felt, reading that card. And there I stood, at the front door of Professor Baussan's very house. I knew that we would play chess; we would simply play chess. But I felt as if I had, not an appointment to see him, but an assignation.

69   CHESS, BENDING SQUARES

Standing outside Professor Baussan's front door, I did not immediately ring the doorbell. The doorbell's button, an off-white disk in a plain, brazen setting, reminded me of the white chess pieces in Burke's portable chess set. The button also reminded me of Burke's (hard, concussive) use of cue balls when shooting pool. Burke's illiberality on the point of gayness invaded the doorbell-disk. I hesitated before pressing it. Further, despite the riverine cartography imagined into the door's wooden grain, Professor Baussan's front door cautioned me, as his office door had cautioned, against self-delusion: You may think you know something about this person, but you really don't. I'd imagined Professor Baussan a family man, straight, unattainable as a lover by the likes of me. I'd gotten something important about him spectacularly wrong. Perhaps I knew nothing at all about his actual nature. I joyed and I cautioned: Tread carefully, fool. Fools rush in—onto slick, oaken floorboards. You broke your arm on a basketball court. Don't break your heart here.

I pressed the doorbell. Two notes floated away within the house. Water drops split. Water drops sounded as if they split glistening. Muffled approach sounded beyond the door. The door moved, came unstuck; Professor Baussan appeared in the opening, smiling more broadly than I'd ever seen him smile. He said something repeated and genial, like: Good to see you, good to see you; please, come in, come in. Taking my hand and shaking my forearm along with it, he towed me into the entry. He looked radiant, happy, and very well-groomed: buffed, clipped, burnished, scrubbed, brushed, and freshly shaven. He wore the same perforation-decorated wingtips that he'd worn the first day I'd seen him; pressed, khaki trousers; a pale yellow dress shirt; a softly thin, brown—caramel-colored—sweater buttoned up to his sternum with every button it possessed. Small, recessed handles in sliding doors to his right looked concavely golden while Professor Baussan's molars, exposed by his grin, looked goldenly convex. We looked at each other. He said, "I was afraid I was dreaming— there for a while." I said, "I had the same feeling." "But here you are," he announced. "And you," I breathed. He ushered me out of the entry (past a columnar statue of the Virgin Mary, wooden and veiled in ancient paint) into the living room. Brushing conventions aside, Professor Baussan offered me a drink, "a little early, I know, but," "but what would you like?" I virtually whispered, "Whatever you're having." Professor Baussan told me to have a seat and to make myself comfortable. Thus, told to stay put—in the living room—while he made drinks in the kitchen, I looked around the room. (Rafters slanted from a massive ridgepole, a beam one end of which rested, set, in the highest part of the stonework that formed the southern half of the far, western wall. Molding regularized the end of the stonework below the beam. A plate-glass window, cut at the top to match the rafters' angle, finished the western wall lightly, beyond the heavy stones. The room looked high and lodge-like; its silvery decoration looked softly palatial. Two baroque tapestries blanketed the two inner walls. The threaded soft blues, ochers, and old reds depicted, as a pair, Rubenesque entertainments in idyllic landscapes—one, a feast about which the participants sprawled amorously, the other, a dance of melting grace in which people amply, if distantly, gave themselves to each other. Furniture looked either glassy or gray—determined not to compete with the tapestries. How had I not noticed them the day before?) I saw the piano (sans Mr. Kuprin, closed). I saw the chess set glimpsed previously, the set unmoved from where I'd glimpsed it, on a long, low, narrow glass table parallel to a sofa in the windowed, northwestern corner of the room. Matching the silver-gray sofa with open arms, a chair sat near the chessboard but placed, with regard to the board, where no one seriously intending to play chess would sit. The chair, the sofa, and the table all looked lower in height than ideal for chess. I began to fear that Professor Baussan didn't actually play chess, that he'd deployed the chess set decoratively, a disturbing idea, but I need not have feared.

Professor Baussan returned, carrying glasses, one in each hand, with his hands raised a little unnaturally, the slight elevation suggesting care not to spill. The glasses glimmered with cut-glass facets, and ice cubes within them jarred their inner sides. The sounds grazed me with remembered lust: Professor Baussan, ponderous in buttoned-up cashmere, stepped through a remembered man in Turkey, through an ailing man who could barely breathe. Health and happiness gilded Professor Baussan. Extending a glimmering rock glass to me, he asked, "Scotch meet with your approval?" "Ah, lord," he sighed, "Neddy. Do you mind if I call you that?" "Neddy, I hate to think: This stuff's older than you are." "To hell with age," I replied. We clinked our glass rims together. (I thought a prodigious toast, unspoken: To health, happiness, long life. I will love you forever.) We simply said, "Cheers." Professor Baussan sank into the window-corner sofa as if he lived there (perhaps he did). "Oh, I'm sorry," he said, setting his drink aside, waving, "Move that chair if you like." Perhaps he gave me the choice, whether to play chess or not.

When Professor Baussan sat down, the cushion receiving his weight—one of three lining the sofa—bent beneath him. Clefts between it and the adjoining cushions didn't actually widen, but they—suggestively—suggested widening. Professor Baussan set his drink aside and sat back, gazing at me. He sat openly, his knees wide-spread. The chessboard sat on the inappropriately low table, near his knees, so near that he almost appeared to hold the board between them. The chessboard, the square-of-squares, looked sharp and hard and flat. It looked sharply hard with colors that, in Professor Baussan, looked soft and curved: flat walnut, in the board, simplified his eyes' brown; flat oak flattened his hair. I felt stunned by the sight. I'd begun to learn chess when revolted by bodies. And there, beyond the chessboard, sat a person in a body, a bodily person with whom I might (finally) feel free.

70 CHESS TO BED

Professor Baussan and I played chess. We met at his house; we played chess repeatedly. We talked before and after play. We spent two weeks in such ritual meetings, talking, playing chess, agreeing to meet again in a day or two to do the same again. We had dinners together, too, dinners at restaurants and dinners which Professor Baussan himself prepared. After one such, he played the piano in his living room and I, rapt, watched his stout figure bend toward the keys while something like passion abounding sounded. But mostly we played chess, calm, strict, temperate chess, chess with its long views of artificial futures, chess with its deliberate moves. In talk, I conveyed much of my life to Lawrence. ("Call me Lawrence," he said. Lawrence, not Larry, Lawrence, an abiding formality. In contrast and without precedent in my experience, Lawrence began calling me Neddy and Ned. "Mind if I call you that?" he asked; I could never object, never scotch his least whim.) Lawrence heard much about Estelle and her sepulchral silverware; much about studious Burke and horsy Christine; much about etching, engraving; much about my father's plans for my way of life. In turn, Professor Baussan talked about his Catholic schooling, about the persistence of its usefulness to him in his professional studies of medieval manuscripts in archives and rare book rooms. I learned that he faithlessly read Latin in many types of handwriting—insular majuscule, Visigothic minuscule—and that he studied so minutely the small works of anonymous artists who had illustrated or who had decorated ancient texts that he, Professor Baussan, might recognize the same style again when it appeared on another far-flung, distant, or otherwise disassociated page. I learned that Professor Baussan had an almost literal taste for works on vellum: he said that odor alone could suggest a manuscript's origin. Professor Baussan's field interested me and, listening to him and looking at what he showed me on his computer and in young books, I felt soothingly reproved, soothingly lectured against a belief, a grievous belief, contracted from my family, the belief that pictures had no place on the superior plane of words.

Professor Baussan and I played chess and played chess and talked. He talked about his work, his opinions of his colleagues, his positions on departmental issues. He talked about committee work expensive in time and energy, all the while giving me hours and hours, whole swathes of acres of his precious time. I began to sense the stringencies of his daily life and slowly, slowly, following the almost soundless steps of chess pieces reset from the air onto a hard, wooden board, we approached bed, sex with each other. I heard what Lawrence chose to tell me about what I primly called his "previous relationships." "Ah, Neddy," he said. A tolling recitation of "he left me" followed. One strip of a Charles left him for the sake of a job, one Mike for a different lover, one Louis ditto but with different reasons. One Matthew Cheviot actually died. "That was a long time ago," Lawrence mournfully mused. I ventured to touch his khaki-dressed thigh; I spread my right hand flat upon it; Lawrence covered my hand with his. I said that I had never had a lover beyond imagined ones. Professor Baussan's eyes widened. He stared at me. He asked a gauchely blunt question: "You're a virgin, Ned?"

I felt embarrassed because I liked to pretend to more sophistication, to more knowledge of the world, than the word "virgin" implied to me; I did not wish to bear a label different, but little different, from "ignorant." I also felt embarrassed because I felt obliged, then, to tell Professor Baussan that I'd fantasized and masturbated and had no sexual partner beyond myself and that, further, I'd almost entirely avoided all sexual touches—other than my own. I made my confession without looking at Lawrence. I felt afraid that he might regard me as a neurotic freak and that he would want to get rid of me, to end our acquaintance, then and there. But, although averted from him during my confession, I heard Lawrence; I heard assurances and nudging questions. And I sensed something amazing: What I said pleased Lawrence. He breathed shortly and when he spoke, he sounded peculiarly enraptured, happily incredulous, and positively desirous to believe me. "Is this true, Neddy? Neddy." "Of course, it's true." I felt like telling Lawrence, I try to lie only when politeness requires. Perhaps my discomfiture convinced him that I spoke truth. He paid me compliments in doubting me: "Someone as attractive as you," he murmured. I told him that I only felt glad that he found me attractive. I said that I couldn't explain my fear of sharing so much as nakedness, much less arousal. "But you would trust me?" Lawrence asked. I gladly recognized that, by that time, he would trust me not to ruin life.

And so it happened that the strangely, the patiently enraptured Professor Baussan led me literally—by one of my quaking hands—away from the chessboard and into his bedroom where an ample bed covered in a puffy, golden-brown duvet looked softly rectangular, definitely not square, definitely not hard, and definitely not like a parquet consisting of contrasting, wooden squares. That the duvet's filled pockets actually had square borders, borders defined by crossed lines of stitching, didn't destroy their air of very soft convexity.

71 ROBE

Lawrence held me around the shoulders as we walked down a hallway and into his bedroom. He talked calmly; I shivered. I whimpered apologies. He said, "Shh, shh, Neddy." He said that he knew "perfectly well" not to "expect wonders" from me. Although we'd hugged a few times, I'd never felt his body as I felt it then. "You good?" he asked. I said, "Yes" and "I'm sorry." He said, "Shh, shh" and "Just so you're all right." I assured him; he squeezed my shoulder. I felt bedded against him before we even lay down.

In his bedroom, in sunlight from windows apparently giving onto such deeply wooded privacy that Lawrence felt no need to close the long, rough, pale mealy-textured curtains which hung superabundantly (ends heaped on the floor), we undressed each other. Ironically, I thought, the strong, warm, confident Lawrence wore far more clothing than I did. I, who feared disclosure, wore nothing under my shirt while Lawrence, who seemed to fear nothing, wore a sweater, a dress shirt, and an undershirt. He stood deliberately still, arms slack at his sides, while I unbuttoned his sweater, untucked and unbuttoned his shirt. By the time that my shaking fingers had methodically slipped every one of his frontal buttons backwards, through its buttonhole; by the time that I'd finished maniacally addressing each button as a separate task, taking comfort in each ordinary act as an ordinary act, acting as if the progressive opening thus effected in Professor Baussan's clothing portended nothing out of the ordinary; by the time that

I'd completely parted the two layers which had concealed his undershirt, I felt that I understood something. Perhaps I read something into the undershirt, into the prim, white integument tight around Lawrence's waist and slack over his breasts. I felt that Lawrence hid, or would have liked to have hidden, the exact extent of his curved centrality. Sensing or imagining that Lawrence regretted his bodily shape, I slid my arms around him and buried my face in his belly. He made a snuffling sound as if amused; he twiddled locks of my hair.

Lawrence, leaning, with one hand spread flat against the top of a chest-of-drawers, let me divest his feet of hard shoes and soft socks. He leaned with that same hand on my back, steadying himself, while stepping out of his trousers, an awkward process which my prudish mind judged fraught with indignity. Holding his removed trousers before him as if he should not mistake them for any others, I asked, "Where should I put these?" Lawrence smiled mightily. He tipped his head toward a chair. I folded his trousers inseam to inseam and laid them carefully—without spilling the pockets—across the arm of one of two chairs flanking a table beside a window. I helped Lawrence off with his opened shirt as formally as a stranger might take a coat. I hung the shirt around the back of the pants-bearing chair. Lawrence then beckoned me to him literally. He said, "Neddy. Come here." Scared, although excited and moved by the sight of him, I neared. He looked strangely cherubic. The strong, warm light in the room, ambient where he stood, converted his body hair into a golden haze and he still looked fully dressed in two shades of white (shorts slightly more blue than the knit which enveloped his torso and the upper parts of his arms). Lawrence also looked younger than I'd ever seen him look, a benefit, perhaps, of the revelation of much perfect skin, skin which looked as if never tanned, never burned. Lawrence stretched his milky-golden arms toward me. I closed my eyes and walked into his embrace.

All went well enough from then on, with Lawrence heartily acting more like a normal person than I did. All went well enough.

We kissed and embraced. Lawrence, embracing, put his erection into it, an undergirding to his grip, which made me feel unhinged with fear and excitement. He grappled with my shirt, unbuttoning it impatiently, kissing my chest in the process, groaning, "My god, Ned. You're thin. You're even thinner than I thought." Making that statement, he happily, he rapturously forgot tact, thinness having positive import to his mind. When he, amid the pressing, the gripping, the kissing—all of which astounded me, seeing his big, golden head nuzzling below my chin, for example—when he began roughly undoing the buttons on my right-hand shirt cuff, I said timidly, "Estelle sewed those on." He groaned. Estelle had "set" the buttons "over" to improve the cuff's fit. Lawrence lavishly kissed the buttons, the little hearts on my sleeve.

All went well enough until, finally, both of us naked, I began shivering again. Lawrence inquired politely, "Would you like to lie down?" I shivered yes. He hurled the tobacco-golden, puffy-pocketed duvet halfway off his bed. The very grand gesture made a terrible wind. White sheets parted; I sat, crouched, barely on the bed. Lawrence sat, caressive, soothing, inquiring, beside me. I asked if he had "a bathrobe or something" that I could put on. He said, "Of course, of course." The bed shifted as he left it. I did not watch Lawrence, but I glimpsed him, turning away from the bed. I glimpsed his distended phallus. I glimpsed him as he returned from a closet, carrying gray-blue-red plaid, the red very retiring, two thin tracks of it of unequal widths threading only one edge of the dark, soft, powdery-looking cerulean stripes. Lawrence, sitting warmly behind me again, draped and pressed the bathrobe around me. And the robe affected me wonderfully. Because of the scents it carried, none strong, none definite, but all together indicative of everyday life, of Lawrence urinating, shaving, and applying deodorant perhaps, I imagined Lawrence as just out of bed, first thing on a cold, dark, winter morning, shaving, et cetera, preparing for a sexless workday made up of meetings, lectures, and research. The imagined glimpse suggested that, whatever I feared, I should not fear him. I turned toward him; we lay down. He seemed very pleased.

72   PLAID PATTERN

Few fabrics felt rigid, but to my mind most existed as grids, as warp and weft threads crossed, as sets of threads crossed, as sets of threads which, although bending, although rising, passing over, and diving beneath other threads as the sets interwove, remained, in my mind, not in fact, perpendicular to each other. Soft fabrics existed as bending systems. The deeply soft bathrobe that Lawrence Baussan draped over me when I crouched shivering on the edge of his bed, Lawrence's bathrobe, as fabric, bent as a threaded system. I did not consider its pattern; I did not consider the plaid's reds, blues, or grays, or the ways in which the colors, crossing systematically, as grids or as parts of grids, created checks and variations through the colors' combinations; I did not consider the mere pattern of colors in Lawrence's bathrobe until long after that first time, my true first time, that first time when Lawrence, contrary to my expectation, sustained his careful, his kind principle that whatever we did sexually, I, the cringing neophyte, I, the timid virgin, should take the assertive lead. I did not consider the grid-patterned colors in Lawrence's bathrobe until well after that time when, through my desire and through my desire to please Lawrence, I pleased him; I fulfilled his desire to feel desired.

I lived with Lawrence after that, after that first match of our desires. Lawrence invited me to live with him immediately, before we'd even left the bed. He said, "Stay, Neddy, uh. Please." I replied lightly, "You mean for supper?" He grinned, squeezed my haunch and rocked it. He said that I knew that he meant "for good." He lay facing me at length, his head braced against the heel of hand-on-bent-arm pillowed. Gazing from scrunched, smiling face, he said, "Hm? Neddy?"

I did not consider the flexible grid, the pattern of checks and bands bending, the pattern of colors filling the fabric, the woven substance of Lawrence's bathrobe, until one night soon after I'd canceled the lease on my dormitory room and told my parents my new address and faced their questions. I did not consider the grid, the bands, the hues passed through each other, until one night when I saw Lawrence wearing the robe over his prim pajamas. The plaid's pattern, then, caught my attention. The robe looked lax, softly overlapped, softly tied around his body. His underlying clothing and his slippers also, like his robe, looked loosely uninsistent, utterly lacking in stringency. But the blue-and-gray, red-threaded plaid struck me in particular. The plaid bent in loose conformity to Lawrence's torso; it struck me as bent by his curvatures, as bent away from some abstract condition of perfect flatness, some inherently inimical quality which my mind ascribed, by biting prejudice, to all or to most grids unaffected by curves. All of the ills of my enemies, "straight lines," seemed rendered toothless by the sight of Lawrence wearing a grid-patterned bathrobe. The plaid, bent in loose fit upon Lawrence, struck me as emblematic of his goodness to me.

I saw the bathrobe's plaid pattern as two grids of broad bands superimposed, positioned with regard to each other so that they left no interstices, no space between them unoccupied. In an abstract state, which one did not actually see, one grid consisted of pale gray bands, one of dark sky blue, cerulean, the cerulean bands each threaded along one edge with very narrow, parallel bands of close, bright red. I did not see the red parallels as grids in their own rights. The broad part of each blue band, the breadth of each blue band beyond the red, equaled the width of each gray band. Where the gray and the blue grids intersected, their colors blended. (The intersection of gray horizontal and vertical blue appeared as cerulean lightened by very fine, pale-gray, diagonal hatching. The intersection of blue horizontal and vertical gray appeared as gray darkened by very fine, cerulean, diagonal hatching.) Where the gray and the blue grids didn't intersect, squares appeared, gray squares where gray bands notionally crossed, blue where blue crossed blue.

Any grids in any colors, bending with Lawrence's form, would probably have moved me with gratitude to him. And I did not need the sight of a mere pattern (bent as if against its own inflexible essence) to prompt me to feel grateful. The sight of Lawrence himself moved me repeatedly. He gave me a home and a way of life, all in a stroke, with his "Stay, Neddy, uh. Please." Thus, however other colors might have affected me, the colors of Lawrence's bathrobe suggested security. The blues and the grays looked wintry; the red which shot through them suggested warmth. A dim urbanity of streets and snowy intersections and cars' taillights—prolonged, as in time-lapse photographs—enlivened the pattern. I did not choose to like grids, but I sensed: Lawrence's orderly life gave my life thrilling order.

73 CUE BALL, BLUE CHALK

Over the first Christmas break after I'd met Lawrence, I visited my family—what remained of it absent Estelle. I'd dreaded my father's reception of me beyond that of the others, Burke and Mother. But Dad, ever unpredictable, all but congratulated me, saying that he had "confidence" in the rightness of my choices for myself and that he wished me happiness in those choices, an astounding endorsement for which I felt an unexpected spring of gratitude, relief, and resurgent love—love like a gusher formerly, fearfully capped. Dad's temperate, trusting, more than tolerant acceptance of the idea of Lawrence and me as a couple fortified me against Mother's predictable tears of wounded vanity, or so I interpreted her initial outburst: shown a photograph of Lawrence, she covered her face with a manicured hand and wept, wailing, "Oh, Edward, Edward. I could understand it better if you took up with someone more your own age." (It, Mother? It?) I did not take that statement of Mother's sympathetically, at face value. Unforgiving, and prejudiced against her by experience, I interpreted that first statement of hers to mean that Mother wished that I'd fallen in love with someone whom she considered physically beautiful, a flattering accoutrement to a flattering son (one of her two flattering, human mirrors). And my father's first response, which I deeply appreciated, wore off like a dream. After a few days, he began advising me backhandedly. While his well-wishing continued, he cautioned me against "counting" on my "relationship" with Lawrence to last, and he resumed his summer's occupation of browbeating me about further schooling and about his "plans" for me. He spoke as if no revolution, no change at all, had occurred in my circumstances. That reversion to a norm disappointed me a little, not much, considering the "confidence" tendered. But Burke's behavior, one evening, Burke's and my behavior that night, disappointed me grievously.

Burke had many things on his mind that Christmas vacation, that break between semesters. He reduced the break to a few days; he had to "get back to work." The previous fall he'd begun what he called his "first real job." He said that he felt "incredibly lucky," "unbelievably lucky," that a "decent" college had offered him an assistant professorship. But then he felt "under the gun" to retain the position, which he hoped to do through prolific scholarship. I wondered if Lawrence, who worked day in and day out, doing his rooting research, writing, answering departmental demands, and more, all the while teaching and "seeing," advising, students, I wondered if Lawrence had felt as beleaguered as Burke apparently felt given a "first real job." I couldn't imagine Lawrence feeling as desperately challenged as Burke evidently felt. But then, I believed that Burke wouldn't have let the pressures of his work bother him as much as they did if he hadn't felt grieved and distracted by personal matters. Christine had gotten married and the woman with whom Burke had lived most recently, one Sandra DeSilva, felt newly abandoned by him and kept telephoning him. Burke wished himself rid of Sandra. Having finished a conversation with Sandra one night, Burke walked into the dining room, commented disparagingly upon Sandra, and told me, in no inviting manner, "I'm going downstairs. Join me if you like." I should have known better than to have joined him.

We went downstairs into the basement. Dust dimmed the dark-brown linoleum tiles. Estelle would not have allowed the accumulation. Tracking through the mournful dust, Burke uncovered the pool table, uncovered accoutrements. "You playing?" he asked all but rhetorically. Burke extracted pool balls, arranged them in the usual round-cornered, otherwise triangular rack. The balls fit its corners; pale-and-striped spheres and spheres of solid colors clustered within the confining straightness. The hues brimmed, bright under overhead light. Highlights reflected from overhead on each of the balls. The highlights moved without rolling as the balls rolled, as Burke dragged the brimming rack into position; one of its pointless tips stopped on a dime. Burke unmolded the cluster, walked away from it, placed a cue ball on the table. I turned aside. The hard, bright, unbreakable nature of pool balls seemed to invite the splitting crack and the—hard on hard, slick on slick—clicking concatenation which immediately followed. A cube of blue chalk, largely paper-covered, visibly worn concave on one unpapered face, sat, exemplar of softness, on the table's rail.

A world of difference lived in my mind between pool cues and paint brushes, between pool balls' hues and pigments' colors, between Burke and myself, and between Burke's mind in general and Burke in his present mood. Burke said, "One in the corner," crouched and took aim. He felled the one, the two, and the three. Aiming, in a feline crouch, he looked ready to kill the dark-violet four. His table-touching, cue-supporting fingers looked greenish with light reflected from the table. Looking fixedly at the distant target, Burke said, "You seem much calmer now." He barely moved; balls clicked. "Now that you've met this." Click. "This Professor Baussan." Weight thudded. Burke sounded snide, saying "this," "this," "Professor Baussan." Perhaps he envied Lawrence Lawrence's tenure, Lawrence's secure rank as full professor. Perhaps, saying "Professor" in the snide tone that he did, Burke mocked me and my own adoring, incautious use of the title. Perhaps, in pronouncing upon my perceived, improved air of calm, Burke meant to pose as a model of tranquility himself. I resented Burke's manner, Burke's condescension, Burke, with his several women, sounding snide about my single love. I growled quietly, "Lawrence. His first name's Lawrence, Burke." Arisen from his crouch, Burke walked away. He glanced at me over his shoulder.

He looked smugly satisfied in that I, by saying the name "Lawrence" with quiet vehemence, had disproved myself improved in calm. Burke continued shooting pool, but with angry dispatch. He crouched; he jabbed; disregarded balls cracked together, plummeted. Walking around the table toward me, he delivered a second pronouncement. Sounding as if angry with me and as if disgusted by me and as if tender for me, all, all at once, he said, "You're such a conflicted little bastard, I can't imagine you fucking anyone." I should have said, "Gee, thanks a lot." Instead, I said meanly, "You imagined well enough when Christine was concerned." Burke looked aside wearily. As if bored with me as an obstacle, he said, "Get out of my way."

I had the sense to obey him. I lay in a chair in the dark end of the room, listening to splitting cracks, thrumming roils. Burke's effects upon pool balls sounded murderous. I listened miserably. Hearing an unusual crack, I looked toward the table. Burke had knocked the cue ball off of it. The ball came speeding along the floor toward me. (It looked, fantastically, as if it fled from Burke and raced desperately to me, as if I had a reputation among pool balls as someone to whom bruised spheres knew to run. The ball bore bruise-like stamps from Burke's cue. I could not see the blue chalk on the moving ball, but I knew from past experience that such hard-hit balls bore such marks.) As the ball rolled over the dust-dimmed darkness of the floor and away from the strong light over Burke's table, it slowed. It rolled slowly as it approached; it approached me nearly; I put my right foot down (gently) on top of it. And I remembered breaking snowballs by stepping on them. I remembered a full moon reflected in puddles on steps, underfoot. I remembered Christine playing jacks as a child in that very room, Chris failing to catch the golf ball she used, the ball rolling away across the room. And I remembered peaches. Burke walked angrily toward me. Carrying a cue in his left hand, he looked like straightness armed with straightness. Looming over me, he barely paused. He swept down, grabbed the ball, turned toward the table again. To retain him, I said, almost sniveling, "You remember those peaches we bought in Izmir?" Burke stopped. His back looked savagely attentive. He turned, obscure face set. I sniveled. I said, "Izmir. Peaches. The size of them. The sweetness. The skins like white cats' ears?" Burke said, "Yeah" as if bored to death and as if daring me to get to the point. I said unwisely, "Lawrence is like that." Burke ground the floor underfoot. He strode back to the table. Over his shoulder, he said in a carrying voice, "You were sick then and you're sick now and I don't want to hear about it."

I'd viewed Burke all my life—for the reflective part of my life—as the voice of reason. Burke usually seemed reasonable, as opposed to our father. Burke usually tried to act temperate, tried not to vent temper. Burke usually tried not to punish people around him with—as if for—his sometimes foul moods. His reasonable, temperate guise failed that night. His noisy attack on pool balls resumed.

I went upstairs. As I passed the table, I stole the chalk off the rail; I swiped the soft blue in passing. I claimed it, clenched it, kept it. The cube bore paper on five sides. Paper, paper, sacred paper. In the cube's one unpapered face, the small ends of pool cues had worn a deep concavity, a concavity softly round and rounding downward, conically, into the cube. The concavity reminded me of places eroded by brushes in pans of watercolor paint. The concavity within the chalk, appearing circular where widest, recalled an abstract pattern, a circle within a square, the circle's diameter equal in length to the length of each of the square's sides. That pattern appealed to me as a conjunction of opposites, and I remembered it fondly from Burke's tutelage under the dome of the Hagia Sophia; the chalk cube reminded me of Burke's usual, temperate, reasonable bearing. And the cube appealed to me, further, as any colored chalk would appeal, as drawing material. The chalk's very softness appealed. The chalk appealed to me for many reasons, but it appealed to me most because of one: its one unpapered face, square-looking despite the concavity, reminded me of Lawrence's bathrobe, of the blue squares in the plaid draped over me when we'd first gone to bed.

Luckily for me, my backwardness about sex interested Lawrence. It interested him; it appealed to him; it did not repulse or repel him. He sat patiently playing chess with me for weeks before we undressed. I sensed him observing me while we played. I bent my mind to assuring us, both of us, of my reasonableness. I had told Lawrence, I'd nervously told Lawrence, "I need to learn to breathe in your presence." So I learned to breathe, half-thinking about chess. Lawrence must have observed (immediately) the mountainous inconsistency between my quickness to say "I love you" and my slowness to touch. That inconsistency must have interested him. He displayed patience, patience, patience, kindly, interested patience. He did not even urge the topic of sex between us. And when I finally confessed to a sex life limited to onanism and Lawrence asked, "You're a virgin, Ned?" he must have asked to confirm a conjecture long entertained, a conjecture long entertained with patient, steady, anticipatory pleasure. Even when we first went to bed, Lawrence acted calm. He acted calm, calmly patient; he acted tenderly encouraging, as if he had all the time in the world to soothe me through my nervous shivering, while I could see that he felt aroused. He acted sweetly beneficent and patient, patient, patient. Perhaps I touched him in his heart of hearts, in his teacherly instincts.

I learned and I learned. I learned that Lawrence enjoyed considering me virgin. I learned that Lawrence enjoyed considering me virgin even during sex. I felt too embarrassed to press Lawrence—much—about what he meant by "virgin" in my case, but I gathered, from the little he volunteered, that the concept of virginity that stirred him had nothing to do with first times, nothing to do with a condition lost with a single, sexual encounter, but that it had everything to do with faithfulness, with fidelity, with having sex with no one beyond one sexual inductor. Apparently Lawrence thought—and enjoyed thinking—that if I had sex with no one but him, I remained virgin to him. I did not ask whether masturbation counted as infidelity; I had no desire to investigate Lawrence's pet concept fully. But I did desire to understand Lawrence insofar as I might, and his concept of virginity belonged to his mind.

Lawrence did not strike me as jealous or possessive. He did not strike me as thrilled by covetous thoughts of exclusivity. Getting to know him, I did come to consider him fastidious, but not maniacally so. If I dismissed fastidiousness and jealousy, if I dismissed possessiveness and mean-minded lust for exclusive distinction, what remained of Lawrence's concept of virginity as applied to me? What else might the plagued word suggest or mean to him—that he should gladly speak it, entertain it, and find it arousing?

I wracked my scant brains over that one. I could only think that I appealed to the teacher in Lawrence, that my experiential ignorance appealed to him, and that I possessed, to his mind, an intriguing uniqueness: he'd never met a potential partner more in need of learning about sex than I.

I supposed Lawrence desirous of shaping my mind, of creating a body of knowledge in me: the only knowledge that I might possess of a man's touch other than my own. If that notion did enliven Lawrence's mind, if that notion did enliven him erotically, I would have to admit that desire to teach me about sex coexisted with desire to keep me in ignorance of other men. Exclusivity and generosity curiously intermingled.

I supposed Lawrence interested in sex as a meeting of minds

through a meeting of bodies. I supposed him grown disinterested—and little interested ever—in the pursuit of pleasure for its own sake or for the sake of adventurous thrill. I supposed Lawrence possessed of sexual gifts, of a certain bodily eloquence, of subtle abilities born of practice, of an ability to communicate love through his moving body. I supposed that Lawrence knew that he possessed such gifts, and that Lawrence longed to deploy his expressive powers with an appreciative partner. And who more appreciative than a bundle of nerves like me, someone afraid of bodies, someone whom Lawrence might slowly calm, someone resonant with love although trepidant, every tissue attentive?

I supposed that Lawrence supposed that his body did not suggest sexual gifts, did not give of his enduring expertise, to the casual observer. I supposed that my very attraction to Lawrence, although hedged around by chess pieces, by fearful inhibitions, might, in Lawrence's warm eyes, prove me insightful, not blind to his gifts.

So I supposed that Lawrence, who taught intellectually by profession, might prize me as his first ever student in a unique course called "sensual appreciation," the scope of which surpassed the five senses and their gratifications to encompass everything, everything that comprised, in effect, the material side of his life's enjoyment.

So I credited Lawrence with giftedness as a teacher. So I supposed that I appealed to him as an appreciative neophyte. I supposed and I supposed. But why thoughts of virginity enlivened Lawrence, I really didn't know; I had no idea.

75   LAWRENCE'S COAT

I did not like applying the word "virgin" to myself. But sometimes, I wondered. I felt so impressed by sex with Lawrence, so lingeringly, so lastingly alive with our mutual touches, that I had to wonder: Did I have the mind of a virgin, astounded by sex, turned inside out by it?

Sometimes Lawrence's touches seemed to linger in me. Long after their cessation, sensations—caresses, pressures, motions of his unspeaking mouth—seemed to live continued in my skin, in my body, to the amazement of my mind. Lawrence's give and take in the flesh seemed to live around me, upon me, and in me as his excited body had done. Thus, Lawrence could seem to exist in two places at once: in his independence and in my registration. Lawrence might move around his kitchen, for instance, putting away dishes and chatting about groceries to buy, while I, helping, conversing with him, felt almost as if our touching hadn't ended. His scent, taste, touch, audibility, and appearance, as I had just known those through the amalgamating blur of excitation, subsisted to such an extent that I felt dressed in Lawrence while he, say, merely shelved dishes. In that instance and in many others, he had clearly moved on, out of bed, while I—or half my mind—remained there with him, greedy of his abundance, feeling his heady sway.

Sometimes after sex, freshly bathed, freshly dressed, freshly ready to go out with Lawrence, I helped him on with his coat. I slipped the coat off a hanger's wooden shoulders, held the garment raised and gaping; Lawrence backed into it. I felt the satin-like lining grasp him; I felt it lie smooth upon his shape and drop, in its woven weight, straight from his front.

Sometimes I teased Lawrence about his overcoat, a thing of caramel-colored cashmere lined with shiny fabric a color of very milky coffee. The coat looked warm to wear and felt soft to my hands when I held it up and open for Lawrence to shoulder his way into it. The coat advertised affluence. (Have you no shame? Apparently not.) I said that "cashmere" meant "sea of money"; I called Lawrence's coat "your stockbroker's overcoat," as if Lawrence didn't own it, but rather his stockbroker did. I called the coat's lining "woven saliva." I imagined it warm, surrounding him.

76 HELPFULNESS

I needed to learn many things, things as basic as breathing in Lawrence's presence, elementary things. Everything about Lawrence and everything about living with him seemed charged with the marvelous. Marvelously Lawrence chopped onions. Marvelously he got dressed in the morning, putting on his pants, as the saying had it, one leg at a time: stunning, extraordinary, marvelous. Marvelous the procedures, the degrees, by which the disheveled, pajama-wearing, just-awakened Lawrence converted himself into the groomed man ready to do his job. Marvelous his mere presence, marvelous his unfamiliar familiarity, marvelous both the knowledge and the act, the knowledge that I might grasp him around the waist, interrupting his getting dressed, marvelous Lawrence's laughing, so grasped, so tackled. Marvelous. Marvelous, my mug shoved into his yielding cheek, the golden splinters of his growing hairs infinitesimal stabs. Even familiarity, even *acting* familiar, impressed me as unusual because dissimilar to most of my previous experience with people. Hence, to me, "virgin" might have meant "a social misfit starting at square one."

Living with Lawrence, I helped him in practical ways. (Marvelous, my varied chances to help.) Although I'd lived, between visits home from college, in undemanding, small rooms for years, I felt that I knew all about living in a house; I threw myself into helping Lawrence with his. He hired the hard work done. A crew cleaned—dusted, scrubbed, vacuumed—his house every two weeks. A man called Albert picked sticks out of the ivy and trimmed whatever needed trimming in the yard. I embraced the remaining, the easy tasks. I took out garbage and recyclables. The night before garbage-pickup day, I trundled the rolling bins down to the street; I returned the emptied bins to the garage. I brought in the mail and placed it, all of it, even the junk, on a corner of the kitchen island where I'd seen Lawrence himself place it before culling it. I washed whatever didn't go into the dishwasher and whatever wouldn't fit into the appliance after a meal. I learned where Lawrence kept things in the kitchen; I put dishes away. I helped him cook, largely by chopping and mincing to his specifications. (He wanted all cubes the same size, all slivers of equal length and thickness.) I cleaned the kitchen zealously in his wake. I learned his likes and dislikes in all concerning laundry. When, for some reason, the standard steps of his mornings lapsed and he and I did not make the bed together (simple, with sheet and duvet), I made it. I washed our cars and pumped their gas. With rare exceptions, I did not buy groceries. Lawrence enjoyed planning meals and picking and choosing ingredients in the low light of a grocery store (an appallingly expensive store by my pinched, frugal standards). He would stroll the grocery aisles meditatively, reading the backs of packages, while I pushed the cart or brought to it some known commodity at his request. I did not choose the foodstuffs, but by and large I bullied Lawrence (deferentially) into letting me carry the groceries into the house from the car; I carried copious sacks through the mud room and into the kitchen while he put the things away. Despite my dislike of burning trees, I learned how to split logs and kindling. (A split-bamboo basket beside the fireplace held kindling. I kept the basket filled.) When we had to park on the street due to unusually heavy snow, I excavated our cars. I cleared a path through snow, from the front door to the street. I removed snow from the balcony. I changed furnace and water filters. I politely repelled solicitors who came to the door. My father used to growl at me, "Make yourself useful for once." Chasing paternal praise? I desired to please Lawrence. I tried to please him, and the sweet truth dazzled me: I did not need to try.

I pleased Lawrence without trying. I pleased his sexual eye, mind, and body. He said things to me like, "Fine one, lie down. Let me look at you. Looking at you excites me." I learned, in learning about sex, that when Lawrence, desiring such a "look," instructed me to lie down, he desired that I lie unclothed, on an undressed bed of expansive white, and that I move little while he toured my body, using his lips, tongue, hands, penis, and more, and all caressively. Kisses witnessed my ribs in sequence; a sweet piece of burliness nosed and probed the backs of my knees. While so roaming, Lawrence spoke magic words to his own mind, words redolent of unmasculine delicacy. Such a "look" usually concluded with Lawrence, seated with his back against the headboard, tormented to orgasm by my fingers-and-mouth. I learned; I learned. I learned, through Lawrence's responses, what holds and motions of mine he most enjoyed. He groaned; he creaked; he bayed; great sounds escaped him. Sometimes, amid his torment, he gasped, "I love you," and I made throaty return, echoing his words with formless murmur, and I felt very happy. Of course, he loved me; he "loved" what I did; he "loved" oral sex; he "loved" what he primly called the "sensations" I "gave" him. "Ah, Neddy," he panted, "That was terrific."

And I loved Lawrence. I loved him like a house afire. I loved him forcefully, all out, with all of my mind and with all of my body. Bodily, I could not embrace him deeply enough. Anointed with lubricant, astounded by the intimacy of his admission, by the smoothness of his surrounding warmth, by the embrace of his swaying, upturned legs, by a view of his face or of the back of his head, I shook and staggered. I felt as if *I* contained Lawrence, as if I could line him, every bit of him, with a praiseful repetition, with a second form of his own body. I lay to fair Lawrence, to him and for him. I pinned and pressed him greedily. My first shyness past, I did not act tentative. I did not need encouragement. But Lawrence enjoyed imagining otherwise. Lawrence enjoyed thinking that I needed encouragement. Lawrence enjoyed thinking of me as tentative and delicate. My initial nervousness had pleased him, and I, with all my might, continued to please him—in my guise as "fine," "fine," "fine," reluctant neophyte. Sometimes I played to his fantasies. Sometimes I acted reluctant; sometimes I acted as if anything but ardent, that I might hear Lawrence purr, "Come on, now," "Don't worry," "Come on," "That's good."

77 EXQUISITE

I embraced clichés. Lawrence Baussan and I seemed made for each other, different as day and night, summer, winter, light and dark, yellow and black, an archery target's heart and rind, the one ball and the eight ball in collisional pool. We differed greatly in temperament, in age, in professional attainment, in income, in the purposes of our activities, and in the nature of the responsibilities implicit in those purposes. We differed extremely in our degree of friendliness, in the interest we took in other people. And Lawrence's mind, grinding carefully, discovered ends through worded thought, whereas I visualized and watched visible materials produce visual effects. Beyond our similar heights and beyond traits necessarily shared through gender and genre, Lawrence and I also differed considerably in physical shape. Loving him in his great sway, I did not regale him with adjectives; the bounteous glory of his lapping flesh wounded his pride as it fed my appetite; the only "big" I ever applied to him, I applied to his pride, to his deserving penis. I spared him the truth about my rowdy zeal for his powerful curves. He did not try to hide his delicacy, his fineness, his excitement by ideas of beauteous fragility. He called every bone in my body and my cartilaginous nose "exquisite," "exquisite" stressed on the "ex." The breathy dactyl revealed his tenderness. I fit him like a glove; he fit me like a sumptuous mitten.

"Exquisite" refined. Naming, judging, calling sensations "exquisite," Lawrence refined, to his desire, our sexual engagements. And, sweet man, gentle and fastidious, Lawrence also would have me, me physically, his "exquisite" partner. Because "exquisite" seemed such a mindful word, such a pointed possession of Lawrence's mind, and because "exquisite" seemed, as Lawrence spoke it, so suggestive of the nature of *his* sensibilities, I tried not to take his use of it, as applied to me, seriously. I did not object; I did not protest against the absurdity of his kissing my ankles and calling them "exquisite"; I did not object to kisses bearing "exquisite" pressed to my atlas vertebra. Lawrence's tender "exqui-site," Lawrence's expressed admiration of my skinny frame, seemed pathetically to mirror, in reverse, my own rough excitation by his deep flesh. Besides that consideration, besides the consideration that Lawrence and I seemed alike in the inscrutable roots of our affinity for each other as each other's bodily opposite, I did not object to Lawrence's "exquisite" because I sensed that the word itself, somehow magically casting a spell over his mind, contributed to Lawrence's arousal (prodigiously reliable). I felt determined not to object to Lawrence's "exquisite," but once I slipped. I objected. On that occasion, he called my face "exquisite." I gripped his wrist. I said, "That word isn't manly." Lawrence looked surprised, round-eyed, then he looked mockingly amused, smiling. He said, "Manly?" as if he had never heard the word, as if I had said something utterly outré, like "ostrichly" or "oryxly." I said quickly, "Never mind," but then I told him, "I look like my mother." I watched his eyes. I saw Lawrence absorb the point I'd made, the sore point he'd touched. He looked briefly penitent and then he lectured. He said, "You should thank your lucky stars you're not plain." I said, "I would rather blame my twisted genes."

I slipped on another occasion, too, when Lawrence grazed my face with too much praise. (Touchy bastard, I, Edward: of course, I didn't know how to take a compliment.) That time, I showed Lawrence a chickenpox scar high on the left side of my forehead. He really might not have noticed the scar until then; my hair usually covered it. "So much for faultlessness," I joked. "What?" Lawrence replied. He looked so dazed, so surprised, that I regretted my action, yet I pointed to the scar with an index finger. I regretted diverting Lawrence from his grazing "exquisite," from his fantastical perusal, to my actual person. He might blind himself to innumerable flaws; he might lose sight of sight in his excitation by visions; he might simply not suffer distraction by details, by incidental marks or moldings about the body of a person whom he loved. I should have made allowances, allowances, allowances upon allowances. If love consisted, in part, of tolerance toward the loved one's foibles, then, at that moment, when I broke into Lawrence's train of thought, into his stream of laudatory whispers, I failed in that part of love. The sight of Lawrence's face—Lawrence's surprised-looking eyes, the looseness of his lips—stirred regret like feathers in me. Yet there I lay, closely facing him, finger like a pistol to my forehead, as if daring him to say something, while I myself had something to say. Lawrence said gently, "That's nothing, Neddy." I said, "I know it's nothing." But its enormity went through me. When, as a child of six, I'd scratched the spot that made that scar, Mother had wept as if inconsolably. I felt that she actually cared little about me. How could she carry on so about my face?

78 WHITE IN WHITE

I remembered lying in bed, feeling comfortably drugged with cold medicine, Mother sitting on the side of the bed, reading to me using a caressive voice. My bed seemed completely white with white sheets and with a white-covered comforter, which did not weigh much because small feathers stuffed it. Direct sunlight and sunlight rebounding from snow outside one floor down lit the room unusually. Mother's left-hand fingers curved under the book's left edge, and rings, paired together on her left hand, scattered motes like miniature reflections from toyed-with mirrors. I watched the white motes on the white sheet shoot away and return as Mother moved her hand. When they fell nearest the rings, the motes looked brightest and most clearly defined. When Mother turned her hand, they sprang apart like kicked gravel. Sleep dragged me from the sight; I held onto the sight as I fell asleep.

Sometimes when I lay in bed, Mother, seated beside me, cut paper into snowflake shapes, her left hand moving paper folded many plies deep, her right moving scissors, long, white-metal, shining pointed blades. I watched scissors' blades creating edges in paper; I watched the blades close, the blades' obscured convergence moving along a visible blade's length. When slits forming in paper met slits previously made or when the long, bright, white-metal blades ran out of substance to cut (as if they would cut, just then, thin air), little folded scraps dropped. Mother brushed the scraps off her lap and off the bed when she'd finished cutting, after she'd given me what she'd cut. Handing me a pointed wedge, she urged, "Go ahead, open it. Open it." "Go ahead. Open it," she urged again. "It'll be like in a kaleidoscope." I told her that it wouldn't. "Why not?" she asked. The paper lacked color and couldn't change.

One November noon, having slept most of the morning, having vomited repeatedly the previous night, I, seventeen, lay along the edge of the bed in my room. I heard Mother's footsteps approach; something with her rattled. I saw her set down a tray and turn on the lamp above it on a bedside table. Sudden light bloomed in the small copper tray, round, no larger than an antique phonograph record. On the warm, shiny copper with its flush that seemed fire-lit and warm with association (Estelle polishing the copper bottoms of pots and pans acerbically, with vinegar and salt in her thrifty manner), objects typical of my mother stood and lay, hard and white both, but imbued with Mother's lacy taste, her playfully frivolous tenderness. A white porcelain rice bowl studded with glaze-filled, colorless, translucent spots (supposedly like grains of rice) and a white china scoop of a spoon, similarly patterned, occupied the warm copper. Mother lightly asked how I felt. I said "fine" and then, in response to plucked eyebrows' mock skepticism, "better." Mother asked if I felt like eating anything; when I indicated that I did, she prompted me to "sit up then" and she moved to hand me the white, white, colorless, white scar-patterned bowl, the riddled, thin vessel of her frivolous choice.

The night before, Estelle, awakened by my retching, had startled me by entering the bathroom behind me. Her eyes looked small with sleep, her long, gray-white hair unbraided, voluminous, deranged. Estelle had clucked over me sympathetically; she'd handed me a washcloth. Breathing through the hot dampness, I'd tried to thank her for that and for care past knowing. She'd dismissed the attempt, "Oh, tush." She'd said, "You go on back to bed. I'll bring you something, poor dear. You shouldn't have to keep getting up." She'd brought, from downstairs upstairs, a stainless steel basin with extensions on its rim. She'd left the basin on a bedside table. After she'd left, heartened by her care, I'd moved the basin; I'd kept it in bed with me. I'd retched bitter strands into it, grateful to Estelle that I hadn't had "to keep getting up" to face the stolid, solid, thick, white, durable, white, thick, thick, thick porcelain toilet bowl.

I saw my mother's thin, riddled dish rise in her fingertips, in the shielded softness of her fingertips beneath her unpainted fingernails filed into curves like curved ends of petals, narrow ellipses. The bowl's glaze-filled holes, its gluey little translucent spots, harmonized in shape with her fingernails. Rain, blown by a gust, sounded against the window, sounded as if it pitted the glass. Mother, who had obviously put herself to some trouble for me on that occasion, Mother, who'd chosen that bowl from among sensible dishes, and who had carried it and its liquid contents all the way up the stairs, held the bowl toward me softly. "This isn't very hot," she said. I remembered, I actually remembered, how she'd badgered me, "What do you say?" when she'd handed me folded-up, riddled white-paper snowflakes. I took the bowl from her. I whispered, "Thanks." I hoped that I learned to see what she *did* do for me, what she did do, as opposed to what she did not.

79   CHIPPED GLASS

One night, Mr. Kuprin, the pianist whose voice and music had calmed me briefly and immediately before I'd thrown myself at Professor Baussan, saying, "I love you, I love you" in Professor Baussan's kitchen, Mr. Kuprin, Lawrence, and I sat in a busy restaurant. We ordered a glass of wine each, all the same kind. A harried woman hastily set a glass before each of us. The rim of my glass shone—interrupted by a deep chip. I imagined my father insisting, with cold politeness, that the woman bring a different glass. I wondered: Would most people accept the glass or would most reject it? I accepted it. I could avoid the chip, and the woman who served us had much to do. Besides, imperfections abounded; why look for perfection in an imperfect world? I sat whole seconds, registering the chipped rim, before Lawrence, holding his glass, about to speak one of his rolling toasts in Latin, noticed the chip. He made a clicking sound with tongue and teeth; he set his glass down abruptly; he said, "Let me take that one"; he switched the glasses in front of us, taking the chipped one himself. Mr. Kuprin groaned; Mr. Kuprin grasped my forearm. Looking at me earnestly, Mr. Kuprin said, "I've always wanted someone to do something like that for me." I felt embarrassed by Lawrence's gentle—and gently stilted—gallantry, by Lawrence's move to protect my precious lips while not considering his own lips imperiled. And I felt embarrassment *for* Mr. Kuprin, that he had ever wished, and that he had "always" wished, the wish that he'd expressed. Because I supposed Mr. Kuprin and Lawrence past lovers, I supposed that by "someone," Mr. Kuprin meant Lawrence: I've always wanted Lawrence to guard me as he just guarded you. Who might not long for another's protection? Mr. Kuprin could not touch Lawrence through vulnerability.

Sometimes Lawrence praised me in a lordly manner. He said, "Oh, my dear boy, you are good to me." On one occasion, I replied to that recurring and maudlin statement by saying that he should not tinge acts of love with charity. Lawrence groaned. He said as if positively marveling, *not* as if afflicted, "What have I done to deserve you?" I said that deserts had nothing to do with it, that no Providence existed to determine deserts or anything else. Lawrence said, "Shh, shh, shh," stroking my hair as if stroking a cat.

Devotion drove me to serve Lawrence Baussan, devotion, gratitude, sympathy: love. In sympathy, I suffered when Lawrence suffered. If Lawrence pressed his hands down upon chair arms as he rose from a chair, if he did not leave a chair with perfect ease, I raged internally with the wish that he not need to labor; I desired to assist him, to spare him labor. I'd felt that wish before I knew the man at all; I'd felt it on my first day of "work" as a slide projectionist, when Professor Baussan, having handed me a slide box, somehow hesitated, somehow arranged himself in preparation, before stepping onto the stage in Room 203. I'd felt it, seeing the preparation and the rising motion of his corduroy-covered back.

I feared overdoing attentiveness. I feared boring Lawrence. I feared oppressing him by my presence, by anticipating his wishes, by scrambling to attention whenever he lifted a finger, by taking every word, sign, hint, or intimation concerning his wishes as a binding directive that I would try to fulfill. I feared offending Lawrence by interfering, by offering him assistance when he did not desire or require my aid. I felt apprehensive on that point one morning when, interrupting his usual routine, I helped him on with his shoes.

Ordinarily, when putting on shoes every morning, Lawrence sat in a chair. He used a shoehorn, which remained—taken up and replaced every day—on a table beside the chair. He carried shoes from shelves to chair, seated himself, placed shoes on the floor. He spread them and eased his feet into them, his head tilted first one way, then the other, as he addressed alternate feet. He didn't tie the laces while bent forward; rather, having settled back into the chair and having laid the shoehorn aside, he placed each ankle in turn athwart the opposite leg's knee. At arm's length, he tied the laces. He tied them quickly, inclemently, as if twisting their necks.

I crouched beside him one morning just when he'd taken up the shoehorn. Looking concertedly downward, I touched his right foot. It wore a soft, thick, dark sock of a type I called "foot bags." I urged the foot to move, to yield to me. It yielded. I spread the appropriate shoe, eased the foot into it, and tied the laces. I treated the obliging left foot the same way and remained crouched, worshipfully bowed, at Lawrence's feet. He sighed. He fingered my hair. He said, "Neddy. You know. You're going to make it so that I can't live without you."

One night I removed Lawrence's shoes and massaged his feet. Usually, when he returned to his house from work, he began preparing supper immediately. That night, instead of moving into the kitchen (and rubbing his hands together and clasping them in zealous-seeming anticipation of pleasurable tasks), he veered into the living room. Lowering himself to a sofa beside a glass coffee table, he said that his feet ached and that he hadn't had a chance to sit down for hours. He began explaining volubly how he'd spent the day. He appeared not to notice as I, conversing, crawled under the table and removed his shoes, scallop-frilled, pip-drilled, perforation-dotted wingtips warm with bodily warmth. I set the hard casings aside, squeezed his feet through his socks, cinnamon-brown foot bags slightly damp on the bottoms. I undressed his feet. Lawrence lay back, sighing, gasping, and exclaiming, "Ah-h-h," "Ha," "Ah, good," while I kneaded his feet and manipulated his corded ankles. (Prominent veins over his ankles resembled the rims of human ears.) I reached up his pant legs and massaged his calves as far up and as freely as cloth allowed. I loved his leg hairs to their roots, the blond stragglers surviving where many hairs had died of abrasion by socks worn routinely for years. I moved into sitting on the floor with my back to Lawrence. He draped a leg over my shoulder. While I massaged the given leg, I imagined a drawing, which I later made and gave to Lawrence as a joke, a drawing in the sinuously linear style of one of his Gothic manuscripts. The drawing, which Lawrence later fondly framed and fondly hung in his study, depicted him with a leg over my shoulder, both of us sitting on tree limbs sprung from large, strong letters, L and B, his first and last initials.

Sitting beside me in an auditorium, waiting for a concert to begin, Lawrence asked, "Does it seem a bit warm to you in here?" Perspiration glistened on his forehead; his eyes looked darkly inquiring. Stricken out of all proportion to Lawrence's slight discomfort, I lied; I said yes, and I told Lawrence truthfully, "You're overdressed." I offered to help him off with his jacket, part of a suit which included a vest. "No, thank you," he said curtly. Visions of aid assailed me. I wanted to blot Lawrence's forehead with his own handkerchief; I wanted to bring him water. Where would I find a paper cup? I wanted to open an inaccessible window high overhead. I wanted to wave a concert program to bring him drafts of cooling air. What moved me to such excess? What prompted imagined ministrations? Prospect of real suffering? Prospect of death?

One night after a concert, walking back to Lawrence's car, which I drove whenever we went anywhere together, Lawrence slipped on some ice. I grabbed him; he didn't truly fall. Restored to balance, he held the small of his back. "Are you all right?" I asked. He murmured, "Not quite," and said that he thought that he'd "pulled something." A fleet of exams yielded "nothing serious." But Lawrence suffered real pain for weeks. All turning and bending hurt him. Sinking to sit in a car and rising to leave one hurt him especially, but he would not forego car trips. Consequently, he learned to hold me, and I him, while we negotiated car doors, I lifting him, his arms around my neck, or I holding him around the torso while he held my shoulders, lowering. Even before that painful period, I'd opened car doors for him—and any other door that stood in his way. After Lawrence recovered, I still opened car doors; I gave him a hand in support as he left passenger seats. Lawrence, recovered, had no need of the hand, but we enjoyed the ceremonious routine.

When his back pained him, Lawrence lay in hot baths. I filled the tub and helped him into it in a variant of the manner established for cars. Lawrence lowered himself carefully into very hot water. He lay back, teeth clenched, eyes closed. The first time, after he, sinking, had released me and settled into the cavity, I asked, "Do you want me to leave?" Lawrence said, "No, Neddy, please." I sat on the floor. Wordlessly I cursed the marmoreal bathroom. I knew nothing about tombs, but the stony room stank of them. The huge tub, holding Lawrence in its maw, resembled a sarcophagus.

Sitting as if dumped on the floor beside tub-held Lawrence, I recalled his fondness for having sex in that room after we'd bathed together. I recalled how overtly he beamed with a fresh erection; how he vaunted his drive in words like, "I'm sorry, Neddy, but it looks like once just wasn't enough"; how he proceeded to work his back happily, freely, sidling and swaggering, while I contained him between gaping basins.

81 SHOVELING SNOW

I felt solicitous for Lawrence; I would spare him effort. Living with Lawrence, I soon learned: he felt solicitous for me. He repeatedly told me that I didn't "need" to go outside at night to shovel snow while snow fell. He said, "No need," "Don't bother," "You don't have to do that." Lawrence paid a man, whom he called Klath, to clear the driveway. Sounds of Mr. Klath's plow awoke me at night. I lay beside Lawrence, listening to the revving, the scraping, the driving strain of the man-driven machine working outside while Lawrence's breath sounded even, sounded peaceful, sounded assuring to me in that it sounded assured of all necessities, assured of shelter, for example, each sweep of it untroubled by (homeless) alternatives. The far machine sounded muscular, assertive, manly, brave, active, pitted against adversity—winter, cold, "facts," pitiless reality. Hearing it, I felt reproached for frivolity because I flippantly said, when preparing to shovel snow, "Time to battle the snowflakes." My mother's paper snowflakes didn't melt in my mind. Mr. Klath didn't "battle snowflakes"; he worked hard for pay. He added nocturnal labor to daily work. Joining cleared driveways to city-cleared streets, he facilitated other people's approaches to work.

One late morning—in full, blazing daylight—after Mr. Klath had rearranged snowfall, Lawrence went outside in shirtsleeves to "survey the damage," to view the helpful trench cut to the street. Standing in bitter cold, he said, "My. It is brisk, isn't it?" Another time Lawrence turned his eyes from one of Mr. Klath's canyons to me and said, "I'm sure you know. You couldn't do that with a shovel." He probably didn't feel sure that I knew that.

Sometimes I shoveled snow for practical reasons, away from cars parked on the street, for instance. Sometimes I shoveled snow as if seeking redemption for the sins of my selfish art. (I readily impressed myself as an overgrown, willful child addicted to using colored crayons on some cloud of my own making while people like Lawrence and like Mr. Klath did the world's work in mind and in space.) Sometimes I shoveled snow out of a pathetic, hopeless, and hopelessly misguided determination to work "like a man," "like a man" paid by the ton for shifting coal, not cold, someone with a dozen mouths to feed, someone who had neither the time nor the inclination to hear snow brushing twigs, the universe whispering. Shoveling snow, by plain exertion, helped me out of such moods.

Perhaps I liked the cold, the snow, the white of supreme lightness, the seen-as-gray sifting. Perhaps I liked putting on heavy clothes and boots at night, going responsibly out into the barn, turning on garage lights, stepping into the cold, roomy enclosure where Lawrence's sturdy workhorse Volvo stood beside—without divide of stall partitions—my pony Mitsubishi. Perhaps I liked imagining that I would harness the horses, drive horses to plow, cut into earth. Perhaps I enjoyed considering Lawrence my employer, imagining that I, sturdy peasant, simply, virtuously worked for him. Perhaps I enjoyed imagining that I enjoyed seeing what I did not enjoy seeing: firewood stacked, provident and dry, along the garage's third bay. Perhaps I enjoyed imagining that I had cut the garaged logs—and many more piled outside—using a tool anathema to me, a chainsaw. Perhaps I enjoyed imagining that I, as hired hand, had stacked the logs, bark-to-bark, in patrician Lawrence's prim racks, the raw, round, sawn, saw-torn ends facing evenly outward like filterless ends of close-packed cigarettes. Perhaps I enjoyed imagining that I enjoyed seeing grim metal, honed implements, ax and hatchet, deadly heads hanging downward; the smooth presence of tools; the way in which a wide-bladed snow shovel hung, not crucified, by its shoulders, blade atop three-penny nails—Jesus Christ—nails sunk in a board nailed along a wall. (I would have hung the shovel up by the handle.) Perhaps I enjoyed seizing the suspended shovel, lowering it, feeling that I maintained the place where I actually lived.

Perhaps I liked the frigidity, the falling snow a flood-lit tail beyond the garage. Perhaps I liked pitching in, driving blade into grayness, throwing light weights aside. Perhaps I liked the rough, ringing, rhythmic sounds that the shovel made, scraping the pebbled pavement, the bottom of the snow's vast development. Perhaps I enjoyed believing sincerely, believing serenely, amid the amplitude of falling snow, that what I did didn't matter: no small scratch in the vast snow mattered at all. And yet I could see what I had done, even having done little. Perhaps I enjoyed working with my whole body, not just with my hands, my hands scratching plates from which to make prints.

I discomfited Lawrence when I shoveled snow. One night, snow drifting thickly, I dressed for work out-of-doors. I entered the living room where Lawrence sat, reading. A brass lamp with an almost spherical shade craned toward his papers. Opposite the sofa in which he sat, a fire burned in the fireplace. I planted myself aggressively between Lawrence and the fire. He looked up, over the tops of half-lens glasses, and I felt proud of myself, foolishly vain, armored in quilted nylon, carrying gauntlets, heavy gloves, in one hand. Lawrence stared at me as if horrified. He said, "You're not going out in this? You're not going out in this, Edward." I blithely maintained the contrary. Lawrence said, "Neddy, Neddy. You know. Klath'll take care of it." He also pleaded, "Shoveling won't help. You know that." I replied that I needed "the exercise." "Neddy, Neddy," Lawrence appealed. He closed a bulging folder, pen squeezed to death in its midst. He stood up, pushing off from the sofa pathetically, with both hands. He came near. I felt the fire warmth on him although he'd sat, sweater draped, far from the source. He touched my jacket, part of my armor, delicately. He said, "I really don't think it's a good idea. Your doing this." I said, "Why not?" He looked at me with seemingly dark-eyed concern; the lighting alone made his eyes look dark. He held his forehead creased in entreating corrugations. I asked, speaking to his eyes, "Are you afraid that I'll hurt myself, that I'll make myself sick?" Lawrence grimaced. Without speaking the dare, I dared Lawrence to speak his protective interest in me, his interest in me as "exquisite," as "fine," as preciously "chiseled," as "delicate." Lawrence delicately mentioned only my hands. "Shouldn't you take care of your fingers, the way you draw?" I said, "Spoken like a pianist." And I left, fled, charged out of the house into cold, began work, shoveling snow. I raked stone-studded paving, tossed snow lightly aside.

82 WHITE SHIRT

One day, Lawrence gave me a telling gift (not that I knew for sure what the telling gift told). He gave me a white shirt with French cuffs. On the brink of receiving that gift, in ignorance of its impending arrival, I sat at the dining-room table, absorbed in trying to draw reflections in a group of clear-glass decanters that stood without contents on a tray in the table's center, under an overhead light. I heard Lawrence's car arrive; he entered the house from the mudroom, through the kitchen. He walked more briskly than usual; a sack with him rustled. Passing quickly through the dining room without pausing—without detour for an expected kiss of greeting, peck on the cheek, "How was your day?"— Lawrence exclaimed, "Ah! There you are. I'm glad you're home." I, slightly disconcerted by his manner, muttered something about how I usually preceded him "home." (A wondrous reverberation still attended the word.) Sweeping through the room, Lawrence impressed me as unusually anxious, on edge. I heard him divesting himself of his overcoat in the entry and of his briefcase in his study. I heard both him and the plastic sack return. Full of boisterous, delayed greetings, he rounded the table, dropped the sack in my lap, seized my shoulders with hands still cold from the out-of-doors, and pressed his lips into the side of my turning face. I meant to kiss him fully, but his lips withdrew to near my ear, and he whispered, "Bear with me, Neddy. Uh, please. I brought you something." I felt relieved. Lawrence seemed anxiously desirous:

both sexually desirous and fearful of displeasing me with his gift. I felt incapable of displeasure. I also felt desirous: moved both to touch and to reassure. "What is it?" I asked. Lawrence stood behind me, cold hands still clasping my shoulders. I rolled my head invitingly against his belly. He said, still anxiously, "Open it. You'll see."

Deliberately I set the sack aside. I extracted myself from Lawrence's hands and from the chair. I washed my hands in the kitchen. (The side of my right hand picked up graphite from pencils.) Deliberately I tore a paper towel from a roll, through perforations; I dried my hands on the short, white, roll-bent, curved-and-rectangular length. I left the crumpled dampness on the counter, considering the towel (sacrificed tree) good for further use. I returned to Lawrence. To my fond press, he said, "Uh. Neddy. Please. Open this first." "This" meant his accursed sack. I sat down in front of Lawrence again; again Lawrence touched my shoulders nervously. I took up the sack and took out of it a thick, floppy, white, clear-plastic-covered oblong. The plastic bore print. No wonder Lawrence felt nervous. He had not bought me a shirt; he had bought himself an erotic prop, a sort of costume for me to wear. "Really," I said. "Bear with me," he repeated. I sighed that I would bear with him to the ends of the earth. He chuckled; releasing my shoulders, he fingered my hair. "Open it," he urged. "All right," I said. Why oh why did I have to brace myself?

I slipped the shirt out of its packaging. From much-folded white cloth, I removed pins, pins, pins, pins and cardboard bracings, pins and clear-plastic slips (one clipped over the throat button, another within the collar). I removed pins, spines, pins (pins, of course, reminiscent of Estelle, little gold-hued safety pins used to mark spills on tablecloths; little yellow clamps pounced on trivial sins). Affixing pins and bracing cardboard had converted the human-shaped shirt into a rectangle. Self-pity tempted me. I imagined myself folded, bent, and jabbed with pins metaphorically, nagged, lectured, shamed into taking on a shape of inexpressive, straight-sided, unnatural containment. I unpacked, unpinned, and unfolded Lawrence's stimulant prop, a white-collar shirt with very long sleeves and with little squinting slits in the overly-long cuffs. Seeing the whole shirt, I told Lawrence, in a wounded tone, "It's white. It needs cufflinks. I don't own any cufflinks." Lawrence spoke as if almost overcome by the humor of the ludicrous suggestion that I might own cufflinks. He gasped, "I didn't suppose you did. You can have some of mine." "Borrow," I said. "Borrow, whatever," Lawrence breathed. He acted relieved, as if the worst had passed. I'd seen the shirt; I'd agreed to borrow cufflinks; I'd agreed to wear the shirt.

Loving Lawrence, I meant to please him. I meant to rise to my martyrdom, to go to the scaffold (serving Lawrence's fantasies), snowy noose around my neck, my workman's hands tied (locked at the wrists as if tied behind me) with little bits of borrowed jewelry. I meant to proceed straight to the bedroom, to undress, to put on the shirt without further delay. But Lawrence granted me a reprieve. Although he could barely keep his mouth shut—for lust for whatever figment his mind saw as me shirted—he wanted to "press" the shirt before he saw me wearing it. We went downstairs to the laundry room, an annex off the large room then called my "studio." Going down the stairs, I followed Lawrence. He carried the shirt casually, flung over one shoulder. That treatment of the shirt reassured me because, to my mind, it diminished the "exquisite" shirt's obscure importance. Lawrence erected an ironing board and prepared an iron. He pulled the shirt off his shoulder, spread it expertly, and covered the small end of the padded-and-silver-cloth-covered ironing board with it. He ironed the shirt's upper back. The ironing board's small end, draped with the shirt, looked tongue-in-cheek. The board's curved end, visible when Lawrence shifted the shirt, looked pleasing, soft, comforting, curved, as opposed to the sharply-pointed iron itself, the iron's soleplate in outline something like a Gothic arch.

The perforated soleplate breathed steam, gusted, and gasped. Lawrence applied himself to ironing; he also talked. He told me that washing the shirt would have removed the worst wrinkles, the deepest creases. "This would have been easier." Ah, but, I didn't say: he couldn't wait. Fastidious Lawrence leaned to the board. The heavy, repetitive, domestic, ironing motions soothed me, and the board creaked slightly as Lawrence pressed. The creaking seemed bed-like, sexy to me. I thought about fondling Lawrence, "bothering" him, but I merely watched him. He looked downward; his facial muscles, relaxed, sagged; the creases between his cheeks and mouth looked deeper than usual; his face looked beautiful, creased, as he removed a shirt's creases. (If smooth youth alone moved him, what would he do as I aged?) Lawrence pressed the long sleeves and the shirt's (damn) cuffs. Lawrence ironed the shirt's front sides. He slid the iron's tip between the buttons expertly. "This isn't the first shirt you've ironed," I observed. Lawrence said, "No, no. I used to do my own." He then thought further than I had thought. He stammered, "But this, for you, uh. This is a first, believe me." He glanced up anxiously. I made a dismissive gesture.

Lawrence ironed the white shirt. He ironed the shirt's spineless back. The spread shirt, naturally, didn't resist. Lawrence extended the ironed shirt to me; it hung by its nape off of two of his fingers, almost as if he blessed me with it. He said, "I'll be up in a moment." I wanted to take the shirt roughly, to snatch it meanly off his sweet fingers, to inflict wrinkles on it by crushing it, but I desired to please Lawrence more. I took the shirt from him respectfully, docilely, obligingly, politely. I ascended the stairs very slowly, listening to Lawrence empty the iron and fold up the board. I hoped that he would follow immediately, but he didn't. Proceeding up the stairs and onward, I imagined him waiting, leaning against the cubical, white-glazed washing machine or the similarly slick, inhuman dryer: Lawrence's body, the precariousness of its living intricacy, leaning against the clinical white.

By the time Lawrence entered the bedroom, I'd undressed; he hadn't. I wore his iron-warmed shirt still unbuttoned. I began buttoning it. "Leave it, leave it," he said. I disliked blunt instructions. But Lawrence looked so entranced—so pathetically entranced—staring, lips sagging, agog, that my irritation vanished. But he would have those cufflinks. He extracted a box from a drawer and held it, opened, toward me. Without looking at it, I said, "You choose." He chose. He chose flat, black, onyx ovals, gold-mounted: black ovals. While I fought back ghosts of Estelle's supposititious, conjoined moonstones, Lawrence eagerly folded the shirt's cuffs and slipped the cufflinks' shanks through buttonholes and turned the links' catches. He kept panting my nickname—as if, in his mind, he would wed my person to his embellishments.

83 WHAT LAWRENCE WANTED

When I first came to live with Lawrence, when I first came to share Lawrence's everyday life, I did not expect him to love me the way I loved him. I sensed that, by simply living, by his having lived a long time, Lawrence had outgrown the sort of responsiveness that I experienced. Or perhaps, possessing a temperament different from mine, he experienced everything differently. I believed, without thinking about it clearly, that Lawrence had loved so many people before me that, in him, the very power of love, like a flood, had ebbed to affection, to fondness and liking, that love had sunk, in him, into its own cut channel. But I also believed that sexual energy ran deep in Lawrence, and that I might please him greatly in that regard.

When I first began living with Lawrence, my low expectations concerning his love mattered not a whit to me; only he mattered, his passing expressions and his abiding traits. That he liked me at all requited me inexpressibly. Spending time with Lawrence, however he desired to spend it, gratified me beyond the shadow of any complaint.

Living with Lawrence, I soon learned what he expected of me. He wished me to conform to his routines; he wished to incorporate me into the well-established pattern of his regular life. I should wake up when he did and eat breakfast with him. I should help him cook supper. I should spend evenings with him or, at least, within his house while he, amid books, computers, photographs and notes, did what he called his "own work," his writing, his research. Lawrence's life revolved around work. I supposed that he loved his work more than anything else. He worked with such zeal, with such immense interest in the arcane issues of medieval book production and in the histories of particular manuscripts (stitching together intellectually, for instance, pages long separated, pages blown all over the world by windy centuries of chance); he worked with such absorption, with such eagerness, with such curious curiosity, that his work impressed me as an expression of his personality, not as a series of imposed tasks irksome or burdensome to him. Lawrence worked prodigiously. And in his scant off hours, he needed company; company seemed essential to him. When not overtly working, he wanted to talk, to share his thoughts, his observations, and his cooking. He needed to share his general warmth. His very nature required a lover, an intimate companion, and he had long had companions sequentially. Thus, I learned early on: Lawrence wanted a lover in the interstices of his work.

As an ad for hired help might have it, Lawrence desired company "mornings, evenings, weekends." He needed, he desired, someone willing to conform to his habits. He needed company after work, a domestic, settled sort of company for which, or for whom, he did not have to search. He wanted no one demanding, disruptive, or eventful. Neither did I. Unlike me, however, Lawrence had a communicative temperament. Perhaps he, himself, in and of himself, embodied contradictory inclinations, one side of him scholarly and mole-like, thriving in an obscure element alive to his ear, the other, sociable, light-loving, and brightly sexual.

Early in our acquaintance, I'd thought, crudely, vaguely, that Lawrence needed a lover because he'd "always" had one. That amounted to tautology: he needed one because he needed one. I'd thought loverly companionship essential to Lawrence, essential to the satisfactions of his mind-temperament-body. Further, I'd thought that Lawrence had lived so much of his life with sequential lovers that his very way of life had become companionably patterned: his habits, his routines, his expectations of days, of everyday life, presumed the presence and the active company of a second person. I all but equated his lovers before me with his furniture, with the wooden redundancies displayed in his bedroom furnished for two people. I came close to believing, crudely, that Lawrence, as the broad strokes of an old song had it, "just" wanted, and that he "just" needed, "somebody to love," and that almost anyone, anyone reasonably intelligent and considerate, would do. I showed up, warm and willing. Interviewed through chess, I got the job.

A contradiction, or something like a contradiction, lay in the differences between my sense that Lawrence needed a lover (almost with the blank impersonality with which he might need a fixture) and the countervailing conviction that I appealed to him uniquely. (I believed my uniqueness far from unique. I believed that Lawrence had loved each of his lovers uniquely, for individual traits.) I believed that Lawrence needed someone, almost anyone, and that, once he'd found that person, he loved as if he had never loved anyone else.

Vainly, I did wonder about how I ranked among Lawrence's loves (if some sort of rank existed in his mind). I believed myself unique to Lawrence in two ways. He enjoyed thinking about my virginity. And my appearance appealed to him. Then, too, I thought that he enjoyed both my talk and my attentiveness to his wishes. I might not top the hierarchy (if such existed) of men whom he'd loved, but soon after we met, Lawrence began talking about our marrying. Assured of my desire to live with him "forever," Lawrence discussed the subject. He discussed it comfortably, like a cat purring. And he aired a contradiction, an unambiguous one: He coveted me; he desired; he desired to "keep me" with him; he desired to help me into conditions favorable to my art. And then, sweet man, sweet creature of routine, he said that he felt uneasy about "subjecting" me to his "middle-aged way of life." "You're so young, Neddy. Would it really be fair to you?" Considering what I had to gain materially by marrying Lawrence, I couldn't exactly beg him to marry me. I couldn't simply dismiss his sensitive doubts.

84 LAWRENCE'S DOUBTS

Lawrence soon knew me well enough to know that his quiet way of life agreed with me. I did not need to explain to him in words that I, as an arch-introvert, as an extended nervous system that reacted powerfully to stimuli, as a one-man-dog-sort-of solitary person, differed from sociable people in general and from many people my age in my conceptions of entertainment, pleasure, excitement, and discovery. Despite knowing me (and my surpassing contentment), Lawrence sometimes worried, or wondered, about my aloofness from my peers. One night, for example, he sat reading in his living room; I fell asleep on the floor, near the hearth. Lawrence awoke me by nudging me with one of his slippered feet. He said, "Neddy. Neddy. Wake up. Shouldn't you be out there partying or something?"

I had lain on the floor, savoring the weightlessness of colors, savoring a sense of how colors in objects (like the moss of the multicolored carpet under me) simply occupied those objects without my moving a muscle. I'd spent the day moving colors that weighed a ton, using very old, very heavy, gray-skinned—gray-cheeked—lithographic stones to place colors on paper, flat, bright patches of unblended hues all too obviously derivative, in their lively contours, from paper cutouts by Matisse. I'd felt gratified and exhausted by the work. I'd fallen asleep, feeling as if I blended into the carpet, as if I seeped into it like water, as if my hair drained away into the underlying blue. When Lawrence's soft toe nudged me and Lawrence spoke, I did not even begin to understand his question.

Lawrence sometimes seemed to think that by living with him and by loving him exclusively, I somehow forfeited experiences that I should not forfeit. Once, lying in bed, restfully sealed, flesh to flesh, both of us eased of semen that the other had consumed, he ran his left hand's fingers along my arm, musing, "You're so young, Neddy. So young." I replied, "You like thinking that I'm young, but I'm really not." "Hm," Lawrence intoned. "'Why should she give her bounty to the dead?'" I rolled aside to look at him sideways. "What are you talking about?" I said. He shifted. He said, "Oh, nothing." I persisted, "Who's dead? Who's bounteous? What are you talking about?" Lawrence shifted again to lie on his left side completely, facing me, his left elbow deeply bent, his left hand's heel sunk deep in his stubbly cheek. Reaching to fidget with my hair, he said, "Maybe you should have a more varied life than what I—" I plunged. I knocked Lawrence onto his back; I clapped my fingers over his mouth. To his rolling and almost comically relieved-looking eyes, I fulminated against "should," "should this," "should that"; "should" followed us around all our lives. I asserted that I could decide my own "shoulds," and that no variety of other people could equal the variety of even one little piece of his little finger. I pounded Lawrence with "I love you," "I love you." He, definitely relieved, laughed and gasped, "All right, all right."

As I have mentioned, the idea, or the cloud of indistinct notions, that Lawrence called my "virginity," stirred Lawrence. Until he ventured to suggest that "maybe" I "should have a more varied life," I had had no inkling that Lawrence might pity me for the limits of my experience, for the very limit that he oddly prized.

One morning at breakfast, during one of his enormous and leisurely Saturday breakfasts, Lawrence again called me "young." I again objected. Lawrence chuckled. He said "Ah, Neddy," as if humoring me through some fit of unreason. His bright knife cut translucent marmalade on his plate; bright metal gleamed through the lifted glob. Raking the amber over toast, Lawrence asked, "Don't you ever just want to—cut loose and—" "And what?" I asked. Lawrence looked at me as if looking with interest over the tops of eyeglasses. He produced a sweet euphemism, "See where the night takes you, hm?" I said, "No." Lawrence smiled. He said, "Young people are a challenge." I said, "You mean to me?" Lawrence nodded. Taking up the half piece of toast which he'd let rest, Lawrence continued, "Don't you ever feel you're missing something?" I asked, "Like what?" Lawrence shrugged. Hesitating to bite the lifted toast near his mouth, he said, "I don't know. Clubbing? Sex with other people?" I pointedly didn't answer.

One night we sat in near darkness, in his living room, having returned late from a dinner party. A small fire twitched in the grate; no other light lit the room. Lawrence sat slumped. Looking toward the fire, he growled, "I'm too old for you, Ned." Frightened, I moved to sit beside him. I barely breathed, "Why do you say that?" Lawrence sighed. He exhaled dubiously, from puffed cheeks, through closed lips. He righted his position; he looked at me squarely, firelight reflected on his eyes. He said, "Weren't you terribly bored tonight? All that talk about music?" I replied honestly, "No. Not at all." Lawrence looked at me searchingly. He said, "You really weren't bored?" I said, "Really, no." Lawrence flexed his forehead. He said, "Well, I guess I was, then. And I thought. Neddy. I thought. It's not fair to you. Making you spend an evening like that."

85   LAWRENCE'S RESERVATIONS

Lawrence voiced only one reservation about our marrying. I supposed that he had others besides the one voiced. Lawrence's spoken reservation suggested that he thought only of me, of my ultimate good. He said, "I'm too old for you"; he suggested that I, Edward, "should" live vibrantly, with people my own age. Once, when he said "I'm too old for you," I said, "You mean, I'm too young for you?" Lawrence groaned. He fell all over himself, moaning, "No, no, no," "oh, no, no, no," "no, Neddy, no." And I, easily, easily, felt assured that Lawrence did not long for a middle-aged companion in my stead. But I supposed that my age did give him pause. I supposed that Lawrence, invested by most accounts with many advantages over me and aware of his status as a more firmly established, more burdened, and hence more adult person than I, knew that, if we married, he would feel lastingly and profoundly responsible for me, however responsible he already felt, however much a sense of responsibility entered into his unmarried care. Marriage would bind him and his resources legally to me.

How large did my liabilities loom in Lawrence's mind? Lawrence did not disclose his thoughts on that subject, and I, perhaps out of pride, did not press, prod, or probe. Although unfrightened myself, I considered my liabilities frighteningly great.

I strongly resembled an overgrown child. When Lawrence first mentioned marriage, my father still paid for my schooling and gave me an allowance. And I lacked adult ambition. I'd sensed my ambition at an early age, and I'd defined it, later, in childish terms: to lie on a floor, scribbling with crayons. I wanted to spend my life drawing and painting without worrying about pay. Of course, many voices, and even a voice in my own head, told me repeatedly that I would "have to grow up," to get a job, to earn money, to pay taxes and bills. But I also—childishly, willfully?—believed that maturity might manifest itself diversely, and that I could live contentedly on a pittance, and that I might contrive to earn that pittance without embracing the obligations of a regular job. So my desires whispered, while common sense shouted, and I had internalized enough puritanism to feel that, in fact, the only way in which marriage with Lawrence might actually hurt me—or impair my development as an adult—lay in the license, which Lawrence did give me, to do just exactly what I wanted to do. Lawrence gave me the structure of peace and quiet in which to draw with crayons.

Wondering about Lawrence's unspoken reservations about marrying, I did not doubt the marriage-justifying power of his affection for me. And I did not doubt that I appealed to him erotically. I did wonder, however, if Lawrence might fear social censure for the visible—and merely visual—mismatch between us. Might he dislike advertising his attraction to men much younger than he? Might Lawrence doubt his own capacity for fidelity, if he did not doubt mine? Might Lawrence fear commitment, legal commitment, to one embodiment of youthful qualities while other such embodiments abounded around him constantly? Might Lawrence fear that he, if not I, might desire diverse partners? And those questions, which I dismissed, aside, I wondered if Lawrence might not view some of his conduct with me, his dressing me in covert costumes, for example, as foolish, undignified, inappropriate, unseemly. Might Lawrence fear that he merely, lustfully, played with me? I did not really doubt; I did not really wonder. I confidently dismissed these and other questions.

Socially, Lawrence possessed a much more firmly established position than I did. His job, his work, his daily interactions with people, and his acquaintances all integrated him into a huge hive of human activity, a buzzing system of interactions economic, intellectual, and personal. As a student, I had a relatively small, often receptive role in that great, nameless enterprise of all that everyone did. And, figuratively, Lawrence's mind and personality together resembled a bunch of very fine tendrils ever spreading, ramifying, and expanding, ever reaching into new places, entering into new areas, whether of learning or of worldly experience. That activity of Lawrence's person, that vigorous growth of diverse interests, added integration to integration. Like a rock wall, his job gave him one kind of standing, and then his mind, plant-like, overran that pile of weighty obligations. I, on the other hand, drifted around, awash like a solitary clump of contented algae.

I wondered about Lawrence's attainments and affiliations and my relative lack thereof because I wondered a little about the concept of power as applied to us. There, I stared a contradiction in the face: I firmly believed that Lawrence and I lived eye-to-eye, side-by-side, day-by-day in our bearings with each other, in a partnership in which neither one of us imposed upon or dominated the other, in an accord between equals. But no facts supported the idea of our equality. The abstract equality attributed to all people, as in, "All men are created equal," did not account for my sense about Lawrence and me. And I did not even act exactly like his equal. I worshiped Lawrence. I rushed to serve him, to dry his feet, to tie his shoelaces, to help him on and off with his coat, to open doors for him, to spare him domestic efforts and irksome errands. I acted fervently servile, as if desperate to earn love. But I did not feel desperate. A demonstrative current drove me. And although Lawrence enjoyed my slavish demonstrations, I felt that he enjoyed them modestly, without mistaking them somehow for his regal due. Did I flatter him? I felt that Lawrence lacked vanity. Did some deep-seated humility in him nourish my sense of our equality?

How could I persist in the blissful conviction of Lawrence's and my essential parity when he obviously possessed power of command over me? I deferred to Lawrence. I trusted his judgment more than I trusted my own (and that, for good reason; that deference in me, that deference of mine, might merely seem sensible). I usually desired to do as Lawrence wished, and even in those rare instances in which his wishes and mine did not coincide, I usually found it easy to abandon my preference. Did that abdication of my will in petty wishes make me the inferior and Lawrence the superior, the two of us unequal? I didn't think so. Perhaps my sense of our equality depended upon Lawrence's nature. He simply did not coerce or dominate. Had he shown a controlling vein, I might not have loved him.

I sometimes, fleetingly, tried to imagine how Lawrence and I might appear to eyes other than mine, to eyes less inclined to slide past simple facts. Totting up facts under the comparative and mutually-dependent headings of "advantages" and "disadvantages," I came up with four bricks of "advantage" and four bricks of "disadvantage." All four "advantages" accrued to Lawrence. (I considered Lawrence's age an advantage. He'd lived two decades longer than I had lived; he'd had that much more time than I in which to learn, and he had learned much, in every mode of learning. Lawrence had a job and I didn't. I thought that any person with any role in The Economy writ large possessed, by virtue of that role, social purpose and social integration, both of which gave an employed person an advantage over anyone without recognizable employment. And Lawrence had money beyond what he earned. He'd inherited it, not a vast fortune, but "enough." My feather-wisp of an inheritance weighted comparatively nothing. Finally, Lawrence owned possessions, and possessions like Lawrence's counted as assets, and assets stacked up like poker chips, stacked up like advantages over anyone lacking anything like such chips.) I did not, I could not, figure out, in the overly abstract, how "power" and "advantages" went together, but "power" seemed to inhere in "advantage," in "advantages." Therefore, by measure of plain, weighty facts, Lawrence had power and I didn't. No belief in equality should survive that undeniable imbalance.

Self-delusion could account for my belief maintained contrary to facts. I could delude myself into thinking that I did not delude myself. But I preferred to think that Lawrence himself possessed the last advantage over me in that, although he had those four bricks, although he had personal, social, financial, and material advantages over me, they existed as a lump, as one massive prerogative, as a prerogative that Lawrence, powerfully, chose not to exercise. Besides, those bricks of difference, those bricks of my invention, did not impinge upon the indefinable; they said nothing about love or about attraction or about compatibility. The existence of differences between two people in terms of age, education, professional attainment, income, and property obviously did not mean that those two people could not love each other or gratify each other.

When Lawrence considered our marriage, before the fact of it, only one of the great differences between us seemed to concern him, the difference between our ages. He sometimes unbearably told me, "I'm too old for you, Ned." I dealt with that pathetic judgment, one of Lawrence's few lapses in good judgment, heartily. Lawrence did not seem concerned with how the great and glaring differences between him and me might appear to the minds of people ignorant of us and to minds unkindly disposed toward gays in general. But Lawrence must have imagined, as I did, how, to such minds, our marriage might appear. Some people might think that I exploited Lawrence, that I used Lorenzo to achieve my unconscionably immature and self-centered ends. (True, I desired to live without working in the usual sense.) Some people might consider me, at the very best of this conceivable worst, blind with naïveté to my own conniving, to my self-serving manipulation of Lawrence. And some people might see Lawrence as rationally incapacitated, as gravely infatuated, as unable to govern an unbecoming, if not almost criminal, lust for willowy Youth. So I, a black-and-white stripe of a gold digger, might appear beside a mountain of available ore, either that or as a walking piece of immaturity in search of security, in search of protection, in search of escape from adult responsibilities, all under the wing of a paternal substitute.

87 PAJAMAS

Learning Lawrence's ways, I immediately learned that he slept in pajamas, solid-colored, soft-colored ensembles, loose shirts and trousers. The shirts, prim with piping, buttoned down the front and overlapped their matching pants as if they'd never heard of tucking. (My father's sharp, barked directive, "Tuck in your shirt," echoed off the tailless shirts; tucked, they would have looked ludicrous.) Although intentionally shaped by manufacture, Lawrence's pajamas looked positively, utterly innocent of tailoring; they appeared mild to the utmost, unassertive in the extreme, utterly lacking in rigor; they suggested unresisting acceptance of the body that bore them, unlike business suits, for example (and yes, my father habitually wore trim, nipped, pin-striped suits). Thus, just as the flaccid fall and drape of Lawrence's bathrobe had struck me, one night, as emblematic of his kindness to me, so Lawrence's pajamas, in their easy conformity to his bodily shape, epitomized, for an instant, one great difference between Lawrence and Dad with regard to me: my father had worked hard to form me; Lawrence accepted me as already formed.

One night in the middle of January, Lawrence and I sat in his living room. Wind drove sleet against windows. A fire pecked and preened in the grate. Lawrence, in pajamas, slippers, bathrobe, sat reading on a sofa opposite the fire. I sat on the floor, holding playing cards, two bridge decks intermixed. Much light blended in the room—light from concealed bulbs above the balcony wall; light from the fire; light from a reading lamp with a brass shade craning beside Lawrence. Lawrence sat with his chin drawn in upon itself. Light from the lamp beside him seemed to come from what it struck: buff-colored pages printed in columns. Lawrence held the publication furled, front cover against back. The round-headed, open-faced, brass-shaded lamp beside Lawrence suggested the head of a fair-haired child reading or hearing a bedtime story, a child tucked in bed beside its father, father, father, protective progenitor.

Lawrence, softly dressed in pajamas, wrapped in his gray-blue-red plaid bathrobe, with lenient shoes—softly deformed, backless, maroon, leather bedroom slippers—on his feet, frequently made cocoa for himself late at night. He ate snacks of cheese, crackers, cocoa. I sat with him while he ate. He urged snacks on me; I declined. Once, so sitting, I mentioned the large, four-square, pitted-as-if-stitched-through soda crackers that Estelle had brought me when I couldn't eat. When I concluded my put-upon complaints about the X- and Y-axes pricked into the crackers, Lawrence laughed. He held up one of his crackers, its broadside to me, in front of my face. He said, "See here, Neddy. You might like these. They're round." I growled amicably, "Don't make fun of me."

One night Lawrence wore pink pajamas. Perhaps the baby-girl hue looked ridiculous on him, ridiculously sweet, sweetly ridiculous. Perhaps the hue looked all rightly wrong with its aura of innocence. In any event, I, naked, clasped the sweetly dressed Lawrence around the waist just as he meant to get into bed to sleep. Embracing him from behind with my left arm, I slid my right hand down and around him, under his pajama shirt's overhang, over the clothed scar which he bore from an appendectomy, through his fly placket, into the covered zone where a glowing tenderness of warm skin filled my hand with spilling shapes. I caressed. Lawrence didn't object. He didn't repel my hand. He didn't plead the late hour, the long day. He didn't say, "Neddy, I'm tired. Can't this wait 'til tomorrow?" No. He did not speak, but he responded—strongly and at odds with his prim, pink pajamas.

One night, unable to sleep, awake as if disturbed by joy, by the joy of living with Lawrence, I left him sleeping in bed, his billowing breath, his snoring seeming, to my ears, too rich to bear, too wonderful in abandonment to let pass unacknowledged. I should have done something to get him to change his sleeping position so that he wouldn't snore, but I let him lie, mind and person dropped in unconscious rest. I slid out of bed, put on the bathrobe that Lawrence had given me for Christmas, and went into the living room where, despite my usual feelings about killing trees and burning wood, I lit a small fire in the fireplace. (I had no reason to touch the poker, which Lawrence frequently used, but I touched it because the bulges of its brazen handle recalled his warm hand.) I lay down on the sofa facing the fire. Darkness pulsed around the fireplace. The fire split and rustled. Lawrence's snoring sounded distantly, in peaceful gusts.

88   PHOTOGRAPHS

Once in a while Lawrence called me "Davie"—"Give me a hand here, uh, Davie," or "Davie, would you mind." Other nicknames from a past further removed from our present than "Davie" also bubbled up, applied to me: "Charlie," "Louie," "Mickey." I liked this evidence of a living past in Lawrence. I would have felt devastated if present liaisons confused him, but a jumble of past loves had the opposite effect by suggesting that Lawrence remembered most of his partners fondly and that a unifying fondness ran through their names.

Lawrence's occasional lapses, his occasional failures to remember exactly with whom he lived, interested me. They didn't worry me because I saw Lawrence at his work, and he talked about his work, and clearly no confusion assailed him there. I thought that perhaps his concerted application in one area—in one diversely demanding area—might actually explain his forgetfulness in another.

Because Dana-Not-Christine had spoken of Lawrence's "type" to my face, and because I harbored the suspicion that Mrs. Callender, who'd hired me as slide projectionist, had, glancing up from her cluttered desk, seen "Lawrence's type" in me, I wondered if I could see "Lawrence's type" myself. I asked Lawrence if he had any photographs that I could see of Davie "or Charlie, Mickey, Louie . . . " My voice trailed off, ignorant among clouds. "Ah," Lawrence said sharply, "Why?" "Why," I repeated, "I'm just curious." Nebulosity continued; I did not say—and Lawrence did not ask—about what did I feel curious. I felt curious about Lawrence's past as well as about type. Lawrence dropped his initial sharpness. He began muttering amicably about "digital photos." Digital photos of manuscripts abounded on his computer. He gazed at the machine as if tyrannized by it and afraid to awaken it. He said, "Here. Just a minute." He took a carton-like shoebox out of a cabinet and said, "This is easier. Let's go into the living room."

The box held many paper photographs in many thick paper packets—very dark yellow, gamboge, saffron. Lawrence, seated, relaxed, handing me photograph after photograph, seemed to melt into remembering people while I saw what the paper held, shadows of people who did not, to my mind, resemble each other physically. I devoured glimpses of Lawrence himself. "I was thinner then," he remarked complacently. He mused over photos. He talked about people whose names I'd never heard. We drank wine. He held photographs carelessly, broadly, between thumb and fingers, not strictly by the edges. (I respected edges. A fingerprint on a printing plate could turn into part of a print made from that plate. And thin edges cut. Lawrence, softly reminiscent, seemed beyond such qualms, such considerations, although, professionally, he handled slides carefully.) Lawrence sprawled, sipping wine, setting his glass down carelessly, handling photographs broadly. He seemed happy, as if doting on photos of family members. He seemed happy, even when he exclaimed fatuous-sounding, yet serious things like, "Lord. He broke my heart. I thought I would never get over it." I said things like, "That was twenty what? Twenty-three years ago?" "Hmm," Lawrence replied as if blissful, contented. He spoke as if gratified by his own recognitions, storytelling, sketching memories, while black-and-white photographs passed between us. I saw photos, heard stories. I tried to memorize names heard, and I tried to learn the sequence in which Lawrence had known the people pictured. Many passed as paper slips. I heard a drumbeat under the names, the beat of Lawrence's sexual vigor.

89   LAWRENCE BEFORE MIRROR

Lawrence had energy for work, for cooking meals after work, for conversing while preparing meals, during meals, and while cleaning the kitchen after meals. He had energy to read and even to write late at night, energy to play the piano, and energy to deal with people as part of his work and for entertainment. He had energy on top of energy, including sexual energy. It embarrassed me to hear him express pride in his mind's own vision of that aspect of his energy. Once, he said with satisfaction, "You wouldn't think it, to look at me." "Oh, yes, I would," I replied.

To my way of thinking, Lawrence owned more than he needed. He did not need his big house; he did not need his four bedrooms plus. He did not need his abundance of furniture, contradictory furniture, furniture austere in Scandinavian simplicity, but any-thing but austere in the quantity that filled every room. His bedroom contained a large bed, four chests-of-drawers (double sets of two types, high and low), a table, two chairs, and two miniature chests, which served as bedside tables. The furniture reflected a history of partners, but, to someone ignorant of that history, it might have suggested mere hope or desire. The furniture might have looked presumptuous as well; it might have conveyed the assumption that Lawrence would have a partner if he happened to lack one. (Not often, but sometimes, I did feel a little bit like a foregone conclusion, like a bit of life required by the wood. I barely knew Lawrence when I came to live with him. He instantly "gave" me two rooms, as if he'd kept them waiting. He spoke of the rooms as "mine," Edward's, one a "study," the other a needless bedroom.)

In the bedroom that Lawrence and I shared, a Japanese screen hung above the bed. The screen's golden vacancy caught light indirectly from two spacious windows. White curtains, which Lawrence would call "drapes," hung formally, in columnar folds, below large, perfectly semicircular, overlapping swags of folds, two paired swags per window. Like a beetle's wings beneath shell casings, further curtains—tissuey, white curtains—hung behind the first. Lawrence called the tissuey curtains "sheers." When closed against strong daylight, either or both sets of curtains, white over white or either white by itself, produced a suffused glow in the room, which Lawrence called "steam-bath-Ingres light." That phrase, as I heard it, cast Lawrence, with his roseate back, as a steamed odalisque, hair-gilded, male. A wide mirror hung above the low bureaus. The mirror struck me as modest in that it did not try to reflect the bed.

One morning, I lay in bed, in the glow of "steam-bath-Ingres light." Lawrence and I had played and wrestled and pressed our pointing bodies upon each other. I felt too happy to move, rooted in utter contentment. The sound of a shower from the bathroom off the bedroom suited the light; the air shimmered as invisible foliage moved; the shower hissed; Lawrence, showering, sang operatically, badly. The shower and the singing stopped. I would have liked to have greeted Lawrence as he, dripping, emerged from the shower; I would have liked to have dried him, to have lifted his sodden, clinging leg hair, for example, to springiness through buffing, but I enjoyed supine indolence more. I lay in the very place where Lawrence, slathered and inseminated, had panted, "Ah, Neddy, Neddy. You make me feel young." "You are young," I'd asserted. "Nah, yah," he'd replied. That reflection shaded happiness slightly. I felt absorbed in the light. After a while, the bathroom door opened; Lawrence appeared. He spoke affectionately, with gusto, calling me "love." I supposed that he would begin dressing, but instead of opening the drawer in which he kept underwear, he strode to the mirror and placed himself bodily in profile to it. He looked along his right shoulder to the unseeing glass, to the thin, framed, brittle, flat, hard, rectangular piece of silvered glass that could not see him as I did. The mirror made the cloth sheets around me feel free, pliant, soft, flexible, bending as if forgiving, in contrast to glass. The sheets conformed to my form while the distant, stiff mirror merely, flatly, reflected Lawrence's body to his eyes. I watched uncomfortably as Lawrence straightened his back and tightened abdominal muscles. He stood straight, slightly contracted. He then relaxed. With widespread hands on his belly and gazing at his reflection, he said, "I feel great, really great. I've never felt better. But." Dropping his hands, he turned toward me. He approached me soberly, soberly climbed into bed, soberly crawled, and soberly embraced me. Kissing my neck, he whispered, "It's been a long, long time since I've tried to lose weight. Would you still love me if I were thinner?" I told him, in shocked, indignant tones, "That's the saddest thing I've ever heard," and "Of course, I would. Of course. I'll always love you. What are you thinking? That I love only this?" I shook his thigh emphatically, meaning his body. Lawrence sheepishly apologized. He dropped his maudlin inquiry, his telling suspicion. He said comfortably, teasingly, "But the fact remains. You're a little odd."

90 BELTS

One day, looking for a misplaced shirt of mine, I found—by invasive mistake—in Lawrence's orderly room-of-a-closet, at the very end of Lawrence's bank of calm, prim, pressed shirts, four old belts hanging from a hanger against the wall. I stopped cold. Perhaps an instinctive fear of snakes stopped me; the clutch of belts dangled vaguely snake-like. The belts hung imperfectly vertically, warped in their lengths, the brazen-metal crook part of the wooden hanger passed through the four stacked buckles. I froze. I should have left well enough alone. I should not have done what I did. Guided by some fearful, fascinated interest, I took the hanger off the rod, took the swaying straps to the bed, removed each from the crook, and laid each leathern length, as I removed it, on the bed lengthwise, the buckles aligned. The four faded, abraded, once-all-chestnut belts stunned me. The belt that had hung atop the collection in the closet lay furthest from the edge of the bed. Below it, progressing toward the bedside, the belts decreased in length by some two inches each. I felt vaguely horrified, horrified by having invaded Lawrence's privacy, horrified by something more than proof of my nosy curiosity, horrified by a subtly erotic charge felt at the sight of the belts even before I'd aligned them on the bed as a sideways histogram.

Sure, I felt erotically charged whenever I opened whatever belt Lawrence wore, whatever taut belt released his girth and more to my further fondling. I very much liked feeling Lawrence released from encirclement, feeling Lawrence uncinched, feeling Lawrence, released to bodily ease, unpinched, unimpeded by civilized conventions like belts. But something other than or in addition to the thought of my lover's opening, opened clothing moved me, to my vague horror, as I observed his long belts.

I had never seen Lawrence wear casual belts like the bent, hunched straps spread before me on the bed. I had not known that he owned belts of that ilk, belts with thick, thick, thick, smoothly molded, curvaceously shaped buckles in metal like unpolished brass, with some applied, preservative coating irregularly worn as if chipped off the brass, buckles which looked as if cast all from the same mold. The buckles' frames, the buckles' shapes made to surround the prong-transfixed portion of a buckled belt, flared in their curvatures where they lay furthest from leather. The buckles' mildly arched, blunt-tipped prongs lay across the frames' almost-lobed vacancies; so, of course, as if unavoidably, to my mind, the frames and prongs suggested testicles and penises, the penis prongs disproportionately slender and lying as if pendent against the brazen scrota. Further, of course, the belts' lengths suggested a series of rumps, of accommodating anuses. Two out of the five openings or prong holds in each belt looked heavily worn by the buckle's embrace, by embraces full of strain which had deformed the leather, strain which had bent the smooth stripes into hillocks or knolls of penetrated bending. I groaned, seeing that—long stretch of sex—in Lawrence's belts.

I understood that, beyond his beloved person, Lawrence fired my desire as a figure of satisfaction. I did not have to imagine; I knew, from Lawrence's own, imminently reliable—sweetly unpretentious—comments and accounts, that he had rarely lived, from maturity onward, without a sexual partner. Seeing the four belts before me on the bed, seeing the four warped, hunched, bent belts outstretched, each with the press of time heavy upon it, I thought of Lawrence naked and full upon many partners. The thought stirred me erotically: my mind's sight of his wagging body and the lining of that sight, my idea of Lawrence as prodigiously satisfied.

That notion, that streak of imagining Lawrence, did not horrify me. But, seeing Lawrence's disused belts even as they hung in the closet before I'd arranged them, a perverse sense swept through me, and I feared my perversity. I'd jumped to a conclusion, a conclusion that the belts on the bed appeared to confirm. I'd felt instantly, seeing the belts, "Poor Lawrence." Feeling pity for Lawrence made me deeply uneasy, but my fear-stirring perversity lay in another feeling. Seeing the belts, judging them instantly of four different lengths—with the longest uppermost on the neck of a hanger—I felt an erotic charge at the thought: Lawrence had gained weight continually, continually, at least since he'd begun saving those belts.

That the assumption I'd made, that the thought of Lawrence's weight gain, should move me, should arouse me furtively (as it did do), scared me. Touching the long, bent, shed strips of animal skin on the bed, I imagined Lawrence's body growing softly, softly broader and deeper, even as I imagined him slipping from belt notch to belt notch, from partner to partner, thickening with experience, as if sexual pleasure additively created his plumpness. Lawrence's amassed plumpness did seem sexy to me. That plumpness stood for pleasure, and the more, the greater, the better. Of course, I'd lived as if wrapped around, tightly bound, by many strictures, belts. Still, sensible—sane and right—strictures bound me: I should not perversely desire excess harmful to health. I should not lust, in Lawrence's flesh, for compensations for my past, pinched existence; I should not imagine his flesh as the flesh of all forbidden pleasures.

91   LASAGNA, GRAPES

Whatever my desire for Lawrence said, I recognized, I believed, that his corpulence hurt his health. Lawrence overate. He seemed sensual about food, both sensual and discriminate. He cooked with pleasure and with care; he said that he "loved" cooking; he did *not* say that he also enjoyed eating. But he did eat—deeply. He frequently ate with a sort of sensual abandonment that I did not understand. Sometimes, tasting, he closed his eyes; his face went lax with relaxation, and some pitch about his slightly lifted eyebrows made his briefly sightless face assume, to my eyes, an air of blissful transport. He did not practice any religion; but religion lingered in him, in remnants of speech. Sometimes he actually said of food, of some sapid dish or other, "This is heavenly" or "This is what they eat in heaven" or "This is divine." I, bewildered, didn't verbally respond to such remarks. I believed that one could find "heaven" only on Earth, if at all; thus, Lawrence's calling food "heavenly," et cetera, seemed almost appropriately earthbound, almost. And Lawrence certainly did not believe in a life-after-death heaven involving excellent meals. He also praised food as "marvelous," "delicious," "extremely good." While I might also find something or other "delicious," I could not say so with anything like Lawrence's fervor. A frisson of extremity ran through his words.

I wondered sometimes if Lawrence, an obscurely burning fireball of energy, ate to relax, if he relaxed through eating. I wondered what stresses he, steadily calm-seeming, actually felt. He seemed to eat with a need beyond me. One night, even by his standards, he overate; he ate to the point of hurting his self-esteem. He'd begun cooking as genially as ever that afternoon, a Saturday. He'd made spinach lasagna for himself from scratch, starting with peacefully dark-green spinach, flour, and eggs. He'd coached me into making an egg-less, meatless dish for myself, slices of fried eggplant sauce-laden and baked. Hot olive oil for the eggplant had perfumed the kitchen. The oil had reeked of silver-green, yellow-flowering Russian olive trees and of molten beeswax. I'd commented on the scent; Lawrence had beamed, "Like that, do you?" He'd smirked as if satisfied, having found a chink, however narrow, a split like a hair of sunlight, in my usual obtuseness about food. We'd cooked two elaborate dishes; Lawrence had sung and had muttered as usual while cooking. We ate in the dining room by candlelight and by rheostat-dimmed, overhead light. Lawrence ate more than usual, lasagna, bread, salad, cheese, and grapes. I stood up to take away the dishes. Lawrence sat, chair pushed back from the table, as if he'd thought about standing up but had dropped the idea. His right hand lay on the table as if it had fallen off the wineglass nearby. The round-bowled glass still held wine, dark and garnet-glowing over the stem. Lawrence sat, gazing at the table, his chin nearer his chest than usual, his lips drooping laxly. I followed his gaze: on a dim, clean dessert plate before him lay the remains of part of a bunch of grapes. The plucked prongs of the stem looked wet with light. One grape remained on the fallen tree. I feared that Lawrence felt ill, perhaps seriously. (Again, I feared for his heart.) Lawrence said almost inaudibly, "I don't do myself any favors." He then seemed to rouse himself. He looked at me (stopped in my tracks). He said, "Uh, Neddy. You know what somebody told me once. Thanksgiving, I think it was. Somebody said, 'Gluttony is when you can't eat one more grape.'" He lifted his right hand and waved it loosely as if a circulating fly bothered him. He turned doleful eyes upon me. He said, "Neddy. Neddy. I can't eat one more grape."

92 GRAPES

Long before I met Lawrence, Burke and I went to a steep place in Greece with a deeply ancient name. Hard hills plunged down to a plain of olive trees, a sea of trees beyond which a sea of water wrinkled. A tourist met previously had told us, if an old woman meets your bus and offers you a room in her house, take it. "Why?" "You'll see." A woman met the bus; we followed her and, coming into her house, I saw heaven: grapes hung in bunches from a trellis over a courtyard. Vines spread from the courtyard's sides upward and over, creating a ceiling of leaves over the entire courtyard, a ceiling of leaves dripping grapes with snatches of sky here and there like the white of white paper left in enlivening flecks in watercolor paintings; sky cut and flecked the living darkness. The sight needed no addition, yet just as we entered and I saw the grapes, church bells began sounding loudly nearby. Sounds piled upward like rounds, over and over the pendulous grapes.

Not immediately upon entering, but later, I walked around the courtyard, admiring the dark silhouettes of leaves and the leafy masses overlapping, the suspended bubbling of grapes-in-abundance, the little, living globes of ruddy grapes' sunset skins. I spread my palms under grape leaves, ears. I caressed the green skins.

The house with the arbor at heart had thick walls, deep window embrasures, shutters, and no window glass. I sat in a window embrasure and drew and painted the festooned courtyard. In that fleeting paradise, in that paradise to which I tried to cling through seeing, though observing, I extravagantly told Burke, "I could live here forever." Burke replied dryly, "How would you earn a living?" I lacked the nerve to say that I might someday sell paintings.

Years later, I returned to the ruins, the rocks, the pine trees, the town of the arbor house. I looked for the house. I thought that I knew where to find it, but neither it nor any house remotely like it existed. Hills held tiers of new places. Moralizing clichés attended that discovery. Perhaps paradise comes only in glimpses.

93   HAZELNUTS

Burke and I went to Trabzon, in Turkey, on the Black Sea coast. There I saw hazelnuts, harvested, drying in the sun. The nuts lay deep on long, canvas swaths. Men turned the nuts with board-ended rakes, rolling the rattling abundance, rowing. The nuts had to dry, Burke said; otherwise, Burke said, they would molder when shipped. Sun beat on the nuts, the nuggets, the russet, shining, the garden-like plots deep as tilled earth. The raking, laboring men resembled gardeners tending. The nuts, turning, sounded like pebbles on pebbles, like pebbles dragged over pebbles on a beach by retreating waves. I walked along the beach, beside the nuts, the wooden wealth, the sea, the land, embracing fantasies that earth flowered in nut-brown furrows at the, to the, mere touch of a rake, that trees actually loved us, that trees gave without labor, without cultivation, without business arrangements, without exploitation. I did not see labor past, trees planted, maintained, nuts harvested. I did not see who owned what or who worked for whom or the laboring angels', the nut rakers', poverty. Earth just sang, yielding. Sunlight reflected from plenteous nuts. If one had waded into the nuts—carefully, shuffling so as not to crush any—nuts would have drunk ones ankles; nuts would have covered them. I knelt down, touched the water, the brown, multi-colored, multi-brown, unconnected cobbling. I touched the heads of the nuts. The rake / wave sounds came over me. The loose shingle scrabbled, the combed nuts' currents clashing. So, people's labor kept the human world going, rowing and rowing. I would have had each of those millions of nuts plucked lovingly, by hand, with appreciative fingers, fingers that cared not a fig for commerce, for business. Burke upbraided me, scoffing: "In your world, people don't eat. People don't lust—to make money." They don't shake money, nuts, coins, pennies, down, out of trees?

Looking around, squinting, I saw, far down a nut path, Burke typically talking, Burke typically trying to converse, this time with one of the angels, one of the rakers. Burke gesticulated, waving a dark-turquoise blob I knew well, a paperback Turkish-English, English-Turkish dictionary. Burke waved both his arms, book included. The aged, stooped angel beside him watched, moved one hand, held no rake. I felt that I had to stand up, to rejoin Burke. I had to stand up slowly, otherwise blackness flooded my brain, crushed my consciousness to a spark, a common symptom of low blood pressure. I stood up, returned to Burke. The man with whom Burke tried to converse had concave cheeks due to missing teeth; he had eyes with pale-rimmed irises. He beamed. Using much more German than Turkish, Burke introduced me, said something or other like "my brother." My sliding mind didn't hold the man's name. The man patted my arm and motioned "stay." He entered a low building nearby, returned with newspaper. He rolled the newspaper into a very large cone, went to the nearest nut stream, filled the cone with nuts. He pressed the cornucopia upon me, literally; once I held it, he pressed the peaked ends of newspaper down, over the cone's open end to close it. Nuts clustered like grapes. Burke and I stumbled through thanks. I supposed that the man had graciously thanked Burke for the courtesy of attempted conversation by giving the generous gift to me.

Wanting to eat nuts in our hotel room, I discovered that nothing among our possessions lent itself to cracking nuts. (Stepping on nuts with shod feet didn't appeal as an option.) Burke had withdrawn into reading; I didn't want to ask him to attempt to communicate "nutcracker" to any hotel employee, and I felt even less inclined to attempt the request myself. I searched the hotel room for something nutcracker-like: nothing. Door and door jamb might have cracked nuts in a pinch, but using them might have damaged woodwork. Finally, I discovered that the sliding window had a strong, metal frame. I put nuts one at a time into a corner of the window track and closed the window on them. I fished shattered nutshells and whole kernels out of the track. I moved the grating window repeatedly. Its sound might have bothered people; I didn't move the window at night. I apologized to Burke for the repeated grating. He replied without lifting eyes from print, "I don't care how you do it so long as you eat."

Long before I met Lawrence, at the very beginning of my lessons in chess from Burke, my family and I stayed in a pension in a small town in Mexico. Rolling pastures—neither hilly nor flat—surrounded the town. Pepper trees grew in the pastures. Black cattle, breeding stock for the corrida, dotted and darkened the yellow fields. From my point of view, the pension consisted of a series of large, dark, cool rooms floored with large, dark, clay tiles. Arcades fronted the rooms; two courtyards lay at their backs. A dining room faced one of the courtyards. One side of the dining room consisted almost entirely of folding doors. The doors made of many glass panes usually stood open; the room opened fully onto the courtyard. The other courtyard contained a small, kidney-shaped swimming pool lined with mosaics. Lawn surrounded the pool. On two sides of the pool courtyard, magenta-flowering bougainvillea grew against shaggy white walls and below windows flanked by turquoise shutters. Orange-flowering trumpet vines covered the pool courtyard's other two walls. Someone cut the vines only just enough to keep them from overrunning a long, L-shaped, red-clay-tile bench built into the walls. I enjoyed swimming in the pool and lying on my back on the earthen-tile bench, looking up into the pouring mass of orange flowers.

A fountain stood in the courtyard off the dining room. A font like a white-painted baluster made of concrete dribbled in the center of the fountain; white tiles lined the fountain; colorful tiles covered its eight outer sides. (In the fountain's outer tiles, the creamy white of their basic clay formed a grill-like pattern. Within the grill-like scrolls, bright colors glowed, lit by the white behind them, and where the pale pattern and the glowing daubs lacked, dark blue covered the tiles like glorious jam.) Atop the fountain's rim sat eight large ceramic frogs facing inwards. Water pipes protruded shortly from their peach-colored mouths. Blue splashed their white chests. Blue-outlined and mustard-golden loops spangled their backs like honorific braid. Their eyes looked lustrous, dark, and widely round. The ring of frogs—sprung from fairy tales—looked wonderful to me, but not as wonderful as did the fish that lived in the fountain's pool, large fish with tails like milk spilled in water: flame-orange fish, gold-yellow fish, black fish with yellows and greens in their black, white fish anything but white, pearly and pinkish, fish spotted and mottled and masked, fish that combined all the other fishes' colors. The fish moved by shouldering without having shoulders. Their fan tails flowed. Their colors shifted iridescently with the light. In the heat of the day, the fish packed themselves into the shadow of the dribbling baluster in the fountain's center. In that, they resembled cattle packing the shadows of trees.

Meals in the pension took forever. Waiting and waiting for food to arrive, sitting with Burke and Estelle and with my sometimes redundant-seeming, actual parents, I often felt bored. One day, more bored than usual, I asked permission to leave the table. Without asking further permission, I took a breadstick from a glass on the table, went through the open side of the dining room, and fed the fish in the fountain. Lured by crumbs, they flooded over, out of shadow, to the fountain's side. They shoved and smacked as if ravenous. I held one end of the breadstick in the water; the fish crowded in, tore at it. Seeing the fish really close for the first time, seeing their heads and backs actually breaking the water, I felt tempted to touch a fish. I felt forbidden to do so. (No one had told me not to touch the fish, but I had had "Look, but don't touch" drilled into me.) I actually considered: What might happen if I did touch a fish? In ignorance, I thought that nothing would happen. And so, with the hand not holding the last of the gobbled breadstick, I reached into the water. I touched an orange-masked, pearly fish; it instantly sank below my fingers. Other fish crowded in, and something cut me. I didn't know then, and I didn't learn for a long time, that gills could cut. The cut hurt like crazy. Worse, it shocked and frightened me. It seemed inexplicable (and undeserved). I felt punished, out of the blue, by the inhuman universe, punished by no agent, by none at all. No agent acted through the fish, but I felt punished for having disobeyed the parent-like promptings of conscience that told me that I should not touch just because I admired.

95   PIER

Lawrence seldom went anywhere far from a library, an archive, or
a collection of rare books, but, at my suggestion, the summer after
we'd met, we went to a state park. We hiked briefly, from a parking
lot through pine woods to a lake, and back. Lawrence surprised
me. He walked zealously, avidly, as if back or knees never pained
him. Pine needles blanketed slopes; pine trunks seeped resin; crows
cawed out of the blue as if dropping coolness. We sweated. Earth
grunted, thudded, sounded hollow when our feet knocked it.
Trudging along, watching Lawrence ahead of me, I felt almost
contented. I would have felt perfectly contented had I not felt
aroused by Lawrence, by his sweaty scrambling, by his unlikely
zeal, by his khaki-and-white-dressed body clambering in front of
me as if he'd never suffered from exiting cars, never looked at me
in dismay when he'd dropped case-housed keys and thought of
bending down, stooping to retrieve them. Aroused by Lawrence,
by the handily grappling manner in which he walked, and aroused
by other stimulants, by the literal heat, the fragrant air, the seeping,
scaly pine trunks, white pines with needle tufts in papery cuticles
high in the trees, by slick banks of pine needles rosy or shadowed
dun, I desired to play at mating, to act as a male might in nature.
I wanted to run at Lawrence, to chase and to nip and to shove
him, to harass him into receptivity, to get him to stand still—on
all fours—for me, with his sweet "back" legs parted, his sides bare
and panting while I, rampant and blind to human love, wild with

instinct, plied him with massive sliding. Had I actually tried to shove, nudge, paw—or even talk—Lawrence into some sunny gully for seclusion; had I actually tried to persuade him, one way or another, into cooperating with my urge or fantasy, with my desire divorced from the usual point of such "drive" "in nature," impregnation, genetic perpetuation; had I actually tire to coax him, the prim, buttoned-down Lawrence, into slipping and sliding with me under the pines, he would probably have squinted at me fondly. He would probably have said something mild and sensible and yet indulgent like, "Later, uh? Neddy? This is a public place. We can't take the risk."

We came to the lake cool after dry trees, after buzzing incitement, cicadas' ratcheting. We walked out a short distance into the lake, onto a low dock with a railing. Water lily leaves, leaves of bullhead lilies not flowering, plated the glossy water near the dock's weathered planks. Lawrence leaned, forearms on railing. He gazed about, said, "This is really quite pleasant." "Mm," I replied, staring at water lily leaves, "Green, too." Deep, deep, calm green, flat, dull, curved leaves, leaves like blind spots, lay on the gleaming water. Bronze-golden-green water moved our reflections, worked them by the edges, near the dock's blackened skirting, skirting partially submerged. "I'm glad you suggested this," Lawrence said. I tipped my head sideways as if I'd provided all nature and, of course, deserved thanks. Lawrence sat down cross-legged; I sat down at length, legs in grayed jeans outstretched, back against railing support. Lawrence's trousers creased behind his knees; beside his light-brown eyes, living creases held sweat. I warned Lawrence against sunburn. "I'll be fine," he replied, larded with sunscreen.

We sat on the ramshackle dock; sun beat, very warm. Pine trees' scaly bark exuded resin unseen. Resin unseen caked white on the bark. Insects pulsed, ticked, whirred. I tilted my head back, face to sky, neck beside a vertical railing support, eyes closed, eyelids orange. I thought of rough pine woods, smooth, green leaves, the bare lily leaves like forms lifted from penises, notch to each leaf suggesting median fold. Lawrence sat breathing near me, full on flat planks. Lilies' stems swayed unseen, tough stems slick and long like hoses and more. I knew the stems' toughness. I'd picked a water lily as a child. I'd swum out, in all my clothes except shoes, to a purple-white flower. Snails clung to the pad's underside. Unable to break the cable stem, I'd bitten through it. Estelle, to whom I gave the flower proudly, gave me hell. She'd scolded me severely, not because I might have drowned, but because I'd stolen a flower out of a neighbor's pond, neighbor by summer rental. Estelle, gray eminence, virtue, had made me telephone the neighbor and report my crime. To my relief and, perhaps, to Estelle's moral consternation, the neighbor had laughed. He'd brushed off the incident as if he'd never heard of lawsuits, trespassing children drowning, death. The slick, tough cable-stems aggravated lust. I opened my eyes, asked Lawrence if he needed water; he replied no. I restlessly opened my ancient backpack, small, peacock-blue nylon, hot in sunlight, black straps, black zippers. One biting zipper's little, gritted teeth parted. I took out cigarettes, matches, lit cigarette, as ever, not for smoking but for watching smoke. I lay my cigarette-holding hand edgewise on a plank so that the smoke's lowest unfurling cast a rippling shadow on silvery wood. Cracks in the silver wood curved, suggested desert terrain under cloud shadow, smoke. The dry wood forming the dock, separate boards over wholeness, water, didn't hold nail heads closely, nails, Jesus Christ. With a finger, I touched the nearest nail head; cigarette tip burned untouched. The rude nail went down unseen but for its browned neck, top. The straight, hard, sun-warmed spike went down into the plank. Spikes, spikes, many spikes, nails, attached boards to boards below us, attached boards to pilings; uprights like telephone poles, once-growing trees, supported the dock. Nails, pilings went down straight, unlike lilies' stems, long, curved, flexible, living beside the rootless planks, the stiff, dead-end sticks. To distract myself from the urge to push into Lawrence, I played a stupid game. I sifted cigarette ash onto water on the sun-struck side of the dock, near at hand. I said,

"Watch for fish." I sat, looking down into translucent bronze, green-golden water. Lawrence shifted over, joined me, watching. After a minute or so, he said, "I don't see anything." I said, "Look way down. Where you can't see any further. See them now?" Fish shapes hung barely distinguishable in the glowing blur. Lawrence watched without comment. The fish rose slowly as if motionlessly, slowly, slowly increasing in size and distinctness. Lawrence said finally, "Ah! Sure enough." Surfacing, the fingerlings dabbled with mouths, minute ellipses. They sucked in ash, submerged, spewed out ash (more finely powdered than I had powdered it) in very small, swirling jets. Lawrence watched the fish. "What kind of fish do you suppose they are?" he asked. Perhaps he marveled. Perhaps, far from archives, far from libraries, he felt grazed by strange ignorance. But I didn't take it that way. "What kind of fish do you suppose they are?" Damn it. Family members of mine would ask questions like that, ever looking for names, "vert Veronese" beside the dazzling hue. "What kind of fish do you suppose they are?" Lawrence asked. I said, "Hungry fish, deceived fish, disappointed fish—insofar as that's possible." But then, I cooperated. For fish species, I told Lawrence, "I don't know. Bullheads, maybe." "Bullheads," water lily heads, aggravated lust.

96   FRIED EGGS

On weekend mornings, Lawrence ate—and ate—breakfast. He ate more and at greater leisure than on workday mornings. A weekend breakfast of his included candied tea thick with milk; whole milk coating a large glass; pink-fleshed, yellow-skinned grapefruit cut—by Lawrence, not by me—through their tender equators and further cut between the septa and spooned up, as Lawrence consumed them, through sugar slush. Lawrence daintily devoured, not at one sitting, but plenteously, in rotating varieties, toast, rolls, croissants, muffins, and "tartines" made with French bread, each baked piece treated as if he viewed it primarily as a vehicle for butter. He ate eggs in many styles, usually boiled softly, socketed in pedestals. He ate fried eggs in threes and thick flats of ham. He'd given up eating sausage links and fat-ruffled bacon when I told him, finally, that seeing him eating those things made me fear for his heart. I spoke the least of my fears for him then. Although his excesses scared me, I usually said nothing against his inordinate feasts.

Lawrence instructed me in breakfast preparations. He would have teapots scalded inwardly with a boiling rinse before one poured boiling water into them, over pierced-metal, egg-shaped containers into which he carefully measured tea. He would have seeds picked from sliced grapefruit with the tip of a knife. And all the while that we warmed rolls and made tea, all the while that we performed Lawrence's equanimous, self-cosseting rituals, National

Public Radio spoke, usually of disasters; climatic disaster enveloped the other disasters; a stream of reported disasters passed in speech around us, and Lawrence would putter and talk and ask—over a shoulder toward me—questions like "How much time left on those eggs?" (as if time coated them and would wear off) and "Have you sliced the bread?" Timed in manageable sequence, reflecting years of practice, his preparations came together simultaneously. Lawrence might tell me, with a touch of acerbity, "Your toast is ready," if I'd missed the toaster's clucked cue.

One Saturday morning, Lawrence stood at the stove, frying eggs. Otherwise fully dressed, he wore bedroom slippers, soft, backless, scuffed, maroon-leather bedroom slippers, over heavy socks. I sat at the breakfast table. Lawrence stood in profile to me, looking steeply downward, over eggs which I could not see. I'd watched him break the eggs' shells. I'd watched him pour the slipping clots, the jellied slime, into a skillet. Lawrence's breaking of eggshells seemed not breaking, but, rather, meticulous tearing. Without seeing them, I knew that three eggs lay outspread in the skillet before him; three outspread eggs bulged softly toward him; Lawrence's central body drooped softly toward the eggs. I would think that the eggs lying before Lawrence and in my mind lay on their backs, on backs which their landing, poured to the round floor of the black, cast-iron skillet, alone established. Three eggs lay rounded over their backs, over their incidental backs, over their flat backs formed by chance, backs which could have formed anywhere, out of whatever substance first met the black. Eggs lay sprawled on their incidental backs softly bulging upward: shell-less, soft eggs which could not help themselves, eggs which lacked tautness, eggs which lacked toughness, eggs which lacked sphericity, eggs which lacked many qualities associated with tough, slick, hard, spherical, not-prone-to-slump pool balls. Eggs lay before Lawrence, pooled piles of raw, soft inwardness. Lawrence, gazing over the eggs, picked up a black, slotted, plastic spatula. He glanced at me; he resumed gazing egg-ward. He said, "I was thinking. I don't know what your plans are today." I didn't have any plans independent of his wishes; I asked what he had in mind. Lawrence said, "Every third Saturday. There's an antiques fair. That's what it's called anyway. Out near Morton. We could drive out that way. Have a look around. If you're interested." I said something agreeable with more enthusiasm than I felt for the idea. Lawrence waved the spatula amiably; he turned the eggs. The spatula made me feel guilty. The thing had long, narrow, straight-sided, round-ended slots parallel to each other in its lifting part. The slots had something abstract about their lengths and their round ends in common with sausage links, and Lawrence had professed that he "loved" sausage links, and I'd begged him deferentially not to eat them for the good of his health. Lawrence maintained that I'd "inspired" him to avoid eating such sausage. Nonetheless, I felt guilty of having committed the crime of—slight yet definite— interference with his habits. Picking up the slotted reminder of missing meat, Lawrence simply turned the eggs. Each of the three seemed to roll over on its own, to show its milky, white underside willingly to him. I sensed that I would sometime interfere over eggs as I had interfered over sausage. Lawrence stood, gazing over eggs, eggs shell-less, outspread in a black, cast-iron nest. Eggshells lay in a saucer to Lawrence's right. A white-china dinner plate matching the saucer lay on the stove, amid the burners, gathering warmth. Saucer and plate seemed, without my seeing them broadly, white and extended and, despite their brittle rigidity, like the eggs' albumen-skirts invisible to me. Lawrence turned a knob on the stove's front; small, blunt-looking, blue fire-claws vanished, backed into holes in the burner ring. Lawrence lifted the sheer dinner plate. He moved the eggs, each wholly enclosed in its own white, to the plate, using the slotted spatula, shaking the turner gently as he tipped it. Each egg, lifted, slipped to the plate. (Eggs slid, lacking legs. Each legless, low, wide-bodied egg slid, shaken slightly; each appeared to waddle as it slipped from the slotted spatula-ramp sideways, onto the plate.) Lawrence walked toward me, bearing his three-breasted plate; his breasts moved slightly. Lawrence, advancing, waved the carried plate. He said mildly—

impervious to my mean intransigence—"Change your mind about these, I can always whip up some more." I almost choked. He had not whipped those eggs. I knew; I'd watched; I'd observed his manner. Whatever else the eggs seemed, they seemed very well-treated. I said muffled thanks. Lawrence lowered the plate, seating himself to my right. White-fabric napkin spread on his lap, he picked up a fork. The fork had pointed tines. No fork substance enclosed the spaces between the tines; unlike the black-plastic spatula's round-ended slots, the long, curved spaces within the fork passed into formlessness beyond angular points. Lawrence, who would call himself "bonne fourchette," "good fork," hearty eater, touched the fork to an egg, to one of the three sprawled softly against the hard, thin, white plate. Using the outer side of an outer tine, Lawrence cut an egg. The fork cut; yellow flooded. I looked away.

97 FAIR

When Lawrence, watching eggs fry (not watching paint dry), suggested going to an "antiques fair," I pretended interest. I had no interest in antiques. Deceased people seemed to cling to their things; life's transience attached to objects adrift, for sale; the very word "antiques" creaked like old machinery. We went. I drove, which gave me something to do other than worry. As Lawrence explained it, the "antiques fair" took place "in the country," at "fairgrounds," "near Morton." Thoughts of my Rawlinson grandfathers haunted the word "country." The narrow ghosts of Rawlinsons radiated dangerous virtues. I imagined "the country" as populated by people hostile to couples like Lawrence and me. A countervailing thought occurred, too, however: Dealers in antiques should recognize the buttered side of bread in people like Lawrence. I relaxed, driving, and Lawrence relaxed even more than I did. He fell asleep, seatbelt across his Aran-sweater-clad chest. The wide, dark-blue, glossy, almost satin-like strap looked sash-like, honorific, despite the casualness of the pale knit under it. I associated Aran knitting with Aran poverty; Lawrence, asleep, breathed relative wealth. Lawrence slept, literally nodding. I felt protective of him: proud, alert, responsible, serene. I wanted to drive on forever, skimming smooth road. In strong, warm, October sunlight, groves clung gray to the hills, some bare branches shining. Mud lots abutted ruddy barns. A house held two evergreens before it, one, two, like ski poles. The state highway's no-passing stripes, redder in their yellowness than the flooding yolk of an egg, looked freshly painted. Lawrence slept. Lawrence awoke. He looked about him, said, "Have we missed our turn?" I blithely replied, "Which of these many turns is ours?" Lawrence smiled and frowned both as he looked searchingly through the side window. Eventually he saw something he recognized. He said, "Ah, good. It's still coming up." When Lawrence said to turn, we turned; we left marginal largeness; fences drew near. A bent, tin sign announced fair-grounds. I had to turn Lawrence's car, Lawrence's smooth, dark blue, into muddy ruts. The ruts suggested trucks; trucks suggested men who drove them; truck-driving men joined my Rawlinson grandfathers as hostile to gays. I had to stop the car in a gateway where an aluminum gate, opened wide in a wire fence, didn't block the soft, soft, soft, yet fear-inducing ruts. I had to stay stopped in the car while an old man, thin, stooped, wearing jeans and a red-black plaid jacket, eyes watering, dented cheeks suggesting back teeth's absence, a day's stubble on cheeks, cap with earflaps tied up, not protecting large ears, arose from a very old lawn chair consisting of frayed, plastic webbing, the straps interwoven on a framework of aluminum tubes, came toward the car. I had to open the car's window—automatically, guilty of smoothness—while the man approached. He stooped from a stooped walk to the opened window. He looked through the window gap and said, "How you folks doing today?" I said, "All right. You?" He said, "Fine and dandy," "Can't complain," and "That'll be ten bucks." Lawrence released his rattling seatbelt. Lawrence, heeling over voluptuously, holding one hip raised, dug out his wallet. I passed a crisp bill, a bill guilty of newness, to a hand gnawed by arthritis, a hand which seemed, surely, one painful complaint despite the man's disclaimer. Two hands, both looking work-crippled, held the bill and tore tickets from a roll of tickets, a roll removed from a jacket pocket. Hands handed me tickets, grayish-pinkish, very thin, cardboard strips bent to a pleasant curve from the roll, two tickets united tenuously by untorn perforations, the compound strip's torn ends rough with torn perforations. Each ticket bore the printed word, "Admission"; "Admission, Admission," they read in sequence. A hand with fingers that didn't straighten raised its palm to face me. A voice said, "You folks enjoy yourselves." I said, "Thank you" and raised the window, a tinted, criminal piece of insulating glass.

We parked in the intended parking area, a field. Long stubble brushed the car's underside. Other cars and many trucks, trucks, trucks stood parked in the grass, parked in loose, spacious, irregular rows, not between straight-painted bands in close-packed lines on asphalt, pavement, man-made flatness. I cut the engine; we sat, sealed in quiet. Wind buffeted the car. Lawrence peered through the windshield toward billowing tents, a town-like extent of billowing, tawny, luffing cloth. Tents seemed to have vomited tables, tables packed indistinctly with objects. The tents heaved as if they would vomit further, further additions to the glinting plethora. Lawrence released his seatbelt again; again the retracting rattled. I unlatched my seatbelt and fed the strap slowly toward a voracious slot. Looking studiously downward, I said, "This is a first." "What is?" Lawrence asked brightly. I told him. "This is the first time we've left town together." I did not say, the first time that we'd left a college-town sanctuary. Lawrence said, "Ah, yes. So it is." He smiled impishly and asked, "Does that make this an ordeal for you?" I said "no" blithely. Perhaps I lied. We broke open the car doors. Lawrence slipped out quickly, something he didn't always do. Lawrence stood, massive in his pale, bulky sweater, his fair hair flaring, his teeth agreeably sun-struck, his eyes pinched to the wind. Altogether he looked as if delighted, sailing. I left the car, shelter, and caused the car to lock itself. Its hood looked blurred in illusory depths by moving clouds. Lawrence came around the car, toward me. I began walking backward in front of him to keep him in view, to cling to the moment, to forestall antiques. Walking backward in front of Lawrence, I told him that I wanted to paint his portrait just as he looked right then, but amid "joyous grass," really tall, yellow grass, not that "drab, crew-cut stubble." Lawrence looked pleased with new pleasure and pleased to humor me, but then, ending that brief view of him, he motioned for me to turn around. He said, "You'd better watch where you're going," not one of my strong points. I ceased walking backwards; Lawrence, catching up, squeezed me around the shoulders. His right arm stayed, familiarly at rest where it had squeezed. Walking under the amiable yoke of his one-armed hug, I wondered if Lawrence intended to advertise us as a couple. Perhaps he didn't think. Perhaps he merely engaged in one of his pleasant habits. Perhaps he intended to encourage me by his easy example, his fond arm saying, "Don't worry. Don't fear." I told him that I felt uneasy. I didn't blame "antiques" for my uneasiness. I said, "This scares me. This." I waved toward the billowing tents, the glinting tables. I called the "antiques fair" a "cosmic lost-and-found." Lawrence laughed. He said, "I love you, Ned," companionably.

We approached a tent. The wrack outside it turned into particulars. Women, mostly women, sat in lawn chairs, tending objects: plastic glassware, dishes in incomplete sets, false oil lamps. "Nothing here older than my grandmother," Lawrence commented. I thought of my grandmotherly great-aunt, Estelle, deceased the previous December. As if responding to my unspoken thoughts of Estelle, Lawrence showed me an oval. He held up his hands cupped opposite each other, not as if he held a platter, but as if framing a vertical oval in air. He told me to "keep" my "eyes open for a platter," "a really big one." I said that I would keep my eyes open. I felt inclinations to shut them. Open-eyed, I saw a cello stringless and downed. I told myself sternly: Look at people, not at objects. However, something, some wayward shyness, some stupid, unusual, resurgent, adolescent self-consciousness, something which would have me conspicuous as Lawrence's lover and not respected as such, made me feel evasive. I usually trusted people not to notice me. Clinging to the vestiges of fact, to the fact of my anonymity, I looked at objects: at a saltshaker missing a mate, at something made of glass, red, yellow, and blue, like a melted macaw. The glass reared short tentacles above a central hollow. Not for the first time in my life, I failed to recognize an ashtray as such instantly. Lawrence and I wandered through the valley of the shadow of junk, into tents, conjoined tents. Canvas tinted the light amber. I spitefully mentioned "flea markets," "collections of junk," "out in the country." Lawrence, who knew the fair's nature from previous visits, said apologetically, "I think there'll be some better things in the barns." As if I cared.

Lawrence cared. I tried to concoct an indirect care by caring for his care, for his interests. We meandered. Objects, objects, objects. "Lesser" or "better," what did it matter? Cars parked on the grass pleased me, but furniture—cabinets, chairs—parked in an unusual situation, on earthen ground, didn't. Did I feel unstable dislocation in tents' temporary rooms? Falling behind Lawrence at one point, I saw a horse collar used as a frame to a mirror. That arrested me. The full-flat combination hung high up, suspended from an object on top of a cabinet. The horse collar itself reminded me of something, but I couldn't remember what it evoked. I stood, staring up at it, until I remembered what I knew I remembered, Tenniel's Jabberwock in *Through the Looking-Glass*, the engraved illustration mass-reproduced. The horse collar's oily droop, its padded, black-leather bows, formally resembled the drawn monster's lips. And the horse collar suggested other things: the broad, dark, oval, convex picture frames around my Rawlinson grandparents' photographic portraits. And, as if in the face of the faces of flat, photographed Rawlinsons, as if to offend the grave figures remembered, as if intentionally to offend them, the horse collar became a gigantic anus, and I thought of—no horse straining at the bows, but my own sexual neck happily wearing Lawrence. Just then, someone suddenly near me asked if I wanted "a closer look" at the collar. Startled, I stammered, "No. No, thank you." I quickly rejoined Lawrence. He asked, "Find anything interesting?" I said no. I did not say, "Yes. Sex in a horse collar with reflection at heart."

Lawrence proceeded, investigating junk. He seemed honestly fond of it, which puzzled me. I did not believe that he owned any junk. But then, to me, whatever Lawrence owned seemed valuable, down to the least paperclip; his owning it gilded it. Wretched, wrecked toys came upon us. Lawrence pounced upon—more sex—a pink, plastic tube with a piston, a slide whistle. A bird in black plastic perched on the tube. "I used to have one of these," Lawrence exclaimed. He parted his lips as if he would blow the whistle. I stared at him: Please, don't. Lawrence contented himself with jiggling the bird's mobile, lower beak. He explained, "You blow into it, this moves. It trills the notes, you see." I nodded disdainfully: I'll take your word for it. Perhaps that incident explained Lawrence's junk-loving. Perhaps, seeing such objects, he roved through his childhood, as I often did mine in mind. I noticed that he didn't buy the things that he enjoyed finding. He seemed temporarily, lightly, unacquisitively nostalgic. Falling behind Lawrence again, I picked up a small, heavy toy bear. Crammed with machinery, it could walk mechanically. The toy felt hard to the touch; rigid, gray-pelted, it suggested a dead rat. I sniffed it and put it down. I sniffed my hand, which stank of dust. Lawrence rejoined me. He said, "Let's move on. Shall we?" We moved on, into barns.

Stained glass hung in the best light, near a barn's opened end: panes removed from houses, from churches. Among new panels, Lawrence discovered a fire screen he liked, a stained-glass fire screen hellish with red. I tried to look at everything in that particular collection other than the fire screen, but Lawrence drew my attention to it. He asked unavoidably, "What do you think of this?" I tried to sound temperate. I said, "I don't think it opens easily." Lawrence tentatively tried to shift one of the object's wings. Gazing wistfully at the thing full of teeth of red lozenges, he said, "It does seem a bit awkward." He didn't take his eyes off it. I leapt to pettiness. (How could he? How could he? How could he, a real, live, flesh-and-blood, publishing medievalist, a person with Chartres and la Sainte-Chapelle lodged in his brain, how could he stand there and look—not once, not twice, but long and loving-ly—at *that thing*, as he did?) I temperately mentioned the carpet nearest his living-room fireplace. Fire screen and carpet "might clash," I said. Lawrence, eyes still on the screen, said uneasily, "Uh. Downstairs. I was thinking, maybe." (Lawrence's wood-eating house overshot a hillside. A large room made the house two-storied at the back. With eager extravagance, Lawrence had offered the large room to me to use as a studio. Having nominally given the room to me, he seemed sweetly shy about purchasing décor for it himself. I'd lived with him for mere weeks.) I told him, "None of your other glass is tinted." And Lawrence smiled brilliantly. He said, "You don't care much for this, do you?" "No, I don't," I said. I said, "The red in it looks sharp." "Ah, well," Lawrence said genially. So begins familiarity? Another first? I had, within the past hour, knowingly thwarted two of Lawrence's wishes.

We wandered further, away from natural light, along electrically-lit aisles. Shops occupied stalls intended for animals. Some shops had floors; others didn't. We passed a garden of black Victrolas, mourning morning glories, black flowers. Emblematic dogs in decals on Victrolas heard their "Master's Voice." We passed fairy-tale coffins, glass cases. Lawrence explained the contents of one of the transparent caskets: "mourning rings" and "mourning brooches," rings and brooches in which tiny, glass compartments held dead people's hair. Who would buy such signs of others' long-lost loss? "Well. It's Victoriana," Lawrence gently replied. (Estelle had made small skeins of crimped thread, small bundles of used, removed sewing thread, thread which she wrapped around a pinch of fingertips to save, scrimping, saving, mending.) We came to a case displaying wedding rings, men's and women's plain bands bound to each other, tied together with thread. The men's rings looked larger than the women's, or perhaps I erred; perhaps the size differences merely made me think "men's," "women's." I paused over the rings without noticing that I'd paused. Lawrence whispered into my ear, "A bit early to plan for this, Neddy. But think about it, hm?" He tapped the glass case as if to say "you and me." I jabbed him fondly with an elbow. I muttered, without looking at him, "Whenever you want." He swayed me happily by the nape. I said, "Don't joke." Lawrence said, "I'm not." In a peculiar closeness of implied engagement, we moved on, past shops.

Glass cases gave way to tables bearing out-and-out junk: a plaster collie perched beside a notched pool of amber glass set in the wood on which the collie sat; camp postcards in stacks; postcards in pockets in clear-plastic pages; slithery, skittish chips, buttons; marbles, wonderfully colored, woefully chipped (as if their parents, paperweights, abused them severely); something like a horizontal windmill with spindles along the radial arms, a spool of thread on one of the spindles, thread from the spool entangled in the vertical axle under the arms; trays heaped with costume jewelry; a paper fan corpse-like in a flimsy box suited exactly to the closed fan's shape, long, narrow, shallow. Lawrence lingered behind me. I saw him far down the dim aisle, a clutch of paperback books in one hand, the other hand rummaging, evidently for books, in an orange crate (boards, slat-prison for succulence). In the clutch of held books, page edges faced me. I looked down, saw the fan lying boxed beside me. Its long, compressed folds merely looked like edges. I usually felt rueful, seeing folds in paper, as if folding paper hurt it. But the fan appealed. I picked it up, opened it, and shut it immediately, stunned. Suddenly, suddenly acquisitive, suddenly intensely acquisitive, I wanted to own the fan, I with my supposed lack of interest in homeless objects, I with my supposed disdain for nugatory knickknacks. I wanted to own the fan. I deemed myself instantly, unquestionably, its rightful owner, I with my past of fences and flowers, of a high, board fence beside lilacs in flower. The painting on the fan, on the softly-browned arc of stave-crossed paper, depicted a globular flower and a straight knife. Spaciously paired, with a graceful vacancy between them, a knife like a straight razor faced the flower with its cutting edge. The knife tilted away from the ball of petals. Some factory painter's hand, some factory painter's brush, had apparently touched the paper once, and once only, in the shaping, in the making, of each illusory petal. Pink faded to white in each petal-touch. The knife looked less skillfully painted. Some staleness, some tiredness of painting by rote, tinged the composition. But I liked the painting very much despite that. I also liked the way in which the two painted objects suited the fan's structure. The knife suited the fan's ribs or staves, and the flower suited the curve of the expansive paper. Petals and blade carried clichés, beauty and death, but I forgave them. Seeing Lawrence, fullness to my narrowness, still digging with dog-like interest in a box full of print, I hastily purchased the fan (priced as a piece of hackwork, which I believed it transcended). I hid the fan in its box under one of my jersey's close-fitting sleeves and rejoined Lawrence. I kept the fan secret from Lawrence until Christmas, when I gave it to him. Separately, on a different day but also for Christmas, I also gave him a set of drawings, quick, erotic, ink drawings in which he looked like Hercules and I, like stringy Nefertiti.

98 FAN

The fan purchased at the antiques fair, the fan purchased surreptitiously, at a distance from Lawrence, purchased not quite behind his back yet indirectly, out of the line of his preoccupied sight, had appealed to me instantly as a gift for him. Contemplating the painted fin in private, I wondered why. I usually disliked seeing folds in paper. The fan closed through twelve folds. I usually disliked the sight of cut flowers because cut. The painting on the fan depicted a cut flower to the left of a knife. I generally had no great fondness for knives. And a phrase existed, "fan painting," a dismissive archaism for trivial, decorative work. The phrase lurked in my head as a nagging offense. (Why within why? Did I wish I could earn a living, painting pastorals on harpsichords?) Lying on a bed in a room called mine in Lawrence's house, I stared at the fan's painted presentation. I appreciated the visual balance of the composition, the round shape of the flower dense with small petals—a China aster, I learned later—and the straight shape of the knife. The painting looked airy and open around those elements placed around a vacant center. The rounded, illusorily almost spherical flower with its many sinking shades of pink (pinkest in the feet of each of its many petals), the flower and the comparatively muddily-painted knife with its slightly curved, almost-rectangular blade, the flower and the knife eventually touched my mind as exemplifying hands and straight lines, that capriciously-applied and vaguely vast, nonsensical, sensual system by which I divided the world into two, and only two, opposing camps. The painting's shapely opposites, in harmony as opposites, appealed to me.

Further, of course, I saw the fan's painting as symbolizing Lawrence and me. Considering our alliance, I ignored the sinister implication of the painting's paired shapes, the seemingly unavoidable assumption that the depicted knife had cut the depicted flower, severing it from a mystical stalk unseen, thus killing it prematurely, before it would have withered naturally, had it existed. I saw Lawrence as a flower of positives, as a coordinated abundance of admirable qualities, most flower-like in open, obvious, socially wholesome friendliness. I, lean knife in the equation, didn't spread into the world, didn't give myself openly to the general air. I would not call myself mean, biting, or unkind, but. But I did qualify as self-involved, more than a little fond of solitude, purposeful, narrow, and edged: knife-like.

I gave the fan to Lawrence after he'd enjoyed the first effects of his gift to me. He had given me a bathrobe. I'd long since outgrown the fear that had prompted me to ask for a robe when we first went to bed. I did not think that Lawrence thought about giving me shelter, about giving me a hiding place for my body, when he gave me a robe, when he gave me the dark mass of plushy fabric that I received, a covert costume, something like a piece of dismal Victoriana, which clearly stimulated his imagination. He trembled with eagerness, fitting it to me. And we went to bed. I gave Lawrence the boxed and wrapped fan—fished from the pool of my shed clothing—when he'd finished imagining whatever had inspired him to have that robe made. When he awakened to happy, spent sanity, I gave him the—chaste—fan. Sitting naked in bed, he spread it before himself. He did not make wafting motions with it. He gazed at the painting on it, and I couldn't resist foisting my view of the fan's double subject upon him; "You" and "me," I said. A full kiss of thanks followed. Lawrence enshrined the fan in glass and made it a permanent part of our bedroom's décor.

99   BURKE'S COAT, GIFTS

During the first Christmas break after I'd met Lawrence, I visited my family. A summer's habitation in Estelle's house hadn't inured me to her absence, and each of my remaining family members variously made me regret the visit. My father's initially supportive talk gave way to his plague of "plans." My mother, shown Lawrence's photograph, wept. And the supposedly liberal Burke turned homophobic, declaring, "You were sick then and you're sick now and I don't want to hear about it." Burke later apologized. He said that he felt ashamed of the judgment he'd pronounced. Making amends, he asked friendly questions; we talked like adults without grievances, and I eventually asked him if he still owned a coat that I knew he still owned because I repeatedly saw it in the downstairs hall closet. I specified the coat: "Long, heavy, navy-blue?" "Yeah," Burke said, "You can have it if you want." I thanked him and claimed the coat. Although it did not fit me as it had fit Burke, it fit well enough. Slipping it on for the first time, I felt soothed, as if dipped in soldierly dignity. I felt as if I'd borrowed fortitude.

When I, wearing Burke's coat, showed it to Lawrence, I squared my shoulders. I said proudly, "This is a great coat." Lawrence, with genially creased face, with a squint-given glint about light-brown eyes, replied, "That's what we used to call them, Neddy, greatcoats. They're overcoats now." I forced him to acknowledge the coat's strong, sober air.

Burke's coat, good for my manly ego, fortified me not to object to Lawrence's Christmas gift to me, a sumptuous bathrobe made of ridiculous plush. Lawrence had fretted about gifts for me. He said, "You're a hard person to buy for," to which I replied, "But I'm easily pleased." Lawrence complained that I didn't "want anything." I laughed, "So contentment's a bad thing?" "Well, no," he grumbled. I told him that I wanted plenty of things: chalks and paints and pens and brushes. I mentioned pen nibs with wiry points "like hummingbirds' tongues," expensive and fragile. At all that, Lawrence frowned. He said that I would have to specify exactly, in writing, anything that I wanted "in that department," "art supplies," and that he did not want to buy gifts off of any such list; he wanted to buy me "something more personal." By "personal" Lawrence usually meant clothing. I'd received several gifts of clothing from him by that time. I'd begun to dread such gifts.

Lawrence outdid himself that Christmas. He fretted; he stopped fretting. One day he said brightly that he had "something" for me "in the works." Complexity lurked in that announcement, and the hint of special machinations didn't reduce my slight dread. Two days before I left to visit my family, Lawrence put his head in at the door of a room called mine. No closed door obstructed him. He peered around the doorframe and cleared his throat— nervously, I thought. He seldom acted nervous. He said, "Uh. Neddy. If you would. If you have a moment. I'll be in the living room." I guessed that the dread gift had arrived. I said, "Just a moment." I set aside my work and slid the boxed and wrapped fan from the antiques fair under the innermost sleeve on my left arm, possibly the same jersey sleeve under which I'd hidden the fan when I'd purchased it. I went into the living room. Lawrence sat in an unaccustomed chair. On a table beyond him lay a large, green-wrapped package bow-tied and cross-tied with green-bordered, golden-yellow grosgrain ribbon, a small, white envelope tucked beneath one of the bands of the crossed ribbon's cross. "You might as well open that now," Lawrence instructed me. I kissed him and thanked him and told him that I had "a small gift" for him hidden about my person and that he would have to search me to find it. I intended that statement to sound inviting, but although Lawrence answered warmly enough, saying, "With pleasure" and "Thank you," he urged me to open his package "first." He appeared preoccupied. I held out my arms, inviting him to frisk me. I tried to pique his interest in my gift to him, describing it as "very much-folded" and "not hurt" either by the folding or by my wearing it. But Lawrence refused to take interest; his forbearing smile suggested a grimace. So I approached the dread package without joking about it, without asking Lawrence, for example, "What is this? A brick from the Emerald City?" I plucked the small, white envelope from beneath the grosgrain ribbon, extracted a small, white card from the envelope, and read the message within the card, warm words in Lawrence's handwriting for which I kissed him again. He then nodded toward the green block. His nod said, get on with it; stop fooling around. I opened the package, which someone using a glue gun had wrapped. Unsealing the glue, I picked carefully; I tried to minimize paper's damage. "Let 'er rip," Lawrence urged. "No way," I replied, intently picking. The dark-emerald paper revealed a large, white coat box. I smoothed the paper; I rolled it neatly into a roll. Released, the cylindrical roll increased in diameter; it did not unroll completely. I took up the enveloped note card and began discussing proportional differences between it and the top of the denuded box, a comparison which Lawrence, genuinely smiling, cut short, saying, "Okay, okay." Get on with it. I had to face opening the box, the berg, the three-dimensional white rectangle that looked as if it could have eaten, for lunch, every other white rectangle that I'd ever seen (except the screen in Room 203). No seal, no tape, no adhesive joined box lid to box body. The lid slipped away from the container. Tissue paper stayed me. Ghostly laps of folded tissue covered a lurking darkness. I remembered Estelle's black-velvet hat, a crown of folds, sitting beneath tissue paper within an octagonal hat box, a sky-blue box, burnt-orange-banded above and below like a toy drum and otherwise dotted with little, golden roses. I parted the immediate paper and saw, I didn't know what. I exclaimed, "What *is* this? Magnificence?" I hoped that I sounded thrilled, not shocked or frightened. "What *is* this?" I repeated. Lawrence did not consider the question rhetorical. Sounding much more sensible than he'd obviously acted in making that purchase, Lawrence replied, "It's a bathrobe. Try it on. Let's see how it looks." I lifted the raiment: ferny turns of golden yellow over green and brown splotches, dark. "You like it?" Lawrence asked, pathetically anxious. I lied. I gasped, "Yes. It's amazing." "Put it on," Lawrence urged. I invested myself with the sumptuous moss. I don't know what got into me. Too much Christmas in the air, too many Christmas enactments of Nativities? I knelt before Lawrence, arms crossed over my chest, all reverently bowed. Lawrence gasped. He floundered out of his chair. Kneeling himself, he fussed around me, touching the robe, adjusting the set and the fall of it, the fold of its collar lap. I whispered one criticism. I said of the robe, "It doesn't go with blue jeans." Lawrence, breathless, excited, fussing, fumbling, tugging, laughed. He said, "No. No, it doesn't. I'll tell you what it goes with, Neddy. Neddy, Neddy." He said secretly to my ear, "It goes with your hair." Dark brown with dark brown, I silently agreed. When Lawrence, dithering, considering cuff or no cuff, folding back the left sleeve, deciding, no, no, the given length fit perfectly, when Lawrence touched my left arm, I said, "Warm," as in "warm, warmer, warmer," in the game about finding hidden objects. I incomprehensibly meant the hint to apply to the hidden fan. Lawrence naturally, understandably, misunderstood me. He breathlessly said, "It's supposed to be warm." He meant the robe itself. "It's supposed to be warm. That's the idea." Whatever idea drove him, I supposed, the robe's insulating properties had nothing to do with it.

100   RINGS

At the antiques fair where I bought the fan later given to Lawrence, I had paused, without realizing that I paused, over a black-lined, glass-topped, wooden case containing wedding rings. Against the sooty cloth, plain band after plain band and matching bands tied together with thread circumscribed absences, the circular gaps common to rings, where fingers belonged. Most of the rings looked plainly worn, worn by the wearing of fingers that no longer wore them. Irregularly placed flat on the soft-napped black cloth, the rings, most of them cheerlessly golden, barked to gold-gray, reminded me of the rings that raindrops made in puddles, raindrops not falling thick or fast: waves from sparse drops appearing, spreading, disappearing, ring upon ring, over the liquid surface. I felt as if I saw people falling away, a rain of vanishing people, the little signals of their leaving lying still on the cloth, and that not for long. Amid that mournful recollection of transience, Lawrence tapped the glass above the rings and said jocularly, to my ear, "A bit early to plan for this, Neddy. But think about it, hm?" Think about marrying him, think about our marrying.

Months passed. Months after that passing moment, Lawrence asked what I planned to do after I finished my master's degree. His face asked a greater question than that. To the pendulously intent and tender-looking face above mine, I said, "I want to stay with you." Lawrence gave. He gave me to feel more of his weight and more of his phallus than I had felt, in that feeling, until then.

Giving, he said, "Marry me, Ned. Let's get married." I might have laughed joyously—in part at his timing. Later, Lawrence raised the question of rings. He said, "I know you hate jewelry. But." I said that I had nothing against wedding rings.

So a jeweler showed us plain, golden bands. Two matching rings lay on a blue-gray pad atop a glass case. A blue of blue spruce trees lay behind the bright circlets. Lawrence's fairness and more filled the very stuff of the bottomless cups. Sentimentally, we ordered our names engraved inside the rings; Lawrence's name would touch my flesh and vice versa. I did not trust myself to do the minute engraving. The man who'd shown us rings separated the two remaining rings unceremoniously. He slipped each into a small, transparent plastic sack red-ribbed at the seal. To the sacks, he brutally stapled paper instructions about the engraving. Before the working salesperson (my age) picked up the rings and packed them off to industry, their brightness on the blue-gray touched me. I hoped to grow old wearing the ring lined with Lawrence's name.

101 MARRIAGE

Lawrence and I married. In an office lined with law books, in an office which, beyond containing books, did not resemble Burke's book-lined study in Estelle's house, Lawrence and I and our two witnesses, Burke and Mr. Kuprin, stood facing a justice of the peace across a desk neatly laden with forgettable evidence of judicial labor. The justice asked Lawrence and me if we had vows to make or "anything special" for him to read before he married us. I replied that Lawrence and I had already said to each other what we wanted to say. The justice, rich in silvery dignity, struck me as unfavorably impressed by such lack of ceremony, but he proceeded to invoke the powers invested in him by the state in which we lived; by those powers he pronounced Lawrence and me married. We, Burke and Mr. Kuprin and Lawrence and I, signed papers which a clerk bore away. The justice used an embossing stamp on a sunny piece of foil affixed to a marriage certificate. He congratulated Lawrence and me and, handing the sun-sealed paper to Lawrence, the justice said jocularly, "Don't lose that. That's the original. It's hard to replace." We thanked him. Lawrence and I hugged; Burke and Mr. Kuprin congratulated us, and we four left the office, the furled flags, the law books, the skeptical justice. I felt oddly that nothing had changed between Lawrence and me but that something informational arising from paper and from pronouncement might change other people's perceptions of our mutual commitment. I also felt braced by the greatness of law, embraced, beyond my ken, by an entire legal system.

Following that unceremonious ceremony, Mr. Kuprin drove Burke and Lawrence and me back to Lawrence's house, which we'd left full of people, including my parents, Lawrence's sister, and a company of caterers. On the drive back, I continued to feel soberly impressed by something that I could not name, something of an ordinary mystery involving the insubstantial operation of actual laws. I held Lawrence's left hand still bare of its engraved ring. At one point, while the car sat motionless, Lawrence's hand squeezed mine; I looked at him. He positively beamed. He looked stuffed with happiness, as if happiness somehow increased the convexity of every convex surface of his face. He squeezed my hand and said, "Husband," as if happily accusing me of something. Then the rush began. I ceased feeling somber. I felt as if happiness flowed from Lawrence into me, and that Lawrence sat there as the source of it, like a generator charged with what it transmitted, a generator steady with charge even as it transmitted.

That happiness carried me blindly through the ensuing party, the clapping, and the toasts, and the moment when Lawrence and I, standing in the middle of the living room, banded each other's hands with rings last seen empty, just then, against Lawrence's sister's right palm. I felt selflessly happy, drunk with happiness, not at all literally drunk; I did not drink much. I later skeptically suspected myself of flying away into happiness as a defense against trepidations caused by the presence of my parents. (If my parents wished for my happiness, as, I thought, most parents wished for that of their children, my parents would have to ponder the evidence of that wish fulfilled.) However passing, rings abounded, celebratory rings. I did not actually see the forty-some-odd, tall, tapering flutes full of true Champagne which, by some feat of organization beyond me, appeared in the hands of our guests just before Lawrence and I laid the golden claims of rings on each other's hands. I did not actually see the glasses' round mouths or the golden, seething streams of bubbles, minute spheres, while Lawrence spoke over the whole room, in his room-draping voice, about how rings, as circles, "once deemed the perfect form," lacking beginnings and lacking ends, and "all one, ever the same," had long "symbolized union and unity" and, thus, "the two become one" by marriage. I did not actually see "the O for my one," the piece of metal warmed by a woman's informal clasp, the ring that Lawrence, looking down (and thus changing my one and sustained view of his eyes), moved along and onto part of my given hand. I had to attend to the remaining ring couched on living flesh. As I seated it on Lawrence's finger, I repeated distinctly the last words he'd spoken, "My one." I had not known that he would speak; I had nothing to add.

103   BURKE AND DANA

That party took place a year after the Christmas of the Ridiculous Robe. It took place during a break between semesters. During the year before Lawrence and I married, I'd finished my master's degree. I'd begun teaching watercolor painting as an unpaid volunteer at an arts cooperative. And, wishing to banish the concept of small scale from the art, I'd made and sold two big watercolors on spliced pieces of extremely stiff, elephantine paper. I'd begun to feel confident that I could earn a living (or my required pittance, pretending independence from Lawrence). I began to feel confident that I could sell paintings, and that I would sell them. I felt rich in potential, and I richly loved Lawrence. Just as I felt more confident about my future in art than I had reason to feel (given life's uncertainty), so I also felt unreasonably certain of Lawrence, fearless of losing him. I felt that well before we married, well before we agreed, for my sake, to marry by civil ceremony, and for Lawrence's, to follow that spareness with an unstinting party. I chose Burke to serve as witness to our marriage; Lawrence chose Mr. Kuprin. My wish to involve Burke virtually determined our court date because Burke, hard-pressed all the way around as an adjunct professor, could not take time off during any semester. Lawrence and I chose a date during the Christmas break, between semesters; Burke agreed to act as witness. I then realized that, for more than a year, for some fourteen months, I'd wanted Burke to meet the Not-Christine, Dana Ferris.

I would have remembered Dana, seen on the steps of Seekford Hall, even if those steps had not later loomed large in my mind as leading to Lawrence. When Lawrence, then Professor Baussan to me, introduced Dana and me in his kitchen, I'd felt too wonderfully shocked to remember much. I barely remembered Dana's name. I did remember that Professor Baussan had told Dana that he hoped to see a "rough draft" of her dissertation "soon." She wrote several drafts—the last smooth and approved—in the fourteen months that followed. During that time, Lawrence sometimes referred to his meetings with her. I would have remembered Dana without those reminders. I might barely have remembered her name; I might barely have remembered the rending, rent foil, the shuddering mirror that Dana "borrowed." But I remembered clearly, because I regretted, how she and I had exchanged words later that night, how we'd exchanged the word "type" in particular. She'd called me Professor Baussan's type; I'd called her Burke's type without mentioning Burke by name. I'd regretted then, and I continued to regret, that I had so much as mentioned "my brother" to Dana. I regretted that mention out of proportion to its brevity. I regretted it although I told myself that Dana might well have thought nothing of it and might have forgotten it (even instantly, on the spot). I regretted mentioning Burke for a hoard of conjoined reasons: because I regretted whatever unhappiness I'd inadvertently caused Burke through my friendship with Christine; because I could not disassociate the two utterly distinct and independent people, Dana and Christine; because I longed without cause to make amends to Burke by supplying him with a replacement for Christine; because I saw Dana as a sort of bait for Burke; because I should not view a woman or any person, ever, as bait; because I should never presume that I knew enough about two people to play matchmaker to them, if anyone ever should play such a role. I could not forget what I'd said to Dana and I could not rid myself of the irrational conviction that Burke and Dana "should" meet. I criticized myself for jumping to conclusions and for letting people's appearances give me ideas.

During the fourteen months that followed my having mentioned "my brother" to Dana, Lawrence occasionally mentioned his consultations with her. He asked if I remembered her; I said yes, I remembered. I didn't breathe a word about "Burke and Dana." But a plan occurred to me as if against my will. Marriage plans seemed to breed further plans. With Burke secured as a witness, it merely remained, my fool brain saw, to invite Dana to the celebratory party. That invitation had to come from Lawrence.

All along, ever since I'd met Dana, throughout the months that followed our kitchen introduction, I'd avoided her. I must have schemed without realizing that I schemed. I must have decided, behind my back, that Burke and Dana should at least see each other, and that I would do something to bring about their meeting. I must have decided, in the dark of my mind, that to avoid all hint of an *unfortunate* parallel with Christine, if Dana and Burke ever met, she should not appear to him in any way, shape, or form as a friend of mine. When I finally realized how easily Burke and Dana might meet, I explained my busybody interest to Lawrence. I felt ashamed of both my proposed meddling and of my groundless belief that Dana could out-Christine Christine in Burke's estimation. As I rattled on to Lawrence about "Burke and Dana," he lifted his chin forbiddingly. He understood: I all but asked him to commit a crime, to tamper with—or to affect—another student's, yet another student's, private life. But Lawrence invited Dana, as requested. He would have invited her without my request. I gathered, from Lawrence's report, that in inviting her to our party, he'd mingled the invitation with congratulations to her on the completion of her thesis.

Of course, I felt guilty of plotting. I told myself that I'd chosen Burke as a witness without thought of Dana, but I knew my mind devious. And I began to worry: Plots aside, should I wish Burke on anyone? Since Christine, he'd not treated women well. But I believed, on the basis of nothing, that Dana possessed the power to tenderize his callousness. Besides, I told myself, Burke and Dana could assess each other for themselves. I merely contrived, if I contrived, an opportunity for them to meet—to see—each other.

They took that opportunity and ran with it. During the party that followed our marriage, while Lawrence and I, separately and together, talked with guests, satisfaction for Burke's sake added to my happiness. Burke appeared very attentive to Dana and she to him. I glancingly saw them talking together, and with other people and, again, together. Eventually, the party thinned to one group, all family members plus Dana. By then, Burke knew something about Lawrence as Dana's "thesis advisor," but he lacked information about Dana and me. "You know each other?" he asked us. Looking at her, I said cordially that we'd met. Dana took my offered hand as if glad to meet me again. I thought that she smiled too frankly to look secretive, and yet I sensed that she remembered my reference to "my brother." Whether she remembered or not, I felt gratified. If I had not actually contrived Burke's and Dana's meeting, I had desired it. I had anticipated that they would like each other.

104　GRATITUDE

One night soon after we'd married, Lawrence and I sat in his—in our—living room, in a pocket of domestic comfort and peace, under a raging blizzard. Wind lashed the house; blown snow flailed its glass as if with sand. A small fire burned in the fireplace. Lawrence sat reading, facing the fire. I sat cross-legged on the floor, near the radiant hearth. I held a hundred and four playing cards intermixed as a single stack, cards with which I often played a game called spider solitaire. (I played cards when I felt too tired to do anything else.) Wind sounded loud, barging and buffeting, yet the small fire burned with the forking, vanishing movements of fire unmoved by wind, and firelight barely survived as an amber tinge moving, reflected, in the distant side of the piano closed beyond Lawrence, beyond his right side's back. Sometimes the fire split and rustled audibly within the wind's sounds. Sometimes a turned page brushed a page previously turned. Sometimes Lawrence made sounds in response to what he read, an abrupt sniff, a snap of the tongue withdrawn with suction from behind his front teeth. And the world raged destructively, beyond the insensate energy of the snow-bearing wind. And a figment of innocence persisted: Lawrence's reading lamp, the almost-spherically-shaded, craning, brass lamp that had once made me think of a child reading—or hearing a story read—while tucked in, beside him, the blond-child's-head-of-a-lamp retained its fascinated, fixated air, poring over Lawrence's pages, although I told it not to do so, although I told myself not to see anything human in the stretch of a neck made of parallel rods or in a hollow, brazen curvature. Fantasies arose from fantasies: the wind barged around the house like a giant escaped from a children's story, like an irate giant armed with a cudgel and bent on beating out of existence all such little burrows of warmth and comfort as the one that Lawrence and I inhabited for the moment. Lawrence stirred on the sofa. He cumbrously arose, walked to the hearth, unhooked a poker from a rack, and prodded the fire. Sparks burst from the abrasion, from the squeaking pivot of stick upon stick, sticks all patterned, burned and burning, like alligator skins of live coals and charcoal. Lawrence resumed his seat, resumed reading. Touched by the sparks' brevity, I shuddered.

I supposed that moments shot through me like sparks, here and gone, vivid and nothing but remembered vividity. I supposed that everyone experienced such twinges of instants of simply living. I supposed that Lawrence, comfortably reading beneath a blizzard, experienced, at the moment, not a moment, but a sustained engagement with what he read. I thought that words on pages usually worked to purposes and usually worked, through the sustained sense that they carried, to the fulfillment of their purposes sequentially, gradually, with logical continuity. I probably read much into the reading Lawrence. He soothed me perpetually. Calm and sensible, not readily disturbed—unlike me—Lawrence, to my eyes, carried about him a comforting aura of continuity. I thought that, like the print he read writ large, Lawrence himself worked, Lawrence himself lived, to a purpose and for a purpose, a purpose that he, as his own, ongoing author, had invented, embraced, and defined for himself. He worked to satisfy and to further professional interests. I supposed that sustained purposes—and other pleasures—sustained Lawrence. I, on the other hand, lived by fits and starts in my art, in little binges of discontinuous effort. I simply made "pictures," paintings, etchings, sketches, and daubs, all separate things, none sustained in the extended manner of arguments or stories. Of course, the plain continuity of biological life (until death) contained these efforts continually. But I felt as if I lived in surges—none quite as predictable as the surging systems of seas. Lawrence, living with Lawrence, knowing Lawrence, gave me a stable, daily life. For that loving matrix, I would always feel grateful.

354

ABOUT THE AUTHOR

Carla Bradsher-Fredrick grew up in Oklahoma, where she was devoted to the equestrian sport of show jumping. After having lived in France and Turkey, she graduated Phi Beta Kappa from Grinnell College and earned an MA in art history from the University of Michigan. There, she also fulfilled the requirements for a PhD in art history except for the writing of a dissertation. She and her husband lived for many years in Saudi Arabia and in Arlington, Virginia, before moving to the Portland, Oregon area. *Hands and Straight Lines* is her first book.